Greig Beck grew up across the Australia. His early days were science fiction on the sand. He then went on to study comp— ence, immerse himself in the financial software industry and later received an MBA. Greig is the director of a software company but still finds time to write and surf. He lives in Sydney, with his wife, son and an enormous black German shepherd.

Also by Greig Beck

Beneath the Dark Ice
Dark Rising
This Green Hell

Available through Momentum

Arcadian Genesis
Return of the Ancients: The Valkeryn Chronicles Book 1

BLACK MOUNTAIN

GREIG BECK

momentum

First published by Pan Macmillan Australia in 2012
This edition published in 2013 by Momentum
Pan Macmillan Australia Pty Ltd
1 Market Street, Sydney 2000

A CIP record for this book is available at the National Library of Australia

Black Mountain

EPUB format: 9781743341650
Mobi format: 9781743341667
Print on Demand format: 9781743341674

Cover design by Jeremy Nicholson
Proofread by Tara Goedjen

Macmillan Digital Australia: www.macmillandigital.com.au

To report a typographical error, please email errors@momentumbooks.com.au

Visit www.momentumbooks.com.au to read more about all our books and to buy books online. You will also find features, author interviews and news of any author events.

*To those wild, imaginative and dedicated
cryptozoologists – just like you, I truly believe
some legends are real*

ACKNOWLEDGMENTS

Once again, thank you to Nicola O'Shea, Cate Paterson, and Samantha Sainsbury for all the guidance and advice. Many times I have been asked: 'does professional editing make a difference?' My answer has always been: 'Only 100 percent of the time!'

PROLOGUE

Southern Appalachians, 11,000 bce

The creature screamed as the arrow punched into its neck. Ripping it free, it turned to roar in frustration. The wound was deep and bled heavily, but the sticky blood quickly froze on its coarse, blunt fingers.

The small ones were coming fast, sending more of their arrows flying through the air. The creature roared again, wanting to rush back and fight, to crush those small, loud man-things down to nothing. But that would mean its own death, and then the end of all of them. There were now barely forty members of the group remaining, and some with young; they would be slaughtered. The leader snorted and drew its clan higher, moving quickly now. When it looked back briefly, the man-things were a crawling multitude that whooped and ran and hurled their sharp sticks.

The time for peaceful coexistence had long since passed. The creature looked to the sky – cold, iron gray with heavy cloud down to the peak – then it grunted, calling the group. There was one place they could go, where they could defend themselves and save their young. The deep, wintering cave that they used for hibernation when the season was unusually long and cold. Down there, deep inside the mountain, where the lichens glowed green and things slid and wormed their way in the darkness, there was safety. Deeper still there was a black river, with pale, sightless things swimming within it – food.

The leader urged the group to greater speed, forcing them on, higher up the mountain, along the old pathways, steep and narrow tracks on the cliff edge that fell away to a depth so great its bottom was invisible in the heavy mist. Up, up, and into the cave, through the small and narrow opening, into the inner world of the mountain. There was no way out, but they could wait. If the man-things followed them in, then they would have to fight; they'd done it before. The small ones wanted their heads as trophies. If they came into the mountain, then *their* heads would be taken.

Deep in the dark they waited, the large adult bodies pressed to the front, the young behind, all breathing heavily, fear sharp and acrid in the air around them. And then the man-things came, but just to the mouth of the cave, throwing fire inside.

The great beasts waited still, but instead of an attack, there came a scraping, grinding and pounding noise, over and over. Then, to the creatures' horror, the light from outside began to diminish. A mighty wall rose up before them, stone by stone.

The adults screamed in rage and surged forward, but were answered with more fire and stinging arrows. They fell back, pounding the ground, their rage loud but impotent as large, interlocking blocks continued to be piled and fixed in place, until the last square of light was blotted out. Still the sounds continued as many more layers were added.

Finally, there was silence, save for the heavy breaths of the creatures themselves. The leader shuffled forward and rested a large and bloody hand against the stone – it could sense the many thick layers and doubted they could break through. It also sensed the man-things on the other side, waiting for them to try.

It turned back to its clan, a decision forming in its mind. There was food, and there would be weak light from the lichens in the deeper caves below. They could survive. They would wait, and eventually their world would be given back to them. They had walked its surface before the man-things had arrived, and they would walk it again.

ONE

Kowloon, Hong Kong, 1935

Charles Albert Schroder paused at the bustling intersection. He knew the main streets were too easily picked over, and so it was down the secretive side alleys that he had navigated this day. Being a head taller than the milling crowd, he should be able to spot the type of shop he was searching for without too much trouble. *There* – the double Chinese 医药 symbols for medicine hung from a shingle out the front of a dark cramped space that emanated the mixed odors of a thousand exotic herbs, fungi and dried animal carcasses.

Schroder watched the doorway for a while. The clientele were a mix of older men, presumably seeking remedies for ailing potency, or young women looking for an elixir to turn a rich man's head. Each left with a small package wrapped in rice paper and stamped with the shop owner's symbol.

Schroder ducked his head as he stepped inside, and blinked a few times to try to adjust his eyes to the gloom of the interior. An ancient Chinese man stood behind a counter, staring at him with a rheumy gaze and resting a pair of reptilian hands on the countertop. Behind him, the wall was completely covered in wooden slots holding powder-filled jars or tiny drawers that were undoubtedly filled with exotic wares. Schroder quickly looked left and right, making sure he was alone with the man. The only other gaze he detected belonged to the milky eyes of a monkey's head suspended in a jar of yellow fluid.

Schroder nodded – he didn't need to look around the shop any further. What he searched for was never on display. He cleared his throat. He didn't know much of the language but had taken pains to memorize a few phrases. His greeting was delivered with a bow, and on receiving a small nod in return he was encouraged to continue.

'*Nǐ yǒu lóng de yáchǐ?*'

The man didn't move, perhaps pretending not to understand. Schroder repeated the sentence, confident his words and pronunciation were correct. Still nothing more than the flat gaze in return. He lifted his billfold from his breast pocket and slowly removed a single note and placed it on the counter. He bowed and tried again.

'*Nǐ yǒu lóng de yáchǐ?*'

The man's eyes flicked down briefly to look at the purple and yellow bill. After a few seconds he nodded and disappeared behind a string curtain, emerging with a wooden tray covered in a soft cloth. He laid it down on the counter and pulled back two-thirds of the material. He waved his small wrinkled hand over the tray's contents and said in a surprisingly deep voice, '*Lóng de yáchǐ.*'

Schroder smiled flatly. His eyes quickly sorted through the tray's contents, mentally cataloguing the species that the pieces had come from – cave bear, giant deer, a boar the size of a rhinoceros. All excellent fossils, but nothing of real interest to him. He went to push back the cloth that still covered a portion of the tray, but the shopkeeper made a sharp noise in his throat and held his hand up. With the other hand, he pushed the single bill back across the table. His meaning was clear: the covered side of the tray was more expensive.

Schroder knew the real thing would be. What he sought was unique, and rarely placed in the hands of unappreciative foreigners. He bowed again and pulled another two bills from his wallet and laid them on the pile. He made a flat gesture indicating that was all he was going to pay. The shopkeeper's eyes narrowed briefly, then with a flourish that would have impressed a stage conjuror he lifted the cloth to reveal several more specimens.

Schroder felt his heart thump in his chest. It wouldn't have mattered if there were a hundred relics laid before him, his paleoanthropologist eyes were immediately drawn to just one. A canine tooth, broken at its base but still easily four inches long from its root to curved tip. With a shaking hand he held it up before him, the breath locked in his chest.

'*Lóng de yáchǐ – gāo pǐnzhǐ.*' The small man pointed one long fingernail at the specimen, obviously satisfied with Schroder's response.

'Yes, yes ... dragon's teeth.' He used English without thinking as he brought the fossil close to his face, studying it, mentally calculating, estimating, extrapolating. In his mind, he turned the fragment of a long dead creature into something living – he could see it in all its terrible glory. He held the relic above his head, standing on his toes to reach up above his six-foot-plus frame, adding another four feet to where the mouth would have been.

He heard the shopkeeper's voice again. '*Lóng de yáchǐ. Guàiwù lóng de yáchǐ!*'

Schroder exhaled and lowered his arm. 'Yes, best quality, but not a dragon. Something just as fantastic.'

He emptied his wallet onto the counter and leaned in towards the man. '*Zài nǎlǐ?*' he asked. 'Where?'

*

Present day

Alex was miles beneath the surface. He stared up at a shimmering mirage of blue light. He clamped his lips shut. Panic was a heartbeat away, and the more he tried to break free, the tighter he was trapped by the black coils of slimy rope that bound his arms and legs, wrapped around his chest and coated his face. He was aware his burning lungs would soon give out, but he dared not open his mouth even to scream, as he knew the mucous-covered strands would find their way inside.

He was dragged deeper down; his feet sinking into the primordial ooze of the lightless depths. With his last fragments of energy he sprang towards the surface. Last time, last chance – he needed to breathe; he wanted to live.

TWO

Southern Appalachians, North Carolina

'I'm cold.' Amanda Jordan put her gloved fists under her arms and gave a little hop to cross yet another puddle of melting snow, trying to keep pace with the long legs of her new husband. The tiny pink metallic camera she had on a cord around her neck bounced against her parka as she skidded on some dark ice.

Brad Jordan turned to walk backwards a few steps, the snow squeaking under the tough rubber soles of his new boots. He pulled a face and scoffed, 'Big baby – and it'll get colder further up.' Then added quickly, 'But it'll be worth it, I promise.'

Amanda raised her eyebrows and tried to laugh, but just ended up coughing. She sucked in another stinging breath and exhaled, her breath steaming in the cold, dry air. She grimaced – even stretching her face hurt. When she dabbed her bottom lip with the back of one gloved hand, she saw a dot of red smeared on its waterproof coating. Damn, she thought, regretting not putting on some lip balm before they left.

Some holiday, she thought grouchily. She felt terrible. Under her bulky clothing, her armpits, back and groin were sweating from the exertion of the climb, but the chilly thirty-degree air was stinging her nose, chin and ears like they were being pricked by a hundred needles. She bet they were as red as beets. If that wasn't enough, she hadn't worn her ski cap. Brad liked her thick hair and she'd wanted him to admire it in the sunlight. Now she didn't care what he thought – she just wanted a big hat she could pull down over her ears to keep them warm.

'Brad, can we at least stop for some coffee soon?'

He turned and stretched out his arms. 'Great idea.' He looked around and spotted a flat rock just off the trail. 'Over there.'

Brad shrugged out of the large backpack and lowered it to the stone. He was a big man – six-two, and broad across the back. Amanda often said he looked like a big, jug-eared Ben Affleck. He'd offered to carry everything on their way up and seemed to haul the weight with ease. He eased himself down and patted the rock beside him, then opened the backpack.

Amanda sat down heavily and frowned. She pulled off one of her gloves and laid her bare hand on the stone. 'It's warm.'

'Yep. Sun's directly overhead, and the stone only needs to catch a few rays to make it a degree or two warmer than the surroundings. Not much, but feels kinda good, huh?'

He pulled the thermos free and pushed his hand back down into the depths of the backpack.

Amanda pulled off her other glove, rolled over and hugged the stone, pressing her face to its warm surface. 'Blisssssss,' she sighed.

Brad lay down on his side next to her. 'How're the feet? We've already been trekking for half a day – not bad for a city girl.'

Amanda rolled onto her back and put her hands behind her head. 'City slicker, huh? I'm from Greensboro, remember, not New York, and I've been hiking before. The feet are just fine.' She sat up. 'Now where's that coffee I ordered, you big moose?'

He laughed as he handed her a cup of steaming liquid. 'I forgot, they breed 'em tough in the Boro, and you're a regular Calamity Jane, aren't you?'

She sipped the coffee, and winced as the hot liquid touched her lip. 'Damn right I'm tough. So, Paul Bunyan, how much further?'

Brad pulled up his sleeve, displaying a variety of dials strapped to his wrist. He consulted them, then nodded at the landscape. 'Notice the darker trees, the Fraser fir and red spruce crowns – we've been into them for quite a while. Altimeter says we're at six one-twenty feet – that's high. Peak's supposed to be sixty-three twenty-seven ... but we're not going there – way too easy.'

Amanda's lip curled in displeasure. 'Oh really? Brad, I said I was tough, not stupid. I'm cold – how much further?'

Brad pulled a face back at her and leaned in close, as though worried about being overheard in the isolated wilderness. 'Did you read about the recent tremors and resulting landslips in the mountains? Well, I have it on good authority that a slip's opened up a new path to the Black Dome – absolutely the highest point in the whole Southern Appalachians. Think of it – we'll probably be the first people up there since the mid-1800s ... and it's only a bit further than the lookout peak.'

Amanda groaned, refusing to be infected by his enthusiasm. '*Sooo*, how much further?'

He shrugged and turned away to pour himself some coffee, saying something Amanda couldn't make out.

'What? I didn't hear you. Come on, Brad, how much higher do we need to go?'

He turned back to her, his cheeks slightly red. 'Eight hundred feet.' He lifted his mug in a salute. 'Maybe one more hour, max. I promise.'

Amanda lay back down on the rock. 'God, where's the ski lift? You are so rubbing my feet tonight, Bradley Henry Jordan.'

He tipped out the dregs of his coffee and lay down next to her. 'I'd have done that anyway – I'll rub everything, promise. Besides, on the way back its *all* downhill – *eeeeeaasy.*'

She laughed. *Putty in his hands*, she thought and sighed, knowing she'd just agreed to the extra trek. 'So how do we get to this Black Dome ... and more importantly, is it safe?'

Brad rummaged around in his back pocket and pulled out a folded piece of paper. He opened it on the rock next to her and traced some lines with his finger. 'Here's where I reckon we are, and this is where we'd normally be able to get access to.'

The paper showed a rough sketch of the mountain peaks with a trail winding up the east face. It then changed to a dotted line marked with zigzags for rockfalls and an underlined notation that said *New Pathway*. Amanda noticed some groupings of small red crosses near the mountain's crest.

'What do these mean?'

'Nothing important.'

'Well, what? Soda machines, phone booths?'

Brad cleared his throat. 'Probably points of interest – lookouts maybe.' He shrugged. 'Not sure; it's not my map.'

Amanda sat up straight and stared at him for several seconds. He kept his gaze on the map, refusing to look at her even though he must have felt the intensity of her gaze. Eventually he turned to her with his usual infectious grin, his thumb and forefinger held up less than an inch apart.

'This far, that's all.'

She nodded slowly, still not convinced he was telling her everything. *Still, one more hour can't hurt*, she thought, and tossed him her empty cup.

*

Brad watched Amanda smack a low branch out of the way as she set off. Even in the bulky cold-weather gear, her tight little figure was visible beneath all the layers. He smiled as he watched for a moment longer, then rolled up his sleeve to check his altimeter and compass again. The dials were illuminated due to the poor light. He looked up and frowned: the sun hadn't reappeared and the low cloud was darker than he would have liked. If it snowed, or got any colder, Amanda would kill him. The trek was turning out to be miles longer than he'd expected, and now he was thinking that they'd be trekking back in the dark for sure. He chewed his lip. If the advice he'd been given was right, it should be less than an hour now to the landslip that had created a short cut to the top of the Black Dome. Maybe he should lift the pace a bit.

He hoisted the pack a little higher on his back and adjusted his belt. As he did, the gun he was carrying dug into his gut. The red crosses on the map indicated bear sightings. Seemed the large animals were on the move early this season. *On the move away from where we're going*, he thought, *which is good*. He'd heard that even the wolves had been coming down off the mountain. *Even better.*

Still, it was better to have a gun and not need it, than to need it and not have it.

*

They looked at the landslip – tons of rock and soil that had been shaken free from the side of the mountain and had settled to create an uneven path up the once inaccessible rock face. Normally this was the spot where hikers gave up and professional climbers took over, but now, even to Amanda, it looked ... well ... possible.

Brad had picked up a stick about four feet long and was pointing it at a few places along the slip. 'We just need to ease across that small gap at the start, then drop down onto the path and stay close to the cliff face – it'll be a piece of cake.'

He leaned in against the stone and hopped across the gap, then turned back to her and held out the stick for her to grab onto and follow. As Amanda leaped across, she noticed that the newly exposed rock was clean – the stark browns and gray of the gneiss and schist probably only laid open to the elements within the last few weeks. A fanciful thought crossed her mind: it looked painful, like a wound cut through to the bone.

Amanda kept hold of the stick and used it as a walking staff. As she moved along the dry wall of stone, she observed crevices and holes in the rock face exposed by the loss of surface soil and debris. Some of them looked deep, and she bent down to peer into one. Even though she put her hands on either side of her face and squinted, it didn't do any good; there was nothing to see but inky blackness.

She wrinkled her nose. 'Phew, smells like something died or pooped in there.'

Brad looked back at her. 'Maybe a falcon, they like to nest in rock faces. Come on, keep up.'

Amanda turned to look out from the mountainside. At over 6000 feet and without the trees to block the view, it was spectacular. True to the name, the mountain looked almost black in the fading light. Low cloud vapor was snaking through the hollows and around the treetops, giving the whole place a primordial atmosphere. She lifted the camera from around her neck and opened the zoom – it buzzed and clicked as it took the snap, then tidied itself away.

It was almost magical to be able to look down on the other mountains from this height. She leaned out towards the edge of the slip – it was a long way down, at least a 1000-foot drop before the slope became a little gentler and tree-covered again.

'*Halloooooo,*' she called.

The word stretched out and she waited, but no echo came back to her. She sucked in a huge breath, preparing for an even bigger shout, when Brad swung around pulling a pained face. As he put his finger to his lips, a rock the size of a mailbox thumped into the dirt between them. They looked at each other with wide eyes ... and waited. Amanda drew her shoulders up and gritted her teeth – she'd forgotten they were in a slip zone.

Brad came back to her. 'It's pretty stable,' he whispered, 'but there could be loose debris that may fall. Best not to bust out with any more karaoke right now, okay?'

She nodded and went to step over the stone that had fallen. She frowned, tapped it with her stick, then squatted. *Odd, it doesn't look like a raw boulder.* The stone seemed to have been shaped, squared, like a large cinderblock, she thought. She brushed it with her hand – and noticed the symbols carved into it.

'Hey, look at this,' she called.

Brad kneeled beside her and pulled the stone out of its slush and dirt crater. He turned it over – the symbols were on all four sides. 'Old. Looks Native American – a figure behind two arrows, one pointing left, the other right. Makes sense – the Black Dome was actually called *Attakulla*, after a Cherokee Indian chief, long before we palefaces renamed it.'

Amanda brushed more soil out of the carving. 'Is that a man?'

'Nah, don't think so; arms are too long. Looks sorta deformed though. See all those other little marks carved into it? Might be symbols, or just where the stone was cut.'

Amanda sat back on her haunches. 'Well, it's very cool – we should take it back with us.'

Brad looked at her with half-lidded eyes. 'My little angel, I know who you mean when you say "we". This piece of stone probably weighs about forty pounds. I'll end up a hunchback if I try lugging it down over 6000 feet of mountain.'

'But it's all downhill on the way back, remember? Like you said, it'll be *eeeeeasy*. Besides, I have the perfect place for it beside the fireplace.'

Brad groaned. 'Let's leave it for now and have another look on the way back, okay?'

'Good idea, I'm sure it'll be lighter then.' She patted his shoulder, then used it to get to her feet. She looked up at the sheer rock wall above them. 'Wonder where it came from? It looks like a giant house brick.'

Brad scanned the rock wall where it had been scoured by the slippage. 'There.' He pointed to an area half-hidden by a small ledge and a tangle of fallen bushes. He squinted. 'Looks like more of them up there.'

Amanda followed his directions about thirty feet straight up, and saw the other stones – dozens of them, stacked one on top of the other, bricking in a natural cavity in the rock wall that had been exposed by the earth sliding away. It was roughly triangular shaped and about nine feet in height. She could see a small dark hole near the top where the fallen stone had come from. She stepped back, closer to the edge of the path, to get a better look.

'The cave's been sealed off – did the Native Americans build walls like that? I thought they only made stone burial mounds.'

'Sure they did. Different tribes built walls for everything from agriculture to defence. In fact, I read archaeologists just found an ancient Indian wall submerged beneath the Hudson River – running 900 feet end to end.' Brad stepped back as well. 'Maybe this was a grain store they needed to hide. Around here, the Catawba and Cherokee were always at war with someone.'

'Pretty secure grain store if you ask me. Maybe it was a prison – you know how the legends go: mess with the chief's daughter, get entombed, problem solved.' She had another thought. 'Hey, could be hidden treasure maybe. You think?'

Brad rolled his eyes. 'They were Indians, not pirates, Amanda. The ancient tribes never valued gold, or jewels. Land, good hunting and honor – these were the things they treasured. Can't seal them up, can you?'

'Guess not.' Amanda stepped back again, craning her neck to see the stones better. The ground shifted under her feet as the lip of the ledge started to move. She felt herself sliding towards the abyss and pinwheeled her arms, trying to regain her balance.

Brad grabbed her by the front of her parka and pulled her roughly forward. 'Stop playing around, will you? Anyway, we've seen all we can from here. Let's go on up to the Dome, and we can report the wall to the ranger when we get back.'

Amanda looked back at the edge of the path and shook her head, trying to clear the image of that long fall to the forest below. She started walking, her legs feeling wobbly, then turned back briefly. 'Okay, we report it, but only after we've got that stone safely in the trunk of my car. Just one second.'

Buzz-click, buzz-click – two more photos for her album.

*

By the time Brad had hauled Amanda up onto an outcrop of rock and declared they were as high as they could go, the occasional speck of sleet had turned to real snow. There was a wind chill that cut through their clothing and made their lips so numb it was hard to talk.

'We might be the first people to have stood here for nearly one hundred and fifty years,' Brad said through gritted teeth.

Amanda tried to give him her best appreciative smile. She was standing as close as possible to his huge frame so he acted as a wind-break. As far as she was concerned, and kept telling him, the view had been just as good from the side of the mountain where the slip had been. She noticed his lips were turning blue and he'd developed the hunched look of someone whose body temperature is rapidly falling.

The snow either drifted down or whipped past them, depending on the gusts of wind, and she had to speak loudly to be heard. 'Let's go, baby. We've seen enough now.'

Brad stared into the wind for a few more seconds, then nodded and took her hand to help her down from the rocks. 'You're right, time to go. I don't like the way the weather's closing in on us.'

There was no sightseeing on the way down. Away from the ex-posed Black Dome, there was more shelter so the needle-sharp cold wind with its haunted moaning was left behind. The falling snow suppressed any sounds around them, except for the squeal of crushed flakes under Brad's large feet as he moved them quickly along. Amanda had her hands firmly tucked up under her arms and only pulled them out to maintain her balance when they had to hop across logs, boulders or particularly slippery-looking drifts.

'You hear that?' Brad said, stopping and half-turning to her with a frown on his face.

She almost bumped into him. On seeing his expression, she stopped to listen to the snow-dampened silence. She didn't hear any-thing ... *no, wait, there* ... It was a thumping sound, like a fist striking a giant pillow. There was no rhythm or pattern to it. She slowly turned her head, trying to determine where the sound was coming from.

'What is it?' she asked.

'Shit, better not be another rockfall. Come on, let's hurry – we're nearly at the slip. I'll feel better once we're back across it.'

'Goddamnit, Brad, I am not staying on this mountain tonight. I warn you – you'll be in big trouble if you've gone and gotten us stuck.'

Brad just frowned before setting off again. *He looks worried*, she thought. She didn't know why she was blaming him, after all she liked to hike and it wasn't as if he'd made it snow or caused the slip to drop more debris. She just felt like venting – and probably would again before they got back down.

It didn't take them long to get to the slip, now white with fresh snow. Its surface looked like a powdery moonscape complete with meteor-strike craters. Brad hung onto a tree, not yet ready to step out. He leaned out and craned his neck to look upwards.

Amanda grabbed a handful of his parka and tried to lean out too. 'What is it?' she whispered. 'Has there been another landslide?'

Brad kept his eyes on the track. 'I think ... yes *and* no. That old Indian wall up on the rock face – it looks like it's finally crumbled. I think that's what's causing the pits in the snow.'

'Is it safe to cross?'

Brad hesitated. 'I guess so ... doesn't look as though there are many stones left to fall. Besides, there's no choice if you want to sleep in a bed tonight.' He still hadn't moved, just kept looking from the path to the cliff face and back again. Finally, he turned to her. 'Just a little over a hundred feet – stay close to the wall, and to me.' But he still didn't move.

'What's wrong? You're scaring me, Brad.'

'Nothing, just a funny smell – reminds me of when we were kids and Scotty found a dead bird and rolled in it. Sort of a rotten, wet-animal-hair, shitty smell – took us two baths before we got the smell out of his fur.'

'Hey, that's what I smelled in that little hole before. Maybe it's that dead falcon again – remember you said that?'

'Yeah, yeah, I do. Stay close.'

Brad stepped out, his foot sinking into the snow to his ankles. He kept one arm up towards the rock face, not touching it, just monitoring where he was in relation to the wall and the sheer drop to the slopes below. Amanda could understand his tentativeness. The late afternoon, combined with the heavy cloud, was creating an early twilight on the mountain. Snow was starting to fall again, making the edge of the cliff path hard to see. The whitening air around them, white sky and a white pathway – all definition was disappearing, making it too easy to step off into limbo.

She hung on to the back of Brad's jacket and tried to test the path with her small staff, but nearly tripped several times as she was pulled along at a speed that better suited his long legs than her shorter ones. Out on the slip path, the lack of trees meant the wind chill was severe again, and the earlier silence was broken by the wind's shriek and moans.

She flinched when Brad stopped dead. He spun around and stood like a statue, his eyes wide and his face frozen as he stared along the bleak pathway. She put her hand on his arm and felt his large bicep shivering under his parka. She hoped it was just from the cold, but deep in the pit of her stomach she knew it was something more. As he gently pushed her behind him, she realized her legs were shaking so hard she could actually felt her knees knocking together. It hurt.

'Please, Brad, let's go.'

Her stomach was fluttering in a tingly, upsetting way. She craned her neck and looked up at his face, hoping to see that big dumb grin splitting his handsome square jaw in an *I gotcha* kind of way. She'd be real angry for a while, sure, but then *real* relieved. But he wasn't smiling; instead, he looked pale … and scared.

Amanda saw his hand go to his waist and lift his parka. There was a gun tucked in behind his belt. Anger flared inside her then, at his secrecy, at bringing a dangerous weapon … And then, just as quickly, the emotion disappeared. *Thank god he did.*

He pulled the revolver free – shiny black metal against the white surroundings. As she stared at it she saw snowflakes melting on the short barrel; the heat from his body was still radiating from within the steel. She was about to speak when he raised the gun slowly to aim down the path. She followed its grim pointer and made out a shape in the swirling snow – roughly man-shaped, but impossibly huge.

'Is it … a bear?' Her voice sounded ridiculously small.

'Back up,' Brad said.

She was pressed up behind him, looking at the shape from under his arm. She lifted her camera on the cord around her neck. *Buzz-click.*

Brad stepped back just as she took the photo and tripped over her crouched body, falling backwards on top of her. The gun went off and she screamed. In a flash Brad was on his feet, the gun pointed back at the shape. But the slip path was empty.

'Shit. Did I hit it?'

'Was it a bear?' she asked. 'It looked like a big deformed bear.'

'I dunno. Must have been. I've heard black bears can get pretty big – 800 pounds and seven feet tall on their hind legs. It was a lot bigger than that, but it had to be a bear ... *had to be.*'

'It seemed to be waiting for us, but I can't see it anymore. Do you think it's gone?' Amanda had both hands on her stick, holding it out in front of herself like Gandalf at Helm's Deep.

'I think the gunfire scared it off. I might have even winged it. We're just lucky we didn't set off any more landslides. Come on, we better get off the path.' Brad looked over his shoulder briefly, then down at Amanda. 'Take my hand and hang on tight. We need to move quickly.'

*

Brad leaped off the path, back into the forest, literally dragging Amanda through the air with him. Being out of the landslide zone should have made him feel more secure, but the thick tree cover did the exact opposite. The wind was muffled, and light snow swirled gently around the tree trunks. The thick cloud, combined with fast-approaching twilight, made the dense stands of spruce and fir trees even darker.

Brad rushed them headlong down the mountain. Several times he stumbled on logs or loose rocks hidden beneath the snow and knew that come tomorrow his ankles would be painful and swollen. *A cheap price to pay*, he thought, *if it gets us off the mountain safely.*

Amanda fell and reached out to a slim tree trunk to save herself. She pulled her gloved hand away quickly when it stuck to something sticky and red.

Brad saw it. 'Hey, I did hit it.'

Good, he thought, and cast his mind back to the shape on the slip path. He'd seen black bears around the Appalachians before, but what had stood in the center of that trail was no bear – he knew that even with the low visibility. It wasn't like anything he recognized.

He could hear Amanda gasping and slowed his pace. He didn't want to stop, but he knew what she was experiencing. Even in an environment of frozen water, dehydration was a danger to both experienced and amateur hikers alike. He slid the pack off his shoulder so he could pull a water bottle free.

'C'mon, sip slowly. You're doing great.'

Twigs snapped behind him. Both of them froze, paralyzed by the sound of movement behind the tree line. Their breath created small plumes around their faces before dissipating into the white landscape.

A creaking beside them made Brad whirl with the gun. He found himself aiming it shakily at a tree that had become overburdened with snow. A huge mound slipped from a branch to fall harmlessly to the ground.

He laughed nervously. 'I knew that was probably all it was.'

He looked down at Amanda, but her face was half-hidden by the hand she held over her nose and lips. Brad had been breathing through his mouth to avoid taking the stinging air into his nostrils, but now he tested the air and it wasn't the cold that assaulted his senses. It was back – that shitty, rank, animal stench.

'God, no.' Amanda buried her face into the side of his parka.

What Brad had taken to be a tree trunk shifted on the darkening slope. The enormous hulking shape swayed slightly, a snow-covered colossus. Though it was partially obscured by the trees and falling snow, Brad could see that his first thought had been correct – the limbs were too long and the head too small for it to be a bear. It also looked to be well over ten feet tall; even a full-grown male grizzly topped out at about seven or eight, max.

'I love you,' he said to Amanda.

She nodded and said something back, but it was muffled by his parka. Brad didn't feel afraid anymore. His wife's frightened shivering brought forth in him a growing anger and a determination to protect her with his life.

He leveled the gun at the creature's enormous barrel chest. *This is gonna hurt you more than it is me, buddy ... I hope*, he thought.

Without taking his eyes off the figure, he leaned down close to Amanda's ear. 'No matter what happens, if I say run, you run. Don't look back. I'll be right behind you, but don't stop until you get to the first trekking station – the one with the emergency callbox. Tell the ranger –'

He stopped as a booming *whoop* caused the snow to fall from the tree branches around them. Brad flinched, then tried to swallow. His throat and mouth were bone dry. The thing thumped the ground with both arms and Brad actually felt the enormous power of the movement through the soles of his feet. The *whoop* came again, then the thing charged ten feet towards them and stopped.

Brad took an involuntary step backwards, dragging Amanda with him. With one hand he pulled her away from his body and shook her until she looked up at him. Her face was wet and her mouth was turned down in fear. He saw that her nose was running.

'You gotta go now,' he said. 'Remember what I told you – run and don't look back.'

He kissed her quickly and she tried to cling onto him.

'Don't look back, baby – I'll catch up.' He pushed her hard.

She seemed about to turn back towards him when the *whoop* came again, followed by deep grunting. She ran.

The creature made to follow the small running figure – until Brad stepped towards it and fired three shots. Things happened quickly then. It charged at him, faster than he'd expected. He fired again, but it was moving so fast he didn't know if he'd hit it.

At twenty feet, it leaped. He didn't feel the impact – everything just went black.

*

As consciousness returned, he felt the pain in his body and knew things inside were broken and torn. The shitty, rank stench was all over him – in his nostrils and mouth, on his skin. He tried to open his eyes but only one worked. He had the sensation of being carried, and looked at the ground. He saw the corner of one of those stones Amanda had wanted, the opposite-pointing arrows clear on its exposed surface. *I need to bring that back for her*, he thought crazily.

The smell was overpowering, and the pain exquisite as the creature adjusted its grip on him. It was climbing now, up towards the cave in the rock face. He watched with his one good eye as the light at the opening faded. The thing was dragging him into the mountain's depths.

He hoped Amanda had made it.

THREE

Asheville, North Carolina

'And what's wrong with you today, mister?'
The trainer scratched his head as he watched the West
African lion circle in its cage. Its golden hide covered 500 pounds of
rippling muscle, and the long fur on its head and at its neck framed a
fearsome visage. Its ribs moved in and out as it panted heavily. It
stopped its pacing to place its large snout against the bars and inhaled, snorting out a sneeze as though wanting to dislodge
something unpleasant from its nostrils. It swung away, making a dis-
agreeable growling sound deep in its chest.

The trainer noticed it kept staring at a spot just over his shoulder.
He turned; there was nothing there but mountain, darkening in the
fading sunlight.

'Settle down, Odin, it's just a big-ass old mountain. C'mon, we've
done this a hundred times.'

The trainer stood at the cage door with broom, mop and bucket,
and a shortened cattle prod under his arm. He knew the lion, and it
knew him. Usually it ignored him, or, at worst, acted like a misbe-
having teenager and swiped at the mop or knocked over his bucket.
But today, something was upsetting the creature – and no one
wanted to get close to a giant lion when it was acting weird.

'Should I call the vet? You got an upset, boy?'

The lion lay down and fixed its golden eyes, sphinx-like, on the
spot in the distance. It remained like that for many minutes, and
the trainer finally shrugged. 'That's more like it.'

He put his cleaning tools down and reached for the slide lock on
the door with one hand while keeping hold of the cattle prod in the

other – a foot-long baton with two exposed electrodes at the business end. He'd never used it – he and Odin were old friends – but still … The lock slid back and he pulled the heavy, metal gate open with a slight squeal, as he had done weekly over many years. He waited at the door for another few seconds, but the lion could have been stuffed and mounted for all the attention it gave him.

'Okay.' He reached down for his bucket, just for a second.

A maelstrom of fur and teeth flashed in his vision, and a roar exploded from mighty jaws. He fell backwards and threw his hands up over his head. Odin leaped over him and was gone.

The lion shot through the circus like an express train, its golden mane rippling in the chilly afternoon's fading light. The trainer lay shivering on the ground, his hands up and crossed over his face. A warm, wet patch spread across his groin.

*

'Chief. It's Jason Van Hortenson again.'

Asheville's police chief, Bill Logan, groaned and rubbed his balding pate. He thought briefly about telling Shelley, his septuagenarian receptionist, to tell the man he wasn't in. Then he shook his head and held both hands open in surrender. It wouldn't do any good to ignore the call – the annoying man would call back on the hour, every freakin' hour.

'I'll take it, Shell.'

A light on his phone started to blink, and he picked up the handset in one large hand, depressing the lit button with his little finger on the way to his ear.

'Mr. Van Hortenson, how are you tod–' He pulled the phone away from his ear slightly as the man's voice blared over him.

Van Hortenson was one of the new breed that had moved into the community in the last few years. Young moneyed sorts, they'd been buying up the smaller farms in the area, spending a fortune on them, then stocking them with some of the best-looking, best-groomed animals in the region. *Hobby farmers*, the locals called them; they worked Monday to Friday in high-paying jobs on the coast, then spent their vacations on the farm. Presumably, it gave them some sort of back-to-nature bragging rights.

Chief Logan grimaced and breathed in evenly through his nose as he looked up at the Asheville Police Department shield on his wall. *Integrity, Fairness, Respect* – the guiding principles of the APD. He tried hard to remember what they meant every time Van Hortenson rang to blast him for the most minor of perceived infringements. This time, he had some sympathy for the man – seemed someone was stealing his expensive Lakenvelder milking cows. Pretty stupid, as the brilliantly black-and-white beasts were pretty rare in these parts. Also, given the man only had two dozen cows, a single animal going missing would be immediately noticed.

'I'm sorry to hear that, sir,' Logan managed to cut in. 'Just to be clear – just the one animal taken again? I'll send a car around, but you might want to consider an aerial search, sir … No, I'm afraid you need to organize that; we just don't have the resources available right now. But, sir, my gut feel is these animals are wandering off –'

He pulled the phone away from his ear again and grinned. Shelley turned to mouth the word *ouch* to him. After another few seconds he put the phone carefully back to his ear and *hmm-hmmed* a few times.

'Might be a good idea to house the cattle closer to town for a few days, Mr. Van Hortenson – be cheaper than losing more head.'

Logan finished by promising to send a man up for another look-see, then hung up. He sat staring at the phone for a few minutes as his mind worked over the details. Three full-grown cattle gone over three nights. They weighed about 1000 pounds each; you couldn't exactly strap one to the hood of your car and speed through the town square.

'That's a helluva lot of free steak,' he said out loud.

He turned to stare out the window. The weather was getting colder. He couldn't see the cattle wandering up into Black Mountain, not when the snow was starting in earnest. Besides, the tree cover up there was too dense for grazing. *So where are those big brutes going?* he wondered.

*

'Higher, Daddy!'

The grin on five-year-old Emma Wilson's face threatened to split her cheeks as she kicked her skinny legs forward on the upswing and then tucked them back under the seat on the backswing.

'Last few times, Emma honey,' Clark Wilson said. 'It's getting cold and dark, and I need to rustle up some dinner for the both of us.'

'Eggs?' she called on the upswing.

'Nope,' Clark replied as she came towards him on the backswing.

'Dogs and ketchup?'

'Nooo. Last guess.' He smiled.

'Um, eggs?'

Clark laughed. 'Mommy left us a nice big pie – but I'll do the extras.'

'Yay. But no peas, Daddy – they're little balls of yuck.'

'Okay, no peas. Last big swing ...'

'Just a bit longer, *pleeease*. I can almost see the top of the mountain when I swing up really high, and I'm not cold at all.'

Clark turned to where his daughter was looking and half-smiled. Sunsets on the mountain were magnificent this time of year. The summer heat was long gone, autumn was just beginning to bite with a few light snows on the higher slopes, and the air at the foot of the mountain was as clean and clear as you could get anywhere on the continent. And she was right – it wasn't that cold. The evening was calm and quiet. It would have been perfect except for a damned funny smell – must be another squirrel gone and died under the house. Why they kept doing that, he never knew.

He looked back at his daughter. She looked so happy on the swing, in her favorite red sweater, pink rubber boots and some big clip-on earrings she'd pestered Helen to buy her from the market – blue glass beads finishing in tiny silver bells that tinkled like music. Emma said they reminded her of Christmas time. Clark shrugged – a few more minutes in this wonderful air wouldn't hurt, he reckoned.

'Okay, Emma-boo. But when I call, you come in ... and no daredevil swings, all right?'

'Never!' But she kicked out hard, her little body almost going horizontal on the swing, the earrings jingling.

'Count up to ten five times – by then you'll be hungry,' Clark told her.

He jumped up onto the small porch and pulled open the swing door. He appeared at the kitchen window, and opened the glass pane so Emma could hear him when he called. Then he started pulling utensils and pans from cupboards, and lifted the pre-baked pie from the refrigerator. *Mmm*, he thought, and broke off some of the crust and popped it in his mouth, raising his eyebrows in delight.

He checked the window – Emma swung back and forth in the repetition the very young enjoyed. He went back to his tasks, humming. The metronomic whine of the swing and the sound of Emma counting drifted in through the window. Life was good; moving to Asheville was the best decision he and Helen had ever made. No traffic, no smog, no street aggro – and access to the internet gave them the same size shop window as the big city boys at a hundredth of the cost. A no-brainer, really.

He grabbed a handful of carrots and potatoes from the pantry, and looked briefly at the bag of fresh peas – *little balls of yuck*. He chuckled; he'd take 'em over brussels sprouts any day.

There was a small squeak and metallic pop from outside the window and the sound of the swing stopped dead. Clark picked up the kitchen cloth to wipe his hands and stepped backwards to peer through the open window, expecting to see Emma skipping up towards the porch.

A cold shock jolted through his body as he saw that the swing was *gone* – the seat, the chains, everything. And Emma was nowhere to be seen.

He called her, still half-expecting to hear her respond, or the slam of the screen door as she came into the house. But there was nothing.

Clark threw the cloth down and leaned right out of the window. There was no sign of his child, just that smell, stronger than ever. He pulled his head in and raced to the back door calling Emma's name. Louder each time.

'Oh no, no, no, please, no.'

He raced into the yard – no trace.

He sprinted around the outside of the house, then the inside, tears filling his eyes. He called her name again – nothing.

Outside, he yelled her name up at Black Mountain. It remained mute.

FOUR

'Fuck it all to hell!' Captain Robert Graham threw the clipboard across the room, making Marshal and several of the scientific assistants duck for cover. 'And clean that stinking mess out of there before the general decides to pay us a surprise visit.'

Graham turned back to the screen and hit a button that caused the glass cell's window to become opaque so he could no longer see the screaming man raking the flesh from his blinded skull.

Lieutenant Alan Marshal turned to the assistants who were still taking notes. 'Batch ARC-044 – gross psychosis, physical manifestations of self-harm. Significant display of strength and resistance to pain – unfortunately, both turned against subjects' own selves.'

Captain Graham rested on his knuckles at a long bench, grinding his teeth. 'More than sixty dead, comatose, insane or exploded test subjects,' he said over his shoulder. 'At this churn rate, we'll end up with more soldiers in body bags than at fucking Pearl Harbor.'

He shook his head and pinched the bridge of his nose for a second, before staring down at his hands. They shook slightly. He slowly lifted his head to look along the remaining row of cell windows.

Years, he thought darkly, his frustration at the constant failure festering inside him. *Only one success, one enhanced soldier, after countless millions spent ... and we weren't ready for him. It was an accident, an aberration, a one-in-a-million shot that was never expected to succeed.* He snorted sourly. Blinded by the hubris of success, he had released the man back to duty, fully expecting that the results would be easily replicated, that the primary subject would be the first of thousands. But reality had kicked him in the teeth.

Human biology is the same ... and different. Identical twins brought up in different environments were subjected to a thousand differing variables that could significantly alter the direction of their physiology and psychology. Whatever Hammerson's soldier had had inside him to begin with had enabled the full absorption, fusion and utilization of the Arcadian treatment. But what the *fuck* had it been?

Years, he thought again, grinding his molars.

He heard the sound of the pressurized dart-gun in the shuttered room as the latest mutilated soul was brought down like a maddened rhino. The man's last days would be spent in an induced coma, until a euthanasia order was approved. Then his brain would be dissected and whatever clues remained would be teased from the corrupted tissue. Even hours after the subjects had been terminated, their flesh was still hot to the touch. It was as if their bodies acted like over-heating reactors, causing a total physiological meltdown. Their skin was covered in blistering sores and their internal organs were little more than soup by the time he got to open them up. It was always the same ... except for that one success.

He cursed again as he recalled how fucking Jack Hammerson had sent the man out into the mission meat grinder. He crushed his eyes shut, his knuckles turning white where they pressed onto the bench top.

Graham knew that impatience was his enemy now. He leaned back and drew in a deep breath. It had taken Jonas Salk seven years to perfect his first polio vaccine, and the man had worked with 220,000 volunteers and 20,000 physicians. Opening his eyes, he looked again along the rows of test rooms. There were just three more cubicles to examine.

He spoke with a deep feeling of lassitude. 'Is Batch Forty ready – the one where you introduced significant levels of cortisol directly into the brain prior to introduction of the Arcadian treatment?'

Marshal came and stood next to his superior officer, holding a clipboard in front of his chest like a shield. 'That's correct, sir – cortisol introduced into the cerebellum in the hypothalamus and thalamus junction. We figured that even though we'd already tried physically traumatizing the brain, maybe the *actual* destruction wasn't the key. Maybe it was only the chemical effects of the destruction, and as cortisol floods the brain following significant trauma ...'

Graham nodded and sucked in a deep breath. He knew that his superiors wouldn't be patient forever, and without the original Arcadian subject to hand they had to resort to a more heuristic approach – trial and error. Or rather, trial and fail, and fail, and fail again.

Fuck that Hammerson for burning the only successful subject's body, he thought.

Then he stood straighter and pressed a button beside the next large window. The darkened glass immediately cleared.

Graham's mouth dropped open. 'Oh, thank you, God.'

The young man in the cubicle sat on the edge of the bed talking to one of the huge male nurses.

Graham rushed to the next window, and then the next. He smiled and lowered his head to shut his eyes for a moment, before glancing up again quickly, as if to make sure his tired brain wasn't playing tricks on him.

A small blush of a rash on the men's cheeks, but they were fine – sane looking, normal. He turned to Lieutenant Marshal, a glow of gratification on his face. 'Ready them for the next round of testing.'

*

Nes Tziyona, Israel – The IIBR, Israel Institute for Biological Research – Deep Core Biohazard Containment Facility II

General Meir Shavit wrinkled his nose at the sight before him. Doctor Moeshe Weisz chuckled softly at the look on his face and turned back to the man on the bed. His body was coated head to foot in an oyster-colored, jelly-like substance that had also stained the pillow and sheets he lay upon – it was a ghastly sight.

'He's physically intact, but lapsing in and out of consciousness,' Weisz told the general. 'Don't be too concerned by the way he looks; his body's still expelling the bacterial residue. Stinks like gasoline and old fish, doesn't it? We also found this when we did a full body scan.' He held up a test tube with a small flesh-colored pellet inside. 'It's quite sophisticated miniaturized electronics – tracking device, I'd say.'

Shavit's eyes narrowed.

Weisz nodded. 'Seems someone wanted to keep an eye on him. We disabled it, of course.'

Shavit turned his attention back to the man on the bed. 'Turn it back on, and have it dropped out in the center of the Negev.'

Weisz had no intention of heading out into the Negev Desert himself. He opened his mouth to tell the general he needed to delegate the task to someone more appropriate, but the general's cold stare spoke of authority and a ruthlessness beyond anything Weisz could summon. Weisz swallowed the words he'd been about to say and simply nodded.

He cleared his throat and read from his clipboard. 'This is the most interesting case I've ever worked on. The microorganism that infected him has a pathogenesis like nothing I've ever seen in my life.' He motioned towards the form on the bed. 'This man should be dead a hundred times over, but his extraordinary physiology and the compounds he was being treated with have made him a unique specimen – a unique and valuable specimen.'

Shavit lit a cigarette and blew smoke into the air, making Weisz wince at the breach of the laboratory's sterile conditions. 'Will he live?'

Weisz paused for a few seconds to consider the question. 'Yes.'

Shavit grunted. 'Good. Send me the file.'

*

General Shavit sat alone in his office. He drew deeply on his cigarette, let the smoke escape through tight lips and tried hard to stifle the wet cough that squeezed up from lungs congested from decades of smoking. He lifted the folder on his desk and smiled grimly at the Hebrew characters on the cover: *Project Golem* – his little joke, or perhaps his wish. All Jews knew the legend of the golem – an ancient mythological figure molded from the clay of the Vltava River by the holiest of rabbis, Judah Loew ben Bezalel. The powerful man-like creature had defended the Jews in their time of need. Unfortunately, the story didn't have a happy ending – the creature that had at first been their saviour had become increasingly violent, until the rabbi returned it to an inert state.

A golem berserker – maybe that is what we now have in our possession, Shavit thought, and his laugh deteriorated into a wheezy cough.

He opened the folder to the report's latest pages and read silently for a few seconds, his brows knitted. Every report produced by the scientific team charged with investigating the American Special Forces soldier both astonished and frustrated him. Every time they learned a little more about Alex Hunter, known as the Arcadian subject, it turned out that they actually understood less.

Colonel Jack Hammerson, commander of the secretive HAWCs division within the US Special Forces, had worked with Mossad, Israel's intelligence and covert operations organization, to get Hunter out of the country before his own medical teams could claim the soldier's near lifeless body for experimentation and dissection. Hammerson had taken a huge gamble by handing Hunter over to a foreign power – both in terms of the man's life and his own career. Hammerson's own agency believed the Arcadian subject was now nothing more than powdered ash in the bottom of one of their powerful military furnaces.

Yes, Hammerson had gambled, but so had Shavit. He had authorized his niece, a Mossad operative, to retrieve the man, even though his body was riddled with a disease that everyone thought would turn it to mush, and which could have devastated Shavit's entire country. But Shavit knew he had no choice: the possible rewards were too great to ignore. Hunter had been brought to the Israeli military's secure laboratory beneath the Negev Desert, where Weisz's team had succeeded not only in eradicating the lethal microorganism but also in reviving the man.

Shavit felt he had won that round, but knew he was still in a race – to unlock the Arcadian's secrets before the man self-destructed. And it was one he fully intended to win; the future of Israel depended on it. The Americans would eventually succeed in reproducing their experimental soldier, but although they were magnificent at creating outstanding advancements, they were terrible at hanging on to them. Within a few years, the Russians and Chinese would have stolen everything they needed to create their own Arcadian soldiers, and then their proxies across the Middle East would soon follow.

The general flipped to the report's next page and started reading the section headed 'Cellular Repair and Revivification'. Analysis of Captain Alex Hunter's DNA showed that the ends of his chromosomes, his telomeres, had stopped fraying. A side note from Weisz explained the significance of this to the layman: a telomere was a biological capstone, like the plastic tip on a shoelace, and its role was to stop the chromosome deteriorating, or fraying. Most cells had an ability to divide about fifty times before they started to deteriorate and shorten, and therefore begin aging. Scientists could read the length of a cell's telomeres and provide an accurate picture of the cell's age and how many more times it would replicate. But Alex Hunter's DNA strands had ceased fraying – in fact, the telomere tips were almost totally intact. Weisz hypothesized that this could be why the man had such enormous potential for rapid cellular repair. It also meant that Alex Hunter might stop aging; or, at the other extreme, his entire system could turn malignant, as the only other cells known to have no finite chronological barrier were cancer cells. Like most of the analysis in these reports, it ended with a brief notation stating that more time and work was needed.

Shavit shook his head. 'Always more work needed. Never anything we can use now.'

He lit another cigarette, and screwed an eye shut as the smoke curled up one side of his face. He turned to the section on neuro-architectural analysis, skipping paragraphs of dense jargon and stopping when he came to several topographical images of Alex Hunter's brain side by side with a normal brain. The normal brain looked like an average-sized pink and gray cauliflower with its folds, bulges and coils. By comparison, Hunter's brain had hundreds more folds. The known sulcus folds were labelled, but other arrows indicated numerous newly identified folds. As with the cellular repair data, however, the notations below the images stated *Uses Unknown* time and time again. Shavit swore.

'Useless,' he said to the empty room.

He frowned as he noticed a paragraph at the bottom of the page stating that the latest neuro-mapping had found no trace of the metallic object that had been embedded deep in Hunter's cortical mass when he came to them. This was puzzling, as all reports on the Arcadian subject had clearly shown that the bullet lodged deep within his cerebellum had been the initial genesis of his condition. How could it suddenly be gone?

Shavit had read of cases where sharp objects had worked their way through people's bodies. There was an old woman in Tel Aviv in 1985 who'd fallen on one of her knitting needles; the tip had broken off in her heart. At the time, surgery was determined to be too high risk an option and so they'd kept the woman in hospital for a number of weeks. While there, she had developed a cough – a cough that had eventually brought up the broken tip of the knitting needle.

Maybe, he thought.

He read on. More notes and diagrams and arrows ... strangely, there was *something* still remaining in Hunter's brain, or perhaps something totally new – a whitish trauma zone with a solid central mass that showed up in the CAT and MRI scans and X-rays. At first, the scientists had thought it was a blood clot, but then found indications that it had a dense biological core. Further scanning had suggested that there was some form of electrical activity taking place within what the report now described as a *synaptic bundle* – it was as though the small mass was firing off its own electrical impulses.

Shavit raised his eyebrows and glanced at the section on further data collection options. *Neurosurgical needle biopsy ... hmm* – he took another deep drag on his cigarette – *maybe, but not yet.* His niece would not react well if the man she had risked everything to retrieve was sent back to her with holes drilled into his skull. Weisz might end up needing surgery of his own. Shavit laughed dryly, and flipped to the last page to review the progress of the recent test subjects. He sighed and scratched his forehead. As with the previous week, the week before that and every week since Hunter's recovery, they had been trying to replicate the process that had led to his condition. But every time they had failed.

Shavit ground out his cigarette in disgust as he read through the new list of names, treatment variations and the familiar, dismal results: *Patient Comatose; Patient Psychologically Disordered; Patient Emergency Termination.* He would love to know how the Americans were approaching the problems his team kept encountering. After several months, they still had *nothing.*

He sat back and placed one gnarled hand behind his head, staring at the ceiling. *Almost nothing.* They still had control of the original Arcadian. Alex Hunter himself was the key: locked away in his memory – if it were still intact – were the events that had led to his superior physical and mental condition. If the information could be extracted ... or, better yet, if he could be encouraged to tell them ... Perhaps the man needed something to jog his memory, such as being with something he remembered or someone he trusted. A friend.

General Shavit lit another cigarette, then lifted his pen and made some notes. When his niece finished her current mission, he'd organize for her to pay Captain Alex Hunter a visit. Maybe even spend some prolonged time with him.

As he signed the order, a sound came from deep in his chest that could have been the beginning of a cough or a rumbling laugh. He liked to gamble, and he liked to win.

FIVE

Beirut, Lebanon

The woman walked slowly with the stiff-ankled rocking motion of the old and arthritic. Her traditional black abaya attracted the heat and must have made the ninety-degree early summer temperature significantly warmer. To anyone watching her pass, she appeared to be a devout Muslim, also wearing a niqab, or face veil, and black gloves. Around her neck, reading glasses with thick black frames hung from a short length of string and banged against her ample bosom as she walked.

She paused and looked back down the steep, cobbled street. Beirut was a mix of ancient and modern, home now to major industry and corporations and even considered as a candidate for the 2024 Summer Olympic Games. A smart black AMG Mercedes shot past, no doubt headed for one of the fine restaurants on the waterfront that did a roaring trade with the tanned and well-heeled locals. The woman inhaled deeply; the city's leafy avenues, rich with the smell of coffee and cinnamon, made it seem a world away from the troubles of the south. Beirut reflected all the magnificence of modern Lebanon, with Christians, Druze, Shias, Sunnis and many more seeming to live together in cultural and political harmony. The modern mixed with the ancient, the religious with the carefree; in Beirut it seemed the Middle East was one of the happiest places on earth.

The woman walked on, towards Gemmayze Street in the Ashrafieh district. The streets narrowed to thin, winding lanes here and it was easier to get lost. She checked her bearings, and hoisted her string bag a little higher; the loaves of fresh bread, cheese and onions would be a welcome breakfast for the men. She paused to rest on an old wooden chair in the shade of a young olive tree. Beirut was a small pool of calm water in a turbulent sea; unlike the south, where the poor begged in the streets, resentment fomented, vengeance was plotted and hatred often boiled over into bloody violence. The south had been the frontline for the Israel–Lebanon conflict for many years. It was where Hezar-Jihadi ruled – the Party of a Thousand Martyrs, they called themselves. They were political, religious and paramilitary; their leaders called for the destruction of Israel, war with the West and a true Islamic state in Lebanon. Violence was their first negotiating tool of choice.

The woman lifted the glasses from her chest and placed them on her face, then sat as immobile as the street's surrounding bricks and mortar as she watched a young man walk quickly up the street towards a solid wooden door recessed into an old-fashioned apartment block. He looked around furtively, then knocked three times.

The woman waited for another minute after he'd disappeared inside, then she got to her feet and hobbled towards the same door.

*

Abu ibn Jbeil opened the door a crack and peered out. He looked the old woman up and down. She lifted her bag a little higher and groaned softly under its weight. The eyes behind the thick glasses were like blurred pools of oil – unreadable. She moaned again, her arm shaking from the weight of the bag.

Abu ibn Jbeil could not care less about her suffering, but she was expected and her food would be welcome. He opened the door a little wider, but as she entered he stopped her with his hand and roughly felt her sides, back and front, searching for guns, knives or explosives. She coughed wetly, and he held his breath, hurrying through his examination. How he detested being so close to the old hag, touching her body. It was probably a waste of time, but it was best to take no chances considering how close they were to their goal.

Finished, he stood back and waved her impatiently towards the kitchen, resisting the strong urge to kick her large behind as she hobbled past him.

*

The woman shuffled slowly towards the five men sitting around the table in the darkened room. All had stopped talking at her arrival, and now sat smoking their thick, pungent shisha tobacco and sipping syrupy-sweet coffee. Though her limbs were slow, her eyes darted from one man to another. She recognized Hezar-Jihadi faces and also some senior Iranian Revolutionary Guards. Unfurled on the table, the corners held in place by a bottle of whisky and several ashtrays, were the schematics for the new Iranian missile, the Shihab-2, the Meteor.

She stopped at the table and turned to the black-eyed young man who had let her in. 'May I use the washroom, *edame*?'

The young man looked to one of the older men at the table, who shook his head without even looking up. 'No,' the young man said. 'Leave the bag and go, *halla, halla*.'

She nodded her understanding and turned towards the kitchen. On the way, she pulled off her gloves and pushed them into a fold of her robe. If the men had been watching, they would have been surprised to see such strong and youthful hands on one so bent and infirm. She lifted the string bag onto the kitchen bench and in the same motion drew up the front of her long abaya. Strapped high between her smooth, muscular thighs was a squat black pistol. She pulled it free of the tape and secreted it in one of her long, loose sleeves. She whispered one word: 'Installed.'

From one arm of her glasses, came the reply: 'Proceed.'

She drew in a deep breath and turned to hobble back out to the men.

The young man who'd let her in was looking at her with ill-concealed disgust and contempt. He felt in his pocket, pulled out some crumpled Lebanese pounds, rolled them into a small ball and dropped it at his feet. The woman slowly bent to retrieve it; however, when she came back up it was not the wrinkled money she had in her hand but an unwavering black Barak pistol. There were no words needed – the gun barked once in the young man's face, and before his body had even begun to fall she turned and fired at the men at the table.

Two went down with precision headshots; the third was taken high in the sternum, throwing a plume of blood and shattered spinal column over the wall behind him. Of the remaining two, one took up a vantage point behind some furniture and the other launched himself at her across the table. Perhaps his mind was fooling him into believing it was an old woman under the dark robes and she would easily buckle under his 200-pound frame. Maybe he realized his error when he was in the air, but by then it was too late.

The woman took up a combat stance and, with perfect balance, launched a flat-soled kick to his face. Even though the man easily outweighed her by over fifty pounds, the muscles in her thighs uncoiled with enough force to smash his nasal septum up into his brain. He was dead before his large body had hit the ground. She dropped and rolled to the left, slamming her back to the wall. She needed to reacquire the final target.

A voice sounded in the quiet from amongst the toppled furniture. 'Bat-Tzion, you have stopped nothing. There are hundreds like us, and we will eventually bulldoze your bodies into the sea.'

The woman remained silent at the threat. Seconds passed as she quickly looked around the room, now heavy with the smell of cordite and coppery blood.

'Bat-Tzion, if you let me leave, I will give you Nazranasha. I know you have been searching for him. He is here, you know, right now, in Beirut.'

Nazranasha was the leader of Hezar-Jihadi and the mastermind behind every assassination, bombing and cross-border raid for a decade. He was the first prize for every Israeli soldier and agent.

Tempting, but not for today, the woman thought. She began to slide forward in the shadowy room, towards where the voice was coming from.

'Israeli, I surrender to you. Here ...' A new Glock handgun clattered on the floor in the center of the room.

A lesser agent would have been momentarily distracted and perhaps have missed the almost imperceptible sound of the flattened steel pin of a stun grenade being removed.

The man stood to throw the explosive. At the same time, the woman also stood and fired twice in quick succession. The man took two shots to the forehead and hit the ground at roughly the same time as the grenade. The woman dived behind a couch, crushed her eyes shut and held her hands over her ears. Stun grenades were designed for maximum disorientation and had little shrapnel; however, they could destroy eardrums or maim if they landed close by.

The small black cylinder exploded with an ear-shattering *whump* and a flash that would have seared the woman's retinas for days. The impact wave blew out all the windows, and the pyrotechnic metal oxidant set fire to the rug and most of the furniture.

The woman stood, her ears still ringing even though they'd been covered. She crossed to the table where the missile schematics lay, stuffed them under her robes, then ran to the kitchen and retrieved her bag. She looked down at the black gun she still gripped; the hand that held it was as steady as a rock. In the meat between her thumb and forefinger was a small tattoo – a blue Star of David.

She quickly wiped the weapon and threw it onto the burning rug, then spoke to the dead man. 'And there will always be thousands more like us waiting for you.'

She pulled on her gloves and slid the glasses back onto her nose. She pressed a small stud at the side of one lens and spoke softly. 'Blue Star requesting immediate extraction.'

The emotionless voice spoke into her ear again: 'Extraction authorized.' And then: 'Be advised, Blue Star, Arcadian conscious.'

She almost stumbled as her body, already awash with adrenaline, kicked up another gear. *Awake*, she thought. *At last.*

She drew in a long breath, calming her urge to rush. She bent slightly at the knees and waist before she pulled open the door. Once again, an old woman suffering from the heat shuffled down a winding street in the city of Beirut.

*

Adira Senesh couldn't take her eyes from the figure on the bed. She found it hard to associate the mucus-covered thing staining the sheets with the strong, handsome HAWC soldier she had known. Alex Hunter had been – *was* – like no human being she had ever seen or probably ever would again. Adira's jaw clenched and she felt her anger rise at fate's cruel joke. She had told Alex she would take him horse riding along the shore of the Sea of Galilee; to stand on the purple cliffs of the Golan Heights. She had wanted to show him *her* Israel. Now he was here and yet he wasn't. It wasn't fair.

Together, they had faced horror and death, and he had saved her life. In turn she had stopped the Americans from cutting him into a thousand pieces for study. She drew in a deep breath. The man she knew was buried in there somewhere. She was sure of it.

She became aware of the scientist next to her talking.

'Although we'd kept the specimen at extremely low temperatures, the bacterium was still active in his system – just slowed to a point of near inactivity.'

'The specimen,' she echoed, feeling her rage increasing further.

Weisz nodded, unaware of her reaction, and continued. 'And then a week ago it inexplicably resumed its vigorous progress. We don't know what triggered it, but it didn't leave us with many options. Nothing has worked against its aggressive progress to date. In my opinion, this thing is straight from Hell. You've seen what it can do to flesh? We extracted and cultivated some of the bacteria immediately on the specimen's arrival at the facility, then injected it directly into several chimpanzees. In twenty-four hours, they were liquid – muscle, hair, even bone. We had to incinerate the remains in an industrial furnace, as the residue was still active and aggressively infectious.'

Weisz nodded towards the bed. 'With the bacterium active again, it would have been the same with this specimen. Within twenty-four to forty-eight hours we would have had nothing left to work with. So we immediately brought the body temperature back up to sixty degrees, just below room temperature, and increased the dosage for the Arcadian treatment that was brought in with him. We have no idea how his body metabolizes the chemical compounds, as they've proved fatal to every other subject they've been administered to. But ever since, his body has been squeezing out the denatured Hades bacterium.'

Weisz looked like he was about to touch the man's face, but instead let his gloved fingers hover just above the slimy flesh. 'The microorganism is now fully degraded; the tertiary and secondary structures, the bonding interactions, are all fully disrupted. Seems the treatment, and the specimen's unique metabolism, are the only systems that can mount a defence to overwhelm the invaders.' He shrugged. 'If only we knew how they do it.' He straightened. 'Every now and then he wakes, yells a few garbled sentences, then lapses back into unconsciousness.'

Adira pushed past the scientist and leaned slightly towards the figure on the bed. When she saw the leather and canvas cuff restraints on his hands and feet, she felt her heart rate start to lift. Anger bloomed in her belly and her lips compressed in displeasure.

Weisz chortled, probably interpreting her expression as disgust at the smell or the man's physical appearance. 'Go ahead, it's safe to be close. Just won't be very pleasant until the body's finished excreting the microorganism's protein shell. The suit I'm wearing is regulation for this level, not specifically for protection from this oily, oversized *goyim*.' He smiled and used his pen to prod Alex's body through a clean section of the sheet. 'I, personally, have taken several slices from the subject and I can guarantee there is no viable infectious agent remaining.'

Adira felt a charge go through her body. It was the same feeling she had before she killed an enemy agent. She steeled herself, closing her eyes momentarily. When she opened them, she turned to face the scientist, using all her will to keep her voice even. She failed, her voice increasing in intensity on each word. 'You are anatomizing? Who authorized this?'

The force of her voice and gaze seemed to make Weisz suddenly unsure of himself.

'Uh, the general, General Shavit. He authorized the increase in temperature on the basis that the subject was useless to us in a nexus between life and death – too alive to dissect, too dead to consciously assist us in our testing. We hoped the raised temperature and dosage would retrieve him to a state we could work with. And it worked.'

Adira felt her mouth go dry. 'You are not working *with* him. You are working *on* him!'

The scientist stepped back as her glare turned volcanic. He must have realized she was no simple functionary sent by the ministry. Adira moved closer to the scientist, not sure what she was intending to do to him. Before she could act, the figure on the bed reached out and grabbed her around the wrist. The thick straps of the heavy leather restraints hung from his wrist like tattered streamers.

Adira grunted, first from shock, then from pain. Alex still hadn't opened his eyes, but he hadn't reached out blindly; he'd seemed to know where she was. She gritted her teeth at the excruciating pain as his grip compressed the bones in her forearm.

Weisz dropped his clipboard and moved to a panel of buttons on the wall, obviously intending to call in security.

'Stay where you are!' Adira's voice froze his hand in midair.

Weisz stood rigid for a few seconds, before edging towards the door.

Adira groaned as Alex dragged her towards the bed. 'Alex, do you know me? Do you know who I am?' She brought her other hand around to try to dislodge his fingers, but she might as well have been working on steel. 'Alex, please.'

His eyes opened and she saw spidery red and black veins ringing the once gray-green pupils.

'It's coming!' he shouted and his grip tightened even more. 'She's scared. She needs me! I need to go.'

He released her wrist and sat up, the restraint on his other arm parting like paper. Blobs of dark jelly slid from his face and torso. He coughed, spraying more black mucus onto the bed. He slowly brought a hand up to the side of his head and groaned deeply. 'It hurts.' He looked at her, and his eyes seemed to register recognition for the first time. 'You.'

The first dart took him in the shoulder, the second directly over the heart. The following four went in anywhere the security detail could hit. His hands dropped, and he looked down at the darts piercing his body in confusion before he slumped back on the bed.

Adira screamed in horror and leaped at Alex to pull one of the hypodermic darts from his chest. Before she could grab another, she was seized from behind – one hand on her arm, one on her hair – and pulled roughly backwards. In her volatile frame of mind, it was a mistake – she reacted violently, spinning quickly to strike the first man under the chin with the flat of her hand. His head shot back on his bull-like neck and he fell backwards like a plank of wood.

She brought the other hand around to use the back of her fist on the next man. He dropped the handcuffs he was carrying and staggered backwards, but not before her other hand had shot out to chop into his windpipe, crushing it. He went down on his knees, his tongue protruding, and clawed at his neck, making a gagging sound as his remaining air ran out.

She turned to the other two men, her legs planted in a fighter's stance, hands up and ready. They held their position, looked from Adira to Alex, then back to her. Her furious gaze burned into them, its meaning clear – *back off*. They shrugged and edged out of the room, dragging their incapacitated colleagues with them.

Adira heard the door lock, and her shoulders slumped. *Now what?*

She walked to a metal sink in the corner of the room and wet a cloth she found there. She returned to sit on the edge of the bed and gently bathed more of the dark, oily substance from Alex's face, smiling as the clear skin shone through.

'Welcome back, my Arcadian.'

SIX

'Young lady's name is Amanda Jordan – big Brad Jordan's wife. I know him – he's a good fella.' Officer Markenson nodded towards the woman on the hospital bed. 'She's busted up pretty bad. But the real problem seems to be more *inside* her head. The doc says she's catatonic, won't say a word, and I don't think she's even blinked once since we pulled her off the slope.'

Markenson waved his hand in front of the woman's face, then made a throwing motion at her staring eyes. She didn't flinch.

'Stop that.' Chief Logan frowned at his officer, then looked at the cuts, abrasions and plaster cast on the young woman's arm, before turning back to Markenson. 'Whatta we know? Where's her husband now?'

Markenson shrugged. 'Still up there. Looks like they decided to trek to the top of the mountain – we think the weather gave them an early taste of winter, and I guess they either got caught in an avalanche or had a fall. Or maybe they had an argument that turned ugly – there was blood on one of her gloves.'

Chief Logan grunted. 'Can't rule anything out until we find him, or she speaks. What about her effects – anything?'

'The blood traces on her glove are being analyzed now. We know from Brad Jordan's driver's licence that he's type A. Medical Examiner's office is gonna give me a call when they're done. There was also a camera around her neck – case was busted, but we think the memory chip inside can still be read. Johnson was going to try and download it back at base.' Markenson shrugged again. 'And that's about it, Chief.'

Logan stepped back from the bed. 'Okay, give Harley a heads-up – we might need his dogs for a ground search.' Logan frowned. 'Not even winter yet – way too early for people to start falling off the mountain. Call me if something interesting turns up on the camera or with the blood trace.'

'You got it, Chief ... And Chief ...?'

Logan paused.

Markenson waved his hand in front of the woman's blank face again. 'It's goddamn freaky though, ain't it?'

Logan rolled his eyes. 'Just have the ME and Johnson send me the information ASAP.'

*

Arriving at the station, Chief Logan eased in behind his desk, making room for a stomach that had seen way too much fast food and cold beer. He pulled the bagel from its bag and laid it gently on the brown paper, then took the lid from his coffee and savored the aroma for a few seconds. He sighed contentedly: his morning ritual – bagel, coffee and the newspaper; a small pool of calm in a sea of chaos. He was in early this morning, even with his stop-off at the hospital, planning to coordinate several searches and investigative cases that ranged from the trivial to the bizarre. That was in addition to slogging through his usual mountain of paperwork. He lifted the bagel and took a bite, then unfolded the stiff newspaper – and stopped chewing.

'Oh fuck, no.'

He closed his eyes briefly and swallowed the dry lump of dough. He opened them and looked at the headline again – he'd read it right the first time: *Lion on the Loose – Two Missing.*

The story, from an unnamed source, mentioned the Wilson girl and Brad Jordan in the first paragraph. Then it had some wonderfully sarcastic quotes from Jason Van Hortenson about his damned missing Lakenvelder cows, and if that wasn't enough, the type was all crowded around a grainy photograph of Amanda Jordan sitting up zombie-like in bed. The picture caption: *Big cat got her tongue?*

Logan's first thought was to track down whoever had breached the hospital's security to take the photograph, but then he realized that it didn't matter – the information was in the open and already traveling like a shockwave out from the town.

You read a headline that says *Joe Citizen Missing on the Moun-*

43

tain, you shrug and move to the sports page. But you see *Lion on the Loose, and Joe Citizen Missing* and you're damn well gonna read the whole story ... and then tell all your friends, who'll tell all their friends.

Logan looked at his bagel, but his appetite had deserted him.

As if on cue, the phone rang. He sucked in a long breath and said to the phone without lifting the receiver, 'Good morning, Mayor; what kept you?'

This was going to get ugly.

He lifted the handset. 'Good morning, Mayor ...'

*

Logan threw the report onto his already overcrowded desk and sat down heavily, swiveling his chair to face his computer. He flipped the folder open with one hand and used the other to open his email. Immediately, his inbox filled with messages. His eyes moved from the report to the messages and then back again as he tried to manage the two things at once. He felt a sense of pressure and urgency ... and the morning was still young.

After the call from the mayor, he'd been straight on to Markenson, taking a big bite out of him for not keeping him in the loop about the lion's escape. Now he was in a race to read the facts report, knowing full well he'd already promised the mayor he'd have things under control in twenty-four hours. *And pigs might fly*. He snorted and shook his head; the damned mayor had been better briefed than he was. He made a note on his pad – *Never talk to the mayor*. He'd make sure that was on his list of items for the next departmental briefing.

He read the email messages with quick darting eyes, deleting most as he went, until he came to the last two. One was from the Asheville Medical Examiner, and the other was from Johnson, with attachments. The man had managed to extract the Jordan woman's photographs from the busted camera.

'Good man,' Logan said over his cold coffee.

There were fifty-five shots – Logan pasted them up on his screen in rows and moved quickly through the timeline of Brad and Amanda's last hours together. There was the smiling couple loading the car, stopping for a sandwich and soda on the way to the mountain, with several shots of the side of Brad's huge jug-eared head as he was driving. Logan flipped through them quickly – there was no sign of any tension, both the young man and woman looked happy and relaxed with each other.

He slowed his review – they had arrived. A shot of Brad pointing up at the Black Dome peak. If nothing else, it gave Logan a place to start, and he should at least be able to identify the path they took.

He stopped at a surprising view out over the other mountains. It was a good shot, and they were high up. White specks told him that the snow had been falling quite heavily. He played around with the image for a while – enlarging, removing shading and brightness, focusing in on certain quadrants. It didn't do any good; he couldn't determine where they were. He'd spent plenty of time up on the mountain and he didn't know anywhere at that height that was so opened up from the trees. Basically, there just shouldn't have been a view like the one in the photograph.

'Must've found a new spot,' he said to the screen.

He tagged the image, moved it to the side of his screen, and stopped again at the next shot – a block of carved stone. The next image was the same, just at a slightly different angle. He shook his head; the symbols meant nothing to him. He tagged the shots and continued.

The next shot made the chief frown and lean forward – there was something on a pathway at the edge of the cliff. He didn't recognize the path or what he was seeing. Was it a figure? Didn't look right. He couldn't work out the scale as there were no trees, and it was hard to make out the content as the snow looked heavier in this shot. It also didn't help that Brad's parka was obscuring half the shot; looked like Amanda had been standing behind him.

Logan finished his coffee while staring at the image, and grimaced at the cold metallic taste. He shrugged and dropped the cup into his wastebasket, moved the photo to the side and went on. The first shot reappeared – so, that was it.

He took down some notes: *Climb towards Dome? New lookout and new path opened up on mountainside – high (6000+ feet) – possible slip? Stone artifact – valuable? Fight because it was valuable? Figure on pathway – man, bear, tree, unknown?*

He looked at his notes – not much to go on. *Better than nothing*, he thought, and reached back to the keyboard to open the message from the ME. His brow furrowed as he read the clinical diagnostic results of the blood analysis from Amanda Jordan's glove.

First-Level Serological Analysis:
Blood antigen type: O
Blood biology: Non-human
Metazoa: Mammalian
First-level match: No match / type unknown

That's a big fucking help, he thought as he continued scrolling down the page.

Second-Level Genetic Analysis:
98% base-for-base genetic match to human

Excessive alpha-haemoglobin genes to human. Lower ALU repeats to human. Chromosomal tips contain DNA not present in human chromosomes, and then 10% more DNA than human.
Second-level match – international zoological database: No match / type unknown

There was another line in a different font, telling Logan that the Medical Examiner had added the note:
Sample is either a fake, or primitive form of blood type more closely resembling that of the great apes. Check the zoos and circuses.
It finished with a smiley face.
'Well, that's an even bigger pile of *no help*, you smartass,' Logan said, sitting back in his chair.
He thought for a moment, then leaned forward to flick through Markenson's report. After a few seconds he folded his arms, smiling.
'*More closely resembling that of the great apes* – and whatta you know, the circus is in town. Priority one, find that fucking lion.'

He pushed back his chair, then paused to look at one of the pictures he'd pasted at the side of his screen, that of the figure standing in falling snow. He frowned. He hoped the disappearances weren't the result of a lion on the loose, but at the same time a small part of him hoped they were.

SEVEN

Alex groaned and sat up, holding his head. The pain was like a blast furnace in his skull. Within the agonized fire, a whirlwind of images flashed across his consciousness – people, places, things monstrous and alien. There was a giant bearded man pointing a gun at his face. With a shaking hand, Alex touched a small scar above his eye.

He rocked back and forth for a few minutes until the pain became bearable: a vice instead of a hot spike. The images faded and he rubbed his face. After another moment, he felt able to open his eyes. He remembered being in a laboratory, and feeling like he was drowning. A foul liquid in his nose, mouth and lungs – a dream perhaps. He flexed his hands and turned them over. There were scars on his forearms and running up his biceps. It looked like skin had been removed or carved out.

'What happened?'

His voice sounded strange to his ears. He blinked a few times and waited for the dizziness to settle.

He looked around. The room was small and sparsely furnished – the bed he was sitting on, a chair, a chest of drawers with a bowl of fruit on top. No windows. There was a small bathroom containing a few toiletries; again, no window.

Alex went to the chest and pulled open the top drawer. There was clothing inside, all new. He lifted a pair of slacks and let them unfold at his side to gauge their length. Satisfied, he pulled them on, and followed with a T-shirt. The smell of the fruit made him hungry. He couldn't remember when he'd last eaten anything. Grabbing a green apple, he lifted it to his mouth, then paused and closed his eyes for a second. The smell reminded him of something. He tried to concentrate, but as soon as he pressed for the answer, the furnace swung open again.

He groaned as the pain intensified, and staggered back to the bed, sitting down heavily. Once again the faces swirled around him, like silent ghosts demanding to be acknowledged. There came a young woman, attractive and dark-haired, with blue eyes that changed color as he watched. Next was an older man, square-headed and brutal-looking, then a woman, older, her face ... comforting somehow. There was a large dog beside her and she called to it, said its name. He strained to hear, but the words were muted.

The pain intensified, and he felt a warm wetness on his top lip that ran quickly down to his chin. Blood, running from his nose. He let the images go and tried to relax his mind. The pain immediately eased.

Alex took off his T-shirt and held it to his face, waiting for the flow to subside. He pulled it away and noticed the dark blood was thick with black oily streaks. 'Nice.' He flung the shirt into the bathroom and got to his feet.

After showering, and finishing off most of the fruit, he decided to check out his surroundings in more detail. He reached for the door handle; the round, metal knob was cool to the touch and only turned a fraction before stopping – locked. He frowned; there was no key or locking mechanism on his side. *Jammed?*

He squeezed the knob and tried again. The handle squealed in protest, then came off in his hand. *Huh?* He held up the steel ball. It was dented and compressed from where he'd gripped it. The part that had attached to the door was twisted as though it had been wrung in an industrial press. He dropped the handle to the floor and pushed at the door – still locked. Now he was trapped, and there was no door handle.

'What the hell?'

His neck prickled. He whipped around, feeling a presence behind him. The room remained silent and empty, but as he was about to turn back he noticed a tiny black dot on the ceiling, no bigger than a match-head. It could have been a housefly, or a spot missed by the painters, but he focused on it and saw it clearly for what it was – a small glass lens.

He gritted his teeth, anger starting to build. 'Fuck you. I'm leaving.'

He took a step back, preparing to kick the center of the door, when the lock rattled and the door opened.

Alex took a step back. 'You.'

*

Adira walked into the room, leaving the door open. Alex looked from her to the open door.

She smiled. 'You're not a prisoner, Alex, you never were. It was locked to ensure you didn't stumble around in a strange place while you were recovering. You've been very sick.'

'Alex.' He tested the name. It sounded familiar. 'I can't remember ...'

Adira ignored his question; instead, she walked around him, nodding. Physically, he looked as if he'd never been sick, let alone spent six months in an induced low-temperature suspended animation to halt the progress of a killer, necrotizing bacteria that was trying to ingest his body.

She smiled at him. 'You were injured, but now you're fine.'

'I know you, don't I? I think ...' He grimaced. 'It hurts when I try to remember things.'

She nodded, fixing a concerned look on her face. It seemed any memory of his ordeal, his early life, even of his time in the Special Forces, had been erased.

Might not be a bad thing, she thought.

She spoke as if reciting a prepared script. 'I'm with the hospital. You were injured, and you've been in a coma. Be patient; the memories will come back slowly. Your name is Alex Horowitz, and for now all you need to know is you're back amongst friends.' She reached out and placed a hand on his shoulder. 'Very good friends.'

She held his eyes. 'You've come back to me – to us – and no one and nothing else matters for now. Okay, Alex?'

He stared back at her, then seemed to give up. 'Nothing else matters,' he repeated.

*

Adira sat motionless, waiting for the general to get to the point. Her uncle had summoned her, undoubtedly to discuss Alex Hunter. She could see the Project Golem folder on his desk, open at the surgical biopsy section. He had obviously meant it to be seen.

She drew in a deep breath through her nose. The smell of cigarettes, aftershave and old leather was familiar and comforting. Still, today she was nervous. Captain Adira Senesh, member of Mossad's elite Metsada unit, had crawled through claustrophobic terrorist tunnels, fought hand to hand with some of the most dangerous killers in the world, and seen things of abject brutality and horror, but at this moment in General Shavit's office, her tension was acute as she waited to hear whether she would be allowed to continue with the project. She loved her uncle dearly, but if he tried to remove her, there'd be trouble ... and she'd make it.

The general's voice came from his lips like the warm smoke of his cigarette. 'Everything has a price, Addy. Stealing Captain Hunter from the Americans, secreting him here in these facilities – there is more than a financial cost, there are political costs: the cost of putting the entire population of Israel at risk of contamination; the cost of embarrassing our remaining American supporters; and the cost to both our careers.'

She heard a slow wheezing intake of breath and then an exhalation like a sigh. 'Addy, did you really think we went through all this just because you felt you needed to repay some sort of personal debt? Or liked the color of the captain's eyes?' He shook his head slowly. 'The Arcadian genesis is a puzzle, and we need our puzzles solved, Addy.'

Adira's burning anger at Weisz for taking samples from Alex had dissipated. Now she just felt confused and disappointed.

'Weisz said he was cutting him up. You know that was never the deal – you promised he would be looked after. We agreed that we'd seek answers from the man, if that was possible, not just from his biology.' She sat forward. 'No one is going to be cutting the answers out of him. I swear this to you: the next person who touches him ...' She left the threat hanging.

The general sighed and shifted in his deep leather chair. Adira felt her foot begin to tap the floor, still at the mercy of her nerves. She saw her uncle's eyes slide from her jumping foot to her face.

'My child, does he even know you?' he asked gently. 'The real you? We know the infection reached his brain. Believe it or not, I worry about your safety – you know what the Arcadian records said about his mental stability. He could tear you in half before he even realized he had done it.'

'No, never. He saw me ... and *he knew me.*' She looked at her wrist, circled by a band of bruises.

More slow wheezing as the general watched her face for a few seconds. 'Maybe, Addy, and maybe not. But we need the secrets he holds – you've always known that. The Hades bacterium forced our hand, but it also brought him back to us. We must make use of the opportunity while we have it. How long until the American military discovers he is here? For now, they think he is dead, but we know Colonel Hammerson wasn't authorized to deliver Hunter's body to you, or to let you take him from the country. This is the age of technology, Addy – nothing, and no one, can stay hidden for long.

'Yes, I promised only to question Hunter, but how could that happen while he was frozen? If he will not talk to us, his cells will – I must have my answers.' The general leaned further back into the chair and his eyes closed. 'I'm sorry, Addy, but the bill is coming in and it must be paid.'

Adira got to her feet and paced to one side of the room, spun and returned. She stood beside his chair, not facing him, talking just as much to herself as to him.

'I'll get your answers. I can get him to talk – I'm the only one he would trust, and I know what he is capable of. The real secrets are in his head, not just in his flesh.'

She paused and waited. There was silence. She heard her uncle's heavy body shift against leather but didn't wait for his reply.

'Besides, no one is touching him until I say. Or you know what I will do to them.'

A coughing sound morphed into a dry laugh. 'Only you would dare to challenge me in my own office,' General Shavit said. 'You are truly your mother's daughter, Captain Senesh. And if I agree, and let you run the debrief, how will that benefit me?'

She finally turned to face him, going down on one knee beside his chair. 'You know what he can do. If he chooses to resist you, there is no one who can stand up to him. You'd have to kill him, and then the secrets in his mind are gone forever. But he *will* talk to me – he trusts me. I can get your answers, and get them quickly.' She gripped his forearm. 'Give me six months.'

Shavit patted her hand, and after a few more seconds nodded his assent. 'I want a daily report on his progress; and he must report weekly to the Mo'ach Center for medical testing. You have sixty days only – this is not negotiable.'

She started to protest, but he held one hand up in front of her face.

'In sixty days, we begin our own testing. If you cannot solve the puzzle in two months, you never will.' He got to his feet, still holding her hand. 'You will *own* this responsibility. Do you understand what I am saying, Captain?'

'Yes, yes, agreed. Thank you, Uncle.'

He nodded again, and led her back to her chair. 'Now finish your tea, and tell me all about Beirut.'

*

That was too easy, Adira thought, as she pushed out through the doors of the nondescript building and inhaled the scents of the street. There was a hint of citrus on the air; she liked it. Tel Aviv was small, but modern and centralized – a pool of highrises, expensive shops and perfect streetscapes surrounded by parkland, gentrified neighborhoods and beautiful beaches. She was part of the only real democracy in the entire Middle East and it made her proud. *It is a jewel worth protecting*, she thought, as she went lightly down the steps. She knew her uncle was just as determined to understand Alex Hunter as she was – they just had differing ideas on how to go about it. In addition, she cared only about Alex. Her uncle wanted a thousand like him.

Adira chewed her lip as she walked quickly. She hoped her uncle had agreed so readily to her request because he had confidence in her. But her time was limited, and Alex's memory loss presented her with a dilemma – there were some things she wanted and needed him to remember, but there were other memories she didn't want him to recover at all. She had no idea whether his full memory would seep back in time, or whether he would be forever a clean slate. The latter presented an opportunity to implant a whole new mosaic of memories, to create an entire matrix of suggestions – ones she wanted him to have. The trick was for her to get enough information from him to satisfy the general and her objectives, but not to open him up so much that she could lose him back to the Americans.

She hurried down the street, feeling the bite of the afternoon heat on her neck. She would take him out of the city, she decided. Somewhere comfortable and relaxing – she knew the perfect place. She smiled. In a week or two, she bet she could coax the answers from him. Her smile broadened; she hadn't felt like this in years.

EIGHT

Hickory, North Carolina

'Will ... *Will!*

Big Will Jordan jerked upright as he heard his mother scream his name. All the Jordan brothers made it their duty to help their folks on weekends with the heavy chores now the pair were getting on. This Saturday it had been his turn. The old folks were as mellow as they came, but his mother's tone now worried him. It spoke of shock, anxiety and not a little fear. Last time he'd heard her like that was when Hank got busted up in a car crash. He dropped the axe he was using, but hung onto a good-sized lump of splintered wood, and sprinted for the back door.

His father stood at the sunroom window, his back turned and a whiskey in his hand. It was way too early for the old man to be drinking. Will's mother paced back and forth. On seeing him, she wiped her hands on her dress, gripped his shoulders and looked up into his broad face.

'That was the Asheville police. It's Brad, he's missing.'

'What? But he's –'

His mother didn't let him finish. 'They found Amanda; she's hurt.' Her lips trembled and the word *hurt* came out long and filled with anguish.

'Have they –'

His father turned. 'Nope; not even started looking yet.'

His father could do that: read his sons like an open book.

His mother wrung her hands some more. 'He's up on the mountain by himself ... and I read about a lion escaping. I thought it was funny at the time.' She crossed herself, as though asking forgiveness for a sin, and turned back to Will. 'Leave it to them, they said, they'll keep us informed.' She shook her head. 'Brad's not as strong as you boys; he's ...' She put her hand over her mouth.

Will felt a flash of anger at the police inactivity. He knew that Brad was their mother's favorite – they used to rib him about it when they were young. Where he, Jackson and Hank were big blocky men of average intelligence, Brad was still big but finer-featured; more of a thinker, his mother used to say.

Will put his arm around his mother's tiny shoulders, and felt her trembling. He asked as gently as he could, 'Can't Amanda tell them what happened?'

She shook her head jerkily. 'She's in Asheville hospital in a sort of coma – not unconscious, but she can't talk. She was hurt, and I get the feeling they think Brad was somehow involved.' She looked up at him. 'They asked me has he ever hit her.'

'That's bullshit!' Will's roar made his mother put her hands to her head.

His father put his drink down. 'Listen, boy, the weather's turning bad and there's a big animal on the loose up there. Young Brad, he's not a mountain man ... and the police are doing jack shit.'

The old man held Will's eyes for a number of seconds. Will got the unspoken communication: *you find him, bring him home.* He nodded once to his father, then said over his shoulder as he stepped towards the back door, 'Call Jackson and Hank, tell 'em I'm on my way to pick 'em up.'

*

Will Jordan stood by the open back door of the dark blue SUV and loaded the supplies his brothers had bought at the local store. Hank sat behind the wheel, eating cereal straight from the box, and Jackson was still inside settling the bill. Will paused and folded his huge arms as an Asheville police cruiser drove by, its single occupant slowing to eyeball him. He eyeballed the officer right back, daring the smaller man to stop and say something. His feelings about the Asheville PD were at about basement level right now, and after driving most of the night to get to the mountain his mood was as dark and dirty as a coalminer's crusties.

The cruiser rolled on, disappearing around the corner, and Will turned to yell at the shop's closed door.

He jammed his hands in his pockets to keep them warm. He knew he should check in on Amanda, but decided she could wait. The weather was getting colder, and she had a roof over her head ... his youngest brother didn't. Unfortunately, the Asheville police either couldn't, or wouldn't, tell Will where they were up to with their search for Brad. And Amanda was still in such a state of shock that she hadn't said a word.

The shop door swung open and Jackson emerged. Will jerked a thumb to the back of the SUV.

'Throw that in, and let's go.'

*

Will Jordan climbed out of the SUV and walked a few paces towards the start of Black Mountain's trail. He stared up at the mist-shrouded peaks. The low cloud obscured the Dome, but he knew it lay many thousands of feet above where he and his brothers stood. A freezing wind stung his exposed jug ears. Will ignored its bite, as did his little brothers – if you could call men over six-two and weighing over 230 pounds each, *little*. Jackson and Hank were silent too, their heads turned towards the distant peak. They knew Amanda had been found on the eastern slope, and pretty high up.

The youngest, Hank, spoke first. 'Gonna be cold up there.'

'Yup, damned cold,' Will answered without turning. 'And maybe wet too, I reckon.'

Hank hitched his pants a little higher and made a *tsking* noise within his cheek. 'A man exposed to those elements for a few days is gonna be in a world of hurt.'

'Uh-huh.' Will exhaled, and watched a small ghost of warm vapor drift away from his mouth. He knew his brothers weren't looking forward to the trek. All three had been hiking and camping in the woods before, but never for longer than a day at these temperatures. But if any of them were lost, Will knew that Brad wouldn't hesitate to hike into Hell to look for his brother – and neither would he.

Jackson gave his eldest brother a flat smile. 'It's okay for you, Frosty; you like being alone in the cold.'

Will just winked in reply. As far as he was concerned, the cold and the discomfort meant nothing. And Jackson was right – he didn't mind being alone at all; he liked it. Fact was, he found people annoying, his family excepted. One day, he'd buy a place in some remote part of the country and live there all by himself.

He zipped up his heavyweight insulated jacket and lifted his pack. It clanked as the bear canisters inside knocked together, then crackled as the covering weather shield molded to the shape of his broad back. He checked the matt black Browning Maxus shotgun, then, satisfied with the lethal-looking twelve-gauge autoloader, he lifted it over his shoulder and slid it down into a side slot in the pack.

Once his brothers had their own packs in place, they checked their firearms – both were carrying large-frame Smith & Wesson revolvers, just like their missing brother.

Will turned to his brothers, his face grim. 'As long as it takes.'

Jackson and Hank nodded solemnly and repeated the vow. 'As long as it takes.'

The three big men started off towards the ominous black peak.

*

Black Mountain, with its dense tree cover, was normally a quiet place at the best of times. But now, with winter coming on, even the wildlife seemed to have disappeared. Any sounds that did intrude on the graveyard-like silence were magnified, alerting potential hunters to an approaching or retreating quarry.

Will was first to detect the faint sounds of heavy movement from further up the slope. Something or someone was ghosting them, staying close but just out of sight.

They were about 5000 feet up, and he reckoned they still had a way to go to get to where Brad had likely hiked. As Will had expected, once off the formal path, the going had been slow and arduous. The morning's clear sky had changed as the day had worn on. Now, in the evening twilight, the low cloud moved quickly overhead and the temperature had dropped from cold to bone chilling. Still, everything had been quiet and uneventful ... until now.

Will put one gloved hand to his mouth and used his teeth to slowly pull on the fingers to remove the glove and let it fall to the cold ground. He held up his hand. His brothers instantly got the message, and pulled their own gloves off and lifted their handguns from their holsters.

Will lowered his hand to the shotgun, his fingers now sliding easily in against the cold trigger. He widened his stance and grounded his feet. The slope was rocky and steep, and the soil hard and unyielding underneath the layer of pine needles and frozen leaves. One loose step and a man could find himself a couple of hundred yards down the side of the mountain before he knew it. And now was not the time for those sorts of mistakes.

He quickly organized his brothers into a loose skirmish line, with Hank closest, at twenty feet out to his right, and Jackson another twenty further along than Hank. Each strained to watch the upper slopes while also trying to keep one eye on Will. Jackson walked ahead a couple of steps so he could see around the bulky shape of Hank's enormous red and yellow checked parka.

Hank looked from the slope to Will, and then back. He breathed out a question, loud enough for Will to hear: 'Could it be Brad?'

Will didn't take his eyes off the hill, but his mouth turned down and he shook his head slowly. He took a step forward, cocked his head slightly and strained to hear – there was a faint sound, like a giant bellows working, just over the small ridge. He was conscious of his fingers starting to numb from the cold – he'd need to replace his glove soon, or when the time came to pull the trigger, he wouldn't be able to.

There was a grinding, snapping sound from over the ridge, as if something was being ripped, bent or broken, followed by a thumping sound Will both heard and felt beneath his boots. From the end of the skirmish line, Jackson whispered loudly, 'What the hell is that?' and leaned forward to look at his brothers.

Will turned briefly to motion for Jackson to stay quiet. The snapping and grinding turned to a deeper bouncing *thump*. As Will's eyes focused on Jackson at the far end of the line, Hank, in the middle, just ... disappeared.

The man-sized boulder that had taken him out hurtled and bounced down the steep mountainside, Hank with it, breaking small trees and ricocheting off larger trunks and outcrops of exposed stone. It struck an enormous spruce a hundred yards further down, leaving Hank's body a flattened riot of color and fluids against the scarred bark. The echoes of the collision with the boulder died away.

'*Haaank!*' Will screamed.

'Jesus Christ,' Jackson moaned, holding both hands to his head.

'Wha-what just happened?' Will whipped his head back and forth. Confusion swirled in his mind like a fog.

'Hank?' Jackson started to walk stiffly down the slope, calling to his younger brother as though trying to rouse him from sleep. 'Are you okay, Hank?'

Will gestured towards the mess against the tree trunk. 'He's not fucking okay, he's –'

Another sound: stealthy but heavy. Will reacted quickly, spinning with his gun up. He flicked the weapon one way and then the next, trying to pinpoint the sound with the long barrel.

'Show yourself!' he shouted, and then a little quieter he said, 'Where are you?'

His breathing came in rapid pants and his heart raced in his chest. He could still hear Jackson bleating Hank's name over and over, and he turned to yell at him to shut up – just in time to see something collide with his brother, something colossal, covered in greasy, matted red fur. In the time it took Will to raise and aim his shotgun, Jackson was lifted and smashed into a tree trunk. There was a brittle snapping sound, which could have been the breaking of branches or the splintering of his brother's bones beneath his thick jacket.

Will groaned, feeling his soul shrink. His whole body was suddenly as cold as the snow. He screamed Jackson's name, then swore and fired his gun, but the distance was too far and the pellets lost much of their penetrative force. The enormous figure bent over Jackson simply turned its head to him in response.

Will froze at the sight of its face – a mask of pink boiled flesh, with features that were almost human, but grossly large and deformed. Its eyes pinned him to the spot – definitely not human, but intelligent ... and cunning.

Jackson moaned and raised one feeble hand. The creature turned its attention back to him, lifted his broken body in both its hands and spun to whip it against the trunk with such force that something flew off the top of Jackson's body. Will hoped it was his brother's cap, even though he couldn't fail to see the spray of red across the white ground.

Will charged with the shotgun raised. He fired, pumped and fired again. The creature made an unnerving *whooping* sound that was almost as loud as the blast of the gun. Will couldn't tell if he'd hit the thing or not – *I should have*, he thought, *I'm a fair shot and the distance isn't so great.* But the creature showed no sign of being injured or even discouraged by the tungsten-iron shot pellets that must have struck its huge frame.

In a flash, it was up the steep hill, much faster than Will could hope to follow. It disappeared over the ridge; Will could hear it moving at speed, presumably towards some form of cover.

He raced to Jackson, but all that remained was blood, a few fragments of ripped clothing and something that could have been hair-covered skull fragments. The body was gone.

Will screamed his brother's name to the sky, then said it again, softly. He looked down the slope to the crumpled mess that was Hank. He felt freezing tears on his cheeks and opened his mouth, but couldn't find the energy to scream again. He sank to his knees amid the ruination that was the last of his brothers. He was alone. Four had become one, and he felt the loss as keenly as if he had forfeited his limbs.

Snow started to float down, bringing a deeper silence with it. People said big Will Jordan always wanted to be alone. He'd finally got his wish.

*

Will regretted pursuing the creature further up the mountain. Though his desire for vengeance was strong, his body was exhausted, as was his ammunition, and he wasn't sure he'd even hit the thing. He could hear the crush of its heavy footsteps as it circled him in the twilight shadows. It was as if it wanted him to hear, was playing with him, always staying just out of sight, just out of range.

Will drew his handgun and tried to sight along its shaking barrel. His fatigue pulled heavily at him as he tried to hold it steady. He knew he needed the creature to come a helluva lot closer to have any chance of hitting it. *Things have gone to shit*, he thought. *And I goddamn walked them all into that shit.*

He looked down the slope; he needed to get away from here. Even though his anger still burned hotly, reason told him that out here by himself he'd soon die. He needed to come back with a bigger gun, a lot more shooters ... maybe some dynamite.

He took a step back, and then another. The wind had come up; it wailed softly through the tops of the trees, sounding sad. That was appropriate. Will's cheeks stung where the tears for his lost brothers had dried; the ice crystals left there burned his skin raw. He took another step back, and looked slowly from the upper slope down the steep incline, judging where to place his feet when he broke into a run.

Time was against him. In another hour it would be pitch dark, and then ... He didn't want to think about being on this mountain in the dark.

The crunch of heavy footsteps came again, and the coarse sound of a giant pair of bellows being worked – in front of him, then beside him, then to the left, then right. *Perhaps it's just the wind in the trees*, he thought without conviction. He looked down the slope again, fear creating an urgency in him.

Will slid the backpack off his shoulders. He wouldn't need its contents; wouldn't need any of the survival gear he'd packed – there was no way he'd survive a night here now. He sucked in a huge lungful of breath, and tensed his muscles, ready to leap. He stole one last look up the slope – and exhaled as if he'd been punched in the gut.

It was Hank ... about fifty feet up, leaning against a tree. His body was slumped against it and he looked hurt, but it was him for sure – his red and yellow checked parka was unmistakable. Maybe it had been his brother moving around all this time, hurt and confused. Inside, Will knew it wasn't possible; he'd seen Hank's body smashed against the trunk of the tree. There was no way he could have survived that. But still ...

'Hank!' Will slogged ten feet up the slope towards him.

He wasn't moving, just sort of leaning, propped against the side of the tree. Will looked around. Silence. Even the wind seemed to be holding its breath, waiting.

He climbed another twenty feet. *Damn this darkness, damn the cold, and damn dropping my pack* – he couldn't see properly and wished he'd at least kept his flashlight.

He climbed another ten feet.

'Oh, God, no ... Hank.'

He made a gagging sound in the back of his throat, and his teeth bared in a disgusted grimace. He didn't need to go any further. The placement of the body and the bulky material had been deceiving. Closer, and from a different angle, he could see Hank's crushed and flattened frame, the broken skull that had been roughly stuffed back inside the jacket's hood. Will knew what this was – a decoy. The same strategy duck hunters and deer stalkers used to draw lone animals in.

He felt fresh tears burning his cheeks as a soft, crunching footstep sounded behind him.

'Bastard!'

He spun, raising his weapon at the same time, but he never got to fire. The booming *whoop* froze his fingers on the trigger and he was lifted roughly into the air.

Will Jordan joined his brothers.

NINE

Matt Kearns pulled into the Asheville University car park and let the pickup's engine rumble to silence. He sat in the cabin and inhaled deeply, enjoying the sylvan charm of the green campus, and the bright blue midmorning.

'Now *this* is stress relief.'

He pushed open the door, which gave a protesting squeal of hinges crying out for oil, and stepped down from the cabin just as two girls in tight, light blue university T-shirts went past. He afforded them a wide smile and ran his hand up through his shoulder-length hair. 'Go Bulldogs,' he said, and made a bat-swinging motion in the air.

One of the girls giggled and flashed a set of the whitest teeth he'd ever seen outside of a toothpaste commercial. He continued watching them as they disappeared around the corner. *Yep, still got it*, he thought, as he put both hands on the center of his back and stretched, breathing in the clear air.

Matt looked around at the campus – some new buildings in amongst the old, but still recognizable. Given its focus on liberal arts, it was hard to call the university *traditional* – it was more progressive, more ... fun. Not academically as rigorous as Harvard, of course, but a different, freer atmosphere. Did anyone not look back on their university days fondly? he wondered.

He smiled. Standing here in the sunshine, he felt an almost physical lightness, as though the warmth and clean air were scouring the dark corners of his soul. It had been several years now since he'd assisted in a joint scientific–military mission below the Antarctic ice. He'd survived, but many hadn't. His comfortable life had been devastated by the revelation of another world, an ancient place where monsters slithered in the dark and people, people he'd loved, had died horribly. He hadn't coped well. His relationships fell away, his work suffered. Though Harvard had extended his time off on compassionate grounds, he knew he'd never be able to remain there, trapped by wretched memories. He'd been looking for a fresh start, and when his old linguistics professor had sent him a message telling him he had retired, Matt had asked for his job.

Asheville had jumped at the opportunity – and why not? Matt was a big fish – internationally respected, many papers published, Harvard pedigree, and references from leading public and private officials. Even from senior military figures – though these he'd kept in his top drawer. If he never saw a military uniform again, he'd die happy.

The job had been formally offered, and now he was down here to meet the faculty. Fact was, he needed this job, not for the money, but for his sanity. He suddenly felt like he had a future again.

Ahh. He tilted his head skyward and let the sunshine bathe his face. It had been nearly a dozen years since he'd left Asheville, but the place that held the best memories for him was the center of the campus universe – the library. Matt sauntered across the quadrangle, his longish hair and boyish looks allowing him to blend smoothly amongst the milling students. The Ramsey Library loomed before him, still able to evoke in him feelings of excitement and anticipation. It was an impressive structure, with square columns giving it an aloof, presidential appearance. Inside it was a different, warmer place, rich with information.

He walked through the front doors and resisted the urge to turn into Cafe Ramsey, still tucked just inside the doorway. As in his day, students sat there sipping coffee, heads down over the books open on their tables. What had changed, though, was that most of them took notes on tablets or computers.

Matt tutted his disappointment when he noticed another change – the automated donut maker had been replaced by an enormous pay coffee machine. *That's progress*, he thought.

He continued through to the library, taking a well-remembered path to his favorite hangout – the Research Center. It was there that his languages professor, Henry van Levin, had imbued in him a sense of wonder at how ancient civilizations could still speak to scholars today through languages that were, in some cases, more works of art than written words. Together they had pored over pencil rubbings of the Rosetta Stone from ancient Egyptian to Classical Greek. He had gotten to know the Persians via 5000-year-old proto-Elamite scripts, and read fragments of the first Hebrew Bible in the Dead Sea Scrolls. It had ignited a passion in him that had turned into his career. He hoped old van Levin was in today; there was so much he wanted to discuss with him.

As Matt made his way towards the front desk, he saw the familiar dark blue uniform of the police force. Two officers, one large, one small with a bristling moustache, were engaged in a muted but animated conversation with a middle-aged woman, possibly the head librarian. Matt approached with his hands jammed in the back pockets of his jeans, acting casual. He suspected he was invisible amongst the milling students. He leaned on the desk beside them and glanced at several glossy prints the officers had spread on the counter top. Each showed a piece of stone covered in symbols. His interest piqued, he edged closer.

The woman had folded her arms and was shaking her head. 'I'm sorry, Chief Logan, but our language anthropology department these days covers how languages interact rather than their linguistic roots. We haven't looked at ancient languages for a while, not since Professor van Levin retired.'

That answers the question of whether he's in today, Matt thought.

The taller officer, Logan, nodded glumly at the woman. 'Thanks, Ms Steinberger, it was a long shot anyway. Thought we'd try locally before sending it outside for assistance.' He made to gather up the photos, then stopped. 'Just one more thing: any ideas on where we *could* get some answers?'

Matt craned his neck to see over the smaller officer's shoulder. The officer turned and made a face at Matt. Matt pulled back slightly and made a face back. The policeman muttered something and turned back to the desk, squaring his shoulders to make it difficult for Matt to see. But Matt was at least six inches taller than the officer and by standing on his toes he was able to look over the man's head.

The officer swung round. 'Whatta ya think you're –'

'Cherokee, possibly Catawba,' Matt said.

The policemen just stared at him, so he went on. 'Strange – looks like a mix of the two. Definitely a Native American proto-language, though. Where'd you get them?'

The two policemen and the librarian stood with their eyebrows raised, still staring. Matt pushed past the smaller officer and went to pick up one of the prints. Chief Logan put a large, blunt finger on it to stop him. 'And who might you be, son?'

Matt stuck a hand out. 'Matt Kearns, professor of archaeological studies at Harvard University. Well, ex-Harvard. I'll be taking up a position at Asheville University. I specialise in ancient civilizations and protolinguistics, and that, sir, looks like a museum-quality artifact. May I?' He stuck out his other hand, palm up.

Chief Logan ignored his outstretched hands and looked into Matt's eyes. Probably trying to check if he was about to spring a student joke on the local police, Matt thought.

The chief shrugged. 'Okay, I'll bite.' He indicated himself and then the man next to him. 'I'm Logan and that's Markenson. What can you tell me about these?' He briefly shook Matt's hand, then swiveled the pictures around for him to see.

Matt lifted the prints carefully, squinting at each, and finally going back to the clear image of the stone with the rough figure behind two arrows. 'I think this predates most of the tribes from around here – the arrow fletch is too simple for it to be Catawba, but maybe very early Cherokee. Ancient, very ancient, even bordering on Paleo-Indian. I've only ever seen this type of imagery in cave art, and that was dated to the First People to arrive after the Ice Age – nearly 10,000 years ago.'

Matt squinted again and brought the picture so close to his nose it almost touched the print. 'The stone itself doesn't look that old though. My guess is that it's a reproduction.'

Markenson crowded in. 'So it's just a copy?'

Matt kept staring at the photograph. 'Uh-huh, produced maybe in the twelfth or thirteenth century from an earlier design – you'd need to carbon date the stone for accuracy. You could say it's a bit like touching up an old painting or sculpture. Someone went to a lot of trouble to keep this warning in place and legible for a very long time – perhaps thousands of years.'

'It's a warning?' Officer Markenson tilted the photo in Matt's hand so he could look at the image again.

Matt leaned one arm on the officer's shoulder and pointed to the carvings. 'There are two things here – a warning, and a protective talisman. See the arrows – one's pointing left and the other's pointing right? The one facing right means protection, and the left one is meant to ward off evil. Not sure what the figure behind the arrows is supposed to represent – never come across that form before. Some sort of mega fauna – cave bear maybe, or a spirit totem?'

Markenson shrugged Matt's arm from his shoulder.

Matt flicked the photograph with his finger. 'Any more stones? I'm betting this warning is part of a longer narrative – images like this rarely exist as stand-alone glyphs, they're nearly always part of a detailed chronicle. That's how the First People handed down their stories through the generations.'

Chief Logan pulled another print from the folder he carried. 'We've got no more pictures of the stones, but what about this?' He handed the picture to Matt.

Matt looked at the snow-shrouded image and frowned. He picked up the photo of the carved stone and held it close to the new print. The figure's hulking shape, the long powerful limbs – it was hard not to see the immediate similarities between the carving and the figure in the other photograph.

He looked at Chief Logan, who raised an eyebrow in question.

Matt shrugged and handed back the prints. 'Curiouser and curiouser.'

'You got that right. Anything else you can tell us, Professor Kearns – about the stone or the figure?'

Matt slowly shook his head. 'No, but I'm around for a while – probably permanently actually. I'd like to see the stone in person, and where it came from. I could probably tell you more about its provenance then, and what its creator was trying to tell us ... or warn us about.' He thought for a second or two. 'It might have come from some sort of ruins, I suppose, which means there could be other valuable artifacts in the area. But the figure ...?' He shrugged again. 'Don't know. Not really my area. Could be a cave bear, as I said, or maybe an ape – but there's nothing like that in the mega-fauna record. At least, not round here.'

Logan nodded and grunted. The ME had thought the blood trace on the Jordan woman's glove had come from some kind of great ape. He turned to his partner. 'Markenson, you checked on the Kringle Brothers' circus, didn't you?'

The smaller officer shrugged. 'Sure, nothing really relevant. All they got is some mangy chimpanzee that's older than Methuselah and has to have his bananas mashed 'cause he's got no teeth.'

Logan nodded, then looked back at Matt as though considering something. He sucked in one cheek and made a clicking sound with his tongue. He turned to the doorway.

'Chief Logan?'

Logan turned back to Matt and raised an eyebrow.

'That strange figure in the photographs ... it looks familiar to me, but it's not my field. I deal in languages and ancient civilizations. But I do know someone who could help us out. I could make a call, maybe get him up here to identify it. Might give you a lead.'

Chief Logan stared at him, but Matt could tell his focus was elsewhere. He shook his head slowly. 'Don't really have any budget for that, Professor Kearns.'

'We'll do it for a round of beers,' Matt said, surprising himself with his determination to help.

Markenson took a step towards Matt and waved his hand back and forth in front of his face. 'Not a chance.'

Logan grasped his officer's shoulder and pulled him back. There was a weariness in his voice when he spoke. 'Professor Kearns, I've got a man lost on the mountain, a woman zoned out in hospital, a lion on the loose and a small child missing. Not to mention weird shit going on all over town. Right about now, we'll take all the expert help we can get.'

'We don't need civvies in on this, Chief,' Markenson protested. 'They'll just –'

'You got it, Chief Logan,' Matt cut in, and reached over the top of Markenson's shoulder to shake Logan's hand.

They swapped contact details, then the large police chief guided his still remonstrating officer out of the building. Matt thought of the chief's words, *weird shit going on*. He stopped dead. *What am I doing?* He felt a chill of fear go through him. Memories threatened to overwhelm him. He shook his head. *No*, he thought. *It is time to live my life again.* He headed out of the library.

He knew exactly what he was doing. He loved mysteries, especially those from ancient times. This would be an exciting professional challenge. And he knew someone else who would dig this job just as much as he did.

*

Matt grinned. 'Is that the best brown-butter pecan you've ever tasted?'

In response, Charles picked up his empty plate and made a show of licking it. His tongue made a squeaking sound as it ringed the plate. An old woman at the next table clicked her tongue in disgust. Matt turned to her and whispered, 'Just out of prison.'

'So this is where you're running away to?' Charles said. 'Not bad. Anything interesting going in anthro for me?'

Charles Schroder was professor of physical anthropology at Harvard and one of the few friends Matt had managed to hang on to after the Antarctic experience. Short, with a round face and thinning blond hair, Charles had been nicknamed 'Charlie Brown' in school, not helped by the fact that his surname, Schroder, was also the name of one of the comic book character's friends.

He looked at the folder Matt had brought with him and became more serious. 'So, what have you got for me, Kook? Why all the excitement?'

'Charlie, this is such a cool town. As well as looking like something out of a postcard and having the best pie in the state, it's given us this ...' He flipped open the folder and spread out the pictures Logan had emailed him like playing cards in front of his friend. Then he removed a sheet of typed paper and placed it face down on the table.

Charles studied the pictures individually, then came back to the hulking figure in the snow.

Matt leaned forward 'It's not a bear, is it?' He was trying hard not to pre-empt anything or put ideas in his colleague's mind.

'Duh ... maybe a man in a bear suit? C'mon, Matt, this is a hoax. Where'd you get these? From some teenager? Or maybe a middle-aged farmer who reported he'd been abducted by aliens and probed – and I bet you know where.' Charles laughed.

Matt raised his eyebrows. 'From a woman who's now in hospital in, so I'm told, a terror-induced catatonic state. Her husband is missing up on the mountain.' He turned the sheet of paper over. 'She had blood on her glove – not hers, not *anyone's* really. The lab only managed to come up with an approximate match ...' He waved his hand over the page, indicating that his friend should read it for himself.

Charles read the ME's report, then frowned. He retrieved the photograph of the snow-shrouded figure and this time drew a magnifying glass from his pocket and studied every inch of the print. He pursed his lips and put down the magnifying glass to sip some coffee, then picked it up again and returned to his examination, this time reciting soft observations.

'Hominid. Long arm-to-leg ratio, broad chest, short lower back, flat face, large domed cranium with bony ridge above forward-facing eye sockets providing stereoscopic vision.' He drew back a bit from the print and squinted. 'Hmm, prominent pectoral girdle and dorsal scapula, powerful ribcage that looks flatter front to back.' He lowered the print, but held onto it. 'And a Medical Examiner's report that indicates a genetic match to some type of unknown primate. *Okaaay*, what is this?'

Matt brought his fist down on the table. 'That's exactly the right question – *what the hell is it?* But I think you know.'

'Maybe.' Charles frowned at the print again.

Matt leaned across the table. 'C'mon, buddy, say it.'

'No.' Charles dropped the print and put his head in his hands. 'No, I won't, I can't, they'll burn me.'

Matt grabbed his friend's arms and chanted, 'Say it, say it ... c'mon, you can do it.'

The woman at the next table clicked her tongue at them again.

Matt turned to her. 'It's for his therapy – the doctor says it's good for him.'

Charles groaned and said something too softly to hear. Matt stopped shaking his arms but held on. 'Louder, Charlie Brown; say it out loud.'

'Momo, Nuk-luk, Mogollon, Skunk Ape, Fouke Creature, Old Great One ...' He looked up as his speech slowed. 'Sasquatch ... Bigfoot.'

Matt let his arms go. 'And ... bingo!'

Charles sighed and sat back. 'Matt, I think you need someone a little more like my uncle, someone who likes to dabble in the exotic.'

'Oh right, your uncle who went missing in Southern China around 1935? That's a big help. Listen, Charles, I think there's something weird going on up in those mountains. I've been doing some research on the history of the area. There's a Native American legend about a place called the Jocassee Gorge – dates back to 1539, when the Spanish explorer Hernando de Soto documented some Southern Cherokee picture-script. Jocassee was supposed to be the daughter of a great chief. On hearing that the young warrior she was in love with had been killed in battle, she paddled out into the center of the Whitewater River. The legend goes that she didn't drown, just disappeared, and the gorge became known as the Place of the Lost Ones.'

An old man sitting at a nearby table moved his head slightly. His face was turned away, but one large rubbery ear was pointed at Matt and Charles.

Matt pulled a pen from his pocket and grabbed a napkin. He drew two sets of symbols on it and turned the napkin around for Charles to see. 'But ... look at this.'

Charles stared at them for a moment, then looked up and shrugged. 'Same.'

'*Almost* the same, Charlie Brown, except for these small wavy lines and some extra shading. The first is the Cherokee symbol for *lost*, but the other symbol's much older – it translates as *great*, in the sense of size. I've seen the de Soto transcripts, and I think he got it wrong. I believe the legend was referring to something a lot older than the missing chief's daughter. I don't think the script referred to the "Lost Ones" but the "Great Ones" – as in a race that was *great in size*.' Matt threw the pen onto the table and sat back folding his arms. 'Charles, we have *got* to check this out.'

Charles mimicked Matt's actions, an I'm-not-convinced-yet half-smile on his face. 'Matt, I'm delighted to see that something has finally fired you up again, but what I see here is a partially obscured simian or protosimian shape. It could be a dozen things, and all you've got to support your theory is a carving and a photograph – and a bad one at that – of a man-shaped thing that could have come straight from the file of Sasquatch sightings that gets a run once a year on the Discovery Channel. If we're not careful, we'll end up driving into a wall that has ridicule and bye-bye career written all over it.'

Matt knew he had his friend hooked the moment Charles started using the word 'we'. He laughed and shook his head. 'Not a chance – I'm way too good a driver. Hey, we're just doing a little consulting for the local police force. Where's the harm in that? And you're probably right – it's probably nothing more than some overdressed camper lost in the snow.' Matt paused for dramatic effect. 'But then again, it might not be. After all, the Native Americans have numerous legends that refer to the Big Man, the Hairy Man or the Big Brother of the Forest. The Cherokee, Dakota, Sioux, Algonquin and dozens of others had stories about the *Chiye-tanka* long before white men showed up. Even the word *Sasquatch* is from a near-extinct First Nation language called Halkomelem – it means *hairy giant*.'

The old man turned to look at Matt and Charles, then turned back to his empty plate. Matt noticed his rising voice was attracting attention so he sat forward to speak more conspiratorially.

'You know, Charles, little people were just legends, or make-believe, until they discovered the hobbit in Indonesia.'

Charles was staring down at the table top, seemingly lost in thought. '*Homo floresiensis*,' he said softly, 'found in the Liang Bua cave on the Indonesian island of Flores in 2003. A magnificent find, and one that proves some legends are real.' He looked up at Matt and narrowed his eyes. 'You said consulting ... they'd pay us as well?'

Matt just jiggled his eyebrows.

Charles's mouth split open in a broad grin. 'Okay, buddy, I'm in.'

*

The old man rose from his seat as soon as the two younger men left the cafe. His thick, slicked-down white hair and faded light blue chambray shirt seemed to glow under the neon lights as he stepped lightly to their table. The perfectly pressed shirt, fastened up to the neck, hung on a frame reduced to sinew and brown leather over the man's nearly ninety years. He placed one brown, wrinkled hand on the napkin, turning it slightly to study the symbols the long-haired young man had drawn. He mouthed the Lakota word he had heard the man use, *Chiye-tanka*, then crushed the napkin and pushed it into his pocket.

He left the cafe and followed the two men along the dark street.

TEN

Kathleen Hunter stared into the fire, the flickering orange tongues reflecting in her eyes. The flames were warm and comforting, and as she watched they opened familiar windows into her past, into her memories. Beside her on the rug lay Jess, fully stretched out like an enormous bear-skin rug – one hundred pounds of German shepherd and her last living family member. Settling further into the old chair, Kathleen let her eyes wander over the angled line of photographs in their wood, silver or plastic frames on the mantelpiece. The first was of Jim Hunter, her husband, in his youth, all whipcord muscle. Beside him, looking even younger, was his best friend Jack Hammerson – soldiers both of them. The next frame held another young man, the face eerily similar to Jim's but the photo was sharper and more modern. It was her son, Alex Hunter. An older version of Jack Hammerson was standing beside him, a hand on his shoulder. *Another soldier sent out to serve and defend the nation. Another soldier who never came home*, she thought morosely. *Except for you, Jack, you could survive anything.*

She looked down at the dog. 'Never love a soldier, Jess – they break your heart even if they don't mean to.'

The dog huffed in her sleep, her feet slowly circling as she chased something in a doggy dream. Kathleen wiped her eyes, cursing softly at the way the pictures could raise her with feelings of love and pride, then cast her down into melancholy and even a little anger.

She sighed and lifted the newspaper resting on her lap to fan her face. 'Phew, someone needs a bath.' She sniffed again. *Odd smell.* 'Did you roll in something?' she asked Jess.

The dog came awake and rolled over to a sphinx-like crouch, eyes round and alert, ears up and pointed towards the window. Kathleen tucked her feet under the dog's large, warm body and looked at the photograph on the front page. A little girl with a gap-toothed smile beamed back at her. Kathleen recognized the face before she read the name, *Emma Wilson*. She was missing, and the police were offering a reward.

'Poor little angel. That's not far from here, Jess. We can help look for her tomorrow.'

Jess hadn't moved, remaining fixated on something outside that only she could sense. The fire popped then settled, making the dog jump. Kathleen looked at the woodpile – it was getting low; there wouldn't be enough to keep the fire burning through the night. Though the big dog was warming her feet now, she knew that by morning the house would be colder than grandpa's crypt. She sighed. She knew she wouldn't feel like going outside to get more wood just after dawn – her old bones complained the most from the cold in the mornings.

She set the newspaper down and pulled her feet from under Jess. 'Should have done it before, old girl.'

As she got to her feet there came the almost imperceptible sound of branches snapping in the trees near the house. The noise carried easily to the dog's ears on the still, cold air and Jess was immediately on her feet, hackles up from her neck to her tail, making her seem twice as large as her usual huge self. Her bark was deep and booming in the small room, and her lips had pulled back to show all her teeth.

Kathleen put her hand on the dog's head, then ran it down over one ear and along her back. 'Stop that, you silly thing. You're scaring me.' She felt the huge chest working like a set of bellows, the muscles bunched and tight.

Jess hadn't taken her eyes off the front of the house, and skittered on the rug now as she rushed to the front door. Kathleen went to the window and looked out into the clear, moonlit yard. The front of the house was clear, and there was nothing visible amongst the large fir and birch trees she had allowed to grow to within fifty feet of the house. *Weird old dog*, she thought, as she looked over to where the firewood had been stacked neatly by that nice Jim Miller boy, who had cut it for her.

Kathleen pulled on her cardigan, picked up the firewood bucket and headed for the front door. On her way, she stepped out of her slippers and into a pair of rubber half-boots. As she approached the door, Jess moved to stand sideways across the frame. The dog looked up at her briefly, before swinging her head back to stare at the door as though seeing straight through the wood and out into the dark night.

'You're not going out if you're going to carry on like that,' Kathleen said. 'I'm not planning on chasing you up the side of the mountain. So move, please.'

Jess took no notice.

Kathleen scowled at the dog, then pointed down beside herself. 'Heel, Jess.'

The dog reluctantly came and sat beside her. She tried to lick Kathleen's hand, whining and obviously highly agitated.

'Stay.' Kathleen walked to the door and looked back. The dog was licking her lips nervously and started to get to her feet. 'Stay!' Jess sat down again, but Kathleen could tell she was struggling to obey the command. She frowned again and shook her head; Jess had never disobeyed her before ... ever.

'I'll just be a couple of minutes.'

Jess got to her feet again, but Kathleen opened the door and went out before the dog could try to stop her.

*

Alex and Adira allowed their horses to amble along the Ashkelon shoreline. Both in T-shirts, jeans and bare feet, they were enjoying the late afternoon sunshine on the coast of the ancient city. Alex inhaled deeply, taking in the smell of salt, warm sand and drying seaweed. He felt Adira watching him and turned to smile at her.

'It's magnificent here – thank you. Smelling the sea, hearing the sound of the waves ... I find it peaceful.' He looked out at the ocean and breathed in deeply again. 'It's strange, I know how to ride a horse, but don't remember ever actually riding.'

'We've been here before; it's one of our favorite spots. Don't worry, it'll come back soon,' Adira said smiling and pointed to a small horseshoe-shaped cove, where the sand was flat and golden. 'Let's give the horses a rest,' she said.

She slid from her horse and Alex followed suit. This far south the beaches were unoccupied – too close to the Gaza Strip to be considered safe, but perfect if you wanted solitude. A few trees stood at the edge of the dunes, and tough grass dared to creep down towards the water. Alex tied his horse up in the shade and walked a few paces to lie down on the sand. He closed his eyes. The gentle sound of the small waves breaking just a few feet away should have made him relax completely. But there was a nagging prickle behind his eyes – as if there was something he needed to do, or remember, and his overactive brain wouldn't let go until he did.

He opened his eyes and lifted one of his arms, examining the skin on both sides. The fresh scars that had been visible a few days ago were gone – not just healed, but vanished entirely. There was something else too: he'd started to sense things ... things beyond sight, smell and hearing. Adira had told him his name was Horowitz, and that he was a soldier in the Israeli army. He'd been injured in battle, concussed, and he'd lost his memory. It *sounded* right, but didn't *feel* right.

Even as they got closer, he couldn't tell whether she wanted to be his bodyguard, or his keeper ... or something more. Back in Israel, he'd seen her talking daily to the man she called his doctor, but he'd known she was lying. She was good at it, but he could tell. He mentally shrugged. *Did it really matter?* Alex didn't feel in any hurry to remember whatever it was that the doctors, or Adira's superiors, desperately wanted him to remember. After all, he had everything he needed here – as Adira kept telling him.

She sat down beside him, and Alex opened one eye and watched her for a minute. She never relaxed, never once closed her eyes and surrendered to the warm sunshine. She was always on guard, on duty; her eyes never stopped moving, from the line of dunes, to the crystal-clear water, to the small stand of trees ...

He tapped her leg to get her attention. 'Do you miss them?'

She looked at him quizzically. 'Miss who?'

'Whoever it is you keep looking for.' He grinned at her, still keeping one eye shut against the glare of the sun.

She laughed and lay down, propping herself on one elbow. 'I just keep a lookout for you.'

'I'm right here,' he said, brushing some sand from her jeans and letting his hand remain on her thigh. 'It's hot. Bring a swimsuit?'

'Very, and no.' She leaned forward, her dark eyes containing amusement and desire.

Alex recognized the gaze, but in a flash Adira's face had morphed into that of another woman, with finer features and soft blue eyes. He tried to put a name to the face, but the prickling he'd felt behind his eyes turned to white-hot pain. He winced and sat up. Something was happening, or about to – he could sense it, he knew it.

Adira pulled back from him and stood quickly. 'Come on, let's get out of the sun. You need to rest.' She sounded disappointed.

*

Adira woke to the sound of crashing and Alex yelling. She switched on the hall light and stood in his doorway, just able to make out his shape sitting on the bed holding his head. *The migraines again,* she thought. He seemed to suffer them most when he tried to reach back into his memory and recover who he was. His past was still locked away from him – behind a redhot door of pain.

'Are you okay, Alex?'

She waited a few seconds for him to respond. When he didn't, she walked into the room and sat on the bed beside him. She poured him a small cup of water and lifted it towards his lips. 'Here.'

He held her hand and the cup, draining it.

'I see faces in my dreams.' His voice was slow, as though he wasn't fully awake. 'I see a soldier, gray-haired and mean-looking. And an old woman on a porch ... there's a mountain in the background. I know her ... *I know her.*'

Alex looked at Adira, but she wasn't sure he actually saw her or whether his mind was still somewhere else. It was hot in the room, hotter than usual, and his body was an unnatural temperature. She had been told to expect it as his metabolism worked well above the normal average range. She used the cuff of her long-sleeved T-shirt to wipe his brow.

'There are other things.' His tone was becoming insistent. 'Things that hide in the dark, or crawl on insect legs – monsters, maybe, from my imagination ... but they seem so real.'

Adira had seen one of those monsters on a mission with Alex in the Iranian desert. They'd been attacked by something that should never have existed outside of a nightmare – and it wasn't only *his* sleep it haunted.

He grabbed her wrist. 'Something's reaching out to me, calling me – it won't stop.' He pulled her closer and stared into her face.

She brushed the damp hair from his forehead. '*Shhh*, you're safe here, Alex.'

'You're all I've got left.' He drew her even closer and she let him. 'You don't know how much I ...' He found her mouth, and the kiss that started softly became hungrier and more urgent.

She clung to him, feeling a warm bloom spread in her belly. Deep down, she knew this was what she had wanted almost since she'd first met him. 'Alex, Alex ...' She kissed him again and again, on the mouth and neck, tasting the salt of his perspiration. It excited her even more.

She wasn't supposed to let anything complicate her mission objectives. She never had before, and it had been easy: she was always a soldier of Israel first. She *was* her duty.

His mouth found hers again.

This is different, she thought. *This is something I want ... something that's just mine.*

She lifted her T-shirt up over her head, and he pulled her down on top of him. The warmth in her belly spread lower.

*

The night was at its darkest; it would be morning soon. Sleep was impossible. She lay on top of the sheets, feeling the perspiration trickle from her temples into her hair. There was a fluttering sensation in her stomach that made her feel euphoric and apprehensive at the same time. The values she held dear and the things she'd thought she wanted suddenly seemed far less important compared to the selfish desires she now harbored. Throughout the night, silly half-dreams of going away together, somewhere far from either of their countries, somewhere no one would find them, had played over in her mind.

Adira could hear Alex's soft breathing beside her, rhythmic like a machine. The feelings of apprehension rose again. She couldn't count on his memory never returning. What would he think when he found out that he was someone completely different from the person she'd told him he was? He'd hate her – she'd lose him.

Her objective was to get Alex Hunter to reveal the elusive element that made the Arcadian treatment work. Science alone was unable to deliver it. Her success would give Israel access to a source of security for the future. Her country was a mere eight million souls surrounded by an Arab world numbering nearly three hundred million, most of whom wanted Israel erased from the map. But once that door in Alex's mind was opened, other corridors back to his past would be available to him.

She groaned and rolled towards him, but couldn't make out his profile in the blackness of the room. When she was a little girl, her uncle, now the general, had told her of a famous Israeli saying: *Alone we are weak, but together we are iron.* She would not abandon Israel, but how could she do that and not lose Alex?

She reached out and touched his shoulder, feeling the heat. She had been faithful to Israel her entire life. Didn't that count for something?

This will not end well, she thought, and closed her eyes.

ELEVEN

Chief Logan stood in the afternoon chill and watched Forensic Services finish up their examination of the Wilson place. He'd managed to persuade Helen and Clark Wilson to stay in a motel in town for the evening so they wouldn't be following the officers around during their investigation. His men needed the freedom to probe everything, from under the beds to the surrounding woods. It would be stressful for the parents if nothing was found; even worse if something was.

An hour earlier, one of his officers had returned from the far tree line at the foot of the mountain carrying a small red sweater in a plastic bag. It matched the description of the clothing Emma was wearing when she disappeared. It was intact, and there was no blood or other signs that could be associated with an animal attack. *At least that's something*, Logan had thought as he watched the head of Forensics, Ted Brandon, open the bag.

Brandon had sniffed the contents then recoiled slightly.

Logan had frowned. 'What?'

Brandon shook his head, shrugged and resealed the bag. He'd thrown it to one of his team and wandered over to Logan.

'What was it?' Logan had asked again.

'Funny smell is all.' Brandon had looked distracted.

'Got something, Chief!'

The shout from the woods startled Logan back to the present. He should have felt elated at the discovery of a clue, but for some reason he was dreading any news at all.

'Whatta you got, Ollie?' he yelled back.

Officer Markenson pointed at several spots amongst the grass and dirt in a clearing. 'Tracks ... plenty of 'em.'

Logan and Ted Brandon moved quickly to where the men had formed a ring around where Markenson was pointing with a flashlight. Brandon crouched down and rested his forearms on his knees. After a moment he nodded. 'Yep.'

Logan went down beside him, squinting at the disturbed soil and twigs. Brandon reached out with one hand and spread his fingers over a group of scuffs and indentations.

'Big pug marks – ten inches at least. Here's your escaped lion, Chief.'

Logan drew in a breath and let it out slowly.

Markenson raised his flashlight and pointed back into the trees. 'Came in from there,' he moved the torch towards the mountains, 'and goes out there. This is as close as it got, I think.'

Logan nodded. 'Good man.'

He felt a glimmer of hope that the tracks didn't come within a hundred feet of the house.

Brandon moved some twigs. 'It was here a while. What was it doing ... just watching?'

Markenson shook his head. 'Lying in wait probably. They do that, you know.'

Logan shook his head. 'Unlikely.' The Kringle Brothers had told him the lion had never attacked anyone in its life.

Markenson crouched down with him and pointed the light at Logan's face. 'I was doing some reading before I came up, Chief. Adult lion eats up to twenty pounds of meat a day. That little Wilson girl was just over forty wringing wet. If it did take her, in a couple of days, there ain't gonna be much left.'

'That's enough of that talk. We don't know the lion took her.'

'It's true, Chief,' Officer Parsons said from behind them. 'And they don't eat their prey right away. They usually take it somewhere quiet and secluded. They like to eat where they –'

Logan shot to his feet. 'Shut the fuck up, both of you.'

Brandon rose slowly, wiping his hands on his thighs. 'Bill, they're right. Big cat, hungry, probably confused and scared. Used to people or not, all bets are off, I reckon.'

Logan looked up at the sky; it was getting dark. He walked a few paces away from the small group and stood with his hands on his hips, looking up into the thick forest cover of Black Mountain. For the first time in his life, he thought the beautiful peaks seemed secretive, even a little threatening.

They probably *were* right about the lion. Decisions mattered, and even minutes probably counted now. He spun back to the group.

'Markenson, Parsons – you two just pulled extra duty. We're going up.'

*

We shoulda done this days ago, Logan thought miserably as he and his three men moved up the side of the mountain, breathing hard, leaving plumes of hot air behind them. Logan was only just managing to keep pace with Harry Erskine, who was being dragged up the steep incline by the twenty feet of leather lead attached to his tracking hound. The large animal was picking up speed in spite of the increasing slope.

Logan tried to remain upbeat. *She's going to be okay. She has to be ... No one gets attacked by a lion in North Carolina, for chrissakes. Might as well put up signs at the Fontana Dam warning of sharks.*

Nevertheless, he felt himself sagging, fatigue and concern weighing him down.

'Get your running shoes on, Chief,' Erskine called. 'Buzz must be getting close.'

Erskine leaped over a log and nearly slipped on the frozen ground. The leash went taut and jerked him forward once again. Logan looked back and frowned; his two officers had fallen nearly fifty feet behind and looked ready to sit down first chance they got. He swore softly, before yelling back down the hill, 'Markenson, Parsons, you get your asses up here, pronto. We got contact.'

Markenson looked up briefly, gave his senior officer a thumbs-up, and started taking larger, though not faster, steps. Pete Parsons nodded, but struggled to get his thick thighs moving at any increased speed. He resorted to using the barrel of his shotgun as a hiking stick, which elicited a torrent of foul language from Logan. Parsons lifted the gun and wiped the stock on his jacket sleeve, then put his head down and ploughed forward, breathing hard in the icy air.

Logan followed Erskine into a thicker stand of trees, and nearly crashed into the man's back. Erskine had reeled the dog in and strapped its snout. It whined softly and danced at his feet, eager to continue the chase and confront whatever it had been tracking for the last few hours.

'What ...' Logan began, but stopped as Erskine held the back of one hand up in front of his face.

'It's just through them bushes,' he whispered without turning, 'moving in and out of the rocks. Must be a cave or shelter or somethin' there.'

Logan followed Erskine's gaze. After a second or two, he saw movement – something large, fur-covered, moving in and out of the shadows. The dog whined again and pulled on its lead.

'What's up?' Markenson's voice made Logan jump.

He turned to scowl at the man, put his finger first to his lips, then pointed through the foliage. Markenson nodded slowly, mouthing, *Got it.*

'What we gonna do?' Parsons gasped as he reached them, his round face the color of boiled beef.

Logan stood, giving up trying to be quiet. 'For fuck's sake, Parsons. Why didn't you bring your bugle? You coulda belted out the cavalry charge. Whatever it is, it's through there. I'm going in, but I want you two ten feet further up near that big oak. Keep watching me, and whatever you do, don't bunch up. And don't fucking shoot each other ... or me.'

He paused and reconsidered that last statement. 'Just stay focused, okay? Keep your barrels to the ground unless you sight something.'

Both men nodded.

Erskine spoke softly out of the corner of his mouth. 'It's movin' again.' He reached down to pat the dog's muzzle. 'Hush up now, boy.'

The dog tried to lick his hand even though its mouth was clamped. Its eyes were rolling in both excitement and fear.

Logan pointed up the slope, then to his men. They hunched down and pushed through the branches of the dark fir trees, which were so tightly packed it was if their stems were woven together. Logan watched them go, then turned back to Erskine.

'You and Buzz stay here. If anything goes wrong for me and the boys, God forbid, head straight back down to the truck and call Chief Winston in Charlotte.' He paused, trying to think of something heroic to say, but all that came to mind were General Douglas MacArthur's wartime quotes – none of which seemed appropriate.

He crept forward, ducked below a branch and stepped out into a small clearing. Some ancient landslip had brought down a jumble of enormous boulders, and the shadowy spaces between them created a series of shelters.

Logan paused to look up the slope. As instructed, Markenson and Parsons were standing in an opening between some trees. They waved, and as he lifted his chin in return he was pleased to see they both had their guns ready but pointed to the ground. Just as well. If he went back to the station full of double-aught he'd never hear the end of it.

He breathed in slowly through his nose: the clearing smelled rank. Something large had been living here, and, by the look of the large bones strewn about, had been feeding up here as well. He took another few steps and motioned with one hand for his men to move forward.

The forest was cemetery quiet, and he was sure he could hear breathing, a deep-chested panting, coming from just up ahead. He lifted his gun. He felt good, his hands were steady as a rock. He remembered two things from his training – don't shoot unless you absolutely have to; and, more importantly, make the first one count.

The panting was getting louder, coming from just behind a large kidney-shaped rock. He gritted his teeth. *This is where training and guts meet reality*, he thought solemnly; then, *Damn, wish I'd thought of that in front of Erskine.* He gripped his gun a little tighter.

The panting stopped. There was silence. Logan held his breath. He waited a few seconds, then slowly brought his gun up, aiming the barrel at the tumble of boulders where he assumed the beast's lair to be. He planted his legs wide apart – a hunter's stance.

The sudden roar was like a monstrous shockwave; he felt it from his scalp all the way down to his clenched sphincter. The creature appeared on the rocks, a colossus of teeth, claw and stinking fur, like something out of a bourbon-soaked nightmare. Its open jaws could have accommodated Logan's entire head and shoulders.

It roared again, but Logan swallowed a dry ball of fear and kept his gun up, level, unwavering. He could see the massive beast coiling its muscles, its face furious, or fear-maddened, or both.

It leaped; he fired.

Other explosive roars quickly followed, then a crushing hot weight landed on top of him.

*

Chief Logan took the canteen, sipped, then allowed Markenson to drag him to his feet. He held on to his deputy's arm for a few seconds, waiting for the wooziness to leave his gut. He guessed he might be suffering delayed shock.

Parsons slapped his shoulder. 'Right between the eyes, Chief.'

Logan looked down at the massive lion. Its skin was torn by numerous bullet and buckshot holes. Someone had used a stick to prop open its jaws, displaying yellowed teeth as long as his fingers.

Markenson kneeled beside the huge head to investigate the cavernous mouth. He turned slowly to look up at the chief. 'You think the Wilson girl is in there?'

Logan went to rub his brow, but noticed there was blood on his hands and wiped them on his pants. He pictured the tiny girl standing alone in front of the 500-pound monster and shuddered. 'You know, Ollie, I sure hope she isn't. But let's call in the ME and find out.'

*

'Over here.' Charles Schroder waved Matt over to where he was crouched beside a tree.

Matt could see his friend's attention was riveted on an area where the dry grasses had been unable to take hold. All that was visible from a distance was bare dirt and a few struggling asters.

Matt looked quickly over his shoulder before heading over. He knew they were probably trespassing. When he'd phoned Chief Logan earlier, he'd been told that he was out at the Wilson place looking for a missing girl. While he was still on the line, he'd heard the chief and some of his men rush in to get kitted out with weapons. Something was up and Matt's radar had gone off the scale. They'd arrived at the Wilson place at dusk, and Charles had been straight on the scent like a bloodhound.

Matt kneeled next to him, adding his own flashlight beam to Charles's, and frowned at the ground. Up close, he still couldn't see anything beyond a few bumps and waves in the dry soil. Charles looked at him, his face excited, eyes wide.

'We got something,' he said, clearing pine needles and twigs away from the soil.

Matt moved his flashlight slowly over the area while Charles fumbled in his pockets. 'I don't see it. What've you got – a track or spoor?'

Charles pulled a small tape measure from his pocket and sat back on his haunches. He lifted his flashlight to shoulder level and shone it at a spot in the dirt. 'Okay, squint and make your eyes go a little out of focus. That'll allow your central vision to include peripheral input.' He raised his other arm, his hand extended flat to the ground. 'Now look where I'm pointing.'

Matt could just make out a rough shape in the dry soil. The small depressions resolved into a pattern, something more than an accident. 'Holy shit, I see it – it's fucking enormous. A footprint, or part of one.'

'Keep your foghorn down,' Charles said. 'You're damned right – we got a clear big toe, and part of the metatarsus pad.'

He expertly extended the tape one way, then the other, then set it down carefully beside the print and pulled a small battered notebook from his pocket. He removed the rubber band binding it, and started to scribble with the pencil stub that rolled free of its pages. He chuckled softly as he looked again at the print. 'Whoa, you're a big 'un, aren't you?'

He held the notebook out so Matt could see his calculations. 'I've used standard anthropoidal biometric ratios. As an example, an average human of about six feet in height has a foot length approximately fifteen per cent of its total height. The big toe is roughly eighteen per cent of *that* ratio.' He looked at Matt, who nodded, so he went on. 'The big toe we have here is around three and a half inches in length, giving us a total stature of ...' He circled a number and tapped it. 'One hundred and twenty-five inches ... over ten fucking feet tall!' He sat back in the dirt, almost panting with excitement.

Matt laughed. 'Hey, take it easy, buddy. Do you need a cigarette after that?'

They both laughed.

Charles shook his head. 'I should have brought a camera. Sorry to doubt you, but I thought this was going to be hoax number one million, and so I didn't bother. I'll come back later and take some casts.'

Matt gave his friend a half-smile. 'I'm glad you came anyway. And hey, all I had to go on was a rock carving and a grainy photo – I kinda doubted it myself.'

Charles's face turned serious. 'You do know, we've got to find this thing before anyone else does? This could make the coelacanth and the Wollemi pine look like sardines and dried flowers. We can't let something this rare be filled with a lot of shotgun pellets.'

'I think Chief Logan took all that firepower after the escaped lion,' Matt said. 'It was probably here too. For all we know, it could have been tracking this creature as well.'

Charles shook his head. 'If this creature is what I think it is, the lion wasn't tracking it. More like *it* was tracking the lion.'

Matt looked up at Black Mountain. It was night now, and a huge moon had lifted up behind the peak, making it look almost prehistoric. He shuddered and felt his fears reemerging. Being out in the dark with a giant creature on the loose brought back memories of another monster that had stalked him and others beneath miles of rock and ice. He took a deep breath. A lot of people had died that time. He hoped history wasn't about to repeat itself.

*

The old man moved through the trees close to the house. He stood looking up at the mountain for several minutes, as still and quiet as the hushed night around him. He took a small leather pouch from his pocket, loosened the looped string around the top and pinched out something that he threw in the air towards the mountain. Some of the substance blew back in his face and he sneezed.

He sliced the air with one arm, his fingers opening and closing, making symbols and shapes in the air. He spoke in a strong voice, a chant that lasted for several minutes. Then he stopped and stood staring once again at the mountain.

As he turned to leave, he kicked dirt over the print that Matt and Charles had been investigating.

TWELVE

Kathleen Hunter shivered on the porch and blew a plume of misty breath from her lips. *Going to be a cold winter this year,* she thought, as she stepped down onto the frosty grass. As she walked around to the side of the house, she could see Jess at the window, up on her back legs, staring down at her. The dog's big black nose was pressed to the glass, leaving a smear. Kathleen laughed softly; on her back legs and backlit like that, the enormous German shepherd looked like a werewolf.

She shook her head as she approached the woodpile. 'Been acting peculiar for days now,' she muttered. 'More like a mother hen.' Could dogs get menopausal, she wondered. Might be time to take her to the vet for a check-up.

Kathleen shivered again. She was always a bit spooked by the trees at night – the clouds crossing the moon made them seem to move and sway even without any wind. They alternated between seeming further away than they were, or closer, as they did tonight. Just a trick of the silvery light, but still a little unsettling.

She reached the woodpile, and stopped to sniff and look around. *Phew, what is that smell? Something must be dead.* No wonder Jess was all stirred up.

In that instant, a booming *whoop* smashed out of the trees beside her. She dropped the bucket and swung around to the noise – to see one of the largest tree trunks moving towards her. Except it wasn't a tree, after all.

Kathleen Hunter screamed.

*

Jess ran from the door to the window and back again. Her hackles were a line of spikes down her back, and flecks of saliva had appeared at the corners of her mouth. The sense of danger was over-powering. A stench leaked in under the door that made her flanks shiver and dredged up a frightful genetic memory from ancestors a million generations back.

As she reached the front of the house again, a booming *whooping* sound made her freeze. She leaped at the door and grabbed the handle in her jaws and pulled. Nothing happened. She scratched at the doorframe with her claws, dragging long splinters from the heavy wood, then bounded back to the window. As she neared it, she heard a sound that made her heart erupt with fury – the scream of her master.

Jess exploded through the glass without a second thought.

*

The creature loomed above Kathleen Hunter like a deformed giant, its long crested head blotting out the moon, its stink filling her nostrils. She scrabbled backwards along the dry ground and screamed again, the first name that came to mind: 'Alex!' The face of her lost son flashed into her mind and she could almost feel him close by.

There was a sound of smashing glass and Jess came out of the darkness like a hundred-pound tan and gold missile. The dog leaped over Kathleen to strike the giant form. She hung on, sinking her teeth in deep and hard. The *whooping* changed to a roar that seemed to blast the leaves from the nearby tree branches.

Kathleen knew Jess could never be a match for the massive brute. As she watched, the creature wrapped one hand around the dog's neck, dragged her free of its putrid-smelling flesh and flung her at the nearest tree as if she weighed nothing. Jess hit hard, bones and cartilage exploding from the impact, before her body shuddered into a heap at its base. Kathleen could see Jess's eyes were still open, staring at her, but probably sightless. She screamed out in agony – her last friend, gone.

The creature shuffled towards her again, its teeth bared, each one longer than her fingers. Its giant hands flexed as if in anticipation of tearing her small frail body apart.

Kathleen fell silent, her mind turning inwards. Nothing mattered any more.

*

Alex's horse thundered along the green tunnel of branches that arched over the narrow track. They burst into a broad clearing and he pulled back on the reins. The powerful animal immediately slowed to a trot and he felt it breathing heavily underneath him. He looked back to see Adira emerge from the tunnel, smiling broadly, obviously enjoying the competition. He grinned back, his mouth forming a quip about her riding prowess, but the breath froze in his chest. A thunderbolt of pain, color and light crashed down on him, like a physical blow, and he fell backwards from his horse. A face swirled into perspective ... the old woman again, the one he'd seen in his dream. Then she'd been on a sunny porch, but now she was wrapped in darkness. She was screaming ... he could feel her terror ... feel it so strongly it was as though he was right there with her. There was something else there too, a huge presence hiding in the darkness. A large dog flew through the air, and a terrifying booming roar sounded all around them. There was blood and pain and fear.

The woman screamed again, and this time it was a name ... *Alex*. She knew him ... and he knew her. His mother. He remembered her now. He remembered lying on a hillside, looking down at her ... it was her farm, she lived there with the dog, Jess. Then he saw her as a younger woman, smiling at him, combing his hair ... he was a boy ... and she was his mother ... Kathleen Hunter. And it was his name she was calling now ... *Alex*. He was Alex Hunter.

He tried to reach out to her, but was condemned to be a powerless observer. The huge presence loomed over her. He felt a surge of frustration and anger. He knew he could save her if he could just reach her. He struck out, thumping the ground, mentally trying to break through the glass. The pain intensified. Blood surged from his nose.

*

Adira leaped from her horse before it had halted and was beside Alex in an instant. His face was contorted in torment and he was holding out an arm, trying to grasp at something only he could see. Adira called his name, softly at first and then more loudly, but he didn't respond.

Alex raised himself to his hands and knees, head down, and pounded his fist hard into the dirt, again and again. Adira could feel the blows through the soles of her feet. He raked up dirt and small rocks in each hand, then crushed his fists hard into the ground, reducing the stones to dust. He rose to his knees and roared in agony. Adira had only heard that sound in battle, from humans suffering mortal wounds.

She realized he was shouting a woman's name ... *Kathleen.*

His mother! she thought in horror. *What is he remembering?*

Alex struck the ground again, as though trying to break through to somewhere below its surface. Blood ran from his nose and she saw that his teeth were gritted. His eyes were open but unfocused. He fell forward onto his hands and shook his head as if to clear it. He was breathing hard.

When he spoke, the words were so soft she couldn't make them out. 'What, Alex? What is it?'

His hand shot out and grabbed the front of her shirt, pulling her to face him. His eyes were focused now, and volcanic with fury. He roared in her face and shook her. 'Why did you lie to me?'

It was the moment she had been dreading: the return of his memories before she was ready – before either of them was ready – to deal with them.

She grabbed his wrist. 'I never lied.'

Alex's other hand came up towards her. She doubted he was going to hit her, but her training took over. Almost automatically she brought her free hand around flat to strike him under his chin with enough force to jam his face upwards. He released her shirt and took a step back, but didn't fall. Instead he came back at her, fast. She needed to slow him down so she could talk to him. She was aware of what he could do if his rage overtook his logic.

She braced herself and struck out twice. The closed fist strikes were part of a Krav Maga combination designed as a fast take-down against the most formidable opponents. Alex took both blows, then swung an arm down to block her next kick. He moved fluidly and Special-Forces-fast.

His mother's name isn't the only memory coming back to him, Adira thought with growing trepidation. For the first time in her life, she realized she couldn't win.

'Stop, Alex.'

He ignored her and yelled again, 'Who am I?' Not one of her punches or kicks landed now; he was in control. His face was furious. 'You're no hospital worker. Who are you?'

She backed up, trying to stay out of his reach. 'Alex, you're still disorientated, you need to –'

'*I need the truth.*' He moved at a speed that left her flat-footed, and before she realized it he had hold of her again. He brought her face close to his own. 'I am Alex Hunter. There is no Horowitz. For the last time, *who are you?*'

She went to strike out again, but knew it was futile. The game was up. She dropped her arms to her sides and went still in his hands. 'Let me go.'

His jaws worked and his eyes burned into hers, but after a few seconds he pushed her away. She took a few steps back, turning away from him so she could think. The voice of her uncle, the general, came to her mind – *sometimes gamblers win.*

And now I must gamble, she thought.

She spun back to him. 'It's true – you *are* Alex Hunter, an American soldier. When you were sick, dying, your country abandoned you and we rescued you ... I rescued you. We saved your life when everyone else had given up on you. We *were* close, you and I ... you just don't remember.'

Alex shook his head, frowning. She could tell he was trying to draw more memories from his fragmented mind, to verify what she'd told him, or to find fault with it. She waited.

'I need to go,' he said. His eyes had lost their fury now; his gaze was level and emotionless.

'Back to the hotel?' She nodded, feeling that perhaps she'd won this round.

He shook his head, and a sudden jolt ran through her. 'You need to go where, Alex?'

He seemed to think for a moment, then looked directly into her eyes. 'Home. With you, or through you, and anyone else who tries to get in my way.'

She held his gaze, her mind working furiously. This was her ground-zero moment – if she lost him, she'd lose everything.

'You'll never make it without me,' she said.

THIRTEEN

Chief Logan sat at his desk scrolling through the Medical Examiner's report on the contents of the lion's digestive tract. He was relieved that he didn't have to make a call to Clark and Helen Wilson to tell them that their little girl had been taken by a lion – *a freakin' lion in Asheville, for Chrissakes*! But he couldn't shake the morbid feeling that something else was out there. There'd just been too many weird goings-on lately.

He really wanted to believe that Emma Wilson was still alive, that she'd wandered off after some late-season deer maybe, and then got lost in the dark. That she was huddled in a sheltered hollow somewhere below the snow line. The reality was, he'd have been satisfied even if they found her small body curled up and frozen solid, proof that she'd gone to sleep in the cold and never woken up. A horrible thought, given the pain her parents would feel, but still better than the crazy alternative that was floating around in his mind.

Logan lifted the cover of a folder on his desk and slid out the photos from Amanda Jordan's camera. The hulking shape in the falling snow caused a knotted feeling of disquiet in his gut. *Yep, finding little Emma frozen, but untouched, would not be the worst thing that could happen*, he thought again as he closed the folder.

The chief sipped his coffee, barely tasting the bitter liquid as his mind continued to work. He had too many questions, and any answers he received only led to more questions. In a month, the snow would start to fall in earnest, and then the winter folk would arrive for skiing, schnapps and fistfights with the locals. He'd prefer to keep everyone off the mountain until he knew exactly what was going on, but that wouldn't win him any friends in the local business community. *Better not take another call from the mayor just yet*, he thought glumly, pushing the folder to the back of his desk. He slumped a little lower in his chair. Truth was, he had no idea what to do next.

The phone beeped, and he frowned at it for a few seconds before picking it up. 'Shelley, I thought I said –' He stopped as he processed her reply: an urgent call from the field. Right now, he needed any information he could get. He sat forward. 'Patch it.'

Logan listened solemnly, his face seeming to age on the spot. 'Good god,' he whispered. 'Time of death?' His voice rose. 'Just freakin' make a guess then.' He closed his eyes. 'Uh-huh, that's probably after the lion was already dead. Okay, tell Ted Brandon to get his boys out there. I'll be on my way in another twenty minutes.'

Logan hung up and sat in silence, wishing he had any other job besides the one he held. The phone beeped again and he lifted the handset slowly to his ear.

'Chief Logan?'

Logan was relieved to hear the young professor's voice; he didn't feel ready for anything else from the field right now. 'Professor Kearns, what can I do for you? I'm a little busy right now.'

'Chief, the Wilson place – we were just out there and –'

Logan felt like being angry with someone; Kearns would do. He cut the man off. 'What the fuck were you doing out there?'

'We found something.'

The angry curl of Logan's lips flattened as he waited for the university professor to continue.

'Some tracks,' Kearns added.

'We know the lion was there, Professor Kearns.'

'No, I mean yes ... we know the lion was there, but these were a different type of print, something ... *strange*. You remember the photographs of the shape in the snow up on Black Mountain? Well, we got a connection.'

Logan pulled the folder back towards him and flicked it open. He tapped the hulking shape with one large finger, thinking. He felt a leaden ball starting to grow in his gut.

'You there, Chief?' Logan grunted and Matt Kearns continued. 'The friend I mentioned, Charles Schroder, he specialises in these types of occurrences. He thinks we might have something up here that we need to be ... cautious with.'

'Cautious? What does that mean – it's dangerous?'

'Maybe ... probably.'

Logan thought furiously, weighing up what he knew against what he didn't. The imbalance was too great not to use everything he had at his disposal.

'Professor Kearns, there's been an attack and a disappearance out at the Hunter place. Might be something else ... strange. I can pick you up out front in ten minutes if you feel like tagging along.'

*

Matt felt a sense of déjà vu as he and Charles watched the police forensics team pick over the Hunter place for clues. Just like Emma Wilson, Kathleen Hunter had disappeared. But unlike the Wilson case, which had offered up very little in the way of evidence for the police, this time there were traces of a struggle. It was unlikely that Kathleen Hunter, a woman in her seventies, could have survived that much blood loss.

Matt put a hand over his nose and mouth to try to mask the thick, coppery scent lingering in the air. He'd never been to a crime scene before, and at first he'd tried not to react to the ghastly tableau, detaching himself from its violence as if it were simply a scene from one of the hundred horror movies he'd watched. But the more he became immersed in the detail, the more nauseated he felt. Matt couldn't help empathizing with the woman, alone and frightened in the night. He'd known terror himself, had seen people he loved brutally killed by a creature that had come out of the stygian deep. It tormented his dreams to this day.

Charles nudged him to get his attention as two police officers carried a stretcher towards their truck. As they came closer, Matt put his hand up to stop them. He lifted the blanket and saw the battered body of an enormous dog. Its eyes had rolled back into its head, and the neck looked soft and boneless beneath the fur. Matt made a sound of regret.

Charles made to lay his hand on the dog's muzzle, but one of the officers yelled a sharp rebuke almost directly into his ear. Matt saw his friend flinch, but to his credit he didn't step back.

Matt held up his hand again, this time in a placating gesture. 'It's okay, officers, we're working with Chief Logan – we're consultants.' He yelled over the men's heads, 'Okay, Chief?'

Logan looked around and seemed to sum up the situation immediately. 'Give 'em what they need, boys,' he yelled back, then went back to talking to Ted Brandon.

Charles lifted his hand to the dog again and ran his fingers deftly from its head down its back and along its limbs, feeling the bone breaks and joint separations and inspecting the lacerations. At the flanks, he worked his hand slowly back up the body, returning eventually to the head. He examined the snout, then lifted the dog's lips. He quickly brought his face closer, then fumbled in his pocket and pulled out a sample tube and a set of surgical tweezers.

'Hold this,' he said to Matt, and held out the small container without turning, his eyes riveted on whatever he'd found in the dog's mouth. He pulled back the heavy lip and used the tweezers to tug something from between the teeth. He exhaled slowly and turned to Matt, his eyes round with excitement. 'Look ... and some of the dermis is still attached.'

The tweezers held a small tuft of reddish-brown hair, coarse and bloody. Matt could see the small plug of glistening flesh that bound it together.

He uncapped the vial and Charles carefully dropped the sample in. He pocketed the tweezers, then took the tube from Matt's hand and capped it. He held it up so they could both examine its contents. The hair was unbelievably thick, and oily looking. Charles shook the vial, uncapped it again and waved it under his nose. He nodded, then extended it for Matt to smell.

Matt recoiled from the rank odor. '*Phew*, what is that?'

Charles didn't answer as he screwed the plastic cap on tightly. 'We need a lab, pronto, before this degrades.'

'Finished?' one of officers asked, looking bored.

Matt stepped closer to the dog on the stretcher and placed his hand on its huge shoulder, stroking the fur. 'Musta been some fight. Where are you taking it?'

The officer covered the dog's head with the blanket again, to keep away an inquisitive fly. 'Chief wants an autopsy.' He nodded to his partner, then motioned with his head to the truck.

Matt yelled after them, 'Hey, any chance of a lift to the university?'

*

The officers dropped Matt and Charles a good mile from the university. Neither complained, however, as the ride had taken place in an uncomfortable silence, Matt's occasional questions eliciting little more than grunts from the two officers. Matt was also glad of the fresh air; the same revolting smell he'd sniffed in the vial emanated from the dog on the stretcher.

The two men walked in silence along the university drive. Matt had given up asking Charles about the sample; the most his friend would give him was, 'Not yet.' The late season sunshine was pleasant on Matt's shoulders, and coaxed a low zumming from crickets and cicadas in the long grasses beside the road. Matt let his mind wander across the strange events of the last few days. He was worried that he might have got himself and Charles into something a lot more complex and dangerous than he'd originally expected. His stomach tightened.

Charles's quiet voice broke his reverie. 'Ten o'clock.'

'Huh?' Matt saw that although Charles was facing forward, his eyes were focused on the field to their left.

'Don't look,' Charles said softly, but of course Matt did.

An old man in an oversized blue chambray shirt stood like a withered fence post amongst the long grass. Even from this distance Matt could see that his rheumy eyes were fixed intently on him and Charles. After they'd passed, Matt could still feel the scrutiny like a laser on the back of his neck. He couldn't resist looking back, but the field was empty. He saw that Charles was looking into the deserted field too.

'Wonder what that was about?' Charles said.

Matt shrugged. 'Forget about it. C'mon.' But he couldn't forget about it. He'd felt as if the old man's stare had held recognition and a hint of ... suspicion.

*

Matt looked around the campus to get his bearings. He felt better being back at the university. 'I figure we need a high-power microscope, access to a computer and the internet, and possibly a fully functioning biology lab. Oh yeah, and an assistant or two.'

Charles looked surprised. 'I'm impressed, you must really have some pull here.'

Matt sucked in a cheek and shook his head. 'Unfortunately, not. I said we needed that stuff; I didn't say we'd get it. Still, I expect to be on staff here soon so that's got to count for something. Let's try the nice approach first, and if that fails I'll invoke the name of the terrifying Chief Logan.'

Charles grinned. 'Sounds like a plan.'

Matt nodded towards an enormous mustard-yellow building on the other side of the quadrangle that towered four stories above its neighbors either side. 'Zeis Hall.'

'Wow, nice facilities. This is no backwoods place of learning, is it?' Charles seemed amazed at the amount of infrastructure for a relatively small town.

'Nice facilities indeed – these guys were teaching molecular biology and robotics fifteen years ago. They'll have what we need, we've just got to get access to it. Come on.'

They moved quickly down a corridor with so highly a polished floor that they experienced the odd sensation of walking on their own reflections. The rooms on either side held banks of computer monitors, electronics equipment, whiteboards sporting literary quotations.

Charles jerked to a stop as if reaching the end of a leash. 'Wow! I mean really, *wow!*'

'What is it?' Matt backed up.

Charles stepped into the unoccupied room. 'What it is, Professor Matthew Kearns, is an FLX genome sequencer – top of the line, one billion runs with a gene-read length of 1000 base pairs per run. Hell, I've been trying to get one of these babies at Harvard for two years. You know, you could decode an entire *E. coli* bacterium's DNA in a single day with this.'

Matt pulled a face. 'Holy shit – *E. coli?* Did anyone else just get a hot flush? Let's go.' He turned to leave.

Charles grabbed at his arm. 'No, really, it's important. We can use it to map our sample's DNA back along its maternal line to analyze its comparative evolution – see what it is, and where it came from.'

Matt looked from the machine to his friend's serious face, then nodded. He turned to check the name on the room's door – *Professor S. Sommer.* 'This must be the guy we need to talk to.'

The next room was a large biology lab, filled with long benches, each with a heating element and waste sink every six feet. Peering through the glass of the door, Matt could see the room was ringed by shelves holding all manner of beakers and tubes, and, most importantly, computers that were double-cabled into walls – power *and* internet access. A woman was typing at one of the computers, her back to them. At the front of the room, writing on a whiteboard, was a tall man with longish silver hair. With his perfectly trimmed beard, half-glasses, neat jacket and corduroy vest, he looked like a Central Casting version of a professor.

'Great, and Dumbledore's home as well,' Matt whispered to Charles. He pushed open the door and cleared his throat. 'Professor Sommer, I presume?'

The man turned and looked at them over the top of his glasses, then, without a word, let his eyes slide slowly past them to the rear of the room. Matt followed his gaze to where the woman who'd been working on the computer now sat with her arms folded, watching him.

'For a scientist, you make a lot of assumptions, Matthew Kearns,' she said. 'But then again, you always did.' She started to thread her way through the tables towards them, pulling off a pair of small glasses as she came, a half-smile at the corner of her mouth. 'I heard you were in town ... and you might be joining us.'

Matt blinked and frowned for a moment, before recognition broke through his confusion. 'What ... Sarah Peterson? You're Professor Sommer?'

'Professor Sarah Sommer – Sommer's my married name. And yes, I run the biology departments at AU, all three of them. This is my assistant, Roger Burrows.'

Matt turned back to the man, ready to apologise, but Burrows gave him an uninterested glance and went back to writing on the board.

'And you are ...?' Sarah held out her hand to Charles.

Charles shot his hand out in response. 'Excuse him; he's not used to social contact. Professor Charles Schroder, Anthropology, Harvard. A pleasure to meet you, Professor Sommer.'

'Sarah, please, and likewise.' She tilted her head. 'Tell me, you're not the Professor Charles Schroder who wrote the paper on comparative analysis of early hominids using DNA markers, are you?'

Matt snorted.

Charles shrugged and stood a little taller. 'Yes, yes, I am.'

Sarah smiled at him. 'That analysis was brilliant work.'

Charles nodded a little too deeply, turning it into a half-bow. Matt groaned.

'Follow me,' Sarah said, motioning to the door. She started towards it, Charles in tow. He looked back over his shoulder at Matt and raised an eyebrow. Matt exhaled slowly and followed. As he left the room, he saw Roger Burrows looking at him over the top of his glasses. This time he was smiling.

*

Matt felt nervous; she made him nervous. He hadn't seen her since his university days, and here he was trying to impress her all over again. He cleared his throat.

'We believe what we have here is unique: a tissue sample of an extremely rare creature. We need to examine it at both cellular and genetic level to determine if we're right. If we are, this could be the biggest news since ... I don't know, since Noah's Ark.'

He groaned inwardly as the words came out of his mouth. They sounded bombastic even to his own ears, and he knew he was recklessly inflating something Charles had only hinted at.

Sarah folded her arms, one eyebrow raised slightly. 'Noah's Ark, you say?'

Charles cut in before Matt could respond. 'We know that's a little melodramatic. But we do have some indeterminate biological material, which leads us to suspect there may be some form of new, or very old, anthropoid species on Black Mountain. We'd like to do some lower-level analysis on the sample just to see if we can identify it according to any of the known taxonomic branches.'

Matt got the drift: lower the expectations; go easy on the details for the moment. He put on his most businesslike expression. 'Charles is right. It might be nothing more than an escaped chimpanzee, or some sort of weird-looking ground squirrel. But we promised the police chief we'd do our best to identify it.'

Sarah's eyebrow went up another notch. 'Uh-huh ... and is this *ground squirrel* responsible for the recent thefts of cows and domestic pets, or potentially involved in the attacks on the farms recently?'

'There's also a lion loose from the circus,' Matt spluttered. 'That's probably resp–'

Sarah leaned forward. 'Lion's dead – the police shot it.'

Matt slowly turned to Charles. Charles just shrugged and pointed to him with a flat, open hand – *over to you, you're doin' great* was the implication. Matt laughed. He shut his eyes for a moment, rubbed them with a thumb and finger, then leaned towards Sarah.

'*Oookay*, we don't really believe it's a squirrel or fugitive chimp. We think there may be some form of early hominid running around on the mountain, and we'd like to try to determine if it's one we know of or something completely new.'

'Go on.'

Matt stared at her for several seconds, torn between telling her everything and wanting to hold back on some of their wilder suspicions until they could prove or disprove them.

Sarah stared back levelly, and the corner of her mouth turned up slightly. 'Listen up, the pair of you. I've lived in this town for most of my life. I love the place, and anything that threatens it or its folk gets my full attention. And one more thing before you start bullshitting: I'm quite a well-respected professor of biology who's pretty highly regarded in the international arena on matters of cellular biology, environmental gene mutations and a dozen other organic micro-matter subjects. Gentlemen, you have two choices. One: you can try and snow me, and you'll be out that door in seconds. Or two: tell me everything, and I may be able to help.' She turned from one to the other, looking them each in the eye. 'Your call, boys.'

Matt looked again at Charles, who nodded slowly. 'We need her,' he said. 'Her and her sequencer.'

Matt compressed his lips, then turned to Sarah. 'Look, there've been stories about something in these mountains for hundreds if not thousands of years. Not just in these mountains, but all over the world.' He sucked in a breath and let it out slowly, preparing for her ridicule. 'We think we may have a tissue fragment from a mega-hominid ... a *living* mega-hominid.' He gritted his teeth, waiting for the mocking laughter.

Instead, she slid her chair across the floor to her computer and began to type. When she'd found what she was looking for, she half-turned the screen for Matt and Charles to see. 'As I said, I've lived here for a long time, and I know every creature in these parts, big and small. But in the last few weeks ... well, I've begun to suspect that there's something else out there. Something that doesn't fit.' She started typing again. 'For several years now, we've had microphones placed around the slopes to collect ornithological data for a number of the local societies. But recently we've picked up something else.'

She hit a key and adjusted the volume. The booming *whoops* and *grunts* were eerie in the small room.

Charles sat forward, his mouth open. When it stopped, he leaped out of his chair. 'Play it again.'

She hit the replay, and folded her arms. 'I've never heard anything like it ... except it reminds me of something at the same time. I just can't place it.'

Charles turned the computer around, then paused. 'May I?' He didn't wait for a response, just started typing furiously. 'Listen.' From the computer came a series of hoots, whoops, snorts and grunts.

'You see, you need a certain shaped larynx without vocal cords to create those sounds,' he said to Sarah. 'Also a heavy jaw, and a deep barrel-chest.' He played the sounds again and swung the screen around for Matt to see. 'God bless you, Dian Fossey.'

On the screen was an image of a black mountain gorilla. Its dark, human-like eyes stared out from under a rubber-thick brow ridge.

Sarah's frown deepened. 'You think it's a gorilla up there?'

Charles smiled and shook his head slowly. 'No, and not by a million years of evolution. But if it is what I think it is, an escaped lion would have been a lot simpler to deal with ... and to explain.'

FOURTEEN

The boat glided in towards the beach and the fisherman leaped out to walk the bow up onto the sand. Adira and Alex picked up their small bags and jumped out, then Alex turned to help pull the boat clear of the water. It was quiet save for the tiny waves *shushing* onto the fine grains of sand. Adira watched as Alex lifted his chin and inhaled the scents of the ocean, before scanning the dark shoreline.

The little open boat had brought them from Eilat, the southernmost town in Israel, to Taba at the start of the Gulf of Aqaba in Egypt. It had taken only twenty minutes to cross the six miles of glass-like ocean, but the trip had cost 1000 US dollars – and there would be much more expense to come. They needed international travel documents, credit cards and new identities. Adira had a contact in Egypt who was one of the best in the Middle East. He, like the fisherman, was part of the large black-market network that operated under the noses of the Israeli and Egyptian authorities. Terrorists used them to get into Israel ... and now she was using them to get out.

She turned to the waiting fisherman. '*Shukran*,' she said, and held out the wad of American notes.

His weathered hand reached for it, but she held on tight, causing the old man to frown and look up into her eyes.

He grunted. 'The car will come. It is my cousin, Bennu, I trust him. As arranged, he will take you as far as Sharm el-Sheikh at the Red Sea, and then ...' He shrugged and tugged again on the notes.

Adira still held fast, examining his eyes for any deception. She spoke in a low, even tone. 'If he does not come, then the next time you see me, it will not only be the money I take from you.'

She let go, and the old man nodded, but Adira could see the hint of a smirk on his face.

Alex helped push the boat off the sand for its return trip. They both saw the small illumination across the dark water as the old man flipped open a mobile phone and started to talk. Adira's stomach knotted – she couldn't believe the risks she was taking. She always thought any plan through from both a strategic and tactical perspective – it was one of the reasons she had stayed alive so long in Mossad's elite Metsada unit. But her decision to help Alex leave Israel had been made in a state of panic. She knew that in doing so, she was betraying her country, her uncle and everything she'd believed in her entire life. The truth was, the woman beneath the lethal exterior wanted a life with Alex Hunter, no matter how remote a fantasy that seemed. At the same time, she was continuing to betray him and his fragmented memory. He already knew she'd lied to him. What would happen if she were proved a liar again? What of her fantasy about a future together then?

It was impossible to know how this crazy plan would turn out. She had to believe that what she was doing was right. She could justify her actions to her country, to her uncle – after all, if she got the answers they wanted about the Arcadian project, then all would be forgiven. In her world, the end *always* justified the means. Today's unorthodox actions were tomorrow's textbook lessons ... as long as they worked.

She reached out and gripped Alex's upper arm and squeezed. 'Come,' she said. She was smart, she would work things out.

Alex smiled and put his hand on her shoulder and she felt its warmth on her skin. *What I'm doing is right*, she thought. *Sometimes logic doesn't matter.*

*

General Meir Shavit watched the surveillance film of his niece and Alex Hunter buying tickets for the domestic flight from Tel Aviv to Eilat. They'd paid cash, and the available CCTV footage had lost them the moment they left the airport. Shavit knew that given Adira's abilities, it was sheer luck that they had managed to catch her on film at all.

Sheer luck, or a deliberate tactic? He tapped his chin with a cigarette lighter. Could she have doubled back into the airport and taken another domestic flight? Or were she and Hunter on an international flight to somewhere else in the Middle East, or even beyond? Or maybe they had sailed across into Egypt or Saudi Arabia? *Too many options*, he thought.

He rubbed a hand over his face and looked at the image of his niece. *What are you up to, Addy? You think you are in love? You think that because one young man shakes you up, everything you have stood for is now worth nothing? Prove me wrong, Addy, before the walls close in*, he thought.

He shook his head and watched the film loop over again. He stopped it and focused in on the young man with her, then gave a long, morose sigh. 'Addy, if you were with anyone else, I might turn a blind eye and let you run ...'

There was a soft knock on the door. The general's assistant opened it, allowing a tall, dark-haired man to enter. The man saluted and stood at attention.

'At ease, Salamon,' Shavit said. He waved the man to a pair of heavy leather chairs, and retrieved a folder from his desk before taking the chair opposite Salamon's. 'You are well?' he asked, smiling.

Salamon's back was straight and he sat uncomfortably in the general's presence. 'Yes, sir.'

Shavit nodded and continued to smile. 'Your Kidon team is available?'

Salamon shifted slightly, the bulge of muscles playing beneath his suit. 'All finished up from previous assignments and ready for duty, sir.'

'Good, good.' Shavit lit a cigarette, sucked in a deep lungful of smoke and blew the plume towards the ceiling. His eyes returned to Salamon. 'I have a small problem. Maybe only a personal one, but it needs urgent, incisive ... and delicate action.'

Shavit handed across the folder and watched as the other man skimmed its contents, quickly and professionally. His hands, although large and with heavily callused knuckles, were nimble.

'Captain Senesh might be having a breakdown,' Shavit added softly. 'I need you to retrieve her.'

Salamon's head jerked up from the file. 'Adira Senesh?'

'Yes, your colleague in Metsada.' Shavit motioned at a photograph of Alex Hunter in the file. 'This man may have corrupted her. Bring her back.'

Salamon's eyes narrowed as he examined the man in the photograph. 'It will not be easy. If she does not want to come with us, she will fight.'

Shavit blew more smoke into the air. 'Bring her back alive, Salamon.'

Salamon nodded and put the picture back into the file. 'What of him ... if he tries to interfere?'

Shavit looked at the young man sitting in front of him. Salamon Eitan, head of the Kidon squad, was his secret weapon; his unit the more brutal side of the secretive Mossad machine. 'Bring him back ... intact. Alive if possible, but his life is of secondary importance. Read the file in detail, Salamon; it will not be an easy mission. Take your squad, because he may also resist, and he *will* be a problem.'

'Not for me,' Salamon said, and bent his head to continue reading.

FIFTEEN

The beast threw the body to the ground, then crouched beside it and sniffed. A thousand rich scents filled its nostrils, almost overpowering its sensory system, which had been dulled by years of living and hunting in the dark. It lifted the small, broken creature, testing its weight and fragility. The limbs flopped and the head rolled on a now boneless neck. The creature held the head up and peered into the bloody face. The eyes had rolled back so only the whites showed, and the mouth hung open in a silent scream.

It reached out with one large, blunt finger, enormous against the prey's small face, and pulled first one pupil down, then the next. It stare, transfixed, into the eyes of the kind that had supposedly driven its people deep into the mountain and imprisoned them there. It snorted. There was nothing to fear from this pitiful creature; the legends must be untrue.

The body was old and its meat would be stringy, but still ambrosia after countless years of living on blind fish, fat grub-like insects and branching lichens. It would make a fitting contribution to the feast to come.

*

'Okay, what have we got?' Matt asked.

Charles and Sarah were working on devices at opposite ends of the laboratory. Charles turned to give Matt an incredulous look, said, 'Come back in a week,' then immediately returned to keying in parameters for his analysis.

Matt raised his eyebrows. 'An hour okay?'

'Deal.'

Charles rushed over to a spinning centrifuge, switched it off so he could look at the separating residues, made a note on a pad, restarted it, then sped back to his computer. Matt grinned. He knew his friend was trying to do several weeks' work in a few hours all by himself; he also knew he was loving every minute of it. Charles bounced over to the digital microscope that was feeding magnified images onto his screen, then quickly noted data from another computer screen about a slice of the tissue sample that had been fed into the mass spectrometer.

While Charles was a turbulent ocean of activity, Sarah, at the other end of the laboratory, was a pool of calm. She lifted her eyes from her own screen and acknowledged Matt with a slight tilt of her head.

Matt put his hands in the back pockets of his jeans and sauntered closer. 'Can I help?'

She folded her arms, her eyes narrowing in suspicion. Then a small smile lifted the corners of her mouth. 'I don't know ... *can* you help me?' Her smile widened. 'And how come you didn't ask Charles if you could help him? He seems to be doing most of the work, and with a lot of unfamiliar equipment. I'm getting my software to do all mine for me.'

Matt looked briefly over his shoulder at Charles, then back to Sarah. He gave her a sheepish smile. 'He's more comfortable working by himself. Besides, by helping you, I'm also helping him. See, we're all happy.'

She laughed, and pulled a disbelieving face. 'Okay, sure. Come around here and I'll show you what I'm doing. Wouldn't hurt to have someone act as a sounding board.'

'I'm your man.'

Matt moved behind her chair and looked at the split screen. Dense rows of figures rapidly scrolled up the left side, and every now and then a line of data was automatically extracted and placed in a table on the right side.

Sara pointed at the table data. 'I'm performing a low-level analysis of the sample's DNA, and looking at the differences *and* similarities between it and that of any other known hominids. At the very least, I'll be able to tell you what *it isn't*, and then maybe what it could be. The gene sampling program I've developed makes use of the mitochondrial DNA to track its descent back along its maternal line, and the new algorithms I've coded extend that lineage reach-back significantly.'

Matt bent closer to the screen but didn't understand it any better. He could decipher hundreds of languages, some that hadn't been spoken for millennia, but when it came to computer stuff, forget it. Nevertheless, he nodded sagely and asked the only question he could think of.

'Yeah, Charles mentioned something about that. But, *um*, why not use both the maternal *and* paternal sources?'

Surprising him, she nodded. 'Fair question, Matthew. Bottom line is, if you want staying power, stick with a woman.' She kept a straight face for a few seconds, then laughed softly, showing a line of near perfect teeth. 'Got ya, Kearns. Fact is, the paternal mito-chondrial DNA is destroyed at fertilization, so the offspring only inherits the mother's mitochondrial DNA, creating an unbroken maternal link to the near and also long-distant past. We can easily track back hundreds of thousands of years, and now, with the new software and the computing power of my FLX, many more again. We've already found that a common ancestor of both modern man and the Neanderthals existed 500,000 years ago.'

Matt was impressed, and let it show.

Then he leaned a little closer to her screen, giving the impression of being more interested in it than her answer to his next question. 'So, Sarah Marie Sommer née Peterson, how's married life in partic-ular and Asheville life in general?'

She snorted. 'Married life is fantastic ... the way it's portrayed in the glossy magazines. In real life ... *weeell*. Ever heard the saying, *Marriages are made in heaven?* No one ever adds the second part, which goes something like this: *Marriages are made in heaven but suffered on a more temporal plane.* Basically, once you come down from the heady heights of the champagne and lovemaking and have to deal with the daily routine, illness, fights and boredom ... well, things aren't quite so rosy.' She looked at him and shrugged. 'Karl was a fantastic guy, but one day we both woke up and looked at each other and realized we didn't want to grow old together.'

'I'm sorry to hear that, Sarah.' Matt put his hand on her shoulder and tried hard to look sympathetic. Inside, he felt like giving her a high-five. 'What was he like – Karl, I mean? Is he still around?'

'No, his family are Swiss – known as the Basel Sommers, owners of the company that makes Sportsuhr wristwatches. Karl's being groomed to take over one day. I met him at a party in New York – he really stood out: tall, blond, broad-shouldered ... and rich. You know the type. He had a real magnetism about him.'

Matt snorted. 'Sounds like a real loser.' He regretted the petulant response the instant it left his lips and hurried to add, 'I mean for letting you go.'

Sarah dismissed the flattery with a slight shake of her head. 'Yeah well, turned out we did have one thing in common – we both loved Karl Sommer.' She half-shrugged in an I-don't-care gesture. 'Anyway, I've been single four years now and I love it. I can do what I want when I want, date who I want ...' She lifted both her eyebrows at him and smiled, then glanced at Charles.

Matt followed the glance, then leaned in close. 'I'm pretty sure he's already involved, and pretty committed.'

She gave him a mock look of disappointment, then turned back to her computer as it pinged softly. She sat down, started typing, then pinched her lip and frowned as she read the presented data.

Charles joined them, a sheaf of printouts in his hands. 'Okay, I've gone as far as I can,' he said. 'I'm afraid the results are either conclusive or inconclusive, depending on your perspective.' He flipped through the pile. 'Okay, some background and basics first. In most mammals and every hominid *except* mankind, the outer layer of every cell carries glycoproteins that contain one specific family of sugar molecules called sialic acid. It's actually one of the first tests we run to determine a human/non-human category. Surprisingly, our sample is totally *without* sialic acid, indicating it came from a human biology.'

Charles paused to look up at them briefly. '*But* I think we're pretty sure it's not from a human.' He raised his eyebrows, then continued reading from his notes.

'Also, I detected switched-on markers for keratin-41 – that's the primary gene for excessive hair growth. This genotype has been switched off in mankind for a quarter of a million years. So we've got a human, or something like a human, but hairy like an ape. Then there's the muscle striation residue – six times longer than human muscle fiber, but shorter than a great ape's. So our hairy, human-like creature would be six times stronger than a man, assuming it was the same size as a man.' He looked at Matt. 'But we know from its footprint that it's a lot larger, so we're talking one powerful being.

'There were extremely high levels of pheomelanin and almost non-existent levels of eumelanin in the sample, which basically means we've got a fair-skinned redhead.' Charles looked up from his notes with a slightly bemused expression. 'The data analysis goes on like this – one result suggesting a human-based life form, another suggesting an ape-like morphology and biology. If I were asked to summarize the findings, I'd say we have a giant redhead with a biology similar to humans and also similar to great apes, but not identical to either ... something in between.'

Matt could tell Charles was both puzzled by and excited at his results.

'Snap!' Sarah said, clicking her fingers. 'I've found the same variance–similarity conundrum. We've got a 98 per cent genetic match to humans, but a 99.1 per cent match to the great apes – close, but no cigar. Data on the genetic structures gives me results similar to yours, Charles – it's in the same family, but a different species. In fact, a whole different branch of hominids, I think. If *I* were asked to summarize, gentlemen, I'd say you've got a potential whole new line, or a very old one that we don't have any living evidence of.'

Sarah walked over to a whiteboard, picked up a marker and waggled it in her fingers as she considered where to begin. She divided the board into three sections: Prosimians; Monkeys; Apes. Under the Apes heading, she divided again, this time into four: Orangutans; Gorillas; Chimpanzees; Man. She tapped the word *orangutans* and turned to Charles. 'I'm betting that's where your gene for red hair originated, Professor Schroder.'

More arrows and names went on the board, forming a detailed family tree divergence model, showing where the different species branched off from one another. Down the side, Sarah drew a timeline. 'Chimps and mankind separated around seven million years ago. *That* root species and the gorillas separated about another two to three million years before that. Now ...' She picked up a different-colored marker and drew a line between the gorillas, orangutans and man. 'Okay, this is what I believe we have – a whole new species that sits somewhere here on the evolutionary line. Something that probably should have died out hundreds of thousands or millions of years ago.' She put down the pen and turned to Matt and Charles. 'Something that modern man hasn't seen for a very, very long time ... if ever.' She narrowed her eyes. 'Come on, guys, you're holding something back. What exactly are we dealing with here?'

Matt turned to Charles and grinned, then motioned for him to proceed.

Charles reached into his pocket and pulled out a small polished wooden box, which he placed on the table between Matt and Sarah. He didn't open it.

Sarah folded her arms. 'So what is it?'

'My grandfather gave this to me when I was eight years old,' Charles said. 'It was given to him by his brother, the original Charles Schroder, who went missing in China in the mid-1930s. It was the trigger for my great-uncle's obsession, one that perhaps killed him, and it's been driving my own love affair ever since I received the gift.'

Charles opened the box but its contents were obscured by a black cloth.

Sarah squinted. 'What is it?'

'Something almost magical. Such treasures are usually sold by the Chinese farmers who find them on their land to apothecaries in the mainland cities or Hong Kong. *Jù lóng de yáchî* – translated as dragon's teeth. Most often they're ground up and used as medicine, for everything from insomnia to improved sexual performance. My great-uncle came across this in a shop in Kowloon in 1935, and sent it back to my grandfather.'

Charles unfolded the cloth to reveal a large, off-white tooth. He looked up into Sarah's face. 'Not a dragon's tooth, but one belonging to Gigantopithecus, the largest hominid ever to have existed on earth. Growing to nearly ten feet in height, twelve to fifteen hundred pounds, omnivorous. These things were big, smart and aggressive – and, for a time, they were probably living side by side with *Homo sapiens*.' He paused. 'Well, maybe. The sad fact is, *Homo sapiens* probably killed them off. Can you imagine the look on some early *Homo sapiens*' face when he came across some pissed-off creature nearly twice his height who ate meat? I'm pretty sure I'd want it out of my neighborhood as well.'

Sarah picked up a pencil and used it to move the tooth around in the box. 'It's enormous. Did your great-uncle find any other evidence?'

Charles shook his head. 'We don't know – he disappeared. The last message he sent was from a small town called Daxin in southern China. He was heading out the next morning to see some huge rock tower riddled with limestone caves – one cave in particular, apparently – a climb of about a hundred feet straight up. My grandfather sent a party to look for him, but the villagers wouldn't talk about him, or even take the search party up to the caves. They said the place was haunted. My grandfather thought dear old Charlie had been robbed and killed and his body hidden. But no one really knows.'

Matt carefully lifted the almost perfect, tusk-like tooth free of the box and tested its weight in the palm of his hand. He nodded to Charles. 'I know you're right – this has gotta be it.'

Charles gave a half-smile, took the tooth from Matt and held it up at eye level, then raised it way above his head, indicating the height of its original owner's mouth. He couldn't know that the previous Charles Schroder had done exactly the same thing around eighty years earlier.

'Anyway, at the time that these rare and fantastic creatures were supposed to have died out,' Charles said, 'the last of the land bridges across Asia and the far north still existed. What if Gigantopithecus was forced to move somewhere without so many little hostile *Homo sapiens*? What if they learned to stay as far away from us as they could – in remote jungles, high on mountain peaks, in inaccessible valleys? Some humans have seen them, but generally they're dismissed as legends. But what if they're not? What if what we're dealing with here is a living fossil – a living Gigantopithecus?'

Sarah was shaking her head, but her eyes were shining. 'But how ... I mean *really*, how? Even if we suspend our disbelief for a moment and say that maybe these creatures have been secretly living among us ... No, sorry, not among us; I mean, living contemporaneously in our most remote and inaccessible places – wouldn't we have at least seen some sign? A portion of a body that's been discovered ... a bone fragment, a rib, or a tooth that's not fossilized?'

Charles snorted softly and carefully placed the tooth back in the box. He smiled as he looked from Matt to Sarah. 'As rare as a black swan? There was a saying in sixteenth-century England that a good person was as impossible to find as a black swan, the idea being that swans could only be white. Well, you know what the English found when they traveled to the west coast of Australia? The swans there were all black.' He laughed at their bemused expressions. 'I know, I know – you're right, Sarah, there should be some remnant of these things, and I certainly don't have all the answers. However, I do have a theory. But consider this first: what I'm suggesting is not *that* fantastic when you consider the amazing things we've found just in the last few decades. There's even a scientific name for these kinds of discoveries – Lazarus taxon. Go on, Google it! It covers things that we thought were extinct for millennia. And I'm not talking about insignificant little gastropods or rainforest orchids – these things can be giants.' Charles ticked them off on his fingers. 'In a hidden valley in Australia they found a tree called the Wollemi pine – it was supposed to have been extinct for ninety million years. Then there's the coelacanth, the limbed fish – that little baby was meant to have been dead and gone for about 360 million years, until scientists found that the Pacific Islanders were eating it all the time – it wasn't rare to them at all. Do you know how many missing prehistoric tribes we find every decade? Dozens. On the Brazil–Peru border, hidden under the dense tree canopy, were the Murunahua – they tried to fight off the helicopters with bows and arrows. And I'm not surprised: once modern man barged in on them, they were nearly wiped out by colds in the first two years of contact.' He clapped his hands. 'And I can't begin to describe some of the strange things that are turning up now that we're doing more deep-sea drill mining in the abyssal zones of the ocean trenches.'

Matt was nodding. He didn't need to be convinced about biological anomalies. Beneath the Antarctic ice, he'd seen things that shouldn't have existed anymore but were very much alive, aggressively so. He looked at Sarah. She was nodding too, but a slight frown still pulled her brows together.

'Maybe these things just hadn't been formally discovered or identified before,' she said to Charles. 'You mentioned you have a theory about why we haven't seen any specimen fragments or more recent-term fossils of Gigantopithecus?'

Charles pursed his lips. 'Two things – firstly, it's the rarity, the *exclusive* rarity.' He pinched his bottom lip, as though looking for a place to start his explanation. 'They remain hidden out in the open for long – so it was the caves that got me thinking. My great-uncle disappeared on a caving expedition, presumably looking for the source of this fossil.' He gestured to the tooth. 'We find new caves all the time, and often we also find weird things living within them. The deep darkness hides a lot of prehistory's secrets.'

'Too right,' Matt said, then looked embarrassed that he'd spoken the thought aloud. 'Sorry, carry on.'

'Secondly: intelligence,' Charles said. 'If we combine what we know about the Gigantopithecus fossils being found in caves and what we've recently been discovering about the ways proto-Neanderthals used to bury their dead deep in caves – well, we now believe, in fact, that they used to hide them – so what if these giant hominids had similar ceremonies? They were rare to begin with, but if they also bury their dead deep in the earth, or even, as with certain tribes, eat their dead, then we've been lucky to find any fossil evidence at all.'

He looked at Matt's and Sarah's expressions and grimaced slightly. 'Yeah, I know, it's a stretch. These things are more likely to be about as smart as gorillas – prehistory's answer to the gentle giant. They were probably wiped out by more modern and aggressive hominids – namely, us.'

Sarah didn't answer. Instead, she stared at the tooth in the box and a slow smile started to spread across her face. 'Okay, so we think we know what it *could* be, but we're a long way from being able to convince anyone else,' she said. 'But there is one way we can be sure.'

She walked quickly to the rear of the laboratory and searched through a few bench drawers, then returned with something that looked a little like an electric toothbrush without the bristles. She placed it on the table so its shining tip was pointing at the box with the tooth in it. It was a bone drill and Matt knew exactly what she wanted to do with it – make a hole in the tooth. The rare fossil that Charles had inherited from his grandfather's dead brother and treasured since he was eight; the tooth that had been the trigger for Charles's entire career.

Ouch, he mouthed, and looked at his friend.

'What do you have in mind?' asked Charles.

He didn't go bananas, Matt thought. *That's got to be a good thing.*

Sarah put her slim fingers on each side of the small box. 'Teeth don't denature as fast as normal bones do – the enamel and dentin are extremely resilient to penetration of groundwater and therefore mineralization. We've extracted viable DNA from the dried pulp of a 130,000-year-old mastodon tooth. We've got the DNA technology right here to fill in any missing base pair blanks – I can match the tooth and the organic sample's DNA in a few hours. Irrefutable proof. You just say the word.'

Charles pinched his lower lip again, thinking. Then he smiled. 'Word.'

*

The old man kneeled in a clearing on the outskirts of town. Before him loomed Black Mountain, its peak shrouded by freezing cloud. His eyes moved along the horizon, tracing the rise and fall of the other dark peaks, before he bent to light the small fire he'd built from sticks collected nearby. Once the fire had taken, he opened a sack and drew out a handful of feathers, nettles and powder. He sprinkled them onto the flames, each causing the tongues of fire to burn a different hue. Lastly, he placed a single bone across the burning twigs. He swore softly and quickly changed its position so the broken tip pointed at the mountain peaks.

The old man got slowly to his feet and chanted in a strong voice over the flames, pointing with a flat hand to each of the peaks, finishing with the tallest – the Dome. He threw another handful of powder at its hidden summit, then stood silently for a moment.

When he was done, he hoisted the bag onto his shoulder and set off for his next destination. There were more fires to be lit before the spirit barrier might have a chance of holding and he could feel the town was secure.

As he walked, he heard a deep *whooping* noise far off in the distance.

SIXTEEN

Alex and Adira had time on their hands while they waited for their documents to be produced. Adira wanted them to stay indoors and undercover, but the sun-filled sky, the ocean and the golden sands of Hauza beach across the road were too much for Alex. He needed to be outside. And even though Adira refused to be convinced it was a good idea, she relented. Alex spent hours in the water, diving below the warm surface, opening his eyes as he swam, enjoying the clarity of the Red Sea. Adira never joined him, preferring to remain on the beach as lookout. But was she his guardian or his supervisor, he wondered.

He ran a hand through his short hair, shaking out the water, and sat beside her on the towel, exhaling contentedly. 'Beautiful,' he said, gazing along the shoreline.

Adira lifted one edge of the towel and dried his back, then leaned forward to kiss his cheek. He smiled, looking into her dark eyes. He wanted to trust her, but wasn't sure he could anymore.

A prickling sensation at the back of his neck caused him to turn to look at the promenade. The small cafes there did a busy trade selling sodas, ice-creams and coffee. He frowned as the crowds of men, women and children seemed to slow, as if time itself was stretching – and then he saw the explosion in his mind, a second before it actually occurred.

He threw himself over Adira on the sand just as one of the busiest cafes was engulfed by an ear-shattering, orange ball that opened like a giant boiling flower. Debris and body parts blew outward, and splintered wood shot overhead in a wave of hot air mixed with blood and small gobbets of flesh. Wreckage rained down around them – remnants of people whose laughter and dreams were now shredded and burning. Screams and moans filled the air.

Alex stared at a small red-black puddle soaking into the sand beside him and the ache in his head intensified and turned to a clenched fist of pain. Anger surged inside him as he realized it wasn't over yet. No sooner had the debris settled on the ground before gunfire rang out over the top of the screaming and the wail of the sirens and alarms set off by the explosion. Four men burst from a van at the head of the promenade, huge packs strapped to their backs, their faces concealed by black and white keffiyehs. They dashed along the promenade, yelling and firing their weapons. Any surviving men were shot; the women and children were dragged towards one of the major hotels along the seafront.

Alex stood up, incredulous at how the calm and beauty of the beach had turned into a hellish maelstrom in seconds. The aggressors fired in all directions as they pulled their captives up the hotel steps. Two Egyptian policemen opened fire with their pistols, but had little chance against men carrying modern assault rifles spewing 800 rounds per minute.

'*Harah!*' Adira cursed. 'Khaybar rifles – must be Hezar-Jihadi. Come on!'

She jumped to her feet, grabbed Alex's arm and dragged him with her. They sprinted along the sand, Adira intent on getting them out of the danger zone. Panicked tourists ran in all directions, many falling as machine-gun fire raked their sun-bronzed bodies. The air was filled with the smell of military-grade explosives and the baked-copper scent of burnt blood.

An inflatable boat roared into the shore, beaching itself in front of the remaining terrified civilians. More attackers leaped out, two of them carrying rocket-propelled grenade launchers on their shoulders. They started up the beach towards the hotel – it was a pincer assault; professional, planned and coordinated.

One of the terrorists came upon a man, obviously wounded, lying next to a woman who was sprawled lifeless on a beach towel. The man was shielding a child; Alex could see her small body huddled beneath him, hands clasped over her ears, her face pressed into a towel. The terrorist screamed something and raised his weapon at the man's chest. At such close range, the bullets would easily travel through the man's frame and into the body of the child he was trying to protect.

Alex yelled, and pulled free of Adira's grasp. Close by were the broken remains of a beach umbrella, its two-inch thick shaft sawn off by gunfire. Alex drew the spike from the sand and threw it with all his strength. The rigid pole with its steel tip traveled the fifty feet to its target almost faster than the human eye could follow. It struck the terrorist in the neck, continued through flesh, cartilage and bone, and landed the same distance again down the beach. The terrorist remained upright for a second, daylight visible through the large hole in his neck. Then his arms dropped to his sides, his knees buckled and his lifeless body fell sideways to the sand.

Alex looked from the fallen man to his hand, wonder on his face.

More gunfire brought his attention back to the attackers racing up the beach. The two men with the rocket launchers had already made it to the hotel foyer, but a third man had stopped to look back at his dead comrade. His dark eyes, visible between the layers of cloth wrapped around his face, widened, first in disbelief, then with a volcanic fury.

Alex's fists balled, his own anger building. It surged through him like a wave of energy. Without realizing it, he took a step forward.

'Not here!' Adira screamed into his ear.

Her words penetrated the red mist that was starting to cloud his vision and reason, and he saw her logic. An unarmed man in bathers was no match for professionals carrying modern gas-powered automatic assault rifles.

Alex grabbed Adira and sprinted to the cover of the promenade and the shelter of the side streets, roughly pushing her in front of him, ignoring her protests. They dodged flying projectiles that sped past like deadly metal wasps, but as they leaped from the sand to the concrete walkway Alex felt a thud on his shoulder. He staggered and grunted in pain but kept going until they'd rounded a corner. There, he let go of Adira and pressed his body up against the wall. The yelling from the front of the hotel receded as the remaining terrorists disappeared inside the large marble foyer.

Adira peered back around the corner, then turned to Alex with anger creasing her face. She wrenched his body away from the wall to look at the hole in his shoulder. A blood smear stained the white stonework.

'*Acch*! You're hit.'

The blood flow slowed but didn't stop. Alex could feel the projectile embedded in the meat of his deltoid muscle; he knew it needed to come out or the wound wouldn't close.

A single muffled shot rang out – this time from inside the hotel, higher up. He angled his head to look at the upper balconies.

Adira put her hand on his chest and pushed him back against the wall. 'No, Alex, you must not even think it. We can't afford to get caught up in this – not here, not now. Our documents must be ready by now. We need to leave – get out.'

He shook his head slowly. 'I can't. You know I can't. I need to help those people.' He gently took her wrist and moved her hand away. 'I *think* this is who I am, and I know what I have to do. You go back to the room. I'll be there soon.'

Adira stood close to him, examining his face. He could tell her mind was working furiously, probably thinking of ways to dissuade him from getting involved. She clenched her hands into fists and muttered something in Hebrew through gritted teeth. After another second, she said with a deadly calm, 'I'm coming with you.'

Alex nodded and said, 'Good,' then scanned the street. He picked up a glass soda bottle from the ground and, holding it by the neck, shattered it against the wall. He handed the jagged top part to Adira. 'Get the bullet out.'

Adira didn't flinch. She took the piece of glass, then pushed him around so he faced the wall. 'Lift your arm slightly. That's it. Now hold it.'

She dug the glass into his flesh and twisted, hard. After a few seconds of agony for Alex, the large bullet popped free and clattered to the ground. Alex immediately felt a tickling sensation as the skin around the wound knitted together. *Amazing*, he thought, and rotated his arm.

'Thanks,' he told Adira, and grinned. 'You've got a delicate touch.'

He walked to the edge of the building and peered into the now deserted street. Bodies and debris lay where they had fallen. A few seagulls had returned to pick through the destruction. Alex hoped they were scavenging food from the destroyed stalls, not feeding on their former customers.

'Let's go,' he said without turning.

Staying close to the hotel's façade, Alex and Adira moved quickly towards the magnificent marble foyer. On the way, Adira retrieved the fallen policemen's handguns. She expertly checked the clips, and offered one to Alex. 'Berettas – 9 millimeter. Both clips nearly full. Small, but they'll do.'

Alex shook his head so she kept both for herself.

Alex concentrated on the doorway. The sliding glass doors had been wedged open in the blast. He focused on the darkened opening, blanking out the surrounding sounds of the ocean and occasional shriek from inside the hotel. He sensed a man hidden behind the reception desk – armed and ready, his mind calm and cold. It was probably the terrorist team's lookout and first line of defence.

Alex backed away and breathed into Adira's ear, 'Man behind the desk.'

Adira made a sound in her throat. 'As expected. The rest will be rigging explosives to themselves, their hostages and perhaps their surroundings. You saw their full backpacks? One word from this man and they could detonate everything.' She looked around, then shook her head. 'The Egyptian police will be here soon. Leave it to them. We *must* not be seen.'

Muffled gunfire came from the third floor.

'We can't go in the front without starting a firefight,' Alex said. 'And they're the ones with the big-caliber guns and backup.'

He looked up along the roofline of the three-story building, and then towards its rear. They didn't have much time. Adira was right: the Egyptian police would arrive soon, and they'd cordon off the entire block so no one, other than their negotiators, could go in or out.

He turned to look at Adira. He could see she was angry – as much with him as with the terrorists, he suspected. But she was armed and ready to do as he asked of her.

'We have time,' he said. 'It's still early in their operation, and we have one element in our favor – they won't be expecting someone from above – or not yet anyway. It's our, and the hostages', only chance. You neutralize the lookout while I –'

She shook her head furiously. 'No! Where you go, I go.'

Alex put his hand softly on her shoulder; her skin was still warm from the sun. 'You need to neutralise this guy, then meet me on the third floor. We'll come at them from both angles. I'll signal you when I'm in.'

Adira's eyes burned into him and he could see her jawline was rigid. She looked ready to swear at him, but instead said, 'What signal?'

'You'll know it.' He bent and kissed her lips.

She said something softly in Hebrew, but he didn't understand.

He jogged to the rear of the building, and turned to see her crouch behind an enormous Mercedes-Benz for cover. He knew that she'd only given in temporarily. Signal or not, he guessed she'd walk in the front door, guns blazing, within the next few minutes. Adira Senesh made her own rules.

At the back of the hotel, tables and chairs stood around the sides of an enormous kidney-shaped swimming pool. Scattered towels, sunglasses and spilled drinks attested to the speed with which the holidaymakers had either scattered or been rounded up following the initial assault on the hotel. Alex picked up a large towel, threw it over his shoulder, and spotted a pair of oversized sunglasses. As he was about to grab them, he noticed a man in wet bathers hiding in a hedge of young ornamental olive trees.

'Yours?' Alex asked.

The man nodded jerkily.

'Can I borrow them?'

Another nod.

Alex tucked the sunglasses into the waistband of his swimming trunks, then examined the building's structure. Drainpipes and window ledges gave plenty of handholds, and within a few minutes he stood on a third-floor balcony peering into an expensively furnished room through a fine gauze curtain. Alex opened the balcony door and moved quickly across the empty room to the main door, intending to put his ear to it to get a sense of what was happening beyond it. However, as soon as his fingers touched the wood, a series of images unfolded in his mind, like watching a movie – except here his hyper-senses were the camera. A corridor led to an enormous room at the front of the hotel with a view of the beach. This was where the terrorists had herded their captives. A single armed man patrolled the corridor, checking rooms and windows.

Alex leaned his forehead against the wood of the door and concentrated harder. He could hear faint screams and the thud of bodies falling. The image sharpened and he realized that the attackers were separating the men from the women and children. If they held them in different rooms, his task would be all the more difficult. There was no more time; Alex needed to be inside that room right now.

He lifted the towel to his head, as if drying his hair after a shower, took a deep breath and pulled open the door.

The terrorist on patrol spun towards him, his eyes wide and nervous. Alex could tell he was young, his beard barely a few wisps on his cheeks, perspiration dampening his keffiyeh. Surprise kept him from speaking at first, but then he began to scream at Alex, raising his gun towards him.

Alex dropped the towel, raised his hands and yelled, '*Français! Français!*' packing as much fear as he could into the word. He saw that the young man's gun was shaking. This was the unknown factor in the plan – if the terrorist pulled the trigger, it was all over. But if he decided Alex was no threat …

Alex stooped to make himself smaller and made his raised hands tremble. He kept his eyes wide and fearful. The terrorist moved cautiously towards him, then drove the barrel of his gun into Alex's stomach. Alex doubled over and the youth grabbed him by the hair and pulled his head back. He was grinning now.

'Holiday over for you, *monsieur*,' he hissed in Alex's ear.

He dragged Alex to his feet and shoved him towards the large doors at the end of the corridor. He turned the door handle and kicked him roughly inside.

At first, Alex's arrival was greeted with startled silence, and then the yelling began. The four terrorists in the room pummelled him on the back and shoulders with their guns, kicked his ribs and screamed at him in a language Alex didn't understand. Their anger had a hard and brutal edge, either because Alex had somehow been missed during their search of the hotel, or simply because their taut nerves needed an outlet.

Pain blossomed deep inside Alex's head, not from the blows but from something within him struggling to break free. He suppressed it, and tried to concentrate on gathering information while he could. Down on his hands on knees, he glanced around: the women and children were on one side of the room, sitting cross-legged, hands on heads. The men were on the other side, same position, but their faces showed signs of brutality. A side door was open, and Alex could just make out the pile of bodies inside the room. Perhaps the terrorists had executed a few of their captives as a warning to the others to behave. It had obviously worked, as the thirty or so captives sat mute and unmoving, barely even glancing over to where the terrorists were beating Alex.

One of the men grabbed him by the hair and dragged his head upwards. Alex went with it, upright onto his knees. He needed to see what he was dealing with. He took it all in within a few seconds. The bad news was that every man was armed with an Iranian Khaybar rifle – gas-rotating, automatic and powerful. No aging AK-47s for this group – they must be well financed. Two RPG-27 Tavolga grenade launchers – expensive Russian disposables. One was mounted at the window, the other was leaning against the wall. Worse, all the men were wearing bomb belts with enough C4 to blow off the top of the hotel. Near the wall, a table was piled with spare ammunition clips for the machine guns – this was a siege armory. Details about the weaponry flooded Alex's mind – the firing rate per second, projectile velocity, jamming potential. He didn't pause to wonder how he knew; he just processed the information and was glad for it.

Three things in particular would inform his action plan. One: the ignition switches for the terrorists' bomb belts were wireless handhelds, which were still on the table beside the ammunition, not yet activated and bound to the men's arms. Two: the C4 packets were stamped with the letter 'T', meaning they were a tannerite mix and could be high-velocity detonated. And three: he had arrived in time – none of the hostages had yet been strapped with explosives.

In his peripheral vision, he saw a gloved fist being raised. There was laughter as the punch came down hard on his cheek. He dropped to the floor again. He heard a whimper and looked across the room to see a small girl surreptitiously watching him, her face streaked with tears of terror. She had obviously seen what had happened to other people the attackers didn't like. He tried to smile at her, wanting her to understand that he'd be okay ... that *she* would be okay, but whatever was building inside him was screaming to be released and he couldn't make his mouth do what he wanted.

Someone grabbed the towel draped around his neck, tightened it and used it to pull him upright again. Alex had all the information he needed now, and came to his feet smiling.

The man who was obviously the leader of the small group, furious at Alex's indifference to the brutal treatment, screamed at him so loudly that spittle flecked Alex's cheeks. He drew a handgun from his holster and backhanded Alex across the face with it. Alex shut his eyes as the savage blow caught him on the cheekbone. Its force should have been enough to fell the largest of opponents, or at least to shatter his jaw. But Alex opened his eyes and smiled. It was not a smile of mirth or pleasure. It was cold and hinted at vengeance and a promise of retribution.

The leader's own satisfied smile became a scowl. '*Qui êtes vous?*' he hissed in thickly accented French. 'Who are you?'

Alex responded in English, without thinking, and without knowing where the words came from. 'I am Alex Hunter, the Arcadian.'

The beast inside him tore free from its chains at the same moment as the leader lifted the gun to point it at Alex's face. 'American,' he screamed in a hate-filled voice, and pulled the trigger.

SEVENTEEN

Alex's body seemed to switch to a different physical plane. His heartbeat sped up and waves of natural steroids and adrenalines flooded his system, combining with the synthetic chemicals already embedded in the flesh and bones of his body. People screamed and rushed about, but to Alex it was as if they were moving through an atmosphere as thickly viscous as honey.

He sensed the pressure exerted on the trigger of the gun pressed into his forehead, and was out of the way of the muzzle flash before the bullet had even exited the barrel. He grabbed the gunman's wrist, twisting the gun from his grasp, then flung him towards the large window at the front of the apartment. As the man smashed through the glass and sailed out into the air, Alex emptied the gun of its bullets – into the crowded packets of explosive circling the man's waist. The effect was devastating.

*

Adira could hear sirens in the distance. She couldn't wait any longer; she had to go in now. She drew in a slow breath, and spoke a small prayer to calm herself.

As she was about to leave cover for the foyer, both handguns up and ready, there was a crash from above. She looked up at the hotel's third floor and saw a body falling from the window. Immediately two shots rang out and the figure detonated in midair, obliterated by an orange and red bloom. The head sailed through the air towards the beach.

Guess that's my signal, Adira thought, and pressed herself back around the corner to avoid the debris of the explosion. She wondered if whoever was up on the third floor had been prepared for the shrapnel that blew back through the balcony windows.

She sprinted to the hotel's front doors and didn't pause as she entered the foyer. As she'd hoped, the lookout had ventured out from behind the desk to investigate the explosion. Perhaps it had come earlier than he'd expected ... or he hadn't expected it at all. His head jerked around towards Adira and his eyes widened. She knew her outfit – a bikini and the two handguns – was distracting. By the time he'd pulled his gaze away from her firm breasts and taut belly, the twin muzzles of the small black pistols were pointed at his face.

*

The hostages in the room were already low on the ground and in no danger from the C4 blast wave. Alex dived to the ground himself as the wave began to move outwards, but only two of the three remaining terrorists had the reflexes to do the same. The standing man only had time to throw up an arm before a dark swarm of hot metal hornets had flung him backwards and shredded his frame. His black and white keffiyeh rapidly turned a dark red, and his body left a wet streak on the wall as he slid down it.

Alex looked over at the hostages – most were frozen in shock, but they would be okay for now.

He turned to deal with the remaining terrorists. One had sprinted from the room into the corridor, and Alex heard his footsteps change as he entered the stairwell. The other made a lunge for the upturned weapons table and the bomb detonators strewn on the floor, then lifted his gun to fire indiscriminately into the group of hostages.

Alex screamed in rage as he heard bullets hit the soft flesh of the women and children. He launched himself at the man and drove him into the wall with his shoulder, and felt his ribs break. When he lifted him, he saw that he'd brought his gun around, but not to shoot at Alex. Instead, he was aiming at the belt of explosives circling his waist.

Alex grabbed the man's wrist and twisted it hard; the splintering bone could be heard throughout the room. Alex drew back his fist and delivered a blow to the man's head that shattered his eye socket and depressed his cheekbone. As he drew back for a second punch, he heard a child wailing behind him. He turned briefly to see the little girl who had been so fearful for his own safety now crying in horror at his ferocious behavior. Alex's eyes locked on the girl's face and his fingers loosened to let the man drop.

A voice stopped him. Its words were indistinct, but he recognized it somehow, even though he didn't know where from. His grip on the man tightened again and he frowned. The voice came again, this time clearer and more urgent.

He'll kill them all if you let him go.

As he hesitated, a furious scream sounded in his mind. *Kill him!*

He turned away from the girl and dragged the semiconscious man out through the door. In the hallway, he held his limp body against the wall, set his teeth and drew his fist back. This time, the final blow landed, causing plaster to rain down on the hostages inside the room.

*

Adira heard an amplified calm Egyptian voice floating up from the street outside. The police had arrived and had immediately commenced their negotiations. Meanwhile, their snipers were undoubtedly in position. She avoided the lift in case it had been booby-trapped and headed for the stairs, now armed with only one gun. It still had a full clip. She went lightly up two floors before freezing. Rushed steps came from above, a single heavy body coming down fast. She tucked the Beretta into her swimsuit and waited. If it was an escaped guest, she'd stay out of their way. If not ... She balanced on her toes and waited.

The barrel of his gun came first, then the flapping keffiyeh framing wide panicked eyes. *Hezar-Jihadi.*

Adira flicked out a hand and jerked the barrel of his machine gun upwards, immediately following with a flat-handed strike up under his chin that knocked him backwards. He hit the ground hard and she moved quickly to stand over him, disgust and loathing written all over her face. So many of her people had been shot in the back, blown up or had their throats slit in the night by these creatures. She pulled her gun free, smiled grimly and pointed at her chest. 'Israeli,' she told him in Arabic. She knew he saw the small blue star tattooed on the skin between the thumb and forefinger of her gun hand.

He quickly pulled free his own handgun, but she was far faster. She fired without even blinking. The bullet shattered both the bones in his forearm, causing him to drop his weapon. She stepped over him, indifferent to his agony, and leaned towards his face. 'How many are you?'

He swore at her, calling her a whore, cursing her family, her country and anything else that came to his pain-filled mind.

Her response was another bullet, this one in his left thigh, skilfully avoiding the femoral artery but puncturing the large quadriceps muscle. She asked again and received the same response. She repeated her own response, but in his other thigh.

She put her bare foot on the new wound and pressed down. 'I have plenty more bullets,' she said with a deadly smile. This time she aimed at his groin.

*

Alex heard the shots, and leaped down the flight of steps, his feet hardly touching the floor. He found Adira standing over the corpse of the last terrorist. The man's body was riddled with bullet wounds, including one in the center of his forehead. He knew now that Adira was a soldier, but her brutality surprised him. Perhaps this was the real Adira Senesh.

'Find out anything?' he asked.

She shook her head, and Alex wondered if she'd even tried.

He listened for a moment, blocking out the police negotiators and sirens outside. Except for the struggling of the hostages upstairs, the hotel was silent. For Adira to have got this far, the man in the foyer must already be dead. The terrorist at their feet was the last.

'Time to go,' he said.

Adira nodded, and dropped the Beretta on top of the corpse.

*

The ground floor of the hotel was suddenly boiling with activity as police, forensics and Egyptian SWAT teams examined every inch of the building. The hostages were brought down from the third floor and escorted out of the hotel with towels draped over their heads to protect them from the media's relentless gaze. This suited Adira and Alex perfectly. Towels over their heads, they mixed in with the crowd of battered and scared people stumbling into the glare of the local television news station's halogen lamps.

Adira pulled her towel a little lower over her face; the sunlight coupled with the artificial lighting was almost blinding. She tensed as one of the policemen lifted Alex's towel to look at him briefly. The police were alert to any surviving terrorists attempting to slip out with the freed captives. Alex's face was still bruised and his upper body coated in dried blood, just like many of the male hostages. His gray-green eyes were enough to clear him of suspicion, but Adira cursed inwardly nonetheless. She hoped the momentary exposure of Alex's face hadn't been picked up by any of the cameras focused on them. As soon as the policeman waved them on, she grabbed Alex's arm and pulled him past the medical teams, not letting go until they were back at their safe house.

They'd waited long enough. They'd go directly to the black-market forgers for their documents and be out of Egypt within the next few hours.

*

General Meir Shavit listened in silence as Salamon called in the incident. A terrorist attack at an Egyptian Red Sea hotel, which had been thwarted by one of the hotel's patrons. Impossible. Unless …

'Some of the hostages thought the man was a guest,' Salamon said. 'They heard him speak French. But others believed he was American. And there's something you should see – it should be coming through now.'

Shavit grunted as his computer pinged. The news clip was attached to an email with the subject line: *Observe from minute 00:02:35.* He opened it, skipped forward to the recommended time, then let it play. He paused the film when a police officer lifted the towel from the face of a man accompanied by a brown-skinned, athletic-looking young woman. It was almost impossible to see the man's face without digital enhancing, but Shavit didn't need to.

'They are your targets. Where are you now, Salamon?'

'We're already on our way.'

'Good, good. They will need documentation so talk to the local forgers. Be as insistent as you need to be – I want this resolved quickly.'

'We'll be there within the hour.'

Shavit hung up, and looked at the large map of the Middle East that dominated one wall. His eyes ranged across Egypt's borders – the Mediterranean to the north; Saudi Arabia; Libya; Sudan. The sub-Saharan countries were not safe by any means, but their airlines carried out very little screening of passengers, and their officials were amenable to corruption.

Still too many options, he thought.

He turned back to his computer and played the clip again from the beginning, this time listening intently to the hostages' descriptions of the carnage the lone man had wrought upon the terrorists – 'a madman', 'insanely powerful'. 'He had a monster inside him,' said a small girl with a tear-streaked face.

Shavit rubbed his forehead. 'What have you got yourself into, Addy?' He sat back and closed his weary eyes. *Good luck, Salamon*, he thought.

*

News of the thwarted terrorist attack was beamed into millions of living rooms and workplaces around the world. Most viewed the report with mild indifference. Such attacks were so commonplace that only the most savage held the general public's attention for more than a few moments.

But there were other eyes that watched, eyes that missed nothing as they scanned thousands of images per second, looking for signs, patterns, faces ... anything that might be of interest to their employers. The towel had been lifted from Alex's face for only a second, but it was enough for his features to be digitized, matched and identified.

A notification signature was sent out. The Arcadian had been found.

*

'That sonofabitch. I knew it.'

Captain Robert Graham leaned back from the surveillance loop he was watching in the empty lab office and thought for a minute. He had personally requested that the Arcadian subject be placed on the global watch list – he hadn't known why; it was just a gut feeling. After all, Alex Hunter was dead.

Now he remembered the soldier's amazing physiology and recuperative powers ... and Jack Hammerson's close bond with the man. There was no way the HAWC commander would have incinerated his best soldier without trying everything in his power to save him. Graham could see now that Hammerson had written Hunter off too easily.

He jabbed the intercom button. 'I need someone tracked. I don't care if it's across the Red Sea, Berlin or the moon – just don't let him out of your sight.'

*

Colonel Jack Hammerson stood at his office window looking down at the unarmed combat classes taking place on the field of the USSTRATCOM compound. *Sloppy*, he thought, and shook his head.

Hammerson had run the HAWCs, the elite Special Forces teams, for five years now. Though he'd succeeded in raising the bar every year when it came to the quality and lethality of his new team members, he couldn't help comparing them to the greatest operative he or his other HAWCs had ever seen ... even though that man was now gone.

He watched the class a little longer, and ground his teeth. *Sloppy, damned sloppy.* He'd send this group home. Better to remain a big fish in their former special ops groups than be an anonymous dead HAWC on some shitty battlefield in some remote area somewhere on the planet.

Hammerson was a tough commander – he had to be. His force was the hardest in the world to join, and even harder to stay in. Like him, the men and women he trained came from either the SEALS, Rangers, Green Berets or Alpha Force, and all needed to be the best at what they did before they were even considered as a candidate for the HAWCs. They also had to have a specialization that Hammerson deemed useful. After the initial assessment and training, only about half were offered a permanent place. Hammerson's people didn't just have to be good; they had to be outstanding. Their missions were always deadly and often classified as *high terminal probability* – suicidal to most other groups. The HAWCs excelled at missions that others had failed at, or couldn't even contemplate attempting.

Hammerson's computer pinged softly behind him, immediately followed by a buzzing from his back pocket and then again from his breast pocket – the alert was obviously of high importance. He turned to see his whole screen flaring red with a single code word: *Lazarus*. His mind didn't comprehend its meaning for a few seconds, even though he had programmed the coded alert himself. Then shock traveled through his entire system.

Freakingodamnhell ...

Hammerson pulled the phone from its cradle. 'Get me Sam Reid, Priority-1.'

He wouldn't have to wait long. Priority-1 was reserved for the most critical of events: Commander in Chief on deck; base infiltration; or, at its worst, the breakout of war. With a P-1, Hammerson's assistant had the authority to break in on any communications system anytime anywhere in the world to find the personnel he needed. First Lieutenant Sam Reid was on leave, but that didn't matter.

After a few seconds, Sam Reid's laidback voice came on the line. 'Reid. Go ahead, boss.'

'Report in,' ordered Hammerson, not bothering with courtesies. 'I have a proximity alert for the Arcadian.'

There was the sound of glass breaking at Sam Reid's end of the line.

EIGHTEEN

Matt swiveled in the driver's seat so he could see both Sarah and Charles. 'Okay,' he said, 'we tell them that we're working for Chief Logan, and that it's absolutely vital we psychologically assess the Jordan woman.'

Charles didn't look convinced. 'What happens if they want to check us out and they call Logan direct?'

'C'mon, with my honest face? Trust me, it won't happen.' Matt reached into the back seat to punch his friend in the arm. 'Stop worrying, buddy, just leave it to me.'

Charles batted Matt's hand away. 'Sarah, what do you think?'

Sarah shrugged. 'Might work. Besides, I can't wait to see the magnificent Matthew Kearns in action.' She did her best hillbilly impression. 'After all, we small-town folk get the wool pulled over our eyes on a daily basis by you big city folk.' She winked at Charles and motioned with her head towards Matt. 'Prince Charming here shouldn't have any trouble at all.'

Matt climbed out of the car and took several deep breaths. 'Let me do the talking.'

The hospital's enormous front desk looked to him like the Great Wall of China – imposing and intimidating. Behind it sat several woman, talking to visitors or patients, taking calls or doing paperwork. They looked very professional and very busy. One woman glanced up and caught Matt's eye. She was a small mountain of flesh with a face hard enough to drill teeth. She wasn't smiling, and probably hadn't for decades. Matt looked around for someone else to talk to, anyone but this woman. She saw straight through him, he could tell.

He stopped and half-turned to Sarah and Charles behind him. 'We're dead.'

Sarah pushed past him. 'Hi Martha, how're the boys?'

To Matt's amazement, Martha the ogress immediately transformed into Martha the friendly mommy.

'Sarah Sommer, I didn't see you there. The boys are both fine. Josh is thinking of staying on at school, maybe even going to college; and Luis is still happy fixing cars. But what are you doing here? Nothing wrong, I hope?'

Sarah smiled and leaned on the desktop. 'I'm fine, just come to visit a friend – Amanda Jordan. Can I see her today?'

Martha typed something on her keyboard, then pulled a face and looked back up at Sarah. 'Well, I suppose you can visit, but I doubt you'll be chatting much as the poor thing's still unresponsive. No sign of her husband yet either ... such a shame.' She leaned forward slightly and lowered her voice. 'Run off after a fight is what I heard.' She nodded sagely, then looked past Sarah to Charles and Matt. 'Are y'all together?'

'Sorry, Martha, yes,' Sarah said. 'These are friends of mine from the city university – meet Charlie Schroder and Matt Kearns. Matt here is actually a UNC Asheville alumnus.'

'Really?' Martha reached out a large hand. She held onto Matt's a bit longer than he'd expected and looked deep into his face, the ogress returning for a second. Matt smiled at her, but it felt like a chimpanzee grin, showing every tooth in his head.

'Room two-oh-five,' Martha told Sarah, 'left out of the lifts. Just pick up any hallway phone and ask for me if you have any trouble, dear.'

'I will, and I'll keep a lookout for Josh if he makes it onto campus,' Sarah called back as she headed for the lifts, Matt and Charles following like docile children.

In the lift, both men relaxed. Sarah gave them a look that was a mixture of satisfaction and amusement. Charles folded his arms and gave Matt a mock stare of deep scepticism.

Matt laughed and leaned back against the elevator wall. 'C'mon, Charlie Brown, did you see the size of that woman? She was terrifying.'

The lift doors slid back, and they walked quickly down the pristine white corridor, stopping at a door with a small glass and mesh window. Sarah briefly peered inside. 'Okay, come on,' she said, and pushed the door open.

Amanda Jordan lay on a cot with two pillows behind her head. Feeding tubes trailed from her arm, and a bag of yellow fluid lay under her bed. She was tiny and bird-like, her face drawn, her blue eyes staring glassily at the ceiling.

Sarah picked up the chart clipped to the railing at the base of the bed and picked out details. 'Age twenty-six, physically and psychologically catatonic, mild muscle rigidity, no facial twitching, no involuntary or dyskinetic movement.' She ran her finger down the page. 'Dry-eye treatment, apply saline drops every twenty minutes, fluid induction ... Basically, guys, the poor girl is a zombie. Why are we here again?'

Matt walked quickly to the door and opened it, looked up and down the corridor. He let it swing shut, then nodded to Charles. Charles stepped closer to the bed and pulled something from his pocket.

'One of the strange things about human beings is that scent perception is directly linked to the part of our brain associated with memory and feelings. It's been proven that smells can trigger memories almost instantaneously.' He looked at Sarah. 'Like when you smell chlorine and immediately remember summer days spent at the swimming pool, or baking bread reminds you of your grandmother's house? Well, those links remain embedded within your brain's limbic system, ready and waiting to call up a memory or a mood.'

Charles opened his hand to reveal the small sample bottle with the ragged piece of hairy flesh inside. He uncapped the bottle and waved it under the young woman's nose. Nothing.

He moved the bottle closer, almost covering one of her nostrils. The effect was both startling and terrifying. Amanda Jordan sat up, her eyes bulging. Her mouth opened wider than seemed humanly possible and she screamed – a wail of sheer terror that bounced around the walls of the small room.

Sarah put her hands over her ears and gritted her teeth. Matt clamped a hand over Amanda's mouth and shouted to Charles, '*Put it away.*'

He grabbed her shoulders and tried to push her down onto the bed, but it was as if her body was electrified. The intravenous needle in her arm began to lift, threatening to tear through her skin. Matt threw his body across hers, trying to use his weight to force her back. Charles, who had recapped the bottle, lunged at her flailing legs. But once the odor was gone, it was if a fire alarm had just been switched off – calm returned and Amanda Jordan sank back into her zombified state.

Matt and Charles stood up slowly, both breathing like they'd just completed a marathon. Charles started to laugh nervously. Matt put his hands on his hips, still gasping, his face clouded.

'Are you insane?' Sarah said furiously. Her face was bright red and her hands were shaking. 'That poor woman looked like she was going to have a heart attack. And if you two idiots expected that stunt was going to bring her out of the catatonia, you failed miserably.'

Charles held out his hands, palms up. 'But don't you see – we couldn't have got a more positive response to the sample. We can conclusively say that whatever happened to Amanda Jordan on that mountain, it involved the creature this piece of flesh came from.'

Sarah wasn't mollified. Charles took her hand. 'Look, I'm sorry if that was a little more … extreme than we expected. But she's the only person who's seen this thing and is still alive. We just needed to make sure.'

'But why?'

Matt looked down at Amanda. Her terror mirrored his own. He knew he'd been letting his fear rule his life. He's been running from it, but now here was an opportunity to face it. He couldn't let the horror continue. It had to stop. He drew in a shaky breath.

'Because,' Matt said slowly. 'We need to … I …'

Sarah withdrew her hand from Charles's. 'The Dome?'

Charles nodded. 'Yeah, the Dome. We need to go up there.'

*

Markenson exploded with laughter. 'A fucking big gorilla?' He clapped his hands together and leaned forward, almost directly into Matt Kearns's face. 'That's what you eggheads think is responsible for the missing people?' He frowned with clownish puzzlement. 'Where's the ship?'

Kearns looked confused. 'What ship?'

'The space-fucking-ship, Daffy. Maybe it's really an a-lee-yan from outta space.'

Logan banged a large hand on his desk. 'That's enough, Markenson.'

'But, Chief, this is a serious investigation,' Markenson said. 'And these *experts* of yours spend days working on it only to tell us we got some sort of big monkey loose in the mountains. I coulda got that advice from one of the drunks down at the Thirsty Bar any Friday night.' He leaned over Logan's desk. 'For the record, I checked with Kringle Brothers a week ago, and guess what? No missing ape. Besides, we were just up there in the mountains ourselves, and we sure didn't see no fucking big monkey.'

Kearns looked at his two colleagues and motioned with his head towards Markenson. 'Any guesses why at his age he's still only a junior officer?'

'You smartass prick!' Markenson leaped at Kearns.

Schroder stepped between them and copped a finger in the eye.

Logan got to his feet, felt his chair tip backwards. 'That's enough!' he roared. 'Markenson, you ever go to assault a citizen in front of me again and you'll be pulling graveyard shifts until you're fifty. Understand? Go and find something to do, now!'

Markenson glared at his commanding officer, then pushed open the door. Logan could hear him swearing as he threaded his way through the desks in the outer office.

'I'm assuming he's not allowed to assault me when he's *not* in front of you either, right?' Kearns said.

Logan rested his hands on his desk and hung his head for a moment, exhaling wearily. He looked up at the three scientists. 'You know who runs this office?'

Schroder jumped in. 'We're sorry, Chief; you do.'

'No, son, not even close. The mayor does.' Logan picked up the notes on the DNA matching that Sarah Sommer had handed him. 'I got a lot of technical information here I can't understand, and a tooth that even I can see is older than Moses. I take this to the mayor to get the money for a full-scale search and by next year I'll be working security out at the mall.' Logan righted his chair and flopped into it. 'A Gigantosaurus! Jesus Christ, couldn't you have at least said it was another lion; or a psycho running around in an ape suit? A psycho we can understand, but a giant ape thing?'

'That's Giganto*pithecus* Chief,' Schroder said, 'and the evidence is almost irrefutable.'

'Aw, c'mon,' Logan said, flicking the papers, 'this is bullshit. Anyone else had brought me this theory and I'd be kicking their ass six ways to Sunday.' He looked at Sarah. 'You go along with this? You've seen this *irrefutable* proof?'

Schroder reached into his pocket. 'Actually, Chief, we were just in at –'

Sarah cut him off with a glare before turning back to Logan. 'No, Bill, I haven't seen *all* the proof yet, but I trust the biology.'

Logan sat back and exhaled. 'I'm sorry, Sarah, gentlemen, but it's not enough. No one but Kearns and Schroder have seen the foot-print, my own ME says the forensics are inconclusive, and all you've given me is a stack of pages with about a million numbers on them that add up to what you yourself say is fragmented and requires "computer-assisted gene speculation". I need more proof. I need ... I dunno, a witness or something.'

'Chief, there are no real witnesses because they're either dead or missing or catatonic,' Kearns said, sounding exasperated. 'Look, if we're right, you'll wish it *was* a lion loose out there. The print we saw out at the Wilson farm puts this thing at around ten feet tall and about twelve hundred pounds. It's big and aggressive and –'

Logan cut in, 'And freakin' extinct, according to you. So what's it doing here now? Where's it been for the last ... what? Million years? Shit, son, where do you hide if you're ten feet tall?'

Kearns put a hand to his temple, as if he was in pain. 'I don't know, Chief, but the answers are probably up on that mountain. I bet this thing has been here before, or something like it – we know the Indians dealt with something similar thousands of years ago. They left us that message written into the stones – you saw it in Amanda Jordan's photographs.'

Logan shook his head. 'Professor Kearns, it's getting colder than a witch's tit up there. If there *is* something wandering around on the Dome, the cold is gonna kill it. It'll drop to twenty below come winter.'

Kearns sorted through the papers on Logan's desk and pulled out a map with small circles drawn on it. 'I doubt the cold's going to kill it. Look at this.' He pointed to the spot where Amanda Jordan was found, where the cows had gone missing, where the Wilson girl and then Kathleen Hunter had disappeared, then grabbed a pen and drew a connecting line between all of them. 'Three things leap out at me here, Chief. One, the creature's making its way down the mountain towards the town. Two, the attacks or abductions are occurring with greater frequency. And three ...' He put his finger on the last circle. 'It's almost here.'

Logan held Kearns's eyes for a moment before looking down at the zigzag line that ran from Black Mountain down onto the plains and up to the outskirts of his town. It scared the shit out of him.

For the first time in his life, he had no idea what he should do next.

*

Logan could hear Ollie Markenson, who trailed behind him, still grumbling at being chosen as accompanying officer at this time of day – or night, depending on your perspective. *Share the pain*, he thought. Being woken at four in the morning wasn't anyone's idea of a good time, and usually meant urgent news, bad news, or both.

Martha Oatson came around the reception desk, her face full of concern. 'She's awake, Chief, and semi-lucid. Still in shock, and needs a lot of rest, but you did say to call immediately if there was any change.'

Logan nodded, but didn't slow. 'You did the right thing, Martha. She's the only witness we've got.' He looked back over his shoulder as he headed for the elevators. 'She okay to talk? We got a lot of questions for her.'

Martha clasped her chubby fingers together as she hurried to keep up with him. 'Yes, but keep it simple, she's suffering from severe distress. I don't think she knows what happened to her husband. She's asking for him. Also, I'm supposed to contact her next of kin to tell them she's awake but I can't get onto anyone.'

'Leave that to us, Martha,' Logan said, standing close to the elevator door to stop the nurse entering with them. 'She probably knows more than she thinks.'

When the doors slid closed, Logan turned to Markenson. 'Get onto the Jordan brothers, Markenson, and inform –'

'Ahh ...' Markenson cut in, pulling a pained face. 'I was meaning to tell you, Chief. The Jordan brothers were in town just a few days back.'

Logan frowned. 'What, all of them. Big Will too? Are they still here?'

Markenson shrugged. 'Maybe ... I mean, yeah. They were all kitted out ... heading up Black Mountain's hiking track, I reckon.'

'Jesus Christ, Ollie, and you let them go up there? How long ago?'

Frustration flashed in Markenson's face. 'I dunno ... three days maybe. Look, Chief, you know the Jordan brothers – they're around two-thirty pounds each. You want to stop those guys doing something, you need a freakin' riot gun and twenty square feet of cargo netting.'

Logan exhaled with exasperation. 'Shit. We'll worry about them later. Let's see what Mrs. Jordan recollects first.'

Logan was shocked by the change in Amanda Jordan. The woman looked like a small, stringy bird; the skin of her face was chalky, her hair lank and greasy. Her eyes, red-rimmed, stared down at her hands, which lay palms up on the bed. The room smelled of antiseptic and an animal, ammonia odor that suggested fear and distress.

Amanda Jordan looked up when she became aware of the two officers. 'Have you found him?'

Logan pulled a plastic chair to the bed so he could talk to her eye to eye. *Take it slow, keep it non-threatening*, he told himself. He didn't want to increase her stress levels. On the other side of the bed, Markenson stood with his arms folded, looming over the tiny woman. Obviously, he wasn't reading from the same rule sheet as his boss.

'We're still looking for your husband, Mrs. Jordan,' Logan said, 'but we need your help. Anything you remember – about the place, what happened, anything at all, even if you think it's silly or insignificant, we'd like to hear about it.'

Her mouth turned down, like a carnival clown's. 'He's still up there then ... with *it*.'

'It?' Markenson had dropped his folded arms.

'He saved me. He let it get him instead.' She began to sob loudly.

Markenson leaned forward. 'Was it a lion?'

She shook her head and squeezed her eyes shut.

Logan took one of her pale hands in his large paw. 'Tell us what you saw, Amanda. What's the *it* you're talking about?'

She opened her red-rimmed eyes and he saw the horror in her stare. 'The monster.'

*

In the elevator, Logan looked at his watch: nearly 5 am. It would still be dark for a while yet. He contemplated going home and trying to get another hour's sleep. But knew that he'd never switch off enough to *really* rest.

The monster got him – oh good Christ. This was turning out to be a nightmare, and he was right at the center of it.

Logan's mind turned over. He needed to get a team up there, but still didn't have anything sane enough to take to the mayor. Perhaps he should listen one more time to those crazy theories Sarah Sommer, Kearns and Schroder had put forward. Then there was the problem of the Jordan brothers out on the peak – he felt a deep fatigue at the thought of trekking up the Dome to find them. Besides, Markenson was right: each of those boys was big enough and bad enough to hold a bull out to piss. They were probably armed to the teeth too. If anyone was going to be all right up there, it was them. *Still, should probably close the hiking track for a while*, he thought, satisfied there was one activity he could implement right away.

As the elevator doors slid open in the hospital foyer, he saw Martha standing there waiting for him. She handed him a sign-out sheet. 'So, next of kin? Be kinda nice for that girl to have some company right now, Chief.'

'Yeah, Markenson's on it,' Logan replied. He started for the door, his mind already onto another problem.

'Maybe Sarah Sommer could come back and visit with her in the meantime,' Martha said.

Logan froze, then turned. 'Come *back*?'

'Yes, Chief – she and a coupla friends from the city came to see Mrs. Jordan earlier.'

Logan groaned. He'd bet good money on what those three amigos were planning to do, or maybe already *doing*. Jesus Christ in heaven, it'd be like Grand Central Station up on that mountain in another day or two.

'Leave them to me, Martha. Maybe you could ask Mrs. Jordan herself if there's anyone she'd like to see – other than her husband.'

He headed to the door fast. Markenson had to break into a jog to keep pace. 'What now, Chief?'

'Well, I'm gonna grab a coffee, have a think, and wait for the sun to come up. You, on the other hand, are gonna break out some cold-terrain equipment for, say, half a dozen officers. Looks like we might have another lion to hunt.'

NINETEEN

Benito Juárez Airport, Mexico

Alex and Adira kept pace with the other disembarking passengers as they headed through the hot and crowded arrivals hall towards the immigration desk. They'd had an exhausting journey via Sudan, Ethiopia, then down the coast of Africa to Johannesburg, South Africa, from where they'd flown to Mexico. Adira's plan was to get through immigration here at the main airport, then take an internal flight to Nuevo Laredo, which was separated from the American city of Laredo by a stretch of just 100 feet of the Rio Bravo. Then it would be a matter of driving to the small speck on the map that represented the town of Asheville – the name Alex had kept repeating to her.

Since the introduction of the biometric eye scanners, it had become difficult to infiltrate the US via any of its own ports, which was why she'd chosen Mexico as their entry point. New software made it possible to identify unique corneal reflections, which meant even prosthetics could be detected. Adira guessed both her and Alex's eye prints would be flagged as soon as they looked into the tiny camera lens. But Benito Juárez was one of the busiest airports in the world, with nearly 30 million passengers annually, so getting lost in the crowd should be relatively easy.

Adira linked arms with Alex as they joined the line for the immigration desk. Outwardly, they looked like a holidaying couple, intent on fun and relaxation. But inside she felt the rising tension. This was a huge risk; Adira knew how intensive the American surveillance was. Coming in via Mexico might buy them some time, but she didn't doubt for a moment that if the US Intelligence Services wanted to look into a window anywhere in the world, they could. She also knew that other eyes would be searching for them. By now, her uncle would have discovered she had disappeared with Alex. *Sorry*, she whispered silently.

'*Pasaportes*,' demanded the woman at the desk, her eyes flicking from Adira to Alex.

Her gaze was unemotional and slightly bored, but Adira knew she'd miss very little. Like most immigration officials, she'd have been trained to assess facial features, eye color and purported ethnicity before checking what her eyes told her against the information in their passports.

Those passports were gold-embossed with the South African coat of arms, and the stamps from numerous countries dating back several years showed a young married couple who liked to travel. The passports had all the necessary watermarks, chips and sophisticated dyes required to pass the forensic testing that may be done by immigration in any country. They were authentic, just not really theirs.

The woman looked at Alex's personal details, then said in heavily accented Afrikaans, '*Waarom kom jy aan Mexiko?*' She watched him closely as he replied.

'*Om jou land te geniet*,' Alex said, smiling broadly at her. He turned to Adira to include her in the conversation. '*Sy kan Afrikaan praat*.'

'*Uitstekend!*' Adira said, stepping forward and beaming at the woman. '*Dit sal 'n wonderlike vakansie liefling*.'

The official's gaze remained flat and bored. 'English?'

'Yes, a little,' Alex said, sounding disappointed that the conversation in Afrikaans was over.

The woman grunted and stamped both little green books. 'Enjoy your holiday, Mr. and Mrs. Jashub. Next.' She waved them out of the way, already focused on the next person in line.

Adira linked her arm through Alex's again and smiled up at him, her eyebrows arched. 'You see, *Benjamin*, a little practice did come in handy, yes?'

Alex smiled back at her. 'Clever girl. You'll make a good spy one day.'

In another hour, they were on their way.

*

Salamon and his three agents watched the young couple walk from the international terminal towards the smaller domestic terminal. He had guessed correctly; he would have made the same choice for a covert entry into America. The convoluted path Captain Senesh and the American had taken had given Salamon and his team plenty of time to arrive to intercept them.

In the back seat of their vehicle, one of his men held what looked like a folded towel at his shoulder. A black tube poked out from it, pointing at the couple. They could take both down in an instant.

'They're about to go undercover,' the man with the gun said. 'We'll lose them.'

Salamon spoke without turning. 'Hold.'

For now, General Shavit had ordered they just be observed; Captain Senesh's intentions were still unclear.

The man in the back seat shifted slightly, his face creasing in concentration. A thin cord ran from the black tube to a small plug in his ear. He pulled the plug free and leaned forward to speak to Salamon. 'Nuevo Laredo.'

'We'll need to move it to catch them if they're flying,' the driver said.

Salamon shook his head. 'No, they're going to cross there. We'll meet them on the other side.'

*

Jack Hammerson and Sam Reid sat in the dark watching the recessed screen that covered half the back wall of Hammerson's office. It was split into several frames, all showing two figures walking quickly towards Benito Juárez's domestic terminal. Both men wore headset comms linked directly to Major Gerry Harris, who was located in an electronics surveillance factory beneath the Offutt Airforce Base in Nebraska. Harris manned the constellation of orbiting birds that fed a lot of the high-altitude intelligence over the United States mainland and also much of the globe.

'Screw down another fifty,' Hammerson said, squinting at the images.

The result made him smile. The man's baseball cap was pulled down, obscuring most of his face from the steep vertical angle, but Jack Hammerson knew that man, knew his walk, his mannerisms, as if he were his own flesh and blood. *Welcome back, son*, he thought.

The woman with him turned her face for just a second and VELA grabbed it. A blurred image appeared in one of the smaller screens to the side; dot points manifested on the facial matrix, joined together, were mapped and enhanced – and a name appeared underneath the photograph in flashing red: *Captain Adira Senesh*. Next to it: *Priority Alert*.

'Trouble,' Sam grunted. He toggled a small stick on his armrest and an electric whine filled the darkened room as his wheelchair moved closer to the screen.

The last mission he and Alex Hunter had worked on together, Sam had suffered a massive trauma to his spine. The creature they had been fighting had broken Sam's back as easily as snapping a twig, severing his spinal cord and shattering his L1 and L2 spinal plates. Sam would never walk again. Or not unless there were significant advancements in stem cell technology, Hammerson thought ... or they managed to convince Alex Hunter to return. The Arcadian's amazing regenerative abilities held so many secrets, so many possible answers.

Hammerson exhaled long and slow. *First things first. We gotta see if we can make contact with him before we start trying to explain to the top brass how a dead soldier's suddenly come back to life.* There would be way too many complications trying to get that one past Graham in Medical.

Sam studied the woman's face up close for a few seconds, then rolled back to Hammerson's side. 'Like a bad penny, huh?'

Hammerson nodded. 'Big time. And if Alex hasn't contacted us, we have to assume he doesn't know us, or doesn't want to. Worst case: she's turned him. Either way, approaching them will be difficult.'

He rose from the chair, pushed the mic wire down from his mouth and went over to his desk. Staying standing, he pulled a keypad forward to start typing, then pressed his palm to the screen. A red line circled his hand, reading the peaks and valleys of his palm and fingerprints. He was accessing MUSE, the Military Universal Search

Engine. The sophisticated USSTRATCOM intelligence system would allow him to enter nearly any website on the planet. There were only a few installations with the technical and intellectual firepower to resists MUSE's invisible intrusions – and one by one they were slowly being broken down.

Hammerson copied a photo of Adira Senesh, then accessed the Mexican immigration arrivals files. Within a few minutes he'd found what he was looking for: *Rebekah and Benjamin Jashub, entering from South Africa on a holiday visa.*

'Sam, take a look.' Hammerson swiveled the screen.

Sam snorted. 'Looks pretty good for someone who was in a steel coffin last time we saw him.' He leaned closer to the passenger information and laughed. 'You gotta be kidding me.'

'What is it?' Hammerson frowned and looked back at the screen.

'Looks like he hasn't lost his sense of humor. *Jashub* comes from the old Hebrew name *Yashuwb*, meaning *he will return*. Expecting us to be watching, maybe?'

'Or perhaps a little warning from Senesh.' Hammerson tapped his chin with one knuckle as he thought. 'Can't afford to go near them; and we certainly can't let the local authorities in on the surveillance. We need to see where they're going, then move to ...' He paused. He wasn't sure yet what he wanted to do with Alex Hunter, or even what he *could* do given Alex's capabilities and unpredictability. 'Move to ... talk to him, I guess,' he finished.

Sam nodded slowly, obviously guessing his HAWC leader's dilemma. 'I'm ready to go whenever you say, boss. He trusts me ... or used to.'

Hammerson nodded. He'd known that, crippled or not, Sam Reid would want the chance to try to bring Alex Hunter back in. Sam knew Alex better than anyone, and had been the closest thing Alex had to a friend. But Hammerson also knew that if Captain Adira Senesh was in any way controlling the Arcadian, Sam Reid would be committing suicide by going after them. And that was if he was fully fit. Stuck in a wheelchair, well ...

'For now, we just watch,' he said, and pushed the mic wire up to his mouth again. 'Captain Harris, I want 24/7 surveillance. Capture every nanosecond of CCTV feed, traffic-control footage and satellite stream we can get ... and patch it through to me, *and only me*. Understood?'

'You got it, Colonel. Recordings?'

'Negative; I'll do that from here – you just follow him. And remember, these guys are the best. They know we're probably watching so they'll be smart.'

'Yes, sir,' Harris responded. 'We'll be smarter. No one can hide from VELA.'

Hammerson was about to sign off when he heard Harris give a grunt of annoyance. 'Got a problem, Colonel – there's a dual-feed loop. I think someone else is watching.'

'Ah shit! Can you find out who?'

'No problem.' There was silence for a moment, then, 'Yep, got it. Feed is being routed to Medical Division.'

Hammerson exhaled a low growl. *Graham probably*, he thought. He leaned forward to rest his knuckles on the edge of his desk. 'Okay, Gerry – just make sure you cover *your* tracks ... and don't lose our man.' He removed his headset and said softly to the screen, 'The game's afoot. Your move, Arcadian.'

*

'They're different,' Lieutenant Marshal told his superior officer.

Captain Robert Graham snorted as he straightened his tie in the mirror. 'Of course they're different, Marshal. We wanted them to be different – we built them that way, remember?'

Marshal stepped a little closer. 'No, I mean that the latest test subjects' personalities have altered. Their strength, reaction times and resistance to pain have increased five fold, but they haven't benefited from the same boost to their cognitive and strategic thinking as the original Arcadian did. In fact, there's something missing ... they're kind of mechanical somehow, like they're just ... I dunno ... like they're just *acting* human.' His voice went down in volume. 'It seems like there's no soul in them anymore.'

Graham managed to snort and sneer at the same time. 'So, we've created a soldier with increased physical capabilities and no conscience – and that's bad because ...? Personally, I think they're magnificent. And so will General Moneybags.' He motioned to the door with his head. 'Speaking of which, time to invite the general in.'

General Wozyniak had three stars and a hell of a lot of pull in the US armed forces. It was he who had wanted the original subject, Alex Hunter, reproduced and had given Graham and Marshal the job of delivering. Money was no object, but time was. Finally, Graham thought, they had something to show him.

Captain Graham saluted, then offered his hand. The general ignored the hand and made a half-salute motion towards his head. 'Show me what you've got, Captain.'

During the next thirty minutes, Graham had their three latest subjects perform individual tasks that showed their strength, speed and resistance to pain and trauma. General Wozyniak nodded at key moments, and at one point Graham was sure he saw a brief smile flick across the man's permanently compressed lips.

The final task was a simple hand-to-hand combat manoeuver that pitted three regular soldiers against one of the ARC-044 batch subjects. The three opponents were large, highly trained and fit. Formidable by themselves, as a trio they should easily overcome a single combatant.

Graham turned to the general. 'Our three attackers have been told they simply need to hold the ARC-044 subject on the floor for five seconds, by any means. They can use full contact, no restrictions, no pulling of punches.'

The general just grunted.

Graham pressed a comm stud on the desk in front of the large window. 'Commence.'

The three men circled the barefoot, unarmed subject. The first attacker came in low from the side, scissoring his legs, expecting to side-sweep the subject off his feet. The subject leapt out of the way of the sweeping leg, then came down hard just as the leg was passing underneath him. Both heels targeted the large bone of the femur; the sickening snap caused the scientists behind the thick glass to grimace.

The remaining two men ignored their fallen comrade, instead taking advantage of his demise to attack at once. One came in fast head-on, the other came from the rear. To the men watching, it was almost as though the ARC-044 subject was waiting for the attack, welcomed it.

The volunteer at the ARC-044 subject's rear wrapped one brawny arm around his throat and the other up beside his head and applied pressure. His teeth were gritted as he strained and seemed to be attempting to separate the small bones in the neck, or shut off the air. It was if the ARC-044 didn't even notice. He continued to face the attacker who came in from the front, who hit out with his large fists in a series of strikes that, had they landed, would have broken jaws or shattered eye sockets. He was quick and his punches were delivered with a professional rolling of the arm and shoulder that told of unarmed combat training. But none of his blows hit their target. All were parried, swiped away or merely swung across empty air where the ARC-044 subject had moved out of the way with an ease that bordered on tormenting.

Finally, Graham's enhanced warrior caught both his combatant's fists, held his attacker for a second and looked into his eyes, before drawing him in close. He shifted his grip to the man's head and twisted violently while still staring into his face. A snapping sound came over the microphone and the soldier's body fell to the floor like an empty sack.

Graham noticed Marshal look sharply at him, but he ignored his subordinate. Wozyniak could have been watching a chess game, but his eyes were unwavering and the hint of a smile had appeared again.

Marshal turned away from the window, but Graham felt his own excitement building as the ARC-044 subject pulled the final man over his shoulder and threw him heavily to the ground. He held him there and pummelled his face, over and over. When the crunches became wetter and softer, Graham switched the window to frost.

'Was he supposed to kill them?' the general asked. His tone was indifferent but his eyes were interested.

Graham shrugged. 'He was supposed to defend himself. He was told his attackers would be ordered to try to kill him so he obviously reacted with what he believed was commensurate force. All the men were Special Ops volunteers and aware of the risks.'

The General nodded. 'Okay. What now?'

Graham smiled. 'Access to the armory, and then test out in the field. I've got something in mind – if you would just sign off on the order.'

TWENTY

Alex and Adira had been in Laredo Nuevo for just two hours and had made their way to the outskirts of the city. Alex searched the darkness, listening for the sound of rushing water.

'This way,' he said.

They had waited for nightfall in a near empty diner, chewing indifferently on stale sandwiches and sipping bitter coffee. Their only other purchase in town had been a pack of black garbage bags. The luggage they'd brought on the flight was padded to avoid suspicion as they came through customs. They had extracted what they needed and left the rest in an alley. By now, it had no doubt been picked over by a dozen different people and its contents dispersed across the border city. Amongst the clothing, cameras and travel booklets in Adira's bag had been a leather roll containing sculptor's tools. Camouflaged among the small chisels, files and spatulas were two slim iron spikes; only another assassin would have recognized them as perfectly balanced throwing knives. These, and cash and credit cards with an unlimited spend, were all they needed. Everything else they required they would buy or steal. There would be no trail.

Alex moved quickly through the darkness to the bank of the Rio Grande. He raised his head and inhaled the desert air, closed his eyes and allowed the rushing images to flood his senses. The link that had exploded into his mind only a few days ago, pulling him towards the small town in North Carolina, was growing weaker. If it was his mother, something was bleeding her of her vitality.

He turned to Adira. 'We need to hurry.' He tore open the pack of garbage bags and began to remove his clothing. 'About a hundred yards,' he said, nodding towards the opposite bank. 'Pretty good current, so I expect we'll come out maybe half a mile further down.'

Adira nodded as she too stripped down. 'Three-fifty miles to Houston – that's five hours' driving at seventy miles per hour; then another eight-fifty or so to Asheville – probably another twelve hours. Maybe on the way you'll tell me a little more about what you are planning?'

Alex looked at her. 'My mother's there. She's in trouble and she needs me ... and I need her. She might be the only person who can tell me truthfully who I am.'

'I can –' Adira began, but stopped when he glared at her. He guessed she could tell his opinion of her truthfulness. After a moment his anger cooled and he gave her a half-smile. 'It's okay. And by the way, in America, seventy miles per hour is the speed your grandmother would drive.'

She laughed nervously and slipped off her underwear. As she stood up straight, she noticed Alex watching her and a small smile curled the corner of her mouth.

'Let's go then,' she said.

*

'Contact.'

Salamon swore softly – he'd bet wrong and was now miles away from the action. There were several spots between Nuevo Laredo and Laredo where a strong swimmer could cross the Rio Grande, but only two that he would choose if he were Senesh. Unfortunately, they were miles apart. He had separated his team accordingly, taking the southern crossing himself – being the highest-skilled operative and, in his opinion, three times as good as his colleagues – and sending his three men to the northern one.

'I'm on my way. Do not engage unless absolutely unavoidable. Understood?'

'Understood.'

Salamon had simplified the objectives for his team. General Shavit wanted his niece alive, but had not been as concerned about the fate of the American. For Salamon, that was as good as a death sentence.

He jogged back to his car. He hoped the Laredo police uniforms his men had stolen would be enough of a distraction to hold Hunter and Senesh until he got there.

Alex and Adira pulled themselves from the water and carried their knotted plastic bags some distance away from the bank, where they both dressed quickly. There was no moon, but the stars gave Alex more than enough illumination to see by. He paused for a few seconds and raised his head, sensing they were being watched. He turned slowly, looking into the brush and beyond, straining to hear the slightest sound – a breath, a wheeze.

Adira noticed his searching and froze. 'What is it?'

He stayed where he was, his head tilted for a few more seconds, until the distant call pulled at him again, urging him on. 'Maybe nothing; let's move.'

He pulled the dark sweater over his head and slipped on the leather jacket. He couldn't waste any more time trying to analyze his suspicions. They needed transport ... and weapons. He had no idea what they would be walking into, but he knew he didn't want to go unarmed.

They made their way through the brush beside the road for ten minutes, not yet trusting the open gravel surface. There may be border patrols nearby, and there was no good reason for anyone other than police, drug runners or illegal immigrants to be wandering around in the dark this close to the extremely porous border. A small knot of pain flared in Alex's head, making him frown and crush his eyes shut for a moment. The pain rippled down his neck and the sensation of being watched grew stronger. He was becoming distracted; he needed to concentrate, pay more attention, needed to ...

'Hold it right there.'

Harsh flashlights shone in their faces and two men came out of the underbrush. Their light blue uniforms looked like those of ice-cream vendors, but signified Laredo City Police. Alex considered dealing with them while he and Adira were still just anonymous bodies in the dark, but held back when a set of car headlights came on across the other side of the wide road. The lights were higher than normal – *SUV or truck,* Alex thought. Another man got out, also uniformed.

'Could I see some ID, please, sir?'

The man who spoke had a deep scar on his chin and his jaw was large and firm, indicating a lot of bunched muscle at the neck and shoulders. He was big and in condition – they all were. Despite the Laredo PD caps pulled down over their eyes, Alex could tell that their gazes never left him for a second. He noticed that the speaker's hand, which held the flashlight at shoulder level, was hard and callused. LPD must have upgraded their recruiting process. The sense of danger bloomed in Alex's head as he reached into his pocket for his wallet.

'We're tourists,' he said, holding it out slowly to the talker.

The man shook his head, his eyes never wavering from Alex's. 'Drop it and kick it over.'

'Careful, there's all my holiday money in there,' Alex said as he obeyed.

He tensed, waiting for the scarred officer to look down at the full wallet, but the man ignored it and reached down to his holster to unclip his gun. He lifted it free in a smooth movement, the weapon comfortable in his hand. It was a big Sig Sauer, a P228, much larger than normal US law enforcement issue. Something wasn't right ... small-town cops were never this sharp and professional.

The man's companions had drawn their weapons too, but their guns were different. There was something about the way they looked that wasn't quite right either, but he couldn't determine what it was with the flashlights in his face.

The men fanned out a little more. They took up equal positions around him and Adira, but all remained facing him, ready and on edge. The scarred officer crouched for the wallet, but still his eyes remained on Alex.

'Cover him while I call this in,' he told his men.

He removed the driver's licence, letting the wallet fall to the ground. He walked a few paces back towards his SUV, pulled a slim phone from his pocket and talked softly into it.

Alex let his eyes slide to Adira. She returned his gaze with a flat stare. Alex guessed what she was thinking: if the cops called in their names, they'd start a trail a mile wide that could be followed. They'd need to trash their cleanskin IDs and start again. He gave her an almost imperceptible shake of his head; he wanted to let it play out a little longer and see what happened.

As he watched her, the air around her seemed to blur, like a cloud of oily smoke was settling over the road, and the burning knot of pain in his skull ramped up its nagging intensity. Fifty feet away, the officer with the scar spoke softly into the phone – out of earshot of everyone except Alex.

'It's them all right.' He paused, then spoke again. 'Yes, but I don't like the look of him – he might be a problem.' His head came up and he turned; his eyes were emotionless as he stared back at Alex. 'Roger that. We've got a plastic sheet to wrap him.'

He came slowly back to the group, his face a mask of indifference. 'Put your hands on your head, turn around and kneel. I'm just going to put some cuffs on you.'

The pain began to flower inside Alex's skull. 'What's the problem, officer?'

'No problem, sir. Just do as you're told.'

Alex grimaced from the explosion of pain behind his eyes as he raised his hands. He turned his back on the officer, and saw that Adira's face had changed to a mask of anger and her fists were balled. He let his eyes travel to the two officers behind her. It dawned on him what he'd thought was out of place. Their uniforms were perfect, expect for one thing – the belts were just plain black leather; no baton, spray, tasers ... or cuffs.

From out of nowhere, a soft insistent voice sounded in his head. Was it Adira? It spoke urgently. *No cuffs. This is an execution – yours. Kill him.*

Alex slowly lowered his hands. 'You're not really police, are you?'

The answer was the almost inaudible sound of pressure on a trigger.

The pain in his head disappeared. *Kill them all.*

Alex exploded into action. He spun and yanked the gun from the man's hand and flung it into the darkness. His hand came away warm and wet, and he noticed that one of the man's fingers was missing. He had ripped the gun free with such force that he'd taken the digit with it.

The man, instead of grabbing his wrist and howling, went into a fighter's stance. He lashed out with a hammer blow that caught Alex on the chin and kicked his head back. He immediately followed with a front snap-kick aimed at Alex's groin. Alex was quick but not enough; he caught part of the boot in his testicles and the burst of pain and nausea made his head swim.

Who are these guys?

Alex lunged forward, taking another blow to his cheek, which he ignored. He grabbed the scarred officer and spun him round so his body shielded Alex's in the same moment as the officer yelled, 'Shoot him!'

Alex heard the men curse as they saw he'd deprived them of an easy kill shot. Alex had planned to simply subdue the scarred officer, but the voice came again in his head – *No survivors* – and it was as if something took over his body. He gripped the man's shoulders harder and pulled him forward, smashing his own forehead into the bridge of his nose with a sickening crunch. Blood ran into Alex's eyes, but it wasn't his own. The scarred man fell like a boneless sack at his feet.

Intuition made Alex leap to the side as bullets came out of the darkness. He was an easy target now, and as he rolled he knew these men, whoever they were, would give him no quarter. These were assassins, and if it was death they sought he'd give it to them.

He saw Adira struggling on the ground with one of the officers. The other stood with legs spread in a marksman stance, trying to track Alex with his weapon. One shaved second was all the man would need, but Alex was moving far too fast for him to get off an accurate shot. He was a blur as he rose up in front of the shooter and in a single motion brought his hand up into the man's neck, his thumb and finger spread either side of his larynx. The blow crushed the man's throat flat and he fell, making small barking coughs as he tried to pull in air.

Alex turned quickly, but saw that Adira was kneeling beside the man she had fought with, drawing one of her lethal spikes out of his ear. The man's legs kicked in a final dance and his eyes registered nothing but surprise.

With all the men down, it was as if a switch had been thrown; his boiling anger began to subside. He crossed back to the officer with the scar on his chin and kneeled to check his status. He was dead; the crushing blow had driven his septum up into his brain.

Alex spoke over his shoulder. 'Get their weapons, and I'll see what else they've got in their cars. And by the way, I didn't need your advice back there.' He glared at her.

Adira looked confused, then she shrugged and moved to the man who was still gasping for breath on the ground. She picked up his gun and looked down at him, her face an unemotional mask. She aimed between his eyes.

'Wait,' Alex said.

She ignored him and pulled the trigger, then smiled at him apologetically. 'I'm sorry, Alex; we're not taking hostages. He was as good as dead anyway – you made sure of that.'

Alex held her eyes a moment, then grunted and went over to the SUV. He watched her through the windscreen. She was examining the gun in her hand, turning it over. She ejected the magazine to look at the bullets, then frowned. '*Shizta*.' She spun and moved quickly from body to body, rapidly turning out their pockets and patting down their torsos and limbs. Alex shook his head and went back to his search of the vehicle's interior. Adira was a strange woman. Sometimes he felt he knew her, even had strong feelings for her. But at other times, she was a complete mystery.

He'd thought it was her voice that had whispered to him: *Kill them all.* But now he wasn't sure.

In the SUV's glove compartment he found two hand grenades. *Nice*, he thought, and stuffed them into his pockets. As he worked, the scarred officer's phone vibrated. Adira rushed to snatch it before Alex. She jammed it to her ear and waited. Alex could hear the silence as someone else did the same on the other end of the line. After another moment, Adira threw the phone over the tree line and they heard it splash into the river.

'Expecting someone?' he said, not thinking she'd answer him.

She stood there quietly, her face dark and unreadable.

'C'mon,' he said, nodding towards the bodies.

It took them another ten minutes to fill the dead men's shirts and trousers with stones and drag them towards the river. The rushing water snatched the bodies away and they quickly disappeared in the torrent. It would be weeks before they were found, and by then they would probably have washed down to Brownsville.

Alex looked at Adira as he dusted off his hands. 'Welcome to America.'

*

Salamon pressed his foot down on the accelerator. From the response to his call, he knew the mission had suffered a serious setback.

By the time he arrived at the interception point, there was little to see. A quick circling of the area showed blood underneath a shallow layer of sand beside the road. In the bushes nearby he found a Sig Sauer with a human finger jammed in the trigger guard. Salamon growled deep in his chest as he remembered the general's words: 'The American will be a problem.'

He flipped open his phone, typed in a long string of numbers, then waited a second or two for the distant connection.

'I need more agents,' he told Shavit.

*

Adira sat in the passenger seat of the SUV they'd salvaged from the attack, while Alex took the first leg of the long drive to Asheville. She felt like she'd been punched in the stomach. The weapon she held on her lap had no part number, but that didn't matter; she'd recognized it instantly – a full-size Jericho 941 pistol, also called an Israeli Uzi Eagle, and weapon of choice of the Mossad Kidon. Now she knew exactly how her uncle had reacted to her running away with Alex. He had sent torpedoes after her. They were marked for termination ... or was it just Alex who was to be executed? She couldn't tell anymore. Nothing was staying together for her; there was no logical plan to follow.

She felt anger burning inside. How had the agents found them so quickly? Her mind ran through their convoluted route – and every time she came back to the Egyptian incident. They must have picked up their trail there. Perhaps they'd been behind them all the way ... or ahead of them.

And now?

She swore again. That phone call had been local. The walls were closing in. The rules had changed again; it was now kill or be killed.

*

Hammerson swore at the empty room. The image from the satellite had been light-enhanced and showed what looked to be three local police officers surrounding Alex Hunter and Adira Senesh. There was nothing the HAWC commander could do but watch and hope things didn't turn bad.

'What the fuck?' Hammerson leaned forward, his face contorting into a frown as, inexplicably, the officer behind Alex lifted a gun to the back of his neck. 'No, no, no.'

Blurringly fast, Alex spun and ripped the gun out of the officer's hand. From there, things went as bad as they could get, real fast. Alex took down the first officer, then a second one. Hammerson was surprised by the amount of resistance they put up – more than he would have expected for local police.

Adira lashed out at the third man, striking him in the ear. By the way he dropped, and then convulsed on the ground, he guessed she had punctured his brain with one of her deadly spikes.

Three dead cops and they've only been on American soil for an hour. Fucking hell!

Hammerson watched Adira search the bodies, while Alex went over to the vehicle parked nearby. She paused to examine something in her hand. 'Okay, what have you found?' he said aloud, and zoomed in to see the gun. He took a still of the weapon, and of the bodies, then watched in silence as the pair dumped the corpses in the river before driving off in the SUV.

He walked slowly to his computer, tapping his chin with one large blunt finger, and pulled up the recording loop, represented as a line on the screen. He tracked back to when the police had first intercepted Alex, then deleted the entire recording up until their departure.

Hammerson blew out a breath through compressed lips and dropped back into his chair. He brought up the image of the gun Adira had been examining; he didn't recognize the make and was certain it hadn't come from any US law enforcement armory he knew of.

He lifted the phone and tapped a few numbers before saying softly, 'I need a clean-up crew ASAP – several bodies in the Rio Grande outside of Laredo. Find 'em, ID 'em, and then incinerate.'

He sat back and let his mind work, trying to piece together the strange events surrounding Alex's sudden reappearance and return to America.

'Why now, son? What's triggered this?' He drummed his large blunt fingers on the desk. 'Are you looking for something?'

He pulled up a map of Texas and printed it out, then drew a circle around it. Dropping the pen, he placed his fingers on his forehead and leaned in close, willing the map to tell him something. Nothing jumped out. He sighed and sat back for a few seconds, then picked up his pen again and wrote a list of names: *Adira Senesh, Jack Hammerson, Sam Reid, Aimee Weir.* He thought for a while, then added two more: *Casey Franks, Kathleen Hunter.* There were very few people Alex knew well, or had remained in contact with from his past. His job as a HAWC hadn't allowed it.

He typed each name into the search engine. The usual scientific information about Aimee Weir came up – she was going well in her career as a petrobiologist. As expected, he got nothing on Reid, Franks or himself. But when he typed in Kathleen Hunter's name, his mouth dropped open.

'Oh, good Christ.'

It was a small piece in the *Asheville Times* – there'd been an attack on the Hunter property, and its owner, Kathleen Joy Hunter, was now a missing person.

'Asheville.' Hammerson got to his feet so quickly his chair fell over behind him. He pressed a button on his intercom. 'Get Sam Reid in here.'

TWENTY-ONE

'Rattlesnake? Perfect,' Matt said, feeling his stomach turn over. He was hardly in the mood for any kind of food, but especially not the exotic variety, which seemed to be all Spirits Native American Diner had on offer.

The attractive olive-skinned waitress smiled broadly and passed around menus and glasses of water, telling them she'd be back in a minute to see if they were ready to order.

'Nice place,' Charles said, watching her go.

'And the food's good too,' Sarah added. 'My version of comfort food.' She leaned across to Matt and gripped his forearm. 'C'mon, cheer up.'

Matt shrugged. 'I'm okay. I just expected more support from Chief Logan. Means we're on our own ... for now.'

Charles waved a hand in the air. 'Don't worry about it – we've got everything we need. The cops'd just get in the way.'

Matt gave him a half-smile. Charles *would* say that. Matt reckoned he wanted any discovery to be made by him first – his great-uncle's blood obviously still flowed strongly through his veins. He leaned back and looked around the wooden ranch-style interior of the restaurant, stopping with a jolt at a nearby table.

'Hey, you're not going to believe this,' he hissed, hunching forward. 'Eleven o'clock – check it out.'

Charles turned slowly and then snapped back. 'You *are* shitting me. That's the guy again.'

'What is it? What guy?' Sarah swiveled in her seat.

'Don't look,' Matt said, hunching down further and lifting his menu to obscure his face.

Sarah swung back. 'What, you mean old Thomas?'

The old man got to his feet and walked towards them. When he reached the table, he didn't say a word; he just stood there looking down at Matt. Matt kept his eyes on the menu, frowning at it with the concentration of someone studying the Magna Carta in its original Latin. He kept it up for as long as he could, but eventually the force of the man's gaze dragged Matt's head up to meet a pair of eyes so intense they would have been more at home on a bald eagle. Matt swallowed audibly.

'Hi, Thomas, how you doin' today?' Sarah said and smiled up at him.

The old man nodded in acknowledgment, 'Miss Sarah,' but kept his eyes on Matt.

'Hello there, sir.' Matt knew his voice sounded feeble.

Up close, the man looked even more antique than he had from a distance, with leathery skin that had been creased a thousand times by sun, sand and dry winds.

Sarah frowned at the strange interaction. 'Thomas, this is Matt Kearns and Charles Schroder, friends of mine from the city. And this here is Mr. Thomas Red Cloud – closest thing we've got to a tribal elder in these parts.' She continued frowning as she looked from Thomas to Matt. 'Ahh, have you two met before?'

No one spoke.

Thomas reached into his jeans pocket and pulled out a small crumpled piece of soft paper. He unfolded it and laid it on the table in front of Matt, then tapped it with one brown, liver-spotted finger. 'Chiye-tanka.'

Matt looked down. It was the napkin he had drawn on in the diner with Charles, when his friend had first arrived. He nodded and met the old man's eyes. 'The Great Ones.'

The old man sat down next to Matt, pushing him along the bench seat, then tapped the napkin again. 'What do you know about them, Mr. Matt Kearns?'

'What do I know?' Matt shrugged. 'I can tell you what *I think* – that there's something big moving around on Black Mountain, and we suspect it might be responsible for the recent disappearances. It's certainly coming closer to town. We also think a lot of people are in danger unless we can convince the authorities to take us, to take *it*, seriously.'

The old man sat like a stone for a few seconds, looking into Matt's eyes. Eventually, he nodded, and spoke slowly. 'Yes, it is true; I believe the Great Ones have returned. My people have been the guardians of their prison for an eternity – a duty that was passed to us by our ancestors, the First People. They enjoyed a land of abundance, with animals of great size and number. But they were not alone; the Great Ones lived high in the mountains. At first, mankind and the giants shared the land, but as the First People's numbers grew, the Great Ones became angry. Without the people even knowing it, a war was declared. Warriors, women and children started to disappear, and the people became angry and fearful. But when the Chief's daughter was stolen, then the war was joined.'

Thomas lifted Matt's glass of water to his lips and drank half of it down before continuing with his story. 'The Chief chose his greatest warrior, Tooantuh, to gather a hundred-strong war party. He also summoned his most powerful sorcerers to force the Great Ones back into the caves and then to seal them away from the light with a wall of stones, each carved with a sacred story and symbols to hold them forever. Many warriors were lost in the battle, and Tooantuh himself never returned. It was a great cost to the tribe, but mankind was saved that day.'

He paused, shut his eyes briefly, then chuckled. 'It'd make a great comic book, huh?' He finished Matt's water.

Matt noticed Thomas wore a small leather bag tied around his neck; it looked soft and slightly oiled, as though it had been rubbed between finger and thumb a thousand times.

Thomas became serious again. 'Whether the story is believed or not, every four generations the wall must be maintained. I am the last of those who know the symbols, but I was not able to repair the wall when I was supposed to and the Great Ones broke free. And now ...' He trailed off.

Matt leaned forward. 'I knew it – something happened, didn't it? Something that broke down the wall? Have you seen this Great One? I mean, do you know where it is?'

Thomas waved a hand at Matt as though batting away his questions. 'The coyote and beaver told me; the eagle spirit screamed it down from heaven; the great-grandfather buzzard came to me in a dream. They said that the earth moved and the wall came down.'

Matt's mouth fell open. 'Wow – no way. Is that true?'

Thomas shook his head. 'Shit no. I read about the earth tremor in the papers like everyone else. But, Mr. Kearns, despite the fact that I might not be a full believer in Native American lore, I have still been lighting sacred fires around the town lately. Anything's worth a try, right?' He shrugged. 'Problem is, I don't really believe in what I'm doing, and perhaps that's why it's not working. Hell, I'm not even sure I'm doing it right. There's not a lot of people left for me to ask.' He reached out and placed his hands over the top of Matt's. 'But I do believe in the Great Ones. At least, now I do.'

Matt nodded. 'I believe in them too, Thomas. Tell me more about the magic symbols – and how we can help.'

Charles pulled a disbelieving face. 'Hang on, Matt – spells? He doesn't even believe in them himself. We aren't going to convince Chief Logan of anything if we start down the mystical path. We need scientific proof now, not magic fires, symbols and dreams. A freakin' elephant gun would be of more use to us than all that.'

Thomas looked at Charles and shook his head slowly. 'You think you see, but you are blind. You think you know all, but you are like a child. Mr. Schroder, how do you stop a force of nature? Can you trap the wind, stop the winter blizzard, or the summer heat? You are nothing but dust before such things.' He pinned Charles with his unblinking stare. 'I said that I had trouble believing, not that it was all make-believe. Sometimes it takes something from ancient times to restore our faith – and not always in a good way.'

Thomas turned to Matt. 'The answers are written on the *ah-u-tsi* stones.' He looked back at Charles. 'That means "prison stones", asshole.'

Charles stared at Thomas Red Cloud, his eyes wide. 'Oookay.' He looked at Sarah and shrugged. 'Well, I'm more than satisfied.'

Matt reached across the table and grabbed his friend's wrist. 'Charles, just hang on a minute and listen. These guys managed to trap it once before, using little more than arrows, spears ... and spells. I think we should at least hear how they did it.'

'C'mon, Matt, you said yourself that was probably over 10,000 years ago. Just give me a hundred milligrams of azaperone, or, better yet, detomidine in a hypodermic dart, and I'll put the big guy to sleep for hours.'

Thomas grunted. 'Science does not have all the answers, Mr. Schroder, and this is no game park rhino you seek. The legend tells that the Great Ones were not merely beasts, they were smart. It would be best if we used our intelligence too and employed everything we have at our disposal.'

Charles groaned, held his head in both hands and shook it slowly.

Thomas looked back at Matt. 'The legend says that Tooantuh's spirit watches over us still and guards us from the Great Ones; and, more importantly, that he will return if he is needed. We must be ready to help him if he comes once again to battle the Great One.' He gripped Matt's hand harder. 'I need to get up there to the wall, to see if I can still repair it.'

'Sarah?' Charles asked with grimace. Matt knew he was hoping she'd come down on his side and stop Matt being side-tracked by the old Indian.

Sarah tightened her lips and tilted her head slightly. 'It all fits – the stone barrier, the Paleo-Indians sealing the creatures away, their reappearance after an earth tremor. Remember the results of the DNA analysis? The red hair, fair skin, near non-existent levels of eumelanin – they all indicate a creature that would be intolerant of sunlight.' She knitted her brows, then pointed at Matt's chest. 'When did the attacks occur – what time of day?'

Matt thought hard for a moment. 'The Jordan woman's believed to have been attacked in the late afternoon, on an overcast day; the Wilson girl disappeared at dusk; Kathleen Hunter was taken at night ... That's it! It's a night hunter, which makes sense if its normal habitat is a cave or underground.'

Charles exhaled loudly, but this time he was nodding. 'You know, my great-uncle Charles disappeared while investigating deep limestone caves in southern China. I don't know ... maybe ...'

Matt clicked his fingers. 'That's how it came to turn up all of a sudden. The stone wall must have been repaired and kept secure by Thomas's ancestors, stretching back to when the first humans came to this area in about 8000 bce. The recent earth tremor destroyed some of the wall, which opened up the cave and let the Gigantopithecus back into our environment,' Matt said. 'This is astonishing.'

Thomas's face was a mask. 'I can show you where the cave opening is. We should leave first thing in the morning.'

'Done,' Matt said.

'Hey, wait a minute.' Charles looked from Matt to Sarah, clearly sceptical about the idea of inviting someone who looked to be at least a hundred years old on an arduous mountain trek.

'I vote we bring Thomas with us,' Matt said. 'Anyone prepared to second me?'

Sarah raised her hand. 'Aye.'

Charles sat back, a look of resignation on his face. 'Okay, but on one condition ...'

Matt raised his eyebrows.

'For scientific purposes, we don't immediately seal the cave opening until we have a significant sample that proves the creature's existence. You know very well, Matt, that this could be the most important scientific find of the century.' Charles folded his arms in a this-is-not-negotiable gesture.

Matt looked at Sarah, who nodded. He turned back to Thomas, whose face was unreadable. 'I'm afraid I agree with him, Thomas. We will help you, in return for you being our guide. But we must obtain proof of the creature's existence first. Deal?'

Thomas stared at Matt for nearly a minute before his leathery face broke into a wide but humorless grin, showing teeth that were far too strong and white to be his own. 'I agree to allow *you* to come with *me*, and I'm sure you will all find what you seek there. I will be ready in the morning.' He patted Matt's forearm as though he were an elderly relative catching up with a favorite nephew.

Matt cleared his throat. 'Ahh, Thomas, one more thing ... how will you know when the Tooantuh arrives, or *if* he arrives?'

Thomas, still holding Matt's arm, stared deep into his eyes. 'Can't you feel it, Mr. Kearns? He is already on his way.'

TWENTY-TWO

Hammerson watched the SUV burn up Highway 20 towards Atlanta, doing 120 miles per hour. The screen faded to a snowy white as the satellite went over the horizon, and he sat back, running one hand across his cropped hair.

'So somehow he's heard about whatever's happened to Kathleen Hunter,' Sam Reid said. 'Or perhaps he sensed it – Arcadian was able to do some pretty weird things.'

'When he had his demons under control,' Hammerson added.

Sam nodded. 'He's heading for Asheville.' He wheeled himself around the desk. 'Head, heart and hands – I've still got 'em all, boss. Let me go – he'll trust me. I just need to get close to him.'

Hammerson shook his head. 'Sorry, Sam, not this time. I'm going to need you looking over my shoulder.'

He headed for the door but Sam cut in front of him. 'Boss, I can do this.'

Jack Hammerson leaned forward to grip the armrests of Sam's chair and look into his broad and battle-scarred face. 'I know you can, soldier – but not this time. If things go bad for me, I've already recommended you take over the HAWC command. Your field skills, strategic thinking and HAWC experience are assets we need – and they're exactly what *I'll* need in my ear when I'm standing in front of the Arcadian trying to bring him in.'

Sam exhaled and started to look away, then quickly turned back to his colonel. 'What about Senesh? If she sees you first, you'll end up in a shit storm.'

Hammerson paused and thought for a second. He nodded. 'You're right. Get me Casey Franks. Tell her she's got thirty minutes to meet me on the chopper pad. Fight fire with fire – one bad-ass woman against another.' He smiled grimly as he went out the door. 'Who said this job can't be fun?'

*

On his way to the chopper pad, Hammerson took a call from the field. Only two bodies had been pulled from the Rio Grande and there was a problem – they weren't Laredo PD. In fact, they showed no DNA, facial, dental or fingerprint matches to anyone in North America. A sense of foreboding grew inside Hammerson as he listened.

'What else?' he asked.

'Analysis of the corpses showed numerous old scars from gunshot and stabbing trauma. In addition, both guys were built like tanks. My bet – Special Forces, just not ours.'

Hammerson groaned. 'Global search?'

'Yes, got something, but not a formal ID. A hit from a Tel Aviv dental laboratory for a crown in a second rear molar.'

'Shit!'

Hammerson crushed the phone hard to his ear and thought through the implications. Tel Aviv could only mean one thing – Mossad. They wanted Alex or Senesh back, and they were prepared to take control of them on US soil. Or at least fucking try. *No wonder they gave Arcadian some trouble*, he thought.

Hammerson ground his teeth. 'Anything else?'

'Nothing else, sir. Orders?'

'Burn them.' He hung up and immediately called Sam. 'Lieutenant, we got a complication. Mossad are here and tracking Hunter and Senesh. Monitor the Tel Aviv communications traffic, and keep the bird watching for anyone following that SUV.'

'On it. Good luck, boss.'

Reckon I'll need it now, Hammerson thought, as he signed off.

*

The helicopter came in low and hovered over a clearing in the Pisgah National Forest, about five miles northeast of Asheville. The machine was small, painted in a black non-reflective coating and surprisingly silent, making more of a *whooshing* sound than the usual rotational whine. When it was within six feet of the ground, a door slid back and two figures jumped lightly from its rear. They jogged away to allow it to lift off, and watched it disappear quietly over the treetops.

Second Lieutenant Casey Franks jogged a few paces into the dense forest circling them, examined the ground for a moment, then removed a small shovel from her pack and started digging. After ten minutes she had excavated a hole roughly three feet deep and the same wide. She and Hammerson dropped their packs and locator beacon into it, and then she covered it over. Once she'd scattered leaves, twigs and other debris over the area, all signs of the surface disturbance had been erased.

Dressed in lumber jackets, jeans and boots, with hunting knives on their belts, she and Hammerson looked like any other weekend campers. The only light arms they allowed themselves were a single Heckler & Koch USP .45 CT pistol each, strapped in a holster at their back.

Jack Hammerson was checking the tracker when Franks joined him, his face illuminated by its screen's soft glow. He motioned towards the west with one flat hand. 'Kathleen Hunter's place is a few miles out of town, at the foot of the mountains. But satellite surveillance confirms the Arcadian is still en route for the town center. So that's where we'll go to wait for him ... them.'

'And if Captain Senesh interferes – what's the engagement level authorization?'

Hammerson slid the tracker back into his pocket. 'Authorization to make life fucking difficult for her ... *only*. Bottom line is, until we know more about the characteristics of her relationship with the Arcadian, we can't afford to do anything that may force him into taking sides. Especially as we're not certain yet which side he's gonna take.'

Franks nodded slowly, but Hammerson knew she'd heard of Adira Senesh and could tell she was excited about the prospect of going head to head with her. Franks was good, probably the best female operative they now had in the HAWCs, but Hammerson knew that might not be enough against Israel's top Metsada operative. Unfortunately, Senesh had also been trained in HAWC attack and defensive techniques – he'd overseen the training himself. There was probably only one HAWC Hammerson would have confidently bet against the Senesh woman – and unfortunately that HAWC was now running with her.

'Double time,' he ordered, and they began a jog towards the town center, five miles away. Hammerson wanted to be there and ready when the Arcadian arrived.

*

Several hundred miles to the north, a dark, nondescript Infiniti G35 with slightly tinted windows sped down Highway 81 in Virginia. It had just entered the outskirts of Marion but it wouldn't stop there ... nor at Abingdon, Bristol or even Johnston City.

The driver could have been part of the machinery of the vehicle. Like his two passengers, he sat mute. All three wore their hats pulled down low, and wraparound sunglasses of the kind favored by seniors, which covered most of the nose and forehead as well as the eyes. The lenses were almost as dark as welding goggles.

The accessories weren't so much for concealment as for protection against direct sunlight. To Captain Graham's frustration, the subjects' superheated metabolisms were weakened by UV radiation. Yet another puzzling flaw to be solved, and even more reason to find the original Arcadian.

One of the men in the backseat lifted his hand to scratch a sore that had opened up on his cheek. The movement of his finger lifted more skin away from his face, but he ignored the fluid that ran down from the open wound. The men had one order, one objective, and they wouldn't stop, sleep or eat until they reached Asheville ... until they found the Arcadian.

*

Hammerson slowed them to a trot as they reached the outskirts of Asheville, and they entered the town center at a brisk walk. It was late, cold and a weeknight, so the streets were empty. They needed a quiet place to wait. Hammerson knew they stood out, even though they'd dressed like regular hikers or hunters. They were too big, too wide and too battle-scarred to blend in with civilians.

'This'll do,' Hammerson said, nodding towards the sign for Old Ron's Bar and Grill.

They pushed the door open and Hammerson inhaled the atmosphere: stale beer, body odor, old grease and bleach – the latter probably used to clean blood from the floor, given the look of some of the patrons lounging at the bar and playing pool further back in the gloom.

A weary-looking woman behind the bar, with a low-cut top that showed her pendulous breasts, raised her eyebrows at Hammerson. Two men who'd obviously been trying their luck with her turned to see what had caught her eye. Hammerson nodded to the woman, then headed to a booth, keeping his cap on to hide his iron-gray buzz cut. Franks slid in next to him.

Hammerson waited a while, until the locals had tired of staring at the newcomers, then pulled the tracker from his pocket and used his finger to scroll down the screen to the information feed he wanted.

'He's about fifty miles out, still headed into town. Should be here within the hour.'

'What do you think?' Franks asked, leaning forward, her angular powerful body made even more solid by the padded lumber jacket.

Hammerson pushed the box back into his pocket. 'Hunter's got to be leading them here. Too much of a coincidence, this being his mother's home town and her just disappearing ... or dead. But how would he know about it?'

He frowned, pulled the box from his pocket again and searched for the Asheville coroner's report on Kathleen Hunter's disappearance. Nothing. He tapped the box on the table top for a second or two. 'Coroner's office hasn't released the information about his mother's death, which smells like an ongoing police investigation.' He tapped some more. 'What if Kathleen Hunter was murdered?' He stopped tapping. 'There'd be a shitload of retribution about to ride into town.'

Franks laughed softly. 'Escorted by a Mossad clean-up crew. Oh yeah, this is getting real interesting.' She slid out of the booth. 'Drink?'

Hammerson replied without looking at her. 'Coffee.'

'Got it.'

Franks took off her heavy jacket, threw it on the seat and headed to the bar.

*

'Two coffees and a Bud,' Franks told the woman behind the bar, pulling off one of her gloves and sliding her sleeves up on her brawny forearms. She could feel the two men nearby staring at her white buzz-cut, ice blue eyes and snub nose. In her teens, Casey Franks had been called attractive once or twice, but the compliments stopped after she got in a fight and picked up a deep facial wound that was never properly repaired. There was no spare cash in her Midwest family for cosmetic surgery. The cleft scar ran from just below her left eye down to her chin and pulled her left cheek up slightly, giving her a permanent sneer. She had multiple tattoos on her forearms – daggers, dragons, names of high-power motorbikes, and one solitary feminine adornment: a rose with the name *Linda* in delicate, curling calligraphy underneath it.

The man closest to her, wearing a greasy-looking cap, nudged his companion and motioned with his head at the rose tattoo. He leaned in close to Franks. 'Hey, this ain't a gay bar ... *mister.*'

He sniggered, and his companion guffawed and leaned around him to have his own say. 'Maybe the young fella's had one of them sex change thingies.'

They both laughed again at their own wit.

The weary barmaid set down the coffees and beer. 'Ignore them, sweetheart, they're drunk. They'll be shown the door soon enough if they don't start behaving.' She scowled at them before walking away.

Franks removed her other glove, exposing raised and callused knuckles. She made no move to take the drinks, instead sending a quick glance to the booth to see if Hammerson was watching. He wasn't, so she smiled and leaned on the bar, turning slightly towards the men towering over her stocky form.

'You know what? Damn shame this ain't a gay bar 'cause I was feelin' a real attraction for both of you ladies.'

Greasy Cap snorted. 'Oh, we're men all right, Butch, but you might not recognize us. Tell me, sweetheart, you ever been with a man before?'

'I bet not as many times as you have.' She thrust her chin out and looked him up and down. 'Hey, I reckon you're about six feet two – I'm impressed. I didn't know they could stack shit that high.' She leaned around him to his friend. 'And you there – where I come from, you need a licence to be as dumb as you are.'

She leaned back, put both elbows on the bar and waited.

Greasy Cap had stopped smiling. 'You should run back to your grandpa now, before you get hurt, you weird little fucker.'

He lifted his jacket front and pulled a twelve-inch bowie knife from a worn leather scabbard attached to his belt. He placed it on the bar, his hand close to it, then turned red, drunk-angry eyes on Franks and leaned in close.

Franks smiled and said calmly, 'That's it? That's all you got? You more used to picking fights down at the local senior citizens' home?' She shook her head, still smiling. 'Listen up, asshole. If I turn around and that blade's still on the bar, I'm going to take it and castrate you, stick your balls down your boyfriend's throat and make him swallow them. I'm not here to make friends to-night ... *fucker*.'

The silence stretched for many seconds, then Greasy Cap made a movement. Whether he was going for the knife or to retreat didn't matter. Franks turned, grabbed the knife, spun expertly and buried the blade an inch into the wooden bar top, between two of Greasy Cap's fingers.

She leaned back on the bar again, still smiling. 'Now, fuck off and play some pool or something.'

Greasy Cap pulled his hand away and looked at it; there was a small split in the skin between his fingers. The seconds stretched as the booze-oiled gears worked in his head. He shot his hand out, grabbed the knife and wrenched it from the bar top. 'Dyke,' he said, and walked off towards the pool table. His friend, following, looked back briefly to flip Franks the bird.

Casey Franks picked up the beer and downed it in a long gulp, then carefully carried the two steaming coffees back to the booth. Hammerson still had his eyes on the tracker, but looked up briefly to scowl at her.

'Making friends there, Franks?'

'Just makin' some space, boss.'

Hammerson grunted. 'We came in here to keep a low profile, not to wipe the floor with the locals. Got that, soldier?'

'Got it, boss.'

She lifted her cup and sipped the dark brew, then turned briefly to see the barmaid smile and nod to her. She winked in return.

'He's reached the outskirts of Asheville – he's coming right to us,' Hammerson said, glancing at her as he spoke.

It was the first time in her life Franks had seen the Hammer look uncertain. It didn't make her feel good.

TWENTY-THREE

Alex let the SUV idle for a moment in the dark street, before switching off the engine and staring blankly through the windscreen. Adira watched him for a few seconds, then scanned the street, looking for anything out of the ordinary. Alex had mentioned a number of times that he felt they were being watched. He was probably right. Now that she knew there were professional Mossad operatives hunting them, her nerves were wire tight. She examined the businesses lining the street but saw nothing of interest.

'What are we looking for?' she asked.

Alex blinked a few times before responding. 'Don't know yet.'

He pushed open the door, climbed out of the SUV and looked around for a few seconds, then stared in one direction. Adira was just about to join him when he said harshly, 'Wait here.'

She sat back, frowning, and watched him head directly towards a commercial building with double glass doors. *Asheville Animal Hospital* the signage announced. He placed his hand on the glass and turned his head slightly. Adira expected him to push the door open, but he seemed to be listening for something. After a moment, he stood back and disappeared around the corner of the building.

Adira opened the car door again and climbed out. A faint glow was just touching the horizon, and she hoped whatever Alex was doing was over with quickly. She looked around slowly. The trained agent part of her hated being out in the open, and she walked quickly across the road to stand in the dark doorway of an apartment block. The entrance hallway stretched away into solid darkness. She walked a few paces into its interior, satisfying herself it was empty. *No need to take chances*, she thought.

She breathed calmly, willing her heartbeat to slow, all her senses focused on the street.

Around the side of the animal surgery, Alex found a fire exit, as he'd hoped. He hefted the external padlock in his hand, feeling its weight, then turned it over to examine its base – and grunted in acknowledgment of the toughened steel shackle and two-and-a-half-inch steel casing. *A good one*, he thought, and smiled. Though the high-grade padlock was near unbreakable without heavy boltcutters, the sliding bolt mechanisms they were attached to were nearly always a lower-grade alloy and much weaker.

Alex gripped the brass case and twisted, turning the steel. It squealed in resistance for a few seconds, but soon broke free from the metal eyelets it was threaded through. He let it drop silently and opened the door, slipped inside and closed it behind him.

Fear, pain, disease and death – the smell of the animals' distress was overpowering. Whimpers and mewling turned to yapping and deeper barks as frightened and lonely animals vied for his attention. He stood in the dark room, still not sure what he was looking for. All he had was a name: *Kathleen Hunter*. But something had drawn him to this place; he knew that somehow he'd find the answers he sought.

He walked quickly through the maelstrom of animal noise and into a room that seemed to be a surgery and office combined. Against one wall stood a large refrigeration unit, with shelves nearby holding drugs, flea treatments and all manner of grooming products. In the corner was a double-steel filing cabinet – probably the place to start. He went to the cabinet and tugged; locked as expected. He braced himself and pulled. The handle bent outwards, threatening to tear free, which would leave him with a flat metal sheet and nothing to grip. He inserted his fingers into the small gap showing at the top. The lock held for a few more seconds, then there was a *pop* as the metal tongue gave away and the drawer slid out.

The files were organized by pet name. He went through them quickly, until he came to one that stood out for some reason. *Jess*. He pulled it out; Jess was a dog, a German shepherd, owner *K. Hunter*. The sheet gave him the address he wanted, and he stuffed it into his pocket and slid the file back into place. He closed the cabinet and tried to bend the door and handle back into some sort of normal shape.

He made his way back through the dark surgery, planning to leave, then paused. There was something else here. His eyes were drawn to the steel refrigeration unit. He moved to it in the dark and pulled open the heavy door. A blast of cold air washed over him and an unsettling odor. On one of the broad trays lay the large body of a dog. He slid it out and looked down at it.

Jess. The dog from his memories.

He rested his hand on the dog's flank, noting the abraded fur and feeling the broken bones beneath the skin. 'So much pain, and you died fighting, didn't you?' He felt an intense sadness that quickly turned to anger. He knew what the brutal death of the loyal animal probably meant.

'Is she dead too?'

He frowned and leaned forward – the smell coming off the dog was revolting. Not the usual scent of unwashed dog but something rank and unfamiliar. He couldn't place it. He closed his eyes and concentrated; tried to visualize the dog, pushing at his memories. A knot of pain flared from the center of his skull all the way down his neck. He saw Kathleen and Jess the sun-warmed porch of a small house ... a meadow beyond leading to a steep hill. Then he was up on the hill, looking down at them. The scene changed to winter, to night-time ... and then the creature came, a grotesquery, hiding in the darkness, moving silently through the shadows towards the house.

Alex ground his teeth as the dog's frustration and fury became his own – he felt danger, fear, the desire to attack and kill. The images came faster, along with urgency and panic. The monster, large but roughly human shaped, came at the woman out of the darkness. He heard her scream and a wave of anguish washed over him.

Alex blinked as the images faded away. The feelings remained, however: a residue of hatred for the *thing*, whatever it was, and a desire to kill it. He lifted his hands to his face and inhaled the bestial odor that emanated from the dog's fur, wanting to remember it.

As he pushed the heavy, metal door shut, he heard a sound from behind him and the lights came on.

'I don't know who you are, son,' said an old man's voice, 'but don't move or there'll be more trouble than you want to be a part of.'

Alex saw the outline of a figure and the black barrel of a gun in the distorted reflection of the metal door in front of him. He responded to the threat without thinking, spinning quickly, one hand ripping the gun from his assailant's hands, the other grasping his throat. The man's feet lifted from the floor and he gagged at the pressure at his neck.

Kill him, the voice inside Alex's head ordered.

Alex grimaced; the man was old and no threat. He lowered him to the ground, and the man folded into a heap, his hands over his face. Alex pulled him upright and shook him.

'Who are you?'

'Ahh, Grinberg,' the man stammered. 'The vet. This is my surgery. There's no money here. Please, let me –'

'What happened?' Alex cut in, motioning towards the freezer.

'What?'

'To the dog? What happened?'

'You mean old Jess?' The old man kept his eyes on the ground. 'Don't know ... neither do the police. Never seen anything like it – must have been a bear, or a pack of wolves, I reckon. Nothing else could have done that to a full-grown shepherd.'

'And the women?' Alex asked.

'Kathleen?' The veterinarian started to raise his head.

'Don't look at me,' Alex ordered.

The old man froze, his eyes still gazing at the floor. He swallowed then said quietly, 'No one knows. She's just ... gone. Same as all the others.'

*

From her hiding place, Adira saw the man enter the street. He was broad, fit and moved too deftly for any normal man of that size. She cursed under her breath. Alex was right – they *were* being watched ... and followed. If the man was Mossad Kidon, he probably wasn't alone. She drew the large Jericho pistol and held it at her side as she pressed herself back into the dark alcove, just the edge of one eye giving her a view of the street.

She waited, her nerves tightening even more. The figure looked briefly at the SUV, then stood there in the center of the dark street, making himself a large target. *What is he doing?* Her breath caught. *Is he drawing my attention?* She whipped around to the impenetrable darkness of the corridor, her arm up, the large gun aimed down the dark passage. Nothing. She gritted her teeth, willing herself to stay calm, and turned back to the lone figure. *Come on, what are you waiting for?*

The man removed his cap and ran a hand through his cropped, iron-gray hair. He lifted his head and now Adira could see his face clearly. *Jack Hammerson. Shitza!* Why was he here in person?

He rolled the cap and tucked it into a pocket, then put his hands on his hips. 'Come out,' he called, and lifted his chin and waited.

Adira glanced across the road to the animal hospital. Hammerson wasn't looking that way so obviously he didn't know Alex was in there. She leaned out slightly, scanning the street from different angles. Would the HAWC leader have come alone? She pulled back, her eyes returning to the blocky figure. Of course he had come alone. He'd had to. It was he who had consigned Alex Hunter into Israel's care and then told his superiors the man's body had been incinerated. Colonel Jack Hammerson wouldn't be able to explain how his man had risen from the dead. He'd lied to the US military, betrayed them, to save Alex Hunter, his creation. Now he was here to clean up his mess ... and she was part of that mess. Was this a retrieval or a termination? She'd have to wait and see.

Hammerson turned to look at the SUV again. They had probably been tracking it, maybe since they'd first set off in it. *Am I that obvious and clumsy now?* She ground her teeth in disgust at her own incompetence.

'Don't waste my time,' Hammerson called again, louder this time. 'Come out *now.*'

Adira channeled her anger at herself towards the HAWC leader. She was confident she could take him, and she would enjoy the fight. Her relationship with Jack Hammerson, her former superior officer, had turned toxic when he found out she was continuing to work for Mossad and thereby was breaching US security. In turn, he had stopped her accompanying Alex on his mission to Paraguay ... the mission during which he had become infected with the horrifying microorganism that had almost killed him. To compound her fury, Hammerson had then refused her offer of using Israeli resources to get Alex out of South America quickly. Alex had been as good as dead by the time Jack Hammerson had crawled back to her to ask for her country's help. She'd agreed, but not for Hammerson, or even for Israel.

And now he was here to threaten her again. She would never let Jack Hammerson get to Alex; never let him expose her desperate inventions to keep Alex by her side. If he succeeded, everything she had done, and sacrificed, would be for nothing.

Adira had trained her mind to be clinical and dispassionate, to remain free of emotion. But as she stared at Hammerson, she felt a deep contempt. She lifted the gun and aimed between his eyes – an easy shot over the distance. But her finger did not tighten on the trigger.

She groaned inwardly at her indecision. She had a thousand reasons to kill Hammerson, but if she did, the amount of force that would rally against her would be insurmountable. And how would Alex react?

She maintained her aim between the HAWC commander's eyes for another second, then lowered her sights to his thigh. She'd wound him. After all, she only needed to slow him down for now. Perhaps he and her Mossad pursuers would trip over each other. Adira tensed, and slowed her breathing for the shot. Behind her, she sensed a slight change in the air density, as if a door or window had been opened somewhere along the darkened hallway.

Stupid, she thought. She kept the gun pointed at Hammerson, but moved up onto her toes and let her other hand drop to her side.

'Don't move.' The voice from behind her was female, but deep.

Adira calmed herself and allowed her focus to turn inwards. In her mind she saw her next move, the countermove of her opponent, and then again her own following action. She coiled the muscles from her shoulders to her thighs and waited for the split-second moment she knew would come. She breathed evenly, and slowly raised her gun to point it straight up, opened her fingers and let it drop.

'Easy now.'

The voice was closer and there was a hint of satisfaction in the words. The cold steel muzzle of a gun pressed into the nape of her neck. It was what she was waiting for. Adira exploded, swinging her other hand, holding a deadly black spike, back towards the voice with blistering speed. The woman managed to block the blow but grunted in surprise. In the deep darkness of the corridor, Adira could make out a stocky form, shorter than herself, but with powerful muscles through the shoulders and neck.

The woman blocked her next strike, but Adira used the tip of her elbow to catch the woman hard on the cheek. The head on the thick neck barely moved. For the next few seconds, furious blows were traded, until both women managed to grip each other and for a few short seconds they stared into each other's faces. Adira looked into the eyes and saw no fear, only ... amusement. The sturdy woman smiled, one side of her face pulling up to match the sneer already made by the terrible slash of a scar on the other cheek.

Adira remained detached, impassive and calculating, her mind still working through the moves and countermoves she anticipated. Jack Hammerson was here, so her opponent would be a HAWC. Adira knew all the HAWC moves ... and many more of her own.

Whatever spell had frozen the two warriors was broken and the frantic combat began again. Spatters of saliva and blood stained the walls as savage blows were met, absorbed or parried. But in the silent doorway no grunts of pain, anger or frustration came from the two professional combat women.

The woman dealt Adira a flat-hand strike under the chin, making her head snap up. She brought it down just as quickly without a sound. Throughout the brutal attack, the small HAWC maintained her smile. The tough woman had the strength of a man, but she was overconfident and underestimated her foe and the battle scenario. Tight-area combat was what Mossad's elite fighters specifically trained for. If you were sent into a Hamas spider hole or tunnel system, you needed to be able to fight within the space of a coffin and win.

Adira brought her knee up, followed a split second after by a head-butt. The knee strike was blocked, but the head-butt caught the smaller woman flush on the bridge of her nose. Adira knew the HAWC's eyes would water for only a second, but it was all she needed. She drew another blade from her sleeve and jammed it into the meat of the woman's shoulder, through the bunching trapezium muscle and just over the clavicle bridge. She left the spike embedded – a calculated strike-and-plant tactic designed to impede movement in the arm and shoulder. The HAWC's gun fell from her near useless hand, but she didn't make a sound, just continued to battle one-armed.

Adira grabbed the arm and used the HAWC's own body weight to slam her forward into the brick wall, face first, then again with even greater force. She wrapped her arm around the woman's throat, holding her in a neck lock, and hissed into her ear, 'You fight well, little HAWC. I won't kill you today because I need you upright. Next time, not so lucky.'

Adira pulled the woman away from the wall and held her as cover in front of the doorway. She bent, dragging the HAWC with her, to retrieve her gun. The woman took the opportunity to reach for her own weapon, and Adira stamped hard on her hand, making the gun go off in the hallway. She slammed the HAWC into the wall again and tightened the grip on her throat.

When she turned back to the street, it was as she had expected. Colonel Jack Hammerson stood just ten feet from the doorway, his gun drawn and pointed at her left eye.

'Let her go, Adira. We're only here for Alex – we just want to speak to him.'

Adira stayed hunched behind the smaller woman. She knew how skilled the HAWCs were; if she exposed even an inch of her flesh as a target, Hammerson would hit it.

'He does not want to speak to you,' she said. 'Any of you. He does not even know you anymore.'

Hammerson moved slightly to her side, improving his angle. 'We both know I could take you down if I wanted. So I'll ask nicely one more time. Let Franks go and let's sort this all out.' His eyes drilled into her, steady, serious. 'Don't make this go bad.'

*

Alex shook his head as the vet's words played over and over in his mind. *She's just gone … same as all the others.* He was too late; he could feel it. His grip on Grinberg tightened. He needed to lash out at something, or someone. He wanted to crush the little man for being in the wrong place at the wrong time.

The vet seemed to shrink in his hands. 'Don't kill me,' he pleaded, his eyes closing.

A gunshot sounded from outside. By the time the old man had opened his eyes, Alex Hunter was gone.

TWENTY-FOUR

Shitza – no time. Adira knew something had to give. Even though the woman she held was partially incapacitated, she was still one of the deadliest soldiers on the planet. Adira couldn't afford to have her begin fighting again when she had an armed HAWC zeroing in on her for a head shot. Adira also suspected there could be more HAWCs creeping up in the shadows all around her.

Then a tall figure stepped into the street behind Hammerson. Adira smiled and raised her gun to point it at the HAWC commander, knowing exactly what would happen. Hammerson immediately moved to a side-on shooter's stance and tightened his grip on the trigger. The figure behind him saw the action and responded at a speed that was both fearsome and unbelievable.

Alex collided with Hammerson and shunted him twenty feet down the street. The older HAWC hit the road surface and rolled several times before coming back to his feet. Alex was already upon him, his fist drawn back.

'Alex ... Arcadian, halt!'

Hammerson still held his gun, but didn't bother bringing it up. He stood there as if waiting, either for recognition or a blow. Neither came. Adira knew she had to act.

She smashed her gun down on the back of the woman's neck, then kicked her forward and shot Hammerson in the outer muscle of his thigh. The tough man went down. Adira knew the flesh wound would probably only slow him temporarily, but that was all they needed.

She ran towards him and aimed the gun point-blank at his face, then saw that he was smiling. She snorted in contempt when she saw the reason why: he had his own gun pointed at her belly. She nodded for him to drop his weapon but he shook his head.

Alex knocked her gun up and kneeled down beside Hammerson, grabbing the front of the HAWC commander's shirt. 'Who are you? I've seen you ... in my head.'

Over in the doorway, the woman struggled upright and pulled the blade from her shoulder. 'You're one of us, you dumb fuck,' she yelled. 'You're –'

Adira fired the rest of her clip into the air. The noise was almost deafening in the silent, pre-dawn street. Lights came on in some of the buildings, and curtains were pulled back.

'Time to go,' she said, and grabbed Alex's arm, ignoring the weapon Hammerson was still pointing at her.

*

Hammerson lowered his gun and swore softly as Senesh and Alex Hunter disappeared around the corner. He saw Franks spin the thin black blade in her hand that she had just pulled from her shoulder. She sprinted towards the corner, clearly intending to launch the spike at its original owner.

'Don't.'

Her arm froze for a second, then wound back further.

'That's a fucking order, soldier.'

Another second passed.

'Fuck!' Franks said, and lowered the blade. She flexed her fingers where the Mossad agent had stamped on them, then headed back to the doorway to retrieve her gun.

Hammerson pulled a handkerchief from his pocket, rolled it, and wound it around his bleeding thigh. He gritted his teeth as he got to his feet, but let out a satisfied snort as he stuck his gun into its concealed holster. The last time he had seen Alex Hunter, the HAWC had been on the verge of death, his body frozen to stop the progress of the Hades bacterium that was eating it. What Hammerson had seen just now was more than he could have hoped for – the soldier he had effectively created, and sometimes thought of as a son, was alive and obviously fully functional, despite the memory loss he was clearly suffering. They had always guessed the bacterium was likely to make its way to his brain and cause some type of complication.

Hammerson smiled; Alex Hunter, the man he knew, the HAWC, was still in there – he knew it. He just needed a few more minutes with him to bring it out, without that damned Mossad woman acting as his minder.

Franks came back, reaching into her shirt to stick something onto her wound. She rolled her shoulder, an angry expression on her face. 'Go after them?'

'No.' Hammerson replied. 'All that'll do is push them into another firefight. We'll let the leash run out a bit, then haul 'em back in later. What we do need to do is separate them, so we can speak to Hunter alone – and for that we need some help.'

'I can take her out if I get another chance.'

Hammerson spoke without looking at her. 'You underestimated her, Franks. I should send you home.'

Franks rebuttoned her shirt. 'She's got a few moves is all. I know I can take her in the open.'

Hammerson glared at her. 'You were instructed to get behind her and hold your position. Next time, you'll be dead. Might even shoot you myself. Clear?'

She muttered something unintelligible.

The glare went up several notches in intensity. 'Are we *clear*, soldier?'

Her head snapped up. 'Crystal.'

That's all I fucking need, Hammerson thought. He knew that if Casey Franks got another opportunity to engage with the Senesh woman, she would – didn't matter what he said or ordered. Franks's skill, competitiveness and aggression had brought her to the attention of the HAWCs, where she had excelled. But Hammerson knew that if she didn't learn to control her impulsiveness, it would be her downfall ... and death.

'Secure us a car,' he told her, then paused, hearing the faint sound of a siren in the distance. 'Belay that order, we've got company. About time they joined the party.' He put his finger to his ear to touch the small comms stud. 'Sam, they're on the move again. Get me some visuals.'

The sky was showing some dawn light. Hammerson took a step, and winced. His leg hurt like a bitch, they'd lost the Arcadian, and Franks now had a seething determination to try her luck again against the Mossad agent. *And it's only morning*, he thought. He needed a drink. Instead, he pulled a wound patch from his pocket and pushed his pants down to reach the deep fissure gouged through the flesh of his thigh.

An Asheville PD cruiser turned into the far end of the street. Its lights and siren shut down, and a large man stepped out and surveyed the scene, including Hammerson and Franks. He reached back into the vehicle to grab the mic and talk into it, before standing and unclipping his holster.

Hammerson raised his ID and walked towards the car. 'FBI,' he called to the cop.

*

Adira heard the sirens and increased her pace. She had deliberately drawn the police to the scene to create trouble for Jack Hammerson, but unless they got well away they'd get caught up in the attention too. She watched Alex from the corner of her eye. He hadn't spoken since she'd dragged him away from the HAWCs, but seemed to have taken charge of their direction.

He stopped and bent to peer in through the window of a large Ford Cruiser. 'This one,' he said, and took off his jacket.

He held it over the back window and punched through the material to shatter the glass, then pushed away the crystalized fragments and reached around to open the driver's door. He jumped in and reached across to unlock Adira's door, then gripped the toughened plastic sleeve behind the steering wheel and ripped it away in one motion.

He held out his hand to Adira. 'Give me one of your spikes.'

She hesitated for a moment and then handed it over. He laid the steel over the exposed solenoid terminal and the engine came to life. He handed back the weapon without a word and stepped on the gas.

Adira knew he wouldn't remember how he knew to do that, but she still didn't like it. His former life was returning too fast. She watched his face as he drove, and could almost feel the waves of simmering rage coming off him, even though his face was as blank as that of an automaton.

She sat back to think. Things were closing in on them. The rapid appearance of the HAWCs meant that it wouldn't be long before they were picked up again. She now had Hammerson on one side, and a Mossad team on the other. Plus, the more Alex remembered of himself, the less he seemed to need her. She had to get him away from this place, the source of his anguish and the trigger for his memories, but she had the feeling that whatever had drawn Alex to this small town was far from resolved. *Time is nearly up for me*, she thought miserably.

'What happened in there?' she asked him. 'Find anything?'

He shook his head. 'Something, but not what I ...' His brow creased in confusion. 'I know she was attacked ...' He grimaced, obviously reliving some painful memory. 'She could still be alive.'

She touched his arm, but he didn't acknowledge her.

'There are too many people tracking us now,' she said. 'We should lie low, go somewhere and wait it out for a while.'

His face changed from confusion to anger, and he turned to her. 'What *I* need to do, *must* do, *you* don't.'

The car accelerated.

'What are you talking about?' she said. 'I'm with you all the way, Alex. Haven't I proved that I want to help you? I can *still* help ... whatever it is you need to do. Just tell me.'

He shook his head, as if trying to clear his vision. The car's speed increased again. 'I need to get up into the mountains, up high. There's a killer up there – the destroyer of my family.' He screwed his face up as if in great pain. 'There's no one left now. My chance to speak to someone who knew me, the *me* I once was, is gone.' His balled fist banged the wheel. 'I don't exist.'

He put a hand to his temple and rubbed. The car jumped forward again, starting to bounce on the icy road, now doing well over a hundred.

Adira reached out again to touch his forearm. 'I can help you find her. I'm not leaving ... and you're not alone, Alex. I'll always be here for you.'

He didn't respond, but the car slowed.

Light snowflakes started to drift down and stick to the glass, and he switched on the wipers. Adira looked up at the low cloud cover. It was a cold morning, and would probably get colder. Up in the mountains, it would be freezing. *Alex might survive, but I won't*, she thought.

'Stop ... back up,' she said.

'No, there's no time.'

'Look, if we're going up there in the snow, we need supplies – hunting supplies.'

The car slowed to a cruising speed and then stopped. Alex stared at her, and she had the feeling he was looking deep inside her, reading her. After a moment, he nodded and reversed the car back down the road.

'Okay ... stop here,' she said when she saw the sign. 'Look – Carroll's Hunting Supplies. Perfect. You might not freeze up there, Alex, but I will – I'm a desert woman. Besides that, I like American knives; they're good steel.' She looked at him and smiled. 'And I'll let you keep the grenades you've been hanging onto.'

She expected some kind of response to her acknowledgment of his secret stash of weapons, but his face remained tight with barely suppressed hostility.

She gently squeezed his shoulder, feeling the knots of tension in the bunched muscles. 'Just one thing, Alex – how will we find who we're looking for?'

At last, Alex looked at her properly, but his expression made her sit back in her seat.

'I have a place to start,' he said. 'Besides, I can still smell it ... I'll know where to find it.'

It, not who. What exactly is it? Adira wondered.

*

The Infiniti G35 coasted to a halt a block from the street where the HAWCs had intercepted Adira and Alex. Its three occupants watched as the Asheville police interviewed residents who had gathered to complain about the early morning's events. After ten minutes or so, the small crowd dispersed, and the police drove slowly down the street and disappeared around the corner.

All three men left the vehicle and walked quickly to the center of the road. One bent down to stick his finger in a small pool of sticky red fluid. He rubbed it slowly between his thumb and forefinger before putting his finger into his mouth.

'Not Arcadian,' he said.

The three men stood there silently, ignoring the steadily building traffic, the cyclists and early morning joggers. The few people who passed them looked quickly away after the initial glance; perhaps because of the cratered skin on their faces, or the way steam seemed to rise from them in the cold morning air.

Like a single entity, the three men turned to stare at the dark doorway where Adira had concealed herself. They looked up and down the street, before their heads swiveled towards the animal hospital. Without a word spoken, they headed to the side of the building.

TWENTY-FIVE

Alex and Adira hunted through the aisles, throwing clothing over their arms as they went – lumber shirts, long johns, boots, socks. Alex stopped at a table covered in hunting knives, his eyes going to just one. He put the clothing down, drew the blade from its sheath and inhaled the scent of fresh oil. He hefted it and turned it over in his hand. 'This'll do.' It was a Blackjack hunting knife, surgically sharpened high-tensile steel, triple-rolled – a bear killer.

As the overhead lights glinted off the razor-sharp edge, Alex's vision turned inwards – he saw long steel coming down again and again, but against dark green fronds and vines ... he was hacking through a jungle. Someone called his name – he turned to see a huge soldier, fearsome-looking and taller than he was. He blinked at the memory, then saw his own reflection in the polished steel. As he watched, it blurred and altered. There were other faces now – the man and woman he had just seen in the street. *You're one of us, you dumb fuck*, the woman had yelled at him.

One of us – what does that mean? he wondered.

His mind sought the answer – and waves of images washed over him again. A dark tunnel, screaming soldiers, a desert, creatures that burrowed beneath the sand. Then that huge soldier again, hacking through jungle vines as thick as knotted cables.

Alex had no idea how long he stood there, frozen, before he felt someone touch his arm.

'You okay?'

'Huh?'

He saw Adira looking up at him, worried.

'Sure,' he told her.

She handed him a tissue. 'Your nose is bleeding.'

He nodded his thanks and held it to his nose. In his other hand, he still grasped the hunting knife. He knew he was going to need it.

*

General Meir Shavit watched Adira and Alex Hunter exit the sporting goods store and climb into their vehicle. The intercepted VELA satellite images were as clear as if they'd been snapped from across the road instead of tens of thousands of miles above the Earth.

Obtaining the pictures had been easy; Israeli intelligence had been accessing the high-value strategic images for years. Getting access to Alex Hunter's sealed files from the technical safes at USSTRATCOM had been more difficult. Shavit had assembled a small group of specialist technicians who had been worming their way through firewalls, trapdoors and spring-loaded tech traps for weeks searching unsuccessfully ... until now. The files had been exactly what Shavit had needed. Hunter's mother's address had immediately been highlighted by the predictive software program as a ninety-nine per cent probability match for likely destinations the pair would head to next.

Shavit lifted the phone, but paused before keying in the numbers. He felt they were no nearer to securing his niece, and that a bloody showdown was imminent. The initial interaction had resulted in three dead agents. He had already given Salamon warning to be careful of the man they pursued. Perhaps the agent's ego had outweighed caution, or was it simply that a good warrior had met a better one?

He had consented to sending Salamon a replacement team; and the new agents had been picked for their specialization in unarmed combat and marksmanship – he knew Salamon's first instruction would be a takedown order on Hunter. He had cautioned his man about extending that order to Adira. He doubted now that she would come in without a fight, but if it was necessary to incapacitate her physically, then so be it. She would live. Alex Hunter was a different matter; capturing him alive was going to be far too difficult and costly. Besides, once the former HAWC had been taken down, Adira would have no reason to fight, or to stay on foreign soil.

Shavit brought the phone to his ear, pressed a string of numbers and waited for the line to be routed through to its destination.

'Salamon, I have an address for you.'

*

Logan took notes as he listened to the rugged-looking FBI agent's explanation as to how he and his strange-looking sidekick had managed to be in town for less than an hour before getting all shot up. Apparently, the FBI had been investigating a series of disappearances up and down the Appalachian slopes, and on the agents' arrival in Asheville someone had taken pot shots at them from a moving car. They hadn't got a look at the shooters so couldn't tell whether the incident was related to their investigation, or just some tanked-up jackass with too much whisky under his belt. Both agents had refused medical treatment, even though the stains on their clothes indicated pretty deep wounds – bloody painful, Logan bet. But both seemed to be moving freely, so it wasn't his problem.

He sat back and folded his huge arms across his chest. 'Bit early in the season for drunken snow-blowers to be in town, throwing up on the sidewalks and shooting up the street signs. And I can't see one of the locals shooting at anyone ... unless you just got caught cheating with their wife.' He looked at the woman, Franks, and grinned. 'Or husband.'

Franks's face turned a couple of degrees harder. *Oops*, Logan thought, and dropped his smile and cleared his throat. He made another note: *FBI sense of humor = zero*.

Jack Hammerson had stopped talking, but Logan continued to stare into the agent's unwavering eyes for a few seconds. His police nose told him something wasn't right, but he couldn't quite put his finger on what that might be. Still, they were the good guys, so they said, and they certainly looked formidable. Every man, woman and dog was welcome to join his investigation right about now.

'Thank you, Agent Hammerson,' he said. 'Let me make a few calls and I'll be right back.'

As he got to his feet, he noticed both agents watching him like they were hungry predators, as if studying every inch of him to identify his strengths and weaknesses. The woman, if that's what she was, made him feel especially uncomfortable. He hoped they checked out; he didn't want to have to try to put cuffs on either of them.

*

Hammerson and Franks waited in silence while the Asheville police chief went out to check their identification. The FBI profiles they'd provided were perfect, and their reproduction IDs came with a divert and intercept technology net over the whole area, which meant any reference checks would be re-routed to their own information centers in Nebraska. Their back stories would survive a far more detailed scrutiny than Chief Logan would be able to bring to bear.

Hammerson reached forward to touch the gouge in his thigh – as expected, no pain and no stiffness. Both he and Franks had covered their wounds with battlefield skin-sheets, plastic-like adhesive patches that were infused with steroids, painkillers and antibiotics. The wound simply felt like it ceased to exist, and rapidly healed beneath the synthetic polymer sheet.

Logan came back into the room with two of his officers, and handed back their IDs.

'Sorry for the inconvenience, but it's unusual for the Feebies to pay us a visit,' he said. 'Especially over a few simple disappearances ahead of the coming snow season.'

Hammerson got to his feet as he took back the small leather ID wallets and studied Logan's face. He liked the man; he seemed old school, just like himself, although he was clearly out of condition. He also seemed in a hurry and under pressure. Hammerson didn't have the time to spend waiting for the man to open up; he needed to give him a little push.

'We're always happy to help the locals – offer our expertise, technology and hardware,' he said, looking the chief in the eyes. 'Now, tell us about Kathleen Hunter. The information we received is that the disappearance was far from simple. In fact, all the disappearances are about as far from simple as you can get.'

Hammerson was fishing; all he knew was that Kathleen Hunter disappeared in undefined circumstances, but the man was too edgy over a single case. There was a lot more he was keeping bottled up.

'We don't have to tell these stiff-collars anything, Chief,' the smaller, moustachioed officer cut in. 'This ain't a federal issue, it's Asheville jurisdiction. End of story.'

Franks got to her feet. 'Wanna bet?'

'Shut up, Markenson,' Logan said, without turning to his officer.

The officer glared at Franks, who smiled. The second, taller officer stepped up beside Markenson and folded his arms. Franks turned side-on and flexed her hands, still smiling.

Hammerson spoke to her. 'At ease.' He could tell she was still pissed after the roughing up Senesh had given her. Nothing she'd like more than an opportunity to let off some steam by caving in a few heads.

He turned back to Logan, his eyes boring into the man. 'We know the disappearances are not routine; we know there have been several abductions. There are identical MOs all over the state. We're here to help, but we'll only offer it once, Chief Logan.'

The chief held Hammerson's eyes for nearly a full minute, before exhaling – probably with a great deal of relief, Hammerson thought. He motioned to the couch. 'Sit down, Agent Hammerson, Agent Franks. Fact is, I could do with your help, and I've got a story to tell that's getting weirder by the hour.'

Logan talked for fifteen minutes, detailing the missing cattle and domestic animals, the disappearance of the Wilson girl, and then the bloody scene at Kathleen Hunter's place and her disappearance. He frowned as he ran through the scientific information he'd been given, seeming doubtful of its veracity, and finished with Amanda Jordan's description of the thing that had attacked her and her husband, who was still missing.

Hammerson sat like stone as he absorbed the information. When Logan had finished, he said, 'Tell me about the scientific consultants again.'

Logan repeated the names, and Hammerson nodded and smiled. Logan lifted his eyebrows. 'You know them?'

'I know one of them – Matthew Kearns.'

Markenson, perched on the edge of Logan's desk, scoffed. 'He's a know-it-all asshole.'

Hammerson ignored him. 'We've worked with him before; he's okay. Where is he now?'

'In town, I hope,' Logan replied. He turned to his deputy. 'Call them will you, Ollie – make sure they're not planning on doing anything stupid.'

Markenson got to his feet. 'Sure, which one?'

Logan scribbled down some numbers and handed the paper to him. 'All of them.'

Markenson headed out, and Logan turned back to Hammerson. 'I gave 'em a blast after they brought me their cockamamie theory on the disappearances.' He snorted with remorse. 'Now I'm thinking I've got a problem on that mountain that looks like it might just be ...' He grimaced and raised his hands palms up, before interlocking his fingers and bringing his large hands down onto his desk.

Hammerson realized he didn't want to put into words what his imagination was telling him.

Markenson poked his head back into the office. 'No answer, Chief, for any of 'em.'

Logan sucked in a deep breath and Hammerson saw him sag. He sat forward. 'What are you thinking, Chief?'

Logan shook his head and exhaled loudly. 'It's my fault – I kicked 'em out, told 'em they needed more proof for their theories. I bet they've headed on up to the high slopes to get that proof.' He stood. 'We need to get up there too, with some firepower, and head off Kearns and his team.' He sighed and rubbed his face. 'Problem is, they'll have half a day on us – and there's no phone reception up there. Best I can do is try to catch up with 'em before they get into too much trouble.'

Hammerson tapped his chin with a gnarled fist. He suddenly knew where Alex Hunter was going. If Kathleen Hunter had been attacked, perhaps taken, by whatever was up on that mountain, then Hunter would find her, or what was left of her. And then he'd take his revenge. If it was up on those slopes, then Hunter would be heading that way too. Hammerson smiled ruefully; *send a beast to kill a beast*, he thought.

'We'll come with you,' he told the police chief.

Logan shook his head. 'Not in that gear – you'll freeze. Look, Agent Hammerson, with all due respect, this isn't gonna be like tracking down some psycho on a New York street, or an accountant who's swindled his bank out of a million bucks. The Dome will be freezing and pretty inhospitable, even at this time of year.'

Hammerson laughed softly. 'I think you'll find we'll manage, Chief. In fact, I insist.'

Markenson eyeballed Franks and made a sceptical noise in the back of his throat.

Logan glanced from Hammerson's rugged face to the brawny and fearsome-looking Casey Franks. 'Okay,' he said, 'but at least allow us to supply you with some cold-weather gear.'

Hammerson shook his head. 'We've got kit. Like I said, don't worry about us, we'll be ready.'

Logan nodded. 'We should get moving. Gonna take us a while to catch up to them, if we can at all. I just hope we're not too late.'

Hammerson got to his feet. 'Would a chopper help?'

TWENTY-SIX

S arah turned the car as Thomas directed, onto a track that was little more than a pair of ruts pressed into the cold, wet grass. Matt jammed his hands up under his armpits – they shook slightly, and much as he tried to convince himself it was from the cold, the knot in his belly told him otherwise. Matt peered through the windscreen from the back seat, where he and Charles were jammed in with their equipment. He noticed that the blanket the old Indian was draped in smelled like cigarette smoke and camphor. Next to him, Charles was holding a long handgun and what looked like a flat plastic lunchbox. As the car bounced into and out of a pothole, the gun poked into Matt's leg.

'Careful with that, cowboy,' Matt said.

Thomas turned in his seat, looked briefly at the gun and made a small sound of contempt in his throat.

Charles shrugged. 'It's okay … tranquilizer only.' He turned the gun sideways, forcing Matt to recoil to avoid the barrel. 'It's an X2 – aluminium, gas-based dart pistol. Twelve shots – short range but silent and very accurate.'

Thomas shook his head.

Sarah spoke over her shoulder. 'What chemical mix are you using?'

Charles opened the small plastic case, and smiled down at a row of four pencil-long darts, each filled with a small amount of clear fluid. 'I doubt we'll actually find anything up there, but just in case I decided on a neuromuscular paralytic – Pavulon actually, 1.44 micrograms. It's pretty powerful stuff, but a good choice for larger … um … targets. It should give us immediate knockdown, and, depending on the size of the creature, at least two hours for study.'

Sarah briefly turned, frowning. 'Pavulon? That's one of the drugs they use in lethal injections, isn't it? How do you know the dosage is right?'

Charles shrugged. 'I don't – everything we're doing is a first. I've prepared the dosage based on a 1200-pound animal. We just have to hope its physiology reacts like any normal mammal.'

Thomas Red Cloud looked at the gun again, then at Charles. 'How big is your anus, Mr. Schroder?'

'What?' Charles looked from Matt to Sarah, and then at Thomas. He frowned. 'Uhh, I didn't quite catch that, Thomas.'

'I asked you how big your anus is. I just want to be sure the gun will fit there after you've fired it at the Chiye-tanka and it's taken from you. 'Cause that's where it's gonna end up.'

Matt burst out laughing, feeling his anxiety lift a little, and patted Charles on the shoulder. 'See, he likes your idea as well.'

Charles pulled a face before resting the long-barreled dart gun on the seat beside him. 'Very funny, Chief. At least I came prepared. What did you bring – some more magic spells and woofle-dust?'

'Yes, Mr. Schroder. I brought the dust of my ancestors, magic bones from Geronimo, and a spirit amulet made from the hair of a wild buffalo.'

Matt sat forward. 'You're shitting me. Really?'

'No, you pair of assholes, I brought a .45 Colt Anaconda.' Thomas looked into Charles's face. 'I do not intend to study this creature, Mr. Schroder. It is the slayer of my ancestors. I intend to put a hole in it the size of a dinner plate.'

Sarah stopped the car. 'That's as far as we can go.' She turned and raised her eyebrows. 'Okay, I guess that's the team-bonding session out the way. Anyone for a nice freezing hike?'

*

The three men returned to their vehicle. They had stuffed the veterinarian's body into one of the cages at the rear of the surgery. It would be hours before anyone found his beaten and tortured remains, and by then they would be out of the city and closing in on their target.

The man in the back seat removed his sunglasses and cap and examined his ulcerated hands in the semi-light that came in through the tinted windows. 'It hurts.'

'Graham will fix us,' said his colleague in the front passenger seat. 'Put your gloves on, we need to hurry.'

The man in the back nodded and slowly pulled his gloves back on over the oozing flesh.

*

Casey Franks narrowed her eyes as the enormous chopper settled onto its three sets of double tires. Beside her, Officer Markenson pulled his hood up to protect his ears from the biting down-draught.

'Holy shit, do you think you could have gotten anything bigger?' he said disagreeably, folding his arms against the swirling icy air.

The single pilot gave Hammerson a thumbs-up; the HAWC leader nodded in return.

Franks felt a surge of pride as the behemoth settled into the cold earth. At nearly 100 feet in length, the CH-53 Stallion had been one of the US army's most formidable transport machines when in service. Despite the fact that Hammerson had raised it up from one of the aeronautical boneyards where newly retired equipment went to be deconstructed and recycled, the chopper still bristled with rocket tubes, machine-gun pivots and sensory equipment, and the tilted rear fin gave it a modern appearance.

She and Hammerson trotted to the open door, climbed in and waited just inside the frame. Logan took this as a sign to load his own officers and pointed to the door, his words lost in the swirling wind. His men ran towards the chopper in a hunched jog, even though the still spinning propeller was at least fifteen feet over their heads.

Franks dropped her duffel bag and flexed her hands to get the circulation going. Inside, it was warmer, but only just. Most of the equipment had been removed from the cavernous interior, leaving a row of attached metal seats down each side of the hold, a few small steel cabinets and netting on the walls, and two powerful-looking winches at either side door.

Hammerson motioned for Chief Logan to join him in the cockpit. Franks watched with amusement as Markenson and his fellow officers took seats along the opposite side of the craft from her. She doubted Logan's men were keen on opening up the social lines anytime soon. Suited her; she wasn't here to make friends.

As Hammerson passed her, he said briefly, 'Suit up.'

She nodded and lifted the duffel bag to the metal seat and unzipped it. She caught Markenson looking at her and paused to smile at him and slightly purse her lips. The moustachioed officer mouthed, *Fuck off,* and stuck his hands in his pockets to keep warm, using his legs to hold his rifle.

Franks kept up her smile – she loved these hard cases. She turned to face him and started to remove her clothing. In no time she was down to her underwear. Most of the men acted like she was invisible, but Markenson shook his head and made a sour face at one of his fellow officers.

She caught one of the men sniggering and leering at her, and turned square on to him, her hands on her hips, displaying her muscled body, its skin crisscrossed and dotted with scars and burns and the swirls of multicolored tattoos, her flattened breasts that were more like a weightlifter's pectorals, the thick white bush crowding out of her underwear. She thrust her tongue out in an aggressively lewd gesture and the man quickly dropped his head to examine something on the floor.

Tiring of the game, she turned to pull her cold-terrain suit from the bag. The dark, close-fitting overalls looked like a combination of wetsuit and insulated body armor, with inch-thick flat ribbing around the torso, thighs and upper arms. The ribbing allowed for maximum movement, while its overlapping structure provided protection. The suits had built-in thermal controls and were fully woven through with a Kevlar fiber; they'd keep the wearer warm in temperatures down to twenty below and also stop a high-caliber slug.

Franks pulled on gloves with similar impact-resistant material over the back of the hand and knuckles. Then, machine-like, she slid two guns into holsters built into the low hips of her suit. She sheathed a long-bladed Ka-Bar into a holster on one thigh, and put a short-bladed Ka-Bar into a holster on the other. Finally, she inserted numerous electronics into concealed pouches and pockets.

She felt good, the suit's warmth immediately infusing her muscles with mobility. She rolled her wounded shoulder, and threw a few air punches, her hands up in a fighter's stance. She spun quickly and punched a metal cabinet, her fist making a deep dent in the steel.

She smiled and nodded to herself. 'Oh yeah.' Then winked at Markenson. 'Let's go do some damage.'

*

Jack Hammerson tapped the pilot on the shoulder and held up three fingers: *Three minutes until takeoff.* The pilot nodded and began his pre-takeoff check.

The blocky HAWC commander sat down, placed some earphones over his head, and motioned Logan to the seat next to him. The police chief strapped himself in and put on his own phones.

Hammerson's voice came through the headset. 'We're in your hands, Chief. Where to?'

Logan pulled from his pocket a small map that had been folded open to show a topographic contour chart of greater Asheville. He placed the map on Hammerson's leg and pointed. 'Far as we can tell, everything seemed to start here.' He jabbed his finger at the center of a series of tight green circles that indicated a high, steep mountainous area. 'The Black Dome. It's where the Jordan couple were initially attacked. If we work through our incident timeline, everything seems to radiate out from that event.'

Hammerson read some of the numbers on the map, then looked out the window. 'The Dome peak is over 6000 feet, and that cloud cover looks down to about 5000. We're gonna have to do some climbing if we need to get to the top.'

Logan pointed at the map's grid lines. 'Too steep to set down up there. I'm guessing we'll need to jump?'

Hammerson grinned and nodded.

Logan grinned back. 'Pick-up?'

Hammerson shook his head. 'Chopper's heading back. We'll be walking home, big fella.'

Logan laughed, then looked around the large military machine, and back at Hammerson's hand where it rested on the map. The knuckles were raised and callused, the fingers large and blunt.

'You're not really city Feds, are you?' he asked.

Hammerson seemed to think over his answer for a few moments, then smiled and shook his head.

'Military?'

Hammerson shrugged.

'What's going on? Why are you really here?'

Hammerson handed back the map and his face became serious. 'To capture a beast ... before too many people get hurt.'

TWENTY-SEVEN

Alex switched off the engine and sat staring at the small house. He'd seen it before – the bed of flowers bordering the front deck, the swing seat on the porch with a pillow at one end, the worn blanket on the boards in front of it that had once held a large dog. Everything was still there and he remembered it all.

He got out of the car and walked trance-like towards the front door, where he stopped to look back at the slopes, now bathed in midmorning sunlight. There was a large rock up on the hill; he had lain there looking down at this very spot ... *When? Months ago ... years?*

He ripped away the police tape at the door and grabbed the handle, pushing hard until he heard the crunch of old wood separating as the metal tongue of the locking mechanism tore through it. The door swung open and he stood for a few seconds inhaling the scents of the house, each one familiar – old smoke and cold ash from the fireplace, his mother's perfume and soap, biscuits. He stepped inside, then half-turned to look at Adira, who was still on the front deck, carefully scanning the slopes surrounding the house. He ignored her and went into the living room.

The pictures on the mantelpiece drew him like powerful magnets. He lifted two. The first was a picture of himself, much younger, with hair falling over his forehead and smiling as if every day held nothing but sunshine. The other was an older photo of a man, shirt off and strongly muscled. He was about the age Alex was now, and it could have been him except the man's features were slightly different. He stared hard at the image, willing the memories to come faster.

There was momentary pain and then they came flooding – he saw a very young boy, himself, and the man pushing him on a swing. He loosened his grip on the chains for a second and flew to the ground, landing face first in the dirt. The man lifted him up and brushed him off. 'You're not hurt, you're strong,' he said. Alex remembered that he hadn't cried, that he'd felt proud at managing to hold in the hurt. The man was his father ... Jim Hunter. What happened to him?

Alex lifted a third picture from the mantelpiece – his father again, but here he was standing with another young man. Alex recognized the square jaw and angular-shaped head, even though the man he'd recently seen was much older. He and his father had their arms around each other's shoulders, friends. Alex shook his head. *Always there in the background – who are you?* He stared hard at the face. *Next time we meet, you'll tell me,* he thought.

He heard Adira moving from room to room. Judging by the short time she spent in each of them, she was satisfying her security concerns rather than exploring. He replaced the pictures and went quickly around the room, pulling open drawers and cabinet doors. A small cardboard box tingled beneath his fingers, demanding his attention. He carefully opened the lid: it held papers – Kathleen and Jim's marriage certificate, his own birth certificate, some school reports, and a death notice from the American government. Alex read it slowly; the language was bureaucratic and cautious, giving little information other than the fact that Lieutenant Jim Hunter had served his country honorably and had been killed in action. No remains were returned for burial.

His mother's voice came to him then, her tone sad: *His job was to protect us, all of us. There was ... an accident, Alex. He was a hero. Be proud of him ... remember him.*

As he touched the last piece of paper in the box, his head began to swim and the air in the room seemed to distort and blur. It was if his own body was warning him, readying him for the shock. It was another death notification, almost a duplicate of the one he'd just read, except this one was written nearly thirty years later and showed his own name. Alex Hunter, killed in action; again, no body retrieved.

Kathleen Hunter would have been devastated; first her husband killed in action, and then her only son. Except he wasn't dead. Why had the US military lied to her; caused her so much pain?

He let the box fall and looked around the familiar room. 'What happened to me? Why did they make me a ghost? Now I don't exist.' He looked across at the photos. 'We're all gone, all dead now.'

Adira appeared beside him and tried to take his arm. 'Alex, are you okay?'

He pushed past her and went out into the yard. He wanted to yell, to explode.

There was a pile of logs, freshly cut, and more tape wound around the outside of a small outbuilding. The ground was trampled there, and he was drawn to it. As he approached, a smell rose up around him, lifted by the morning's warmth – rank, acrid and bestial. It was the same stench he'd smelled on the dog's fur in the animal hospital.

His head pounded, and he reached down to grab some of the dirt and rub it between his fingers. *It* had been here. The ground had been raked clean, probably by the police forensics clean-up crew, but he could still sense the creature's presence.

He moved quickly to the edge of the tree line, and entered a few paces. He turned back to look at the small cottage. The beast had stood here, watching the house – watching *her*. He looked up at the trunk of the nearest large tree; about twelve feet up, a section of bark had been torn away. Alex visualized the creature hanging onto the tree in the dark, watching his mother inside the house, its blood lust building, its fingers closing on the outer layer of wood and ripping it free.

The impressions started to become more solid. Alex moved to the center of the trampled clearing. He saw Adira watching him from the back deck, but she kept her distance. To her, he was undoubtedly seeming more and more manic. He crouched down and closed his eyes. The impressions became images ... and then he saw his mother, saw her lifting her arms to protect her head, terrified of the thing that loomed over her. It attacked, lifted her body only to throw it to the ground, smashing her like a bundle of twigs. It lifted her rag-like body again to sniff it, then carried her away under its arm. She might have still been alive, but it was unlikely ...

The images faded and Alex stood up, his teeth gritted, a boiling anger exploding up from his belly. He lifted his head and roared. He had been kept from her; they had told her he was dead and then hidden him away. He doubled over as if in extreme pain. *If I'd been here, she might still be alive.*

*

Thomas moved up the snow-covered slope like a machine. Matt had to work hard to catch up to him. The old man was probably fifty years older but seemed in better condition than all three of them.

'It's getting colder,' he said when he was finally plodding alongside him.

'Yes, the cloud is falling lower – maybe more snow coming.'

Matt breathed hard, trying to keep pace with the old man. 'Thomas, I've been thinking back to the legend of the First People and the Great Ones. I've studied hundreds of ancient races and their cultural mythology, but I've never heard of that battle, or the warrior you called Tooantuh. Surprises me, considering it's literally in my backyard.'

Thomas grunted. 'You probably have, but didn't recognize it. I have heard the tale many times, and not only in the form of the legend told around Black Mountain. Like a lot of Native American history, it travels with the people and the tribes, and sometimes ends up far away from its first telling.' He turned his narrowed gaze on Matt. 'Ever hear of the Seven Devils Gorge?'

Matt nodded. 'Sure, the deepest gorge in North America. Also called Hell's Canyon.'

'Uh-huh. Well, you know the seven peaks on the Idaho side?' Thomas didn't wait for Matt's reply. 'Then you'll know they're called the Seven Devil Mountains. The tribes have a legend, handed down from the First People, about how they were formed. It tells of a time when the world was very young and the animals and men talked together. It also tells of seven brothers, evil giants, who lived in the forests. They were as tall as mountains, and the First People feared them because they stole and ate their children, then wore their heads around their necks like decorations. Each year the monsters came out of the forest and devoured all the children they could find. Mothers ran away with their babies, tried to hide them, but the giants still found many of them. The wise men in the villages feared that their tribe would soon be wiped out, and yet no one in all the land was brave enough to fight even one of the monsters.'

Thomas looked at Matt, perhaps checking he wasn't about to make fun of him. He didn't need to; Matt was spellbound by the tale.

'The final straw was when the giants took the king's favored child. The wise men of the tribe decided to ask the eagle to help them. They said to the king, "Eagle is our father; he will know how to kill these monsters." And he did. Eagle told the king to ask his best men to help him dig seven deep holes in the ground. When the giants next came out of the forest, they held their heads high, not bothering to look down for they feared nothing below them. Each fell into a hole, and no matter how he struggled, he could not break free and just became more tightly wedged.

'Eagle flew overhead and the giants roared out to him to free them, but he said to the monsters, "You have attacked the people, and eaten them. You must be punished for all time so that everyone who sees you will know what you have done. I will change you into mountains, as dark as your evil sins, and I will make a barrier to seal you inside and keep you from the people forever."

'With that, Eagle struck each giant on the head with his tips of his wings, and each fell silent and grew dark and even larger and turned into a mighty peak. Eagle lowered his talons and scraped the earth for many miles, creating a deep impassable gorge – the Devil's Gorge – so the monsters could never cross again to the world of man.'

Matt nodded. 'Of course, the stolen favored child – the princess of Jocassee. And I'm guessing the eagle was Tooantuh, the barrier was the sacred wall, and the seven dark peaks are Black Mountain and its surrounding peaks – it all fits.'

'Yes, Mr. Kearns, I believe this is another example of the story of Tooantuh and the defeat of the Great Ones.' Thomas exhaled loudly and stopped. 'We're here.'

Matt looked at where he was gesturing, into a green funnel-like gorge.

'It's a short cut,' the old man said, 'and our secret. You won't find it on any guide maps.'

Sarah and Charles caught up, and all four of them stood looking into the gorge. Perhaps hundreds of thousands of years ago, land had slipped to create a small ravine in the side of the mountain. Trees had grown up its sides and around its top, spreading their canopies over it. The result was a dark cave that ran for nearly one hundred feet, broader at the start, so Thomas told them, before funneling tighter and eventually opening out onto an alternative route to the Black Dome.

'Okay. Sorta cool ... I guess,' Matt said, gazing down into the dark crevasse but making no move towards it.

'This is where Tooantuh and the other warriors held their final battle with the Chiye-tanka before forcing it back into its lair,' Thomas said. He looked around briefly, then back at the three professors. 'Hundreds of the First People's warriors were massacred here.'

Sarah looked up at the sides of the slip valley and nodded slowly. 'Yes. Makes sense. Perfect killing zone – for one or both parties.' She looked behind her, back down the steep slope. 'Is this the only way up?'

'Of course not,' Thomas said. 'But the only way if you want to save about three hours' climbing.'

'Okay, we've come this far,' Matt said drawing in a deep breath. He took a step forward, but Thomas grabbed his arm, making him jump.

'Wait ... I need to make it safe for us to pass through.'

The old man took a piece of cloth from his pocket, closed his eyes and started to chant. He hopped from foot to foot, waving the material in a circular motion above his head. He finished, opened one eye to peer at his companions, then burst out laughing and blew his nose wetly on the handkerchief.

'You guys really do beat all. C'mon, I'm not spending the night up here.'

None of them moved. Thomas stuck his fists under his arms, flapped his elbows up and down and made clucking sounds.

Matt looked at Charles. 'He's really something, isn't he?'

Charles shook his head, and led the way into the dark gully.

*

Alex dived to the ground and tunneled into the snow the instant he heard the helicopter's approach. With just his head exposed, he watched the gigantic green machine float above him. Information flooded his mind: US-model CH-53 transport helicopter, seventy-nine feet in length, pinion-based 50-cal machine guns, both missing, and launch tubes for AIM-9 sidewinder missiles, also empty. He immediately knew the machine's strengths and weaknesses should he need to take control of it, or act against it.

It passed over low enough for him to see inside the cockpit. *He* was in there, the man from the photograph. Alex felt a rush of adrenaline, but couldn't tell whether his senses were recognizing a forgotten friend or giving him a warning. He tried to dredge up more information – fragments of conversations, images – but just as something coherent began to form, a fist of pain crushed it. Until he knew more, he would stay out of sight and trust his instincts. He watched as the machine headed towards the dark peak, now shrouded in low cloud.

When it had disappeared, he turned to look behind him. A mile or so down the steep slope, Adira was struggling through the snow, her athletic body fatigued from trying to keep pace with him. They had a way to go yet, high into the dark forest, and he wondered if she would make it.

A boiling fury welled up inside him every time he thought of that creature attacking his mother. He felt her agony, could see the terror on her face as the monster loomed over her, heard her screams as it brutalized her small frame. That voice inside his head was always there now, urging him to kill the beast, destroy it, crush its shattered bones to dust. He felt that his mind might destroy itself if he did not sate that urge to kill the creature.

The snow started to melt around him as his body temperature heated well above normal. His head throbbed constantly. He pulled himself out of the snow tunnel, and picked up the smell of death in the cold air. His senses screamed a warning and he looked around slowly, his body tense, until he found the source of the odor. A riot of exploded meat and bone matter adorned a tree trunk off to his left, along with fragments of red and yellow material. He stared at the remains and the image of his quarry formed again in his mind.

Grinding his teeth, he burst from the snow in a blur of pumping legs and clenched fists. He sprinted up the steep incline, kicking up snow behind him, dodging trees and boulders on his way to the Black Dome.

*

The helicopter slowed as the pilot searched for a drop spot, its rotor chopping and spreading the icy fog below them. Above, the mist grew thicker. With twilight rapidly approaching, it would soon be an impenetrable black curtain.

Hammerson used the thermal scanner in the cockpit to trace for heat signatures on the mountain. 'Got some strong readings about ten miles up,' he told Logan. 'Multiple bodies – mass profiles indicate human. Also a larger mass, or at least a big thermal signature – shape undefined. Not sure what that is.'

Logan raised his eyebrows. 'I know what I hope it's not.' He pointed at the contour lines on the screen. 'That's about where we think the Jordan photographs were taken, somewhere on the way to the Black Dome.'

Hammerson narrowed his eyes, studying the terrain and the surrounding geological formations, looking for trap or ambush zones, defensive positions, or steep drop-offs. He noted that where the heat signatures were located, there was a near vertical rock face on one side and a bloody great drop on the other. *Good for defence, as long as you've got a back door*, he thought.

The pilot spoke. 'Requesting orders, sir.'

'Find us a space to thread our way down,' Hammerson said.

He took one last look at the thermal scanner, then out through the window at the cloud cover and the terrain. 'Steep. Much as I don't like it, we're going to have to split up. We need to be up there ASAP, and your boys will never keep pace with us.'

'Yup, figured that. We should stay in contact though.' Logan pulled his phone free and held it up. 'Not much good up here.'

Hammerson nodded and reached into a pouch pocket. He pulled out a small box holding several flesh-colored buttons. He pulled one free, fiddled with it for a moment, then handed it to Logan and pointed to his ear, before holding one of his earpieces away from his head to show he already had a button inserted.

Chief Logan looked at it briefly, then took off his headphones and stuck it into his right ear.

'Online; check 1-2–3,' Hammerson said.

Logan nodded and gave a thumbs-up.

The pilot motioned with his head. 'Ten o'clock, some open ground – not enough to land. Going to have to drop from approximately twenty feet.'

Hammerson nodded, and pressed his ear button. 'Franks, gonna be a rappel in five. Prepare and instruct the officers.'

*

Franks looked out the small window and moved her eyes quickly over the piling snow, taking in how steep the slope was. She reached into a pouch at her side to remove a black cylinder, which she screwed onto the end of her handgun.

'Silencers – are you shitting me?' Markenson scoffed. 'Who's gonna hear? The fucking bears?'

Franks spoke without looking up from her task. 'Just a precaution when operating in a steep snow theater.'

Markenson made another sound of derision in his throat.

Franks looked at him. 'Ever seen an avalanche, Officer Markenson? Ever seen a 100-foot-high wall of snow and ice moving at about 200 miles per hour? Did you know that if it doesn't immediately crush you or freeze you solid, you can be entombed in the ice until your tongue dry-freezes in your mouth.'

When the man made no response, she snorted and went back to her task.

TWENTY-EIGHT

Matt, Sarah and Charles stood hunched over, hands on their knees, at the start of the slip path, sucking in deep breaths and blowing huge plumes of steam out into the freezing air. Thomas walked cautiously ahead, then paused and looked from the slip path up at the scoured mountainside. He made a low rumbling sound of annoyance deep in his chest.

'This is new. It can only have happened in the last few months. The cave mouth should not be exposed like this. This place was originally chosen because it was hidden, known only to our people.'

Matt noticed Thomas reach for the small leather pouch hanging around his neck. He rubbed it between his fingers as he gazed at the uneven new path that led around the side of the mountain, formed by the settling of the fallen rocks, soil and debris.

Sarah dropped her pack and leaned backwards, stretching her spine, then stared out over the edge of the path. 'That is *some* view.'

Though they were up at the cloud line and surrounded by heavy mist, the lower peaks were visible, their greenish-black trees dusted with snow. At this height of about 6500 feet, at least 1000 feet above the next-highest point, the scenery was awe-inspiring.

Sarah motioned with her arm out over the misty panorama. 'How's that make you two city boys feel?'

Matt scoffed and walked closer to the edge. 'City boys now, is it? Listen, Sheena, Queen of the Jungle, for your information, I've climbed 15,000 feet to the Chachapoyas Ruins in the Andes Mountains – and they weren't called the Cloud People for nothing, you know. Then there was the time I went below the ice in the Antarctic – that was no party either. Another time –'

'Shut up,' Thomas said, staring ahead along the path. 'You all talk too much. Listen ...'

Matt and his colleagues quieted immediately, their heads turning towards Thomas. They waited in silence while the old Indian turned his head first one way, then the other, his eyes closed, his head slightly cocked.

Matt watched the old man, marveling at how he kept his body perfectly still, only his head slowly turning. He was like a graying stump of an old tree on the snow-covered path. At last, he shook his head and looked at them, his mouth turned down.

'It's gone now, but there was definitely something there.'

Matt frowned. 'What was it? What did you hear?'

Thomas shrugged, his hand going again to the pouch around his neck. 'Don't know. Sounded a little like ... music.'

Matt noticed that Sarah had her eyes closed, as if listening for something too. She opened them and frowned. 'Yes, I thought there was something ...' She shook her head, as if the thought had evaporated.

Thomas stepped out onto the path, his feet making scrunching sounds in the fresh snow. He stayed close to the rock wall, clearly not trusting the stability of the edge. A few paces along, he paused to feel around with his foot, then kneeled and began pulling at something. He gave up and settled for clearing away some of the snow.

Matt plodded towards him as fast as he could, and hunched down beside him. Sarah and Charles quickly followed. Thomas shook his head and reached up to grip the small pouch again.

'This is worse than I thought.' He sighed. 'I should have known better.'

He took off his pack and pulled out a pink bath towel, which he spread out on the snow. 'Give me a hand.'

Matt helped the old man to heft several cinderblock-sized pieces of stone onto the towel, Thomas groaning from the effort. When they were done, he stood slowly and exhaled.

'They must all be out,' he said. 'All the wall stones have been removed. I did not bring enough cement to replace this many.'

Sarah leaned forward to examine the stones. 'They all look different.'

Matt pointed at one of the roughly square blocks. 'This one's fairly new – maybe a few hundred years old. But this one's probably ten times that. And this one,' he indicated a stone that was crumbling and black with age, 'well, it's probably the oldest representation of Paleo-Indian stonemasonry I've ever seen in my life.' He placed his fingertips on the ancient stonework.

Thomas made a sound of confirmation in his throat. 'It must be from the inner wall.' He looked over his shoulder, before turning back to Matt. 'According to the legend, there were three layers of wall – the first to contain the beast, the second to bind its spirit, and the third to keep *us* out.' He ran a gnarled hand over the oldest stone's rough edges. 'The walls were mighty; they needed to be, considering what was being sealed inside. The inner layer of stone has never been seen since it was originally built by the First People.' He sat back on his haunches and looked up into their faces. 'I never expected ...' he shook his head. 'It's too much work. I can't rebuild it.'

They all stood silently for a moment. Matt pushed the stone over, and over again. It was blank on all sides. 'This doesn't have the same carved warning as the outer stones.'

'That's odd,' Thomas said. 'Perhaps the ancient ones felt the warning wasn't needed on the inner walls ... or maybe the rest of the tale is in the cave itself.'

He looked up, and the three scientists followed his eyes. A triangular-shaped black maw was just visible in the side of the mountain, before the steep angle of the cliff swallowed it up.

Matt wiped his hands and stood up. 'What now?'

Thomas got to his feet too. 'Now ... we're fucked. Unless you brought some dynamite.'

He pulled a ten-pound bag of cement out of his pack and dropped it onto the path. It instantly sank into the snow. 'We should get out of here.'

'Wait, wait, wait,' Charles said, holding up his hands. 'Look, Mr. Red Cloud, I'm still not totally convinced that the Gigantopithecus even came out of that hole. Seems unbelievable that something could survive for millennia walled up in a cave; and I doubt it's been brought back to life somehow. These creatures were undoubtedly troglo*philes,* but I'm sure they weren't fully troglobiont.'

Thomas blinked at Charles, then shook his head slowly. 'Sonny,' he said, as if talking to a child on the verge of a tantrum, 'I don't understand a word of what you just said. But the stones came out of that cave there, followed by something larger, which then went back in. Do you know what dried blood looks like, Mr. Schroder?'

Charles's head moved in a gesture that could have indicated yes, no or both.

'Well, sonny, it looks like that.' Thomas pointed to a large streak of rusty brown on the wall about twenty feet along the path. 'Yep, just like that. I reckon something dragged fresh meat into that hole up there.'

Sarah put her hands on her hips. 'Fresh meat. Great. That's it – we're leaving.'

Thomas nodded at her. 'I agree, Ms Sommer. We need to make our way back down and work out what to bring with us next time. I was serious about the dynamite.' He looked up at the sky. 'We've only a few hours until we lose the light. This time of year, twilight comes around three o'clock.'

Charles looked from Sarah to Thomas, his face twisted into a mask of disbelief. 'What? No! We've got nothing – no samples, no pictures, no proof. Matt, buddy, c'mon, back me on this. We need to take a look. For Chrissake, *you're* the guy that freakin' dragged me out here.'

Matt looked up at the rock wall, then back at his friend. He pulled off his knitted cap and scratched his head, thinking.

'You want to go *into* the cave?' Thomas said incredulously. 'What exactly do you think you'll find in there, Mr. Schroder? Other than a lot of bones, maybe fresh bones ... maybe soon your own bones.'

'Sorry, Charles,' Matt said. 'He's right. We're not prepared to go into a cave – believe me, I've been caving before and you need a truckload more equipment than we've brought. Besides, I get the feeling that if we run across the Gigantopithecus, it isn't exactly going to happily say hello in sign language, like Koko the ape.'

But Charles was furiously shaking his head. He looked up at the cave mouth, seeming to measure the angle, as though planning to try to run up the wall by himself.

'For God's sake, Charles – can't you feel it?' Sarah said. 'Can't you smell it? There's a large carnivore in this area, maybe not a troglobiont but probably nocturnal. We aren't ready to deal with it out in the open, in the light, let alone in the fucking dark. I thought we'd just be taking some long-distance photographs, collecting spore samples and maybe footprints. But climbing into its lair?' She made a chopping motion with her hand. 'No way!'

She turned and walked a few paces back towards the cliff wall, her arms wrapped around herself, then stopped and crouched down to the snow.

'There's something else here,' she said. 'I felt my foot press down on it.'

She dug around for a few seconds, then lifted her prize slowly, her face turning into a mask of horror. 'Oh. Oh no ... look.' It was a small pink rubber boot. Sarah's hand was shaking as she held it. 'The Wilson girl – she was only about five, I think.'

She held the boot out to Thomas, who just looked away, muttering something. Sarah stood and looked up and down the path, holding the boot out as though offering it to its owner. 'Emma,' she called, then louder, 'Emma!'

Thomas shook his head, put his hands over his ears and walked a few paces back along the path.

'Foxes pick up junk, you know,' Matt said. 'Maybe one of them brought it up here.'

'So do apes,' Charles said.

'No!' Sarah yelled, her face turning red.

Both Matt and Charles froze as the echo bounced around them.

Matt turned to Charles. 'Way to go, Charlie Brown. You didn't need to say that bit about apes out loud, you know.'

'Shut up, all of you.' Thomas had turned back towards them. 'I can hear that damned music again. Everyone, spread out along the path. Let's see if we can determine where it's coming from.'

Sarah's eyes went wide for a moment, then she nodded vigorously and headed further up the path. Matt walked a few paces back the way they'd come, towards the edge of the drop-off. Charles did the same in the opposite direction, closer to the cave wall. Thomas stayed where he was in the center of the newly formed track.

As Matt went to pull his boot from the snow to take another step, he heard something just above the low moan of the wind. He paused and listened, and heard it again – a tinkling sound that seemed to rise as the wind did. He slowly took the step, pulled the hood of his parka away from one ear and turned his head slightly – there it was again. He raised his hand. 'I got it.'

Charles confirmed straight after that he also could hear a faint sound.

'I can hear it now,' Sarah said.

They all waited in silence, watching Thomas. He slowly turned his head back and forth, his eyes closed. He opened them and looked at each of the young scientists. 'Point to where you think the sound is coming from.'

Matt, Charles and Sarah stayed silent for another moment, then each raised an arm, fingers pointing. At the same time, Thomas raised his own arm. He grunted as he saw that all four of them were pointing to the cave opening directly above them.

*

Bill Logan punched the harness release disc on his chest and the straps fell away, to be immediately drawn back up inside the helicopter. It had been a stomach-churning drop in the swirling and freezing air, powdery snow blowing ferociously around them. Rappelling down onto a slope of about forty-five degrees made finding your footing treacherous, and had presented problems to even his youngest officers.

Logan squinted up to see Colonel Jack Hammerson coming down fast and easy, as though he rappelled every day of his life. He shook his head; the man was obviously older than him, but about five times as fit, Logan guessed, and ten times as deadly. If Jack Hammerson was regular army, then he was Lucille Ball.

On the ground, Hammerson took a quick look around then gave the chopper a thumbs-up. The pilot returned the gesture, and the enormous machine slowly swung away. Logan noticed that the Franks woman had gone into some sort of well-rehearsed action plan. She went out to the right first, facing away from the group, holding a small scope up to her eye. Then she swung to the left to repeat the pattern.

Hammerson was gazing at the sky. Logan knew what he was looking at: the cloud cover was now slate-colored and there were no more shadows. He reckoned they had less than an hour of light. It'd be cold and dark soon and they were a long way from home ... and in the territory of something that he hoped Kearns and his friends had been damned wrong about.

Earning my pay today, he thought, as Hammerson made his way over.

'Going to be dark soon, Chief. We should arrive at the track in about an hour. I'd like to suggest you wait here – secure the rear position. Maybe set up a safe area in the event we all need to spend the night here, or fall back in a hurry.'

Logan smiled. 'And miss the party? No chance. Besides, I get a feeling that you're tracking more than whatever's been bothering my town and sent those three fools up to the Black Dome. Me and my men can make it a little further – you may need us.'

Hammerson nodded and stuck out his hand. 'Okay, and good luck, Bill.'

Logan shook it. 'Hope we don't need it. But you too, Jack.'

*

The creature lifted its head and sniffed deeply. It could sense the small animals approaching – many scents from many different directions. Close by was the smell of fresh meat, slightly masked by the sweet odors of whatever they anointed their bodies with. Underlying them, the scent of fear, which excited it.

A heavy, unfamiliar vibration filled the air, along with the smell of metal. The vibration faded, leaving behind more animal smells.

Lastly, from another direction, came something else. A strange scent, with an edge of violence, rage and with a blood lust that rivaled its own.

The creature pulled further back into the deep caves.

TWENTY-NINE

The Infiniti G35 coasted to a stop next to the solitary dark blue SUV. Its three occupants stepped out and stood looking up towards the top of the mountain that was now completely obscured by low cloud. The green spikes of the trees were frosted right down to where they stood at the beginning of the track. Each man wore a white padded coverall with the hood up. Beneath the hoods sat ski masks, which gave the men a non-human, featureless appearance. Wisps of steam rose from their torsos.

One of them inspected the interior of the SUV, while another pulled a large duffel bag from the rear of their own car. It sagged under the weight of its contents. He placed it on the car hood, unzipped it and removed several pieces of equipment and handguns with unusually long barrels and large square grips. Each man strapped his weapons around his waist, and slid other items into his coverall's pockets.

One of them walked a few paces towards the mountain and looked up at it through a small metallic scope. He swiveled it to gain perspective, then, satisfied, slid it back into its pouch. He listened for a moment to some near silent instructions and then spoke quickly as if to the mountain itself. He turned to the other two and motioned flat-handed up the slope.

The three men began to sprint the many miles to the Arcadian's position.

*

Sam Reid sat in Hammerson's darkened office observing the images from the VELA satellite on the wall-sized screen. He was receiving a real-time image feed of the activity on the mountain, and was able to zoom down to the treetops or pull back to the height of the peaks if he so wished. The images were still resolving through the cloud cover, but becoming slightly grainy as the natural light started to fade.

Major Gerry Harris had told him that the dual feed was still occurring and he was pretty sure it was Medical Division that was siphoning off the data. What alarmed the technician even more was that he'd detected another periodic extraction – someone had inserted a data sniffer into his code. Every now and then the tiny bot would wake up, vacuum up information and then go dormant, which made it impossible to find. He didn't want to call in an alert, he told Sam, because then Hammerson's own data views would be questioned. As Harris described the intrusion, Sam detected a note of admiration in the man's voice – whoever was looking over their shoulder was good. Sam had an idea who it could be, but he'd decided to let it run for now, as things on the mountain looked to be coming to a head.

He watched Hammerson's team hit the ground, and saw the big chopper swoop away into one of the mountain's valleys. He had been following Alex and Senesh ever since they'd left their car and could see that the boss and Casey Franks had set down well above them. The HAWCs would be waiting for the pair when they arrived.

He zoomed in on Alex again, and his mouth curved into a half-smile. The man moved like a locomotive through the snow, no slowing or deviating, his arms and legs pumping like machines. The Arcadian – perfect warrior, or perfect killing machine? Hammerson would find out soon enough.

Sam remembered the unique soldier's strength when he and Alex had fought the priest in the jungle – or, rather, the thing that had taken over the body of the priest. It had snapped Sam's spine, and Alex had carried all two-twenty pounds of his friend on his back through that tangled green hell all the way to the rescue chopper. Sam owed Alex Hunter. He wished he was out there on the mountain; wished he could just speak to the man.

He brought his fist down on one of his useless legs. 'Fuck it all!'

He exhaled and tried to relax. Turning back to the screen, he pulled the view up to a few miles overhead the slopes, and immediately sat forward. 'Hello.'

Coming into the frame on Senesh's trail were four men, large and moving in single file. Still a few miles back from her, but keeping pace. He thought of the bot that had been planted into the data feed, and the expertise that operation had required, and smiled. 'Welcome to the party, Mossad,' he said to the screen.

He pulled the wire mic back down over his mouth and opened the secure line. 'Boss, you got some gatecrashers about to join you on the hill.'

*

Adira slammed into the tree and hung on, her lungs pumping huge plumes of steam into the frigid air. 'Alex!' Her shout was raspy, the dryness making her throat hoarse and painful.

He didn't answer, and she didn't bother calling again. By now he was probably too far ahead to hear. The trail he'd left was a furrow through the surface snow, but every step she took was agony to her fatigued muscles. She straightened and put her hands on her hips. *What am I doing?*

Without Alex present, it was as if some sort of spell had been broken and she could think clearly. She had given up everything – her uncle, who was her sole remaining family; her country; her career – all for someone who probably didn't even care about her anymore. Adira felt like she was waking from a dream. She looked back down the slope. The thick trees and leaden sky took on a milky texture in the weird hazy twilight. Her breathing slowed. *What would happen if I returned home now? Could I make peace with my uncle?*

Turning back up the slope, she saw a bird flitter away from a strange shape on a tree trunk. A moment later it returned to peck at the area, then flew off again with something in its beak.

She took a few steps towards the tree, and made out the mess of human remains crushed against the trunk. Adira had seen many dead bodies in her time, and this looked like the unfortunate person had been hit by a truck. Someone had died badly at this spot; not just killed but obliterated. She tensed, her guard up. What kind of forest creature could have done that?

She looked up the hill, sucking in deep breaths again. She remembered Alex's cryptic words: *I'll know where to find it.* And began to feel concerned about what that 'it' might turn out to be.

*

Salamon Eitan held up his hand and his three agents immediately halted as though turned to stone. He walked ahead a few paces and looked at the furrowed trail in the snow. He smirked. The trail indicated one large body moving at speed, and another smaller one, moving slowly, his or her feet occasionally dragging. While he watched, the snow on the edges of the furrows crumbled in on the little valleys. They weren't far behind, maybe only minutes.

He grunted in satisfaction and waved his compatriots forward. Salamon's role in Mossad's Kidon was to hunt down and kill the enemies of Israel. It was his duty, an honor, and one he had never failed at. It wasn't emotional. There was no other perspective than to obey orders, and win or die. But Adira Senesh was a special case; a prominent and celebrated Mossad agent – brave, skilled and deadly. Perhaps as good as him, perhaps not.

Salamon's orders were to bring Senesh in alive. Unfortunately for Senesh, he just didn't want to. He felt no camaraderie for the killer of his men; rather, he believed she deserved to be punished for her betrayal of her country. And Salamon's punishment for the betrayal of Israel was death.

*

'You said it yourself – it could be *her*. Maybe she got lost and climbed up to find shelter. Kids are smart and resilient. If there's any chance Emma Wilson is up there, we need to check.' Sarah jabbed her gloved finger first at Matt and then at Charles. 'I'll never be able to look her parents in the face again if I don't take a look, especially after finding this.' She held up the small rubber boot.

Matt noticed that Charles avoided her volcanic stare just as much as he did. They both turned to Thomas, who was staring at the ground. Matt spoke first, his voice heavy with resignation. 'Is there a way up?'

Thomas nodded slowly, then said almost sadly, 'Have you noticed there is no snow or ice around the cave?'

Matt looked at the cave mouth and raised his eyebrows. Thomas was right. Everywhere else was coated with the sheen of thin ice, except the area immediately outside the cave.

'What does that mean, exactly?' Sarah asked.

'It means it's warm in there.' He looked up at the black hole. He didn't see it as a cave mouth anymore; instead, he thought of it as a doorway. And something had come out of that doorway that should have been extinct.

A ripple of nausea ran through his gut as he remembered another cave from his past. It wasn't true that deep caves were always dead and sterile places. Some caves were very much alive, and held secrets that were horrifying and deadly.

THIRTY

The climb up to the cave entrance was more difficult than Matt had anticipated. It was only about thirty feet, and he'd done much more complicated no-rig ascents many times in the past, but the exposed rock and the muddy, greasy soil around the cave made it slippery. Thomas was right behind him, yelling instructions, with Sarah just starting the climb, and Charles stepping from foot to foot on the path, impatient to begin.

Matt levered himself into the triangular opening, and kneeled at the edge to look down at the path and beyond. His view was obscured by a grainy haze of the cloud that formed a thick curtain just past the slip path's drop-off point, which also reduced any vertigo he might have experienced. He drew in a long breath, and immediately noticed the acrid smell – a shitty, rank animal odor emanating from the interior of the cave. Beneath it was something raw and decaying, like old mushrooms or bad hamburger. The smell wafted towards him on a draught of warm air that heated the cold skin on his face and made his nose and cheeks tingle.

He squinted into the dark hole and got to his feet, taking comfort from the fact that the breeze was blowing outwards. If there *was* anything inhabiting the cave, his own scent wouldn't be carried inwards. *Important if it's a predator*, he thought.

He took a few steps into the interior, and halted at the remains of the first wall. There were fresh cracks in the rock ceiling, and the stones on the floor were mixed with debris from the cave roof – all proof of their theory that an earthquake had caused the wall to crumble.

He had left his pack down on the slip path, but fumbled in his pocket for the small plastic flashlight he'd taken from it, even though it was more suited to reading a book in a sleeping bag than exploring stygian darkness.

'Phew. Something's dead in there.'

Matt jumped at the voice behind him. Thomas walked past and began to examine the fallen rocks of the first barrier. Sarah appeared in another few minutes, holding the top edge of the small pink boot in her teeth. Charles came immediately after her, his impatient expression suggesting he'd been held up by everyone's slow ascent.

Thomas tapped one of the broken stones with the toe of his boot. 'You know, I've never been beyond this point ... and I bet no other human has for a hundred generations.'

He took a large theatrical step over the tumbled stones.

Twilight had descended on the mountain peak, reducing the light at the mouth of the cave to little more than a gray glow. Thomas tried to direct Matt's hand holding the flashlight to where he wanted, but soon gave up and used his cigarette lighter instead. A barely perceptible warm breeze caused the tiny orange flame to bend towards the cave opening now twenty feet behind them.

Thomas lifted his lighter to the closest wall. 'This what you're looking for, Mr. Kearns?'

The wall was covered in paintings and carvings. Matt's face broke into a smile as he moved quickly to where Thomas stood and traced the images with his hand while not actually touching the artwork.

'This is amazing,' he said. 'The figures are definitely Paleo-Indian ... but some of the characters are much older ... more like Mesoamerican. Strange, though – it's like they're not reproduced correctly.' His fingers traced more of the designs. 'As if someone was drawing them from memory without really knowing what they meant.'

Thomas crowded in closer with his lighter. 'I've never seen many of these symbols; and I've never heard of any of my people or ancestors using them. They've been hidden behind this barrier for many, many centuries.'

Matt frowned, his lips moving as he vocalized the symbols and images, teasing out their meaning. After a while, he nodded. 'Okay, it's like a story, or maybe some kind of record. There's mention of Tooantuh, and the battle with the Great Ones.'

He traced some more symbols and frowned again, looking confused or like he'd lost his place. He stood back and rubbed his chin with the back of his hand, then leaned forward. 'Of course! I couldn't work out the flow, but it's actually telling the story backwards. This shows the defeat of the Great Ones, so the start must be further in.'

He moved his small circle of light further along into the cave. 'Just as I thought – look at this.' He pointed to the glyphs on the wall. 'These characters are much older, more like *real* Mesoamerican ... in fact, a little like Mayan. It's telling the same tale as in the outer chamber, but it's more detailed, richer and ... complete.'

He indicated to Thomas where the more primitive Paleo-Indian work was gradually overtaken by the Mesoamerican – with fewer instances of the two-dimensional shapes and many more detailed drawings and carvings. Then he pointed at one central image. 'Tell me I'm not seeing this. This can't be real.'

The old Indian grunted and nodded. 'So that is why they hate us,' he said slowly. 'They were slaves.'

The image showed several hulking beasts with ropes around their necks and waists. They were pulling carts loaded with the smaller human figures, some of whom were lashing the creatures' huge bent backs.

Sarah made a sound of disgust in her throat. 'Then I'd say it was more a case of revolt than attack.' She held the small boot up and shook it, 'Let's look for the girl and then go.'

Charles added his torch beam to Matt's. 'Are you saying the Indians somehow tamed or domesticated these great anthropoids? Bullshit.' He looked from Matt to Thomas.

Thomas shook his head. 'This is not part of the legend I know of the Chiye-tanka. I have never heard this.'

'It might not have been something they were proud of,' Matt said. 'But forget that for now. Look – don't you see something in the picture that *shouldn't* be there?' He paused, but the trio looked blank. 'Remember, this is thousands of years old.' He waited again, before giving up and answering his own question. '*Wheels*! The Paleo-Indians never had wheels; they never invented them. This looks like a totally different race. And judging by the fact that the ochers and dyes are nearly fully faded, I'd say the language script is much older as well.'

Matt walked back to the other side of the second wall and briefly re-examined the carvings. He shook his head. 'I knew it: it *is* different. There's no doubt – the work on the other side of the outer wall must have been done thousands of years later.'

He moved deeper into the cave, stumbling as he focused on the wall rather than his feet. Sarah and Thomas followed, transfixed by the story Matt was deciphering from the strange images on the wall.

He couldn't contain a small laugh of excitement. 'Look ... more proof. The glyphs are now fully carved; there are no paintings at all. The style is almost pure Mesoamerican in its detail and precision – maybe even Zoque Indian, which is more than 1000 years older than the Mayans. This inner work was done by artisans rather than rock painters or stonemasons. My guess is that each story block was created millennia apart, which is why the work's so different in style and content. The tale was probably handed down and then reproduced.'

He shone the flashlight at the third section. 'And that's why the story moves from myth to chronicle. What we're seeing now is a transcript of what *actually* happened right here, over 10,000 years ago.'

Matt pointed out a warrior that was taller than the rest. The detail was magnificent – he stood on a large rock, his arms outstretched, holding a spear in one hand and what might have been a staff in the other. 'Tooantuxla,' he said to Thomas. 'Wow. I'm guessing that's your original Tooantuh.'

Thomas touched the stone. 'The mightiest warrior ever to have lived in our land. He will always be "Tooantuh" for me and my people.'

Matt's brow screwed up in confusion as he tried to make sense of the ancient story. 'This will take years to unravel,' he murmured. 'Basically, the humans fought the mighty creatures all the way into the caves, but they didn't just use bows and arrows – they had swords and shields too, more akin to ancient Greek or Roman warriors.' He shook his head. 'It's all mixed up.'

He moved along a few steps to the very first images, which chronicled the arrival of both the First People and the Great Ones, and his mouth dropped open.

'*Arks*! The Gigantopithecus didn't cross the land bridge, they were *brought here* in boats. Charles, look at this!'

But Charles wasn't there.

*

The cave twisted slightly before opening into a larger chamber, with several tunnels leading away into impenetrable blackness. Charles loosened his jacket – the air was warmer the further in he went. He examined the ground ... as he'd hoped, it was churned and scuffed, suggesting frequent passage. This was an active, inhabited environment.

His torchlight caught something glinting on the ground. He removed his gloves and stuffed them in his pockets, then bent to pick the fragment free. He rolled it around in his palm and frowned. It was a gold tooth. He scanned around with his light, then moved a bit further along. He had to breathe through his mouth as the smell was becoming overpowering.

He opened his jacket, exposing the dart gun. He was in no doubt that he was in an animal's lair. If the creature was as big as he suspected, he didn't want to startle it and cause it to rush him. Then again, it would be worse if it fled as soon as it saw him. He went on another few feet, trying to quiet his breathing. *If I can get close enough to see it clearly, just a peek, I'll be satisfied,* he thought.

He paused mid-step. There was a noise from ahead ... that soft tinkling sound again. He tilted his head to listen. The tinkling lifted and fell in time with the movement of the warm breeze that blew past him as the humid air inside the cave was sucked out into the colder atmosphere outside.

Charles walked forward, waving his flashlight back and forth as he searched for the sound. He stuck his hand in his pocket and pulled out a handkerchief to cover his face. The stench was so acrid that it was stinging his eyes. He was creeping now, hunched over, even though the roof of the cave was a dozen feet above his head. The dark and the smell were claustrophobic, pressing in heavily all around him, making him feel smothered.

He rounded a huge column of stone that had probably started as a few drips of mineralized water from the ceiling of the cavern centuries ago, and stopped to wave his flashlight around. At first, it seemed to be a dead end, but then he spotted openings behind several smaller columns. He took a small step forward, but the air was becoming ominously heavy. He contemplated calling to Matt and the others, but rejected the idea even as he drew in a breath to shout. For some reason, he felt a strong urge to remain silent, his own animal senses warning him to be cautious.

Charles willed himself to enter the nearest smaller cave, drawn on by his curiosity and the strange tinkling sound. But as he stepped into the blackness, both the warm breeze and the music ceased. He waved his flashlight back and forth but the weak circle of light wasn't powerful enough to illuminate the space ahead. It was as if something was blocking the tunnel.

As he turned back to the main chamber, he felt something crunch under his boot. He shone the flashlight down at his feet and grimaced. He was standing on a raft of bones of different hues of brown and red. Most had been broken open and sucked of their marrow, but many were still joined together by gristly tendons.

He stepped back and swung his flashlight to illuminate the walls. What looked like cloth or material was piled against one wall. He held the light closer, and saw that the strips of cloth were actually the remains of clothing, roughly torn and heaped in a mound.

Charles screwed up his face in trepidation as both the breeze and the tinkling sound came again – closer now.

'Emma?'

He knew it was insane to consider the girl might be alive, given what he was standing on, but Sarah's earlier desperate calls hung in his mind. *It's what she would do*, he thought.

He closed his eyes briefly to concentrate on the sound, then took a few crunching steps towards where he thought it was coming from. He shone his flashlight up along the wall near the smaller cave, and then fell to his knees, gagging.

There was a natural shelf of rock about seven feet up from the ground, and on it sat a row of heads, many of them trailing glistening lengths of windpipe and spinal column. The necks were twisted, as though a giant child had screwed them off, like pulling apart a doll. The faces were imprinted with panic, terror, agony – visual proof of the horror they had experienced during their last moments alive.

In the center of the adult heads, as if in pride of place, sat that of a small girl, her tiny features frozen into a wail. One ear held a clip-on earring with a small string of blue glass beads ending in tiny silver bells; as the soft, foetid breeze stirred them, they made a tinkling sound.

Charles retched onto the bones beneath his feet, his near empty stomach reluctantly giving up a long string of yellow bile that stuck to his chin. As he wiped his mouth, he heard a soft, crunching sound behind him and breathing.

He lifted his flashlight, expecting to see Matt or Sarah, or even Thomas Red Cloud. He raised the beam higher, and then higher again, and his mouth dropped open.

'Oh my God.'

He fumbled for the dart gun.

THIRTY-ONE

'Charles?' Matt swung around to the cave's dark interior, and then back the way they had come. He held up his hand to Thomas who was about to speak, and tilted his head to listen for another few seconds. 'Charles? Hey, where the hell did Charlie Brown go?'

Sarah glanced around, then crowded in close to him, the small boot still tucked under her arm. 'He's not here. I didn't see him go.'

Matt swung his flashlight back and forth, taking a few steps deeper into the cave. 'Charles ... Charlie Brown ... you there?'

Sarah joined in the calling, her voice bouncing away into the darkness.

'Keep your voices down,' Thomas said sharply.

Matt turned his flashlight on the old Indian. His usually impassive face held a look of resignation, and something else ... fear perhaps. Matt didn't like it. In the flashlight's glare, Thomas was bleached of all colour, and even the cynical half-smile he seemed to permanently wear had fallen away.

Thomas motioned with his head towards the cave's dark interior. 'Mr. Schroder's tracks lead that way ... along with tracks from the thing I feared we might find.' He looked briefly back the way they had come. 'I say it again: I think we should leave ... now.'

'We're not leaving without our friend, or without knowing what happened to Emma Wilson,' Sarah said.

Thomas lifted his arm and pointed to one of the passages off the main cave. 'He went in there. If you choose to follow, I think you will find what you seek, Ms Sommer.'

Sarah moved towards the passage, but Matt grabbed her arm. 'Hang on a minute.' He turned to Thomas. 'What if ...' He couldn't finish. The words he wanted wouldn't come. Already his mind was becoming crowded with memories of a terrifying journey miles beneath the Antarctic ice ... a trip that had ended badly for a lot of people.

'Can you ...' Matt swallowed and tried again. 'Thomas, can you please stay here ... and, ah, cover us?'

Thomas unzipped his jacket, the noise extraordinarily loud in the darkness, to expose the oversized grip of the Colt Anaconda. He touched it briefly as if for reassurance, but didn't pull it free. Instead, his hand traveled up to the small leather bag around his neck. With a swift tug, he ripped it free and wrapped the leather string around his fist, tucking the cord ends under the loops to keep it fastened to his hand. The gesture seemed so ... final. It scared Matt more than the sight of the huge gun sticking out of the old man's belt.

'I will wait for you,' Thomas said.

Sarah made a *tsking* sound at the sight of the gun, then pulled away from Matt and stepped into the smaller cave. Almost immediately, she vanished into the darkness.

Matt took a half-step after her, then turned back to Thomas. He felt his heart pounding in his chest. 'Okay ... thanks,' he said, and held the old man's eyes.

'Matthew Kearns,' Thomas said softly, barely above a whisper.

Matt blinked as if a spell had been broken.

'Be careful ... some legends are real.'

Matt nodded. He'd heard that phrase before, but couldn't remember where. He turned to jog after Sarah and found her fifty or so paces ahead along the dark tunnel.

A rank stench filled his nostrils, and he held his hand over his nose and mouth and spoke in a pinched whisper. 'Holy crap, this can't be good for you.'

Sarah stumbled, and stopped. She moved her torch beam in broad arcs over the cave floor. 'Bones,' she said.

Matt caught up with her and grabbed her upper arm. 'Slow down. If Charles isn't here, we'll try the next cave. I don't want to go too deep ... *Huh*, what did you say?'

He took another step and heard something brittle crunch underfoot. He swung his beam to his feet and saw a piece of smashed molded plastic – part of the dart gun Charles had been carrying.

'Charles?' he whispered, and swung his beam in wider arcs, stopping it on a rivulet of dark lumpy fluid that ran down the wall twenty feet in front of them.

'Oh no, that's clotting blood,' Sarah said.

Together, they lifted their flashlights up along the blood trail ... to illuminate a ghastly sight.

Sarah screamed, a high-pitched sound that threatened to damage Matt's ears in the small space.

Charles's head sat at a slight angle on a natural rock shelf, his mouth pulled open in a scream that would never end, the stump of his neck ragged and uneven where it had been torn from his body. It rested next to other heads – some fresh, some desiccating.

Matt doubled over, a whining mewl coming from his mouth in the instant before he vomited onto the bones at his feet. The repulsive, pervasive stench was in the air all around him – *in* him, in his nose, his mouth, his lungs. *I killed him*, he thought. *I brought him here and now he's dead.*

He straightened, wiping his mouth, and lifted a shaky hand to take hold of Sarah. Behind him, a sound smashed out, so loud and close it was like a physical blow to the back of his head.

Matt spun quickly, nearly slipping on his vomit. At the back of the cave stood a hulking form, so large he could barely adjust his eyes to take it in. Its face was that of a gargoyle, with pink boiled-looking skin, flaring nostrils, and patchy hair that peaked to a crest on its crown. Its mouth looked like that of a grotesquely painted harlot, its lips garish red with blood. From one of its shovel-sized hands dangled Charles's limp and mangled remains.

The monster roared again, revealing enormous yellow canines as long as Matt's fingers.

Matt did the only thing he could think of. He threw his flashlight into the creature's face, grabbed Sarah and yelled, 'Run!' as loudly as his strangled voice would allow.

*

Thomas's scalp crawled when Sarah's scream came bouncing out of the dark cave. He had hoped they would find nothing, but in his soul he had known it was a vain wish.

A small glow appeared in the passage, becoming a beam of light that waved around madly as Matt dragged Sarah and her torch back to the main cave and the exit. He grabbed at Thomas as they passed, but the Indian shrugged out of his hand. He could see Sarah's white face, hear her terror in her panting breath. Matt was babbling something about heads and bones, but there was no time for talk.

'Go!' Thomas shouted into the young man's face. 'The killing must stop tonight. Tooantuh will come and you must be ready for him. Help him to push the beast back into the mountain, or you will all die – like your friend.' He gave Matt an almighty shove towards the cave mouth. '*Go!*'

Matt looked as though he was about to speak, but Thomas turned away. In another few seconds, he was inside the passageway and swallowed by the dark. He closed his eyes for a moment, trusting his senses. The warm breeze that flowed from the inner caves was snuffed out, as if something had moved to block the source of the draught. *It is here.*

Thomas began to chant softly. The words that he had only half-believed for most of his life, he now sang as if they were the only words that had ever mattered to him. He called on his forefathers for strength and courage. He asked them to prepare the welcome fire for he would be joining them soon.

It is close now.

He opened his eyes, but could see nothing in the pitch dark. A revolting smell enveloped him, along with a sensation of body warmth – something was moving stealthily around him, displacing minuscule amounts of air.

Thomas raised his gun and fired. The recoil jolted his thin arm all the way back to the shoulder, and his ears rang with the sound of a thousand sirens. But in that split second of muzzle flash, he saw the face of his ancestors' enemy above him, a harbinger of agony and death. He brought the gun up again and fired, trying to locate the thing by the flash – but it was useless after the bullet had already flown. The only way he was going to hit it was through luck or the will of his ancestors.

He stood in the blackness, the ringing in his ears making them as useless as his eyes. His arm shook from the strain of holding up the heavy Colt, but as he contemplated changing hands a savage blow smashed into his forearm, its force almost dislocating his shoulder. His hand immediately felt light. He knew the gun was gone, but there was no pain. He brought his other hand up to rub his forearm, but there was nothing there – the arm had been severed at the elbow. His fingers came away hot and wet with blood.

Thomas sank to his knees, and hoped he had given Matt and Sarah enough of a head start.

He laughed softly in the dark and tilted his head upwards. 'Oh, Great One, may your next battle be with a stronger warrior than an old man.'

He didn't feel the horrific blow that came down on his upturned face.

*

The cold, the darkness, the closeness of the trees pressing in all around them; it was just like last time beneath the ice. Matt's frightening memories began to overwhelm him. He sprinted down the path, trying to keep pace with Sarah, whose long legs seemed to dance over the deepening snowdrifts rather than sink into them like his did. He glanced frantically over his shoulder many times, even though whatever had been pursuing them seemed to have fallen back. He didn't think for a moment it was Thomas; he'd heard gunshots from inside the cave. He also didn't believe they'd outpaced their follower, and was damned sure he wasn't going to stop or let it get in front of them.

Sarah carried the only flashlight, and he prayed that she was following the trail Thomas had brought them up on. It was too dark and too cold to get lost. He almost laughed; the cold was the least of their worries right now.

He thought again of Charles, his waxen face that would sit screaming in that dark cave until it dried to a leathery skull; a grisly trophy for a creature that he'd only half-believed existed. A wave of nausea washed over him. He wasn't going to let Sarah or himself suffer the same fate.

'Faster!' he screamed at Sarah's back, even as he knew that if *she* had any speed left in her legs, he certainly didn't.

THIRTY-TWO

'**G**ive me something, Reid. It's getting real dark up here.'

As Hammerson's voice sounded in his ear, Sam Reid was already changing the VELA imaging vector to thermal to pick out the heat signatures of the various bodies on the mountain. The image slant dipped another few degrees, and he tried again to improve the angle but it still dragged to the side.

Shit! Not now, he thought, as his fingers flew over the satellite commands. Nothing made a difference; the image still slipped.

'Sorry, boss, only got a few more minutes here. About to move over the horizon and lose my line of sight. But frankly, it looks like goddamn Main Street down there. Gotta be a dozen people moving on that mountainside now.'

Sam pulled back to look at the multiple fluorescing blips. The two HAWCs carried tracers in their suits that allowed them to be easily identified.

'Okay, I got two bodies coming down at you fast. I also got five, repeat five, warm bodies I can see intermittently in and out of a satellite shadow … they must be in an overhang or ravine.'

The HAWC commander grunted in reply, his breathing ragged as he ran up the steep slope. 'That'll be Logan and his team. Go on.'

'Then I got multiple groups coming up from different angles. Four bodies coming at a rapid rate, approximately three miles back on your five o'clock. They're in a standard tracking formation – my guess is they're your Mossad ghosts.' He moved to another section and zeroed in. 'Okay, I got two more coming up from your seven, one of them moving at extreme speed … and he's hot … very hot. Body heat off the scale. One guess, boss.'

'That's our man. Can you –'

Sam cut him off. 'Wait – that's not all. You got another three bodies on their way, also at extreme speed. Oh shit – they're hot, boss, way too hot for anyone normal, and they're ...'

Sam's words froze in his mouth as he saw an enormous shape appear on the slope behind the two figures coming down from above the HAWCs' position. It moved downwards first, then shifted sharply in another direction. To a military man like Sam, its intention was clear – intercept or ambush.

'Boss, something huge just appeared a few klicks above you. I'm about to pass over the horizon any second and my window will close. But looks like you're about to have a massive new guest at your party – definitely non-human.'

The screen image fuzzed momentarily and then cleared. Sam focused on two particular shapes – the enormous one moving into an ambush position, and the one coming up towards it at a speed faster than any normal human could manage.

In another second, the screen fuzzed again and went white.

'Sorry, boss ... I'm over the rim and blind. You're on your own. Good luck.'

Hammerson responded with a brief acknowledgment and signed out.

Sam sat back in his chair, frustration balling in his stomach. He wanted to be out there ... he *needed* to be out there. If it was Alex coming up the slope, as they suspected, Sam was the best person to talk to him. Sam's size, skill and experience also made him the best choice to deal with the unknown adversary approaching Hammerson and Franks.

Or used to make me the best, he thought.

He stared at the white screen, unaware that he was punching his fist into one of his dead thighs, over and over. Finally, he lifted his hand and brought it down hard on the steel armrest of his wheelchair.

'Fuck these legs, and fuck this chair!'

*

Hammerson and Franks jogged up the slope. It was now full night, and they'd inserted night-vision contacts into their eyes, which made them bulge slightly. The tiny discs included infrared and thermal-vision technology operated through a combination of eye blinks – another useful tool from the HAWC weapons labs.

Hammerson pulled in deep lungfuls of air as he made his way up the slope. The forty-five-degree incline and the soft snowdrifts made a good spring-off impossible; the result – each stride sapped a lot of energy. The communication pellet in his ear pinged and he touched it briefly. It was Chief Logan.

'Jack, me and the boys have tracked the Kearns party to where they entered a small cleft in the mountainside. With the amount of vegetation growing over the top, it's more like a dark green tunnel. We're holding for the moment. What's your position? Over.'

Hammerson sucked in another breath. 'Good work, Bill. Hold it there. We've had intel that there are bodies coming down at us – two of the Kearns's group we think. Also multiple bodies on the way up – not sure if they're friendlies, so you need to dig in deep there. We'll pick up the two coming down in approximately ten minutes, then return to your location ASAP. Over.'

Hammerson thought Logan sounded relieved as he signed off. He didn't doubt for a minute that Logan's men would consider trekking any higher in the cold dark as smart an idea as rolling in the snow naked.

He looked up at Franks and saw she was starting to leave him behind, even though she paused every so often to change her vision from light-enhancing to thermal imaging to scan the steep slope ahead. He reached into a pouch in his suit and pulled free a small foil pack. He tore it open and extracted a small gel capsule, which he broke under his nose, inhaling the stimulants. The chemical explosion went off in his head first, then traveled down his chest to bloom in his extremities. Suddenly, old legs became young. He increased his pace.

*

Markenson had pulled off his gloves. In each hand, he held a mug of steaming coffee. He handed one to Chief Logan, then took a drink from the other. 'Can we light a fire, Chief? It's freezing up here.'

Logan looked at his team; the bulky clothing they wore made them look like overstuffed bears. They'd been grumbling for a while now as it got darker. To his credit, Markenson had made sure they each had a coffee to warm them up. Logan wished he could agree to the fire.

'Sorry, Ollie, this isn't a cookout. Hammerson tells me there are people above us coming down, and more people below us coming up – we're about to be sandwiched. Best we keep a low profile until we see what everyone's up to.'

Markenson shrugged. 'Hey, maybe some of them are the three Jordan brothers.'

Logan nodded. 'That wouldn't be a bad thing – we could sure do with their help.' He motioned towards the other three officers with his head. 'Tell the boys to keep it quiet. I'm going to have a quick look around. And no fire, Ollie. Got it?'

'Got it, Chief.' Markenson raised his mug in a salute, then sipped again.

*

Salamon held the scope to his eye. Captain Senesh was in sight now, moving slowly in the snow; he could tell she was heavily fatigued. He scanned the terrain but could find no trace of Alex Hunter. He switched back to Senesh. The tracks she moved in told him that she was following the ex-HAWC, but had probably dropped well back. They'd take her first then.

He made a single flat chopping motion in the air and his men fanned out, running fast and drawing their weapons.

Salamon lifted his gun. The long silencer would deliver a high level of sound-baffling, and the extended barrel added projectile stability for greater accuracy. He held the gun in a two-handed grip and sighted high on Senesh's back and just at the base of her neck – a kill shot. He gently squeezed the trigger. The hammer drawing back and releasing made no more noise than the tick of a clock.

The gun spat softly and the figure jerked forward and fell into the snow, partially obscured by a massive tree trunk.

That's for my first team, traitor. Now for Hunter, he thought confidently.

*

Alex came to a stop. He swiveled his head ... behind, sideways, then back up the slope. *So many people, so many noises.* He could hear men laughing in one direction; and Adira's heavy breaths far behind him as she continued up the slope; and rushing footsteps – multiple bodies, heavy, moving without any fatigue. *Elite soldiers, two teams,* he thought. Further up, there was a larger group, spread out.

He closed his eyes to concentrate, and placed his hand against the bark of a tree. He immediately felt the vibrations of the moving people. He ground his teeth and focused harder, searching for something else ... *There it is.* Its footfalls were slow and stealthy, as if it was tracking something.

An explosion of pain rippled from Alex's forehead all the way to the back of his skull and down his spine. An image of his mother screaming in the dark blasted his senses, almost causing him to cry out in anguish. His fingers gripped the tree trunk, tearing away a length of bark, and the rapid increase in his body heat melted the snow around him.

A muffled gunshot jerked his head upright; he felt the impact as if it had struck his own flesh. He spun and stared into the darkness, slowing his breathing, listening. Behind him, the cold landscape was as quiet as a whisper – just the soft *shush* of a snowdrift as it shifted under its own weight, a branch creaking as its wood contracted, the distant rustle of some nocturnal creature on the evening hunt.

He couldn't hear Adira anymore, but sensed she was hurt. That bullet had been meant for her ... she needed him.

Alex's mind was torn. He stared down to where the Israeli woman probably lay. He knew he should return to help her; even though his trust in her had leaked away long ago, he still owed her ... something. But another voice commanded him to continue onward, towards the thing that was coming nearer, the beast he had to confront.

He balled his fist and punched the tree trunk.

He took a last look up the mountainside, then turned to sprint down the slope, gathering speed with every step.

THIRTY-THREE

Matt had caught up with Sarah and for the last few minutes they'd been running side by side. His legs felt like rubber and he was worried he'd fall and break a bone. Given what was somewhere behind them, that would be a death sentence.

Sarah held the flashlight in front of her, but Matt knew they probably weren't on the same path they'd come up on. In fact, he didn't think they were on *any* sort of path anymore. He wasn't surprised: there were no landmarks, it was dark, and they were traveling blindly at speed. *Still, we haven't fallen off a cliff ledge, so not bad, considering*, he thought.

As they passed through a narrow space between two massive tree trunks, something slammed them both hard to the ground. The soft snow cushioned the fall, and before either of them could yell out in shock, hands were pressed over their mouths.

It was too dark to make out features, but Matt thought the shape of his captor's head and shoulders were somehow familiar. Then a deep voice he recognized said, 'Nice night for a stroll, Professor Kearns.'

The hand was removed and he was pulled to his feet.

'Major Jack Hammerson? I don't believe it. Thank God.' Matt bent over, taking in deep breaths and allowing his heart rate to slow.

Hammerson's companion had pulled Sarah to her feet, and now pushed her a little roughly towards Matt.

'It's colonel now,' Hammerson said, 'but good to see you too, Matt. Now, quickly: where are the other members of your party? Are they recoverable?'

Matt had been with HAWCs before; he knew exactly what Hammerson was asking. 'No, sir, both dead, and we've got –'

A tree trunk sailed over their heads and crashed into two large trees not five feet away. The HAWCs pulled him and Sarah out of the way as the massive log bounced back to the ground, exactly where they had been standing.

'It's here,' Matt said.

He looked around for Sarah, found her sprawled in the snow and quickly pulled her to her feet. Hammerson and the other HAWC were already up, guns in their hands.

Hammerson grabbed Matt and Sarah and gave them an almighty shove down the slope. 'Head west,' he yelled. 'There's a drop-off that way. I'll be right behind you!'

Matt did as he was told, dragging Sarah with him.

*

Hammerson watched them for a second, then turned to Franks and motioned up the slope with his head. 'See to that giant irritation, will you? I've got to get these two back to Logan and then intercept the Arcadian. Rendezvous at the ravine with the cops, ASAP.'

Franks grinned and blinked her lenses to infrared. 'Roger that, boss. With pleasure.'

She took a look up the slope and sprinted off into the dark.

Hammerson made off after Matt and Sarah, running hard in the dark, adrenaline moving his muscles like pistons. He caught up to them easily and kept them going at a fast pace.

*

The snow was numbing her face but she remained as still as death. The almost imperceptible sound of the gun's hammer drawing back had triggered an automatic trained response that had saved her life. She'd thrown herself forward, the projectile only catching the top of her shoulder. A small piece of trapezium muscle was gone, but she lived.

Through the powdery snow she could hear the crush of the ice crystals as the men circled her. She was dragged upright by her hair and punched hard in the face. She grunted from the impact and went down onto her knees. Anger boiled inside her, and she refused to let them see her pain. Adira immediately got back to her feet and her attacker went to throw another punch but this one she blocked and she struck out with one of her legs. She made contact but, frustratingly, the blow was feeble and her aim was off. One of her eyes was already swelling closed from the first blow.

The man who had blocked the strike swung his fist back into her stomach, doubling her over, and then brought his knee up into her exposed face. Through blurring vision, she saw her own brilliant red blood splash the magnificent white snow. She went down again, coughing.

She wondered why they didn't just kill her. She now knew there were four of them, and their spoke to each other in Hebrew – they were her own countrymen. No random group of mercenaries but all soldiers, Mossad Special Op cleaners, sent to kill her. Adira spat blood and looked up as one slightly larger than the rest called a halt to the beating. Her mouth turned up in a bloody smile.

'I knew it had to be you.' Her words sounded mushy through her swollen lips.

She was dragged to her feet again, and held in place. She met the stare of the man; her own gaze matching it for ferocity and defiance.

'Salamon Eitan, killing unarmed fellow countrywomen now?'

The man's mouth turned down as he spoke. 'I looked up to you; we all did. But you steal our vital secrets, you shoot dead our brothers ... *your brothers* ... and Captain Senesh, you are never unarmed.'

He raised his gun to her face. 'This is my pleasure.'

Adira half smiled but her eyes radiated nothing but contempt. She stood as straight as she could manage – not feeling fear, only anger that she was about to lose something that was more important than her pointless life.

Salamon took a step back – she knew why. She closed her eyes.

'Goodbye Alex,' she whispered.

*

Alex crashed to a stop behind a tree – he'd found her. His jaw clenched as he saw what she was up against – four highly trained fighters; and Adira seemed to be injured.

Alex felt his heart rate begin to rise. He knew he couldn't cover the open ground between them, through the deep snow, no matter how fast he was. Either he'd take several bullets, or Adira would. Still, his body took over, urging him to action.

The man pressing the gun to Adira's forehead took a step back, his arm outstretched. Alex knew this was to avoid the brain spatter that would come from a close-range headshot. He needed to act *now*. He couldn't go over the snow so ...

He dived beneath its surface and churned through it like a machine. He calculated he needed to cover around eighty feet.

Alex burst from the snow ten feet short of the group, but it was enough. In the seconds before the men reacted, Adira pulled away from the gun at her head and dived and rolled.

Bullets flew, and the closest of the agents came at Alex in a Krav Maga move, hands up, one higher than the other. The first blow struck Alex between the eyes. It was rock hard and would have felled a normal man, but Alex caught the man's forearm before he could pull it back and wrenched it with enough force to pull the shoulder from its socket. The point of his elbow continued on into the man's windpipe. Alex held the choking soldier fast, using him as a shield against his comrades' bullets.

One of the men was tracking Adira with his weapon, waiting for a clear shot to finish their mission. In a single move, Alex had covered the ten feet between them. He grabbed the man, batted his gun upwards and slammed him repeatedly against a tree trunk until he hung limp.

Alex dropped the crushed body and ducked below a spray of bullets at his back. He swiveled and kicked backwards into the shooter's diaphragm with enough force to stop his heart.

Alex searched for the final agent, the team's leader, and saw that Adira had grabbed one of the dropped guns and put a bullet in his leg. In the second it took the man to shift his aim from Alex to Adira, Alex was on him, grabbing at the gun and disarming him. He lifted the man's body until his feet came out of the snow and drew his fist back. *Finish it,* screamed the voice in his head. The agent glared at Alex, but, like Adira moments before, showed no fear of death.

'Don't!' Adira shouted.

Alex stayed the fist that was about to cannon into the man's defiant face.

Adira walked up to him and held the gun to his head. 'Salamon Eitan ... my uncle sent you, yes?'

The man remained silent. The snow around him was stained red from the wound in his leg.

Adira pressed the gun into the flesh between his eyes. 'To kill me, or to kill both of us?'

Salamon stared first at Adira, then Alex, defiance burning in his eyes. 'Just Hunter. It was my decision to kill you. You deserve to die for the deaths of my men, your own people.'

Adira lowered the gun, and Alex let the man drop, knowing the fight was over.

Adira rubbed blood from her cheek. 'We didn't know the men at the river were Mossad until it was over. They attacked first.' She shook her fist in his face. 'Stupid.'

She tucked the gun into her belt, swaying slightly from the damage the man and his soldiers had inflicted on her. '*Stupid!*' she yelled again, and kicked out at him, knocking him backwards. She pointed a finger into his face. 'Your life is my gift this day. Tell my uncle ... I know what my mission is.'

Salamon got to his feet, his fists balled, looking like he wanted to continue the fight. Then his eyes moved to Alex and he seemed to change his mind.

He spoke to Adira through gritted teeth. 'Never come home. You are not one of us anymore.'

He turned and struggled down the slope, one of his legs dragging and leaving a furrowed trail of blood in the snow.

Adira watched him go, then slumped against the closest tree, looking tired and deflated. She turned to Alex and half-smiled. 'You saved me again.' She snorted softly and leaned her head back against the trunk. 'All our lives are used up now. We need to get out.'

Alex looked down at the battered woman. She would survive, and he felt his debt was repaid.

'No, *you* need to get out of here,' he said. 'Your fight is finished but mine is still to come. This is the last time we will see each other, Adira Senesh.'

'Don't, Alex. Please wait –'

But Alex was already sprinting up the slope, back towards the enemy he knew was waiting for him.

THIRTY-FOUR

Franks hid behind the trunk of a large spruce, and blinked back and forth between light sensor and thermal vision. She smiled and then whispered, 'I *love* hot, naked bodies.' About 200 feet further up the slope, an outcrop of stone showed a warm patch – something had just been leaning against it, something large.

Franks sprinted between some trees to improve her position, and flattened herself behind one of the trunks. She and the thing she was tracking had been playing cat and mouse for a while. It was leaving traces for her, moving heavily just out of her field of vision, then disappearing like smoke. She knew it was large, fast and feral, but was starting to doubt it was just a dumb animal. In fact, it was displaying all the traits of a hunter, and that made her feel this was becoming less a hunt and more a contest.

She leaned around the trunk – and something enormous rushed at her, its body heat and size making her thermal lens flare bright orange. She had time to raise her gun and deliver two rounds, then dive, before she was caught by the ankle. She screamed as the creature's grip crushed most of her lower leg.

It dragged her from the ground, but she managed to twist in its huge hand and fire another few rounds. It spun her and slammed her to the ground. Her partially armored suit protected her from the worst, but her head swam. The next time it lifted her, the gun that had been in her hand ... wasn't.

The animal's rank stink filled her nose, and her head throbbed as it held her upside down like some giant ragdoll. She tried to hang on to a passing tree trunk, but the attempt was futile; the thing's strength seemed to exceed hers a hundredfold. She guessed she was being hauled eastward, as she caught sight of a pale moon when the low clouds broke apart for a moment.

The giant hand swung her again, and this time she went with it, using the momentum to bend her body and reach up to her thighs and her knife sheaths. She pulled both blades free, one in each hand, and on the next swing she used the pendulum action to bring both blades together and into each side of the mighty arm that held her.

A bellow of pain roared from the monster's mouth.

'How's that, motherfucker?' Franks yelled into the darkness, and changed her lens from thermal to infrared. The colossal figure that held her immediately went from a flaring orange to nightshade green.

'Shit!'

The creature hadn't released its grip. It bent its head towards her and she saw its huge broad face, the heavy ridged brow, and teeth that looked as long as a tiger's. She bared her own teeth at the grotesque features. It continued to stare at her, and she saw intelligence in those glaring black orbs, and experienced a moment of self-doubt.

She swore her defiance at it again, and it snorted and pulled away, seeming to lose interest in her. She took the opportunity to examine its torso – its anatomy was very similar to a human's.

A single deep liver strike and Kong's gonna bleed out, she thought.

She coiled her muscles in preparation for the strike, but the beast seemed to anticipate her move. It shook her and then slammed her into a tree. The night-vision lens in her left eye cracked but didn't dislodge. However, she felt warmth and wetness on her face – blood.

They stopped. It had gone eerily quiet. Franks felt a sensation of ... openness. Like they were in a clearing, or ...

She was flung out into space.

As she fell, she looked up to see the giant figure standing on a cliff edge, watching as she plummeted to the forest below.

Aw, fuck it, she thought.

*

The creature watched the small animal fall away into the void. If it had more time it would have taken the head and carried the meat back to the caves. But it sensed too many threats on the mountain and all close to its lair. This was its territory now, and it was being invaded.

It lifted its huge head and sniffed. There was the smell of fresh blood on the air, and other strange scents. In the distance, it saw a flare of brightness and knew that its enemies were gathered there. They could not be allowed to stay. Never again would it allow those beings to push it back into the deep, dark world inside the mountain.

They would all be meat before the sun came up again.

*

Ollie Markenson crouched beside the small circle of stones, feeding twigs into the tongues of orange flame that lifted off the fire they'd started with the ball of toilet paper Parsons always carried in his pack. He half-turned to wink at the grinning men standing around him.

'Don't forget, when the boss asks, it was *everyone's* idea.'

The cloud cover was gradually breaking up, but the overhang at the start of the long green tunnel they were huddled in didn't benefit from the occasional moonlight. Markenson figured that if they were going to be stuck here for a while, he'd be damned if he was going to do it in the pitch dark, or risk freezing while they waited for those two bullshit FBI pricks to come back down.

He blinked away the floating retinal images of the flames that ruined his night vision and moved his hand a little closer to the warmth. 'Hey, Pete, bring anything to cook?' he asked Parsons. 'I'm starving.'

There was a small cough from out of the dark and a tiny red hole appeared in Officer Parsons' forehead. His large body fell sideways and landed heavily.

There was another cough and Oakleigh, their youngest officer, fell across the small fire. His body didn't put it out; instead, his cheap stuffed jacket began to melt and then ignited.

Williams's forehead exploded outwards, covering the horrified Markenson in a spray of red.

'What the fuck!'

The only man still alive, Markenson dived for his rifle and the cover of a boulder. As he did, a bullet caught him and mule-kicked him back onto the snow. He managed to scrabble back amongst some rocks and peered around to see where the shots had come from.

The flames were higher now, feeding on Oakleigh's burning body, and their glow extended up and along the ravine. In their light, Markenson saw three pale ghosts come down the crevasse's steep side. All were completely white, save for the large guns they carried and the black slits where their eyes should have been. To Markenson, they looked like a squad of futuristic robots coming to send him to his death.

He tried to lift his gun, but the bullet had smashed through the muscle and bone on his left shoulder and his arm refused to work. *Shit, no.*

He raised the gun with his other arm and balanced it on his knee, using his leg to aim the barrel. He held his breath and fired, but in the time it took him to rebalance the gun for a second shot, one of the white ghosts was ripping the rifle from his hands and jerking him upright.

Up close, its eyes were soulless.

THIRTY-FIVE

'Stop right there!' Logan shouted, pulling his weapon and flattening himself against a tree.

Two people collapsed into the snow at his feet: Matt Kearns and Sarah Sommers. The police chief reached down and pushed the woman's hair back off her face. 'Sarah, thank God you're okay.'

Jack Hammerson, who was with them, nodded to Logan, then turned to look back up the slope. He put a hand up to his ear and spoke softly into the dark, waited a few seconds, then spoke again.

Matt got to his feet, but remained bent over as his chest heaved. He tried to speak but nothing would come, his throat constricted by fear and exhaustion. He straightened, gulping air, and pointing wildly towards slope. The words finally came out – too fast. 'We've got to ...'

'What is it?' Logan asked. 'What's going on?'

Before Kearns could answer, Hammerson returned to the group.

'Can't raise Franks,' he said. 'Kearns is right, Bill, you better grab your men and get these two off the mountain. And keep them in tight – there's a freight train coming at us fast.'

Logan holstered his gun. 'Okay, let's get back to the boys. We'll be fine – we brought plenty of firepower with us.'

Hammerson looked him in the eye. 'Chief, with all due respect, if the thing that's following us has got through Franks, it's gonna go through your men like a shark through a school of sardines. I'm heading back up the slope to see if I can buy you some time – make sure you damn well use it!'

A gunshot bounced past them, followed by its echo.

Logan swung his head around. 'Where did that come from? Markenson?'

Hammerson turned to Matt and Sarah. 'Get down, and stay down. Do not move. If we're not back in five minutes, you head down that slope – don't wait for us, don't stop, don't look back until you're in Asheville. Understood?'

Matt nodded shakily. 'Okay, sir. Five minutes.'

Logan tried to pull his face into a reassuring smile, but couldn't. 'Don't worry; we've got this.'

*

Hammerson and Logan split as they closed in on the ravine, taking up positions a few hundred feet away. Hammerson looked at the glow through the trees. A freaking fire, when they were supposed to be laying low. *Real smart, boys.* He shook his head and quickly checked his weapons – all ready.

He tried Casey Franks one more time; still nothing. She'd either turn up, or he'd grieve for her later. He nodded to Logan, and started to weave through the dark trees, the big police chief doing the same on a slightly different angle.

Hammerson blinked off the light-enhancement lenses as he neared the fire. The flames were leaping six feet in the air and Hammerson groaned when he smelled charred flesh. His unease was confirmed when he saw one of Logan's men lying in the fire. Two other men lay nearby, obviously dead.

A large figure dressed in snow fatigues was holding the only remaining officer, Markenson, upright and shaking him. He pushed his ski-masked face close to the officer's, obviously interrogating him.

Hammerson studied the man – he was big, fit, and was actually holding Markenson up off the ground. *Alex?* Hammerson wondered. The man's carriage suggested military.

He saw Logan start to lift from his crouch, clearly unable to remain a spectator as his last living officer was brutalized by an unknown assailant.

Hammerson touched his ear and whispered, 'Logan, you stay the fuck down until we've reconned the entire area.'

Out of the corner of his eye, he saw Logan pause.

The figure in white changed his grip, now holding Markenson with just one hand. With his other, the man pulled free a handgun that was way too familiar to Hammerson.

What the fuck?

Hammerson mentally ticked off the weapon's capabilities and schematics: rotational gas projectile pistol; multi-round air-baffled silencer; small round size but high velocity, giving a small entry hole but a punch power that would drive it through just about anything. The gun was designed for immediate kill capabilities and it was one of theirs.

A nagging seed of doubt planted itself in his gut. There was only one department that might have access to enhanced warrior stock. He knew the Medical Division was continuing its work on the Arcadian project, hoping to generate more soldiers like Alex Hunter. Had Graham succeeded – and sent his protégés to find Alex?

Hammerson hoped to hell he was wrong.

The white-clad figure held the gun to Markenson's temple and seemed to speak again, because the dazed officer shook his head and started to struggle. The figure shrugged.

Hammerson knew the end of an interrogation when he saw it. *Oh, fuck, no.*

The bullet went in one side of the officer's head and blew a giant hole out the other. The soldier dropped Markenson's body in a heap at his feet.

'No!'

Hammerson heard Logan's yell as he charged, firing his weapon. The bullets from his Sig P220 smacked into the white figure's chest, causing him to stagger backwards a step ... but not fall.

Great, armored as well, Hammerson thought.

Instead of going to the ground, the figure turned side-on and started to bring his gun up towards Logan.

Hammerson exhaled, and sighted along the barrel of his handgun. It'd be a long shot with a pistol, and in flickering light, but ...

His bullet took the man in the center of the forehead. The man's head was flung back and the top of his ski mask bloomed red. But instead of dropping, as he should have done from a head shot, the man's hands flew up to each side of his skull and clawed at the mask, as though trying to dig out the bullet.

Hammerson fired again. This time the bullet entered the back of the man's gloved hand, passing on into the skull. The man's arms dropped and he fell backwards onto the bloodied snow.

Hammerson grunted and got to his feet. *Just like riding a bike*, he thought.

As he went to step out of the trees, a zipper of small, silent explosions ran across the snow in front of Logan, then traced along his thigh, up his torso and out to his left shoulder. The big police chief was thrown backwards to the ground, blood, cloth and flesh blowing out behind him.

The body strikes were debilitating but not fatal, and Hammerson knew they were designed to put Logan out of action long enough for his assailant to question him. After which he would undoubtedly suffer the same fate as Markenson.

Hammerson had blended back into the trees, and now he watched as another white-clad figure, identical to the first, leaped down from his concealment position on the side of the ravine. Hammerson edged sideways, intending to follow the dense tree cover and get behind the man, when an almost imperceptible scrunching of snow behind him made him crouch and spin.

A third white-overalled figure, his face covered by a white ski mask, stood before him, his deadly calm almost unnatural. The hand that shot out to grip the barrel of Hammerson's pistol moved faster than any normal man's could. It ripped the gun from Hammerson's grip and flung it out into the darkness, then the figure moved forward to grab Hammerson's still-raised arm.

Hammerson rolled away, spinning as he went, and kicked out hard from the ground. His armored boot struck the side of the man's knee with a satisfying *crunch*. If a strong leg had a point of weakness, the knee was it – just sixteen pounds of sharp pressure per square inch could take it out. The leg bent at an unnatural angle, but the knee held.

Hammerson came up fast, expecting the man to grab him in a standard bear hug and maybe use his forehead as a battering ram. The soldier did just as Hammerson hoped, which made him confident that his opponent would be unlikely to anticipate higher-order combat moves. The man *was* military, but thankfully not Special Ops.

The HAWC commander moved his body to the side in the grip and struck once with his fist into the man's left eye, allowing his arm to travel past the head so he could bring the point of his elbow into the soft space just behind the ear on the back swing. It was a deft strike, and should have rendered the man unconscious at minimum.

Instead, he staggered back, allowing Hammerson to momentarily break the bear hug.

Standing toe to toe in the dark, the two men traded blows. Hammerson managed to block most, but the man's speed and dumb luck allowed a few through and they struck him like a battering ram. This man was strong and fast – unnaturally so, Hammerson thought irritably. The nagging seed of doubt bloomed.

As Hammerson got to his feet after a particularly vicious punch, he noticed the man's knee, the one he'd damaged, was now fully functional. His suspicion was confirmed: Graham was field-testing his latest Arcadian subjects. He and Logan had just got in the way. They were here for Alex, which was why they'd questioned Markenson before killing him – they wanted information about the original Arcadian.

Hammerson sucked in a deep breath, and tasted blood. *Gonna be a long night*, he thought, as the man closed in on him once again. *Or a short and very ugly one.*

*

Alex heard the sounds of fighting – grunts, the hard impact of blows on flesh and bone – but could sense the creature he sought wasn't involved. Still, the glow in the distance drew him; it looked like firelight.

He sprinted on, and came to a natural gorge in the mountain that, with the fire burning within it, looked like the glowing entrance to hell. By the greasy, oily smell, he guessed that the flames weren't feeding on wood.

He scaled the outer wall, scrambling up a rock face which at times was so steep and devoid of vegetation that he had to haul himself up using the tips of his fingers and toes of his boots. At the rim, a dense covering of trees grew out and over the ravine, which he guessed probably made it invisible from overhead. His eyes adjusted quickly, giving him all the night vision he needed, and when the moon broke through, the scene below was as clear as daylight.

The man from the photograph in Kathleen Hunter's home was fighting a man who wore a white mask and white fatigues, and the battle was clearly one-sided. The strength and speed of the white figure was astonishing. Though Hammerson managed to get the occasional strike through his opponent's defences, the well-aimed blows did little to slow his assailant. He seemed to simply absorb them, without any reaction or indication of pain or trauma. Alex wondered whether the mask and coveralls were some sort of body armor.

He looked over to the tree line away from the mouth of the deep green tunnel, and made out two figures concealed there, also watching the fight. At least, the man was watching; the woman was staring back up the slope. Both looked scared.

Down and to the left, another white-clad figure was leaning over a large overweight man who was obviously suffering from gunshot wounds. The white figure pulled him roughly to a sitting position and spoke to him. Alex concentrated and picked up the words.

'Where is he? Where is the Arcadian?'

Alex frowned. The man fighting in the ravine below had called him 'Arcadian' when Alex had seen him in the street outside the animal hospital. Was he the Arcadian? Were these men looking for him? *Why? What does 'Arcadian' mean?*

The man being questioned groaned and shook his head, then spat into his interrogator's face, spattering the white ski mask with blood. The masked man grabbed the other man's head and twisted it violently. The snapping sound bounced up the rock face towards Alex. He frowned and leaned further out over the edge. *Why kill the man for not knowing anything?*

The white figure pushed the dead body roughly aside and moved towards where his comrade was fighting with the soldier from the photograph. He froze mid-step and looked around the ravine, then up to the spot where Alex was concealed. Alex flattened himself to the ground. *Did he hear me?* That should have been impossible over the distance. There was something strange about these men; they weren't like normal humans.

Maybe they're like me, Alex thought.

And, if so, maybe they'd have answers to his questions about who he was, where he'd come from, and why he was capable of the things that made him so different from others.

The ski-masked man moved his head slowly, scanning the entire cliff line. Eventually, he gave up, rolled his shoulders, and continued over to where his comrade was still battling the older soldier. The older man was rapidly tiring and it wouldn't be long before his assailant overpowered him. The new arrival stopped a few paces away, arms hanging by his side and his whole body now motionless. He seemed content simply to watch.

Alex got to his feet, his eyes fixed on the brutal scene below.

*

Jack Hammerson was exhausted and sore. He felt every one of his fifty-plus years as the ski-masked soldier hit him again. The armored suit he wore had prevented any bones being shattered, but he was sure his cheekbone was depressed, and there was a gap in his mouth where two molars had been just a few minutes ago.

What was worrying him was the fact that his suit's ceramic plating, designed to withstand anything from a car crash to a high-caliber slug, was beginning to deteriorate. Black flakes of the synthetically toughened material littered the snow at his feet.

Hammerson spat blood, and circled the man, keeping his hands up and head tucked down low. He expected to die, but he'd make it count, make Graham's freakish creation know he'd been in a battle.

He knew that taking his opponent head-on was a waste of time – it played to his strengths rather than Hammerson's own. The white figure looked as fresh now as when he had first engaged Hammerson in combat, while Hammerson himself was being ground down with every punch and kick he absorbed. He needed a game-changer; it was all-or-nothing time.

Hammerson pulled his long-bladed knife, expecting his opponent to do the same. Instead, the man nodded and made a come-and-try-it motion with his hands. Not the slightest hint of caution, fear or even a defensive combat stance. Hammerson suddenly felt the man was playing with him.

He feinted to the left and slashed back quickly, hoping to catch the man across the torso. Hammerson was trained and fast, but this man was unnatural. *Just like Alex*, he thought.

He spun back and came in again low and fast, but Ski Mask was ready. In one motion, he grabbed Hammerson's wrist and twisted it. Hammerson felt the bones crack and the tendons stretch and pop.

He tried to hang on to the knife, but his fingers went dead and it fell from his hand.

The man used his hold on the HAWC's wrist to pull him forward and punch him in the eye. Hammerson felt the explosion go off all over one side of his head, and only his iron-hard physical condition stopped him from blacking out completely. He would have fallen, except the man reached out and caught him and spun him round. He swiftly removed a plastic cuff from his pocket, fastened Hammerson's hands behind him, then pushed him towards his waiting comrade.

Hammerson shook his head to clear the lingering muzziness from the blow to his skull. He slowed his breathing and worked on assessing the damage to his body, mentally ticking off what worked and what was impaired. He was still armed, and while he was alive he could fight, and kill.

In the center of the ravine, the interrogation began. Hammerson's captor shook him roughly to ensure he had his full attention, then gripped him by his cropped gray hair.

The second man leaned in close. 'Where is the Arcadian?'

Hammerson stared into the black slits of the ski mask. 'Identify yourself, soldier.'

He was shaken again, harder. 'Where is the man called Alex Hunter, the Arcadian?'

I wish I knew, asshole.

Hammerson laughed into his interrogator's face. He didn't see the punch coming to his other eye, just felt the blow and then a warm wetness on his cheek. Felt like a significant cut. *Gonna be sore in the morning*, he thought, and laughed again. The optical devices gave him some protection, but he couldn't take many more hard blows to the eyes without losing his sight – and to a fighter, that meant end game. He'd never make another hour, let alone the morning.

The two men looked at each other, some kind of silent communication passing between them. One stood back a pace, while the other knocked Hammerson to his knees, in preparation for the execution.

A brilliant silver moon broke through the clouds and Hammerson looked up at it. *Beautiful*, he thought, and remembered what his father used to say. *Good light, good night-hunting*. But there would be no more hunting for him.

His eyes traveled along the edge of the cliff, and saw a figure standing there. The shape of the body, the strength and confidence in the stance, told him who it was. He knew the man as well as he'd have known his own son. As he watched, the figure grasped a tree trunk and began to climb down it into the ravine.

'Arcadian!' Hammerson yelled.

The word and its echo bounced around the small valley and traveled up the mountainside.

The white-clad men looked at each other, then one of them spoke softly. 'He's here.'

'Then we have him trapped,' the other said.

Hammerson grinned. *You think you've trapped him in here with you? Wrong, assholes – you're trapped in here with him.*

THIRTY-SIX

Captain Robert Graham tried once again to raise his test subjects on the mountain. None of the three men were responding, and one of their lifelines had gone dead on his screen.

'Shit.' Graham bit the edge off a fingernail and spat it onto the desk. Those idiots couldn't be out there forever. The operation needed to be over quickly.

His major concern wasn't the potential confrontation with Alex Hunter. He had equipped the three soldiers with more than enough capability to accomplish the task. They easily matched the original Arcadian's strength and speed, and they were three to his one. His worry was the instability of the compound and its effects on the men's physiology.

The ARC-044 treatments seemed to start a war within the subjects' bodies. Their increased physical capabilities fired their metabolism to a level far above that of a normal person – basically their recuperative and regenerative powers had to work overtime to keep rebuilding what their own bodies were continually tearing down and consuming in a bid to feed an engine permanently stuck in high gear.

He looked again at the blank screen. He needed to know what was going on, which meant going to see Jack Hammerson. That brickheaded old soldier had kept enough secrets from him.

*

'Don't say a word; that's an order. This is between me and your boss,' Graham said, pointing his finger into the face of Annie Fletcher, Hammerson's personal assistant.

She removed her hand from the phone and narrowed her eyes as Graham opened Hammerson's office door without knocking.

It was dark in the large room, so Graham left the door ajar a crack. The big viewing screen on the wall was fizzing with white noise. He saw a figure sitting near the desk, its back turned, its head resting on one hand.

'Hammerson, you must think we're all stupid,' Graham burst out. 'I know the Arcadian is alive and on US soil. Your submission to the Joint Chiefs was a total fabrication.'

He paused; the large figure just sat there, unresponsive.

'It doesn't really matter,' Graham went on, determined to get a reaction. 'We don't need him in the field anymore. We've reproduced the treatment – Hunter can be retired immediately.' He took a step closer. 'But that doesn't mean I don't need him at all. We can work together – you scratch my back, et cetera. General Wozyniak is delighted with my results, but I know the compound's still a little unstable. I can't seem to balance the subjects' metabolisms. Wozyniak might not be so happy if I told him the men could burn themselves out, literally, in a month – not a great return for a hundred million taxpayers' bucks. Now, if I could take a quick look at Hunter's hypothalamus ...'

Graham reached the seated figure and realized it was too big to be Hammerson. 'Jack?'

'He can be *retired*? You mean fucking *terminated*.'

An enormous hand shot out and caught Graham's wrist, then pulled and twisted, bringing Graham to his knees beside what he now saw was a wheelchair. In it sat Lieutenant Sam Reid.

Graham screamed.

Annie Fletcher came to the door, smiled sweetly, and pulled it fully closed.

Sam tugged on Graham's arm again. 'You want to kill him, you little weasel? You fucking killed him years ago when you pumped that shit into him! He doesn't even know if he's human anymore.'

Graham wailed and banged at Sam's hand with his fist, but the HAWC just tightened his grip.

'I'll see you in chains, Reid,' Graham yelled.

Sam laughed softly and applied more pressure to the scientist's thin arm. 'Haven't you noticed – I'm already in chains, you asshole. Guess I must be suffering from battlefield trauma – happens to us HAWCs, you know. We can go psycho sometimes, real loony – been known to actually kill people.' He laughed again. 'By the way, that reminds me, I'm due for another coffee with my old friend General Wozyniak. Got something real interesting to tell him now. In fact, why don't I –'

'I could make you walk again.'

It was like all the air had been sucked out of the room.

Sam let go of Graham's arm. 'Fuck off.'

Graham stumbled backwards, then stood up. He rubbed his wrist. Both an idea and an opportunity sprang to his mind. He looked at the huge frame packed into the wheelchair.

'Not much of a life for a man of action, is it?'

Sam sat motionless again, staring at the fizzing screen.

Graham took a cautious step forward. 'The Arcadian treatment works, Lieutenant Reid – you know that. But did you know that it can be used to regenerate tissue, bone matter, internal organs ... even the nervous tubular bundle of the spinal cord? That part's easy. Imagine being able to get out of that chair. Imagine being able to run, fight, defend your country again. I could give you all that. I just need –'

Sam jerked his body forward at the scientist. 'I said *fuck off*!'

'Okay, okay.' Graham backed away, holding his hands in front of him. 'We're both a little stressed at the moment. By the way, I saved Hunter's life when everyone else had given up. I'm not the bad guy, Sam. Remember that.'

The HAWC turned his head away, but Graham knew he'd got to him.

He reached behind his back to touch the door handle. 'Think about it,' he said. 'I helped Alex, and I can help you. You know where to find me.'

THIRTY-SEVEN

Matt stayed hunkered down above the ravine, paralyzed by the brutal action below. Sarah sat with her back jammed up against his, keeping watch on the upper slope, but he knew that she was blind in the darkness. She wouldn't see anything coming until it was right on top of them.

He looked around for something he could use as a weapon ... anything. There were a few loose branches nearby – not much use against the beast they'd seen in the cave, or against the guns in the fight below. Then he remembered ... and moved his hands frantically around under the snow's surface. His fingers touched Chief Logan's handgun.

Matt had seen how fast those white-clothed men moved, how just one of them had beaten down Hammerson. Even armed with the handgun, he reckoned he'd probably last about thirty seconds ... and that included twenty seconds to raise and fire it.

Jack Hammerson's last order had been to wait five minutes, then head back down the mountain. Matt knew he needed to honor it. Also, he didn't want to watch a brave man get beaten to death.

He was just about to grab Sarah when Hammerson's voice boomed out: '*Arcadian!*'

Matt's head snapped back to the ravine; he hadn't heard that word in years. He scanned the rock face leading into the valley, then the snowy slope behind him. When he turned back to the cliff edge, he saw a figure silhouetted against the moonlight, arms outstretched, strength radiating from him.

The sight reminded Matt of the last carving he and Thomas had seen in the cave: Tooantuh, Thomas's people's mighty warrior.

The old Indian had been sure his ancestor would return when needed.

'Tooantuh will come and you must be ready for him,' he had told Matt. 'Help him to push the beast back into the mountain.'

The beast. Matt looked over his shoulder again at the dark slope.

*

Alex jumped the last thirty feet to the valley floor, going down on one knee and fist with the landing impact. He stood and walked towards the masked soldiers, stopping a few dozen feet away.

'Who are you?' he asked. 'Where are you from?'

The men moved towards him, fanning out one to each side.

'You are Captain Alex Hunter, formerly of the HAWCs,' said the man without the blood-spattered mask. 'The one they call the Arcadian. You are to come with us.'

Alex didn't move. 'Who are you?' he repeated. 'How did you get to be ... like you are?'

Neither man answered the questions, nor even looked like they understood them.

'You will come with us, Hunter,' the leader said again. 'That is our order, and all you need to know.'

The man's head tilted slightly, studying Alex, then the emotionless voice came again. 'You will come with us. If not, we are authorized to use extreme force.'

Caution flared within Alex and the skin on his neck crawled. These men were like him, he could sense it, but they appeared non-human, disconnected – almost robotic.

When Alex still made no move, both men slowly lowered their hands to their guns. Alex held his hands up, trying to slow them down.

'Wait, I need to talk to you. If I come with you, will you –'

'You will come with us,' the man said again. 'Alive would be better, but our mission will still be complete if we retrieve just your head. Your choice.'

Alex couldn't think straight. He could tell the men wanted to attack him. Perhaps their orders were to bring him in dead or alive, but he knew they wanted to test their own skills against him first. Frustration writhed and coiled inside him. He wanted to talk to the men, but his heartbeat was rising and a fire was igniting deep within him.

The other man got shakily to his feet. 'Alex,' he called out, 'if they get you back to the lab, you'll end up as nothing more than tissue in formaldehyde. Graham wants to cut you up. *I* have the answers you need. *I* can tell you who you are, and where you began. I'm Colonel Jack Hammerson, your former commander. I know about your mother ... Kathleen.' He took a pace forward. 'I know everything – your father, Jim, was my friend ... He was more like you than you know.'

Hammerson ... the name felt familiar. But before Alex could speak, the white-clad man closest to the gray-haired soldier had raised his strange bulbous gun at his face.

'No!' Alex yelled, and charged.

Hammerson dived and rolled, but the shooter was already spinning away from him and bringing his gun up to Alex. The other man turned side-on and did the same.

For Alex, the world slowed. He drew his own weapon and started firing as he crossed in seconds the twenty feet that separated him from the white-clad soldiers. The men twisted and dodged the projectiles, without receiving even a graze.

Their own gas-powered bullets were two streams, kicking up snow as they raced towards Alex.

He dived, spear-like, at the closest man, rolling and coming up in front of him, grabbing his gun and forcing it straight up in the air. The man responded with the same manoeuvre, so each was now gripping the other's weapon, twisting and pushing, their strength matched. As Alex fought, he knew he was vulnerable to the other man, who was circling the struggling pair, looking for the smallest opportunity to put a bullet in him.

He released his gun into his attacker's grip, freeing his own hand and bringing its fist around hard into the man's jaw. The man pulled away and Alex's blow glanced off his chin. Alex knew he should have planned better; they shared the same speed and anticipation skills, so trying to be simply quicker or stronger wasn't going to cut it.

The man must have seen the logic in Alex's move for he released his own gun. Alex took it and threw it to Hammerson. He didn't understand why he felt he could trust the HAWC, but he did. Perhaps it was simply down to the oldest military truism: *my enemy's enemy is my friend.* If he was wrong, he was as good as dead.

In the millisecond it took Alex to hurl the weapon, his opponent took advantage of his exposure and landed a stunning blow to the side of his head. Alex heard the man's fist break on the bone of his brow. His vision blurred for an instant and he felt like he'd been hit by a speeding car. Nevertheless, he grabbed the man's wrist, extended from the blow, and hung on ... and saw the smashed metacarpals slide back into place below the skin.

'*Who are you?*' he yelled into the blank, featureless face.

The black eyes stared back at him through the slits of the ski mask, indicating no understanding or emotion.

In Special Forces training, every hard point on your body is a potential weapon. The knowledge came to Alex from somewhere deep inside, and his body took over. He pulled the man towards him and lowered his elbows to smash them into his cheeks. The blow disorientated Alex's opponent, giving him time to bring a knee up into the man's ribs. The grip on his gun arm loosened enough to allow him to pull it free and grab the ski mask. Alex needed to find out who this man was; to see some flicker of humanity beneath the robotic responses.

He pulled the mask free, and recoiled. Pustules crusted the man's tormented flesh; black-rimmed ulcers exposed the bone of his skull. Alex smelled antiseptic and realized that the ski mask wasn't just to keep the cold out or hide the man's identity; it was a medicinal bandage.

The man screamed and went berserk in Alex's grasp. His fury escalated his strength and he picked Alex up and threw him ten feet across the valley floor. As soon as Alex landed, another zipper of bullets raced towards him, fired by the soldier still wearing his mask.

Immediately, the barrage was answered by return fire, causing the white figure to leap back into cover. Hammerson was making good use of the weapon Alex had thrown him.

The unmasked soldier came at Alex like a charging bull, head down, arms spread wide. The collision threw them both down into the snow. Alex tried to hang onto the berserker and hold him down. He could see that his eyes were red-rimmed and furious.

'Stop and listen to me!' he yelled.

The man was literally frothing at the mouth, and some of the deep cankers on his face had erupted, dripping black, infected blood onto the snow. Alex could feel the heat coming off his body – it was way beyond normal, even way beyond Alex's own overheated metabolism. The soldier punched, clawed and raked at him, his mouth spitting words and sounds that didn't make sense. Alex struggled to hold him down.

They rolled together across the ground, crashing into the cliff face and dislodging rocks that bounced down and buried themselves in the snow around them. A piece of granite the size of a loaf of bread landed near Alex's head, and he quickly reached into the snow to seize it. He smashed it into the man's skull and a crackling crunch told him he had caved in the bone.

The man immediately fell still. Alex released him and pressed his fingers to his neck, feeling for a pulse, but his flesh was too hot to touch for long. The snow around him started to melt, then the white suit he wore began to steam and smoke. Alex backed away, shaking his head. He couldn't believe what he was seeing.

He reached out to touch the blistered face; a gesture of comfort for whatever hell the man had been subjected to in the name of science. He wished he could have talked to him, discussed their similarities, shared the mutual pain of their situation. It was clear to Alex that the man had suffered the rages that sometimes consumed *him*. He had been learning to control his fury, but this man's demons had broken free – and eventually killed him.

Is this how I'll end up, he thought, *consumed and destroyed by rage?*

Was this his own future playing out before him like some ghastly movie?

As Alex watched, the disfigured face collapsed in on itself, the flesh liquefying and bubbling in the cavity of the skull. He cried out in horror, and scooped snow over the putrefying mass that had been a man only minutes before.

THIRTY-EIGHT

Adira drew in cold air and then blew it out in huge smoking plumes. She had vomited onto the snow from exhaustion a few minutes ago, but still continued to push herself up the slope. She grabbed another handful of snow and held it to her battered face. She had taken a blade to her eye, slicing the outer corner away from the palpebrae muscle to release the enormous build-up of blood that was forcing the eyelid down over the eyeball. The viscous fluid had run hot and fast, and her eye was now open enough for her to see, but she dreaded another blow.

The sound of gunfire drew her on with as much urgency as her fatigued muscles would allow, anxiety fuelling her desperation. She had invested so much in Alex Hunter; the idea of bringing him this far, only to lose him to some mad personal vendetta was too much to contemplate. More gunfire came, and she jerked her head up to stare into the darkness. If anyone put a bullet in Alex, she would destroy whoever was responsible or had been involved in the event.

She cursed and punched both of her thighs as hard as she could, the pain bringing a small jolt of adrenaline into the rubbery muscles. Through pain-gritted teeth, she clambered up the steep slope, at times having to drop to all fours to keep going.

At the edge of a small slip valley, she crouched against a tree, breathing heavily but doing her best to remain silent. Blows and grunts from below drew her eyes to the bottom of the ravine, where a number of large men were fighting viciously – Alex among them, and also Jack Hammerson. She couldn't make out their opponents – *more Mossad agents?*

She kneeled up to look closer, then immediately hunkered back down as she saw two figures huddled beside a tree trunk a short distance away. She wormed her way forward, staying low, and drew her weapon. In another moment she was behind them, wrapping a hand around the woman's mouth and aiming the gun into the young man's startled face as he turned.

He dropped his gun, and held up his hands. 'Don't shoot.'

Adira released the woman, who immediately huddled closer to the man. She saw shock and terror on their faces, and guessed some of it came from the sight of her own swollen, blood-streaked features.

'Identify yourselves,' she ordered.

The couple talked over the top of one another, and she managed to pick out references to the *thing* Alex had alluded to, as well as some connection with Jack Hammerson and also Alex himself. She could use that. She needed to get them off the mountain; there were too many people around, and in such a situation confusion would be the killer.

'I am also a HAWC,' she said. 'Part of Colonel Hammerson's team. You need to get out of here, now!' She nodded down to where the fight was still raging. 'I will look after them from here. Go.'

'But –' the man began, pointing back up the mountainside, but Adira gave him a push.

He grabbed the woman by the arm and together they started to run, but the man kept glancing back. Adira wondered whether he intended to obey her instruction. She watched them disappear into the dark, then crouched low and started to move in closer to the fighting.

She stopped and sniffed through her blood-clogged nose – there was something acrid and animalistic floating on the air.

*

The creature reached the high edge of the sharp ridge and stared down at the small creatures as they beat and tore at each other. The aggression and blood lust excited it.

As it tensed its tree-thick limbs, ready to launch itself into the battle, there was movement to its right. Two shapes sprinted away into the darkness, and it was drawn to pursue them. After a few paces, it slid to a stop as the intoxicating odor of fresh blood and raw flesh filled its broad nostrils. Hunger flared and it bared its teeth.

It would take the meat first.

It moved closer, readying itself.

*

The single remaining attacker turned side-on in a shooter's stance and aimed at Alex Hunter as he threw snow over his decomposing comrade. Hammerson brought his own gun up and fired several rounds at the man, keeping the trigger depressed for full automatic. The bullets blistered out from the long barrel like a swarm of hot angry wasps. In this mode, the small compact weapon delivered more bullets, but the force of the recoil made it extremely difficult for even the most accomplished marksman to control the spread. Only a couple of bullets struck the white-clad figure's armored torso before he flung himself out of the way and rolled.

Hammerson tried to track the rapidly moving figure. He was astonished when, instead of seeking cover, the man came to his feet and sprinted directly towards him in a blur of white. The man's speed made it impossible for Hammerson to draw a bead; and when about fifteen feet out, the figure dived, Hammerson didn't have time to recalibrate his aim or even dodge. The six-foot-two-inch missile hit him mid-chest, slamming him painfully backwards.

The man easily wrenched the gun from Hammerson's hand, and a blow just under his diaphragm knocked the wind out of him. Hammerson heard the crack of his ceramic armor plating as the man's fist connected, then pulled back to strike again.

The HAWC commander felt himself lifted and spun. He struggled in his captor's unnaturally powerful grip, but might as well try to break lengths of steel cable. There was a hand around his neck, the other holding the gun up beside his face – but it was pointed not at him, but at Alex. Hammerson realized that he had never been a real threat ... it had been about Alex all along.

Hammerson was pushed towards his former protégé, who seemed to be focused on something along the top of the ridge rather than what was going on in his immediate vicinity. Hammerson knew exactly what was happening – the masked soldier was using him as a shield to get himself close to Alex so he could take him out at point-blank range.

Hammerson struggled again, but every time he did, the grip on his neck tightened. Breathing was becoming difficult. He strained against the iron-like fingers around his throat and tried to reach down to the last weapon he had – the shorter Ka-Bar strapped to his leg. It was only seven inches long, but lethally sharp. Unfortunately, the way he was being held kept it just out of reach.

*

Alex was aware of Hammerson shooting at the last white-clad figure and then being overpowered, but his attention was elsewhere. There was something moving stealthily along the top of the ravine, trying not to be seen or heard, but he could tell that it was big and breathing deep and slow.

Alex knew the creature was hunting them, stalking them.

THIRTY-NINE

Hammerson saw Alex turn his head slightly so he was staring towards him and his captor, but he seemed to be looking through them rather than at them. There came a thundering roar from behind Hammerson – the undeniable sound of a challenge – followed by a loud thump, and then blinding pain as he and his assailant were smashed to the ground.

The HAWC commander tried to roll over, but his arm wouldn't work. His shoulder was much lower on his frame than it should have been. Lying in the snow, his face half-buried, he saw a colossus standing where he and the ski-masked soldier had been seconds ago. Hammerson's eyes traveled upwards, but the creature seemed to go on forever. At last he caught sight of an enormous crested head framed by the moonlight.

Well, Chief, he thought wryly, *looks like the Kearns kid was right – there is something up here, after all.*

The white-clad man got to his feet, his super-charged physicality allowing him to recover much more quickly than Hammerson. He brought his gun up at the giant and fired. The bullet struck its leathery hide but elicited no more than a howl of annoyance.

The beast reached forward, seized the man by his gun arm and pulled him off his feet as easily as lifting a doll. In its grip, the man's unnatural strength counted for little. The creature outweighed him by easily 1000 pounds, and its bunched simian muscles gave it more than enough power to deal with his smaller frame. It roared again, and brought its broad gargoyle-like face close to the man's head, its enormous mouth opening wide to reveal long curved canines. It closed them around the soldier's skull, the ski mask affording a perfect non-slip surface. The man rained blow after frantic blow on the creature's broad face, but it ignored them.

Hammerson grimaced as the massive jaws shifted their grip with a grinding noise. For the first time, he heard the unnatural soldier react to pain – his screech made him sound all too human. There was a crunch and pop as his head burst, to splash thick fluid onto the snow at the creature's feet.

The beast flung the body down the ravine. It disappeared into the trees fifty feet below. Hammerson lay still, hoping to be taken for dead. Years of watching *Animal Planet* had taught him that, to a carnivore, a dead animal was far less interesting than a live one.

'Hey!' a voice yelled. Alex's.

Oh, shit no, thought Hammerson.

*

The silence stretched – the only sound the slight squeak of leather as Alex clenched the knife handle tighter, readying himself for the beast's charge.

It came, fast and heavy, its arms opening wide. Alex knew what it intended: to crush him in an embrace, then tear him to pieces. But when it reached Alex, he was no longer there. He'd darted under one of its seven-foot-long arms and flicked his blade across the leathery torso, opening a gash that splashed crimson blood onto the snow.

The beast spun quickly, then paused and blinked. A huge hand came up to touch the wound. It snuffed and blew out its cheeks, then smashed fists the size of basketballs into the snow. It screamed in rage and pounded the ground again and again, its fury building.

Alex moved around to its side, judging his next point of attack or defence.

The creature came again, but, unbelievably, it feinted to one side. Alex was forced to step and then correct himself. He had underestimated its intelligence and ability to adapt. In the split second it took for him to change his balance, the mighty beast charged again.

Alex dived, but it threw out an arm in a backhanded motion that caught Alex's hip and spun him in the air. When he got to his feet, he felt his hip joint grind beneath the skin.

Hammerson was limping towards them, at the creature's rear. He had the gun up, but his injuries made it difficult for him to aim. The enormous beast glanced briefly at the approaching HAWC, then returned its attention to Alex, circling him. With a flash of speed incongruous for something so huge, it twisted and flew towards Hammerson, grabbing him by the shoulder and flinging him bodily at Alex.

Hammerson had no chance; he spun in the air, arms and legs loose. He crashed into Alex and both men went flying, skidding several feet through the snow.

Alex flung the older soldier's body off him. He knew what was coming next – the creature had used Hammerson as a diversion. And it had worked. His knife was trapped beneath him and the thing was already on top of him. It leaped and landed across his body, pinning him beneath its bulk of muscle and stinking fur and bringing its open mouth close to Alex's face. Its jaws were as wide as his entire skull, and its hot breath smelled of rotten meat and death.

Alex used both arms to hold the thing back from him, one hand on a throat that was as broad as his own waist, and another grasping a tree-trunk-sized arm. But even his unnatural strength struggled to contain the titan, and slowly the tusked jaws came closer. Eyes that held a cunning intelligence met his, and Alex was sure that the corners of its vile maw turned up in triumph.

Just as the teeth grazed Alex's skin, he heard a scream from behind and a small figure landed on the creature's back. Adira. She screamed again and stabbed a metal spike into each side of the beast's neck.

It arched its torso and roared down into Alex's face, the sound near deafening, the vile shitty stench even worse. Its jaws pulled back, but it still lay across his body, crushing him deeper into the snow.

Before the Israeli woman could leap out of the way, an enormous arm flew up to grab her. The beast pounded her body into the ground, then flung her roughly to the valley floor, where she landed hard with a grunt, seemingly dazed.

The creature tried to pull the spikes free from its neck, but they were too deeply embedded or too small for it to grip with its giant leathery fingers. It gave up and leaped furiously to its feet, the motion grinding Alex's body further into the ground.

Alex felt rather than heard the cracking of multiple ribs being fractured in his chest as the beast's 1000 pounds of pressure was magnified by its sudden movement. Immediately, breath was gone from his lungs and his heart ceased beating, making his vision swim and giving a sensation of falling into a dark pit. But like a car receiving a jump-start, his body refused to give in, and commenced to pump blood once again. Strange chemical combinations in his body rushed to repair the damage, as Adira's sounds of pain acted like an electrical charge across his consciousness. *Enough – finish it!* His mind screamed to him.

The giant rose to its full height and gave a booming *whoop* that turned to an enraged roar. It rushed towards Adira and lifted a massive foot over her prone body. Adira weakly held up one hand, as if it were possible to ward off the crushing blow that was about to stamp the life from her.

As the foot came down, Alex struck the creature's torso like a missile. This time, he buried his steel blade all the way to the hilt in the tough hide. As the creature reached to grab hold of him, he used the swinging momentum to twist his knife and open the wound even further.

A massive fist pounded him into the snow. He looked up to see the beast pulling the blade from its side. It flung it away into the dark, then, in a human-like gesture, felt its side, looked at its bloody hand and whined.

Alex rolled and shook his head to clear away a fog of pain and disorientation. Slowly, he moved his hands about in the snow, searching for something he knew should be there. As he stretched out to search a wider area, the beast came down hard on his back. Cartilage and ribs popped under the weight, and he felt the hot blast of its foul breath on his neck. He guessed the giant mouth was opening over the back of his head. His time was up … unless he could defend himself.

His hand closed on the object he sought and he rolled under the massive weight, coming around to jam the gun that had belonged to one of the masked soldiers into the creature's open jaws. The blast of high-velocity projectiles blew out the top of its crested skull and it thumped flat across his body.

FORTY

Alex lay still for a moment, breathing heavily, blinking away pain from a hundred different spots on his battered body. Then he lifted one of the creature's shoulders and eased out from under the massive torso. He knelt in the snow for a few seconds, sucking in deep breaths.

Adira lay some distance away, and he crawled to her. Blood smeared her lips, and her face was disfigured from the beatings she had received. She took his forearm and tried to smile through split lips.

'I think I'm broken.'

He put his hand over hers. 'You always turn up when I need it most.'

'I am your guardian angel ... didn't you know?' she replied softly.

Alex half-smiled. He would never trust her again, but, for a time, he had loved her; and she had loved and protected him.

She groaned as she shifted, and looked away from him. 'I can't go back. Better I die here, Alex.'

He shook his head. 'Not a chance.'

He quickly ran his hands over her body, feeling the breaks and for other injuries. He pulled her to a sitting position and she grunted in pain and coughed blood.

She squeezed his arm. 'What is there to live for? I know I have lost ...'

She couldn't finish her sentence, and he saw that her eyes were shining with tears. She gritted her teeth and pulled him closer.

'I need to tell you ... Everything I did, I did for you. I lied to you because I had to. Now it doesn't matter.' She swallowed. 'You are Alex Hunter, a HAWC agent, part of the American Special Forces. You were dying with an incurable sickness and your superior, Jack

Hammerson, took a big risk and sent you to us, to Israel. We saved you ... *I* saved you! I took you to my homeland, and you were cured there ... but not fully. Your memory did not return, and so you lost your old life. I thought I could fill the gap for you.'

Her voice became urgent. 'Your people wanted to kill you, Alex, to cut you up to see what makes you what you are. They still do. And now I think my people want to do the same.' She glanced over at Hammerson. 'But not that man. He is not your enemy. It was through him that you were saved.'

Alex stared at her, absorbing the information. Everything seemed to click into place, as though the missing details had plugged themselves into the blank areas of his memory. He reached down and pushed the hair from her face, but sticky blood held it there.

She turned away from his gaze. 'I was weak and selfish, Alex. I thought we could both run away from our lives. I wanted you for myself ... Stupid.'

A small pack landed in the snow beside Alex. He looked up to see that Hammerson had dragged himself over to them. The stocky man didn't look in much better shape than Adira. Alex stared at him, the shattered fragments of memory rebuilding themselves. 'Jack?'

Hammerson nodded and smiled. 'Welcome back, son.' He gestured to Adira. 'Get her on her feet.'

Alex picked up the packet and tore it open, then broke the gel cap under the battered woman's nose. 'Breathe in,' he told her.

She did and coughed, before inhaling several more times. Then she pushed his hand away from her face, and he grabbed her around the waist to help her up. Adira shook her head as if to clear it, and sucked in a few deep breaths. She staggered a bit, but managed to remain upright.

Hammerson rolled a shoulder under his shattered armor. 'That'll give her an hour or so. After that, she's going to need help, or she'll probably die. In fact, we all need to get the hell out of here.'

Alex walked over to the creature's massive corpse and pulled the spikes from its neck. He returned and handed them to Adira. She lifted her dark eyes to Hammerson and Alex edged between them. He knew what she could do with the deadly throwing spikes.

After another second, she spun the weapons in her fingers, bringing them back towards herself, and they disappeared into a small sheath at her belt. She pushed her hair back with a shaky hand and looked across to the massive corpse. She inhaled deeply and then slowly let her steaming breath out through her nose before speaking.

'So, now it's over.'

Alex remained still for a few moments before his eyes moved from the creature's body, up once again to the sharp edge of the ravine. He shook his head slowly. 'No, not yet, but soon. She's close – my answers are close, I can sense it.'

*

Matt and Sarah came out of the trees a few hundred feet down the hill. Matt's curiosity had overridden his sense of self-preservation, and now the fight was over, he needed to see if Jack Hammerson had survived ... and maybe get a glimpse of the massive creature they had encountered.

Leading Sarah cautiously over the rim of the ravine, he looked down to see Hammerson and the HAWC woman standing by the body of the most magnificent thing Matt had ever seen. He climbed as swiftly as he could manage down the rock face, keeping an eye on Sarah, who followed him more slowly. She had been subdued ever since they'd fled the cave and its grisly sights.

When they reached the valley floor, he noticed the HAWC woman's face was ravaged by more than just her wounds. She looked as if she was grieving.

He looked around. 'Where are the guys in white?'

'Dead,' the woman replied, her eyes lifeless.

'And Alex Hunter?'

She looked up at the snow-covered ridge towards the dark peak. 'Gone.'

'Gone where?' Matt asked, frustrated by her terse replies.

'To fight his demons.' She shrugged and turned away.

Matt looked at Hammerson, but he just shook his head.

Matt pointed at the large creature. 'Is it dead?'

'All yours,' Hammerson said.

Matt knelt beside the beast, and Sarah joined him. She placed her hands on the massive back, her eyebrows pulled together in a frown.

'It's real. It actually exists,' she said, her tone incredulous. She ran her hands over the creature almost tenderly, brushed the blood-matted fur off its gargoyle face. 'An inglorious end to a magnificent creature. Its first encounter with humans in 10,000 years, and it turns out to be its last. No wonder they rebelled against us all those millennia ago. Now, we may never –'

'It killed Charles and Emma Wilson.' Matt's voice was flat.

Sarah pulled her hands back as if burnt.

*

Alex scaled the sheer rock wall. In a few seconds, he was standing in the cave's entrance. The revolting stench he'd smelled on the creature itself became stronger the further he went into the pitch-dark interior.

He ignored the cave drawings and the battered headless body of an old Indian man on the ground, only pausing to lift a large Colt revolver from the dry soil. He could smell that the big handgun had been fired. Opening it, he saw there were two bullets left. He tucked the weapon into his belt and continued towards the rear of the cave and the passages that led off it.

The light was so faint it was barely enough even for Alex's enhanced vision, but he could just make out the scuff marks in the dirt that told him which passageway to take. A short way in, he made out a ledge, a tiny shelf of bloody stone, and as he stared harder, the row of grisly trophies come into focus. He recoiled – the pain, suffering, and terror pressed into the flesh of their faces was horrifying. Pale windpipes and red and blue tendons, stained with dried black blood, hung from the ragged stumps of the necks of men, women and children. Just when he felt able to tear his eyes away, he saw her, his mother, or what was left of her. The skin was drawn tight on her skull, and the ligaments of her jaw had shortened in the dry atmosphere, setting her face in an eternal scream.

He reached out to touch the cold flesh. 'I'm sorry I wasn't there to save you,' he said. 'I was *never* there for you.'

He kept his hand on the dead woman's cheek and rested his head against the cold, damp stone. The soft rustling sounds from deeper in the caves, the stench of death and decay, faded; time became meaningless as his mind retrieved fragmented images of his mother, his parents, his childhood, and played them over and over.

He couldn't tell how long he stood there remembering. After a while, the memories became distorted, a soft fuzziness, like white noise, interrupting them.

Returning to his grim surroundings, Alex looked down at his feet. His boots stood amid a mess of bones. Most were adult, the meat recently scraped or chewed away. But there were smaller bones too ... a femur still attached to the tibia by gristle and tendon at the knee. Far too tiny to belong even to a small adult. Men, women and children – all had been prey; brought here dead or alive, he couldn't know. But this was where it had ended for them ... for his mother.

He looked at the hellish desecration all around him, the heads lined up on the ledge. *So many of them, and all killed so brutally*, he thought miserably. He stared again into his mother's face. *I wish I could have helped you ...*

The thought disappeared as he jerked his head back towards the mouth of the cave. There were too many remains here for only the one predator.

Idiot!

Alex sprinted for the entrance.

FORTY-ONE

Hammerson held up his hand. 'Quiet.'

'Huh?' Matt said, looking up from the creature's body.

He saw that the HAWC commander was focused on something along the ridge. Matt stood, and Sarah came up quickly beside him and took his hand. As they watched, a hulking figure appeared at the rim of the ravine, outlined against the moon. Sarah gasped and crowded even closer to Matt.

The HAWC woman said something in what sounded like Hebrew, and edged towards Hammerson.

All four of them were backed together, forming a ring in the snow and staring up at the many creatures that now surrounded the ravine.

The beasts were silent at first, but then their eyes found their fallen kind. Low grunts and rumbles built to a whooping sound, a terrifying cacophony that made Sarah cover her ears. When Matt turned to her, he saw that her eyes were crushed shut too.

Some of the massive creatures rocked from side to side, but others uprooted huge trees and flung them down at the group. Others pounded the ground, the resulting tremors causing debris and snow to slide down into the ravine.

'Don't move,' Matt said, reaching out to take Sarah's hand again.

She grabbed it, and pressed closer to him. 'Like that's gonna happen!'

The HAWC woman held a throwing spike in her hand, which looked comical as a defence against the horde that would soon be bearing down on them. She whispered over her shoulder, 'No, I think we *should* move – away from the body.'

Matt nodded, keeping his eyes on the ridge. 'She might be right, Sarah. Mountain gorillas have been known to grieve for their dead, and these things' behavior seems a lot higher order than that.'

Sarah nodded jerkily. 'Okay, let's do it ... slowly.'

Like a single, many-legged beast, they edged towards the center of the small valley. As they moved, the howling, whooping clamor increased, then stopped. The largest of the creatures had roared them all to silence. Now, it moved down the slope towards the small group, sometimes on all fours, sometimes in a shambling man-like stance.

'Do not make eye contact,' Hammerson ordered in a whisper.

*

Alex saw the creatures ringing the edge of the rift, silently staring down at the humans below. He got as close as he dared, then stayed low and watched. He could feel the fear emanating from the small group huddled together on the valley floor. One of the beasts was climbing down towards them. As it came upright, Alex saw that it stood a foot taller again than the creature he had slain. The moonlight glinted off the silvered hair on its impossibly wide shoulders and back, and in one massive hand it grasped a tree trunk that probably weighed as much as a man.

Alex marveled at its size and power, and wondered what the world must have looked like all those millennia ago when it ruled the land. His admiration evaporated when he recalled what he'd seen in the cave – proof of the creatures' thirst for human blood.

They killed your mother, the voice inside his head reminded him. *They killed the last of your family; your chance to know your history.*

Alex saw his mother's face silently screaming in the stinking pitch-black cave. Those monsters had mutilated her ... had *eaten* her.

As the giant leader roared and charged the group below, Alex leaped. He landed in the snow between it and the humans, his arms wide. He screamed into the enormous face and it halted, probably more out of surprise than fear. It came up onto its hind legs, its fist-sized eyes showing white around the dark pupils.

'No old women or children here,' Alex yelled.

He held the large Colt at his side, waiting. He knew he could never kill all the creatures if they decided to come at him at once. But he would send as many as he could straight to hell.

The beast blew out its cheeks in disdain as it passed Alex to crouch and sniff at the giant corpse in the snow. It closed its eyes and slid its hand over the face and chest, slowing at the gash in its side. It brought its fingers to its lips and tasted the blood, then touched the corpse again, this time on the face.

Alex looked at the two creatures nearby, then up at the ring of beasts lining the edge of the ridge. Even though their boiled pink gargoyle-like faces looked the same, there were differences in the features – just as there were amongst humans. He looked back at the two on the valley floor; they shared a similarity that suggested a blood tie.

Alex smiled grimly. 'An eye for an eye then.'

He had spoken softly but the creature straightened as it heard his voice and wheeled and charged at him. He heard the civilian woman in the group scream.

The mountain of flesh and stinking fur stopped a few paces short of Alex and roared down into his upturned face. Alex didn't flinch.

'It hurts to have your family killed, doesn't it?' he yelled.

The beast's face loomed closer and its eyes narrowed. Alex sensed the emotions coming off it – fury, hate, contempt, the promise of re-tribution.

Its nostrils flared as it inhaled Alex's scent and then it screamed, so loud that Alex thought his eardrums might burst. Had it detected the blood of its kin on Alex's body? It swung a huge arm at him, striking him in the chest with a sickening crunch and propelling him dozens of feet back into the snow. Alex lay still as the creature stared at his prone body, the gun still ready in his grasp.

But it seemed to be finished with him. It blew air out through its puffed cheeks again, showing disdain, then swung back to its fallen kin. It tapped the body several times, then took hold of one of its mighty arms and started to drag it away.

After a moment, it made a guttural sound in its throat, and several of its kind clambered down the slope to help. Together, they carried the body back up to the ridge.

Alex got to his feet and followed.

FORTY-TWO

Hammerson took a few painful steps towards Alex. 'Arcadian – wait! Alex! *Ah, shit!*'

The ex-HAWC moved up and over the steep ridge faster than Hammerson could have hoped to follow, even if he was in good shape.

He shook his head and turned back to the small group, keeping his injured arm pressed to his side. The ceramic plating in his suit crackled as he moved, and in many places it had simply fallen away. He could feel the searing cold through the rips in the toughened, insulated material. He could tell the young woman, Sarah, was about to go into shock. Matt Kearns looked cold and disorientated. Senesh was still staring up at where Alex had disappeared. Her fists were balled and her demeanor was far from being approachable.

Hammerson knew the Israeli agent harbored ill feelings towards him, but she had done what he had intended: she had kept Alex Hunter alive, and had brought him back. He couldn't have hoped for more. She just needed to realize her job was done.

He spoke softly to her. 'You said you owed him a life – you've given it to him. Now let him go. If he needs you, you know he'll find you.'

She didn't turn, and he could see her hands flexing. Her mind must be working furiously, processing options that would give the best outcome for herself, and perhaps what she thought was best for Alex as well. Hammerson walked a little closer.

'You need to go home,' he said.

She spun around, one of the deadly throwing spikes in her hand. 'You used me,' she spat.

She didn't release the spike, just held it pointed at his face. He waited; there was nothing else he could do. His suit was shredded, and he was too battered to try to leap out of the way.

He waited and watched. She hissed something in Hebrew, through clenched teeth, but he couldn't make it out. Her head dropped, but her arm and the spike stayed raised. Hammerson stood his ground.

'The general, your uncle, wanted answers,' he said, 'so give him some.' She looked up and he pointed to the crushed white-clad soldier. 'Those men have undergone some form of the Arcadian treatment. Take one of them back with you. Have your people cut it into a thousand pieces and see what made it tick. I'm sure as hell not going to miss it.'

She dropped her arm, and, muttering to herself, walked to a rock near one of the dead soldiers and sat down ... but for only a second. She jumped to her feet and launched a vicious kick at the corpse, then sat down hard again and grabbed her head with both hands.

'They want me dead,' she said, staring at the snow. 'My *own uncle* wants me dead.'

Hammerson moved closer a few paces. 'I don't believe that. He wants his asset back. You need to help him save face, though. Take the body. I'll help, make a few calls ... Meir still owes me.'

When Senesh didn't respond, Hammerson looked around for Logan's body. He needed his comms pellet – his own had been smashed from his ear long ago. He saw the police chief's body, went over to it and crouched down next to the bulky shape.

'Sorry I got you into this, Bill,' he said, and pulled the pellet from Logan's ear and stuck it into his own. 'Sam ... come in.'

'Boss, thank God. What's been happening? I'm blind here.'

'We need to get some warm and cold bodies off this freakin' mountain ASAP,' Hammerson told Sam Reid.

'Yes, sir, I expected that. There's a car already en route from Raleigh. Should be there in thirty minutes. You'll need to get down to the east-side car park to rendezvous.'

'Copy that.'

Hammerson walked back to where Adira was sitting and, facing her, spoke again. 'Sam, I also want you to get a message to General Meir Shavit, direct from me. Tell him that Captain Senesh has successfully completed her mission and has an Arcadian subject for retrieval, with our blessing.'

Sam spluttered a response, but Hammerson cut him off.

'At ease, it's not Hunter. One of Graham's abominations, I reckon.' He thought for a moment. 'Tell Meir that I'll permit a single chopper to do a clean-up on the mountain and retrieve the asset, but after that I don't want to see any more Mossad torpedoes on our soil or I'll make it my personal mission to send every one of them home ... horizontally. Oh yeah, one more thing – tell him to get the fuck out of our VELA satellite.'

Sam laughed darkly. 'You got it, boss. And, ah, where is Alex now? Is he with you? And what about Franks?'

Hammerson walked away from Adira. 'Unknown on both counts. There'll be two for pick-up – Kearns and Ms Sommer. Don't worry about me – I'm fine. I'll check in later, once I've done a search.'

He suppressed a groan as he felt the cold on his damaged side. He wasn't really fine. Still, he'd been worse. He turned back to the Israeli woman. She was looking at him with a flat smile.

'Thank you. Maybe after some time, we ...' she trailed off and shrugged.

'Maybe? Maybe next life. You're good at what you do, damn good. Perhaps we can work together in the future; who knows. But like I told the general – right now, you need to get off our soil.'

He looked up at the dark sky as she got to her feet.

'Don't worry, they'll find me,' she said. 'And also the other agents' bodies. I bet they are already on their way – Salamon would have been in contact with the general by now.'

She held out her hand and he shook it.

'I may see you again, and I may not,' she said. 'Our stories rarely have happy endings, Jack Hammerson.' She shrugged. 'It is not in my hands now.'

'It never is,' Hammerson said, and walked away.

*

Alex skidded to a stop at the edge of a precipice. The path he had been following through the interior of the mountain for the last half-mile had dwindled to little more than a slim ledge alongside a dark void that stretched several hundred feet across. At its center was a nothingness that swallowed even the sound of his footsteps.

Along the way, he'd passed sections of rock art etched into the brilliant blues and greens of the deep-earth mineral salts. Not the sophisticated drawings or carvings that had so excited Matt Kearns in the outer caves, but crude drawings of the hulking shapes he pursued. If Matt had been there, he might have shown Alex the beginnings of a whole new language, or might have explained the creatures' talent for storytelling, their desire to be free from slavery and from the darkness of their mountain prison. But Alex wasn't interested in the wonders of science. His objective was to pursue and acquire the targets.

He strained his eyes to make out the figures ahead of him. He could see the silver of their nocturnal eyes in the dark, their huge shapes attempting to conceal themselves along the narrow path. They were waiting for him, clearly intending an ambush. Perhaps they thought he was like the others of his kind they had mutilated – blind, weak and fearful.

Taking my head won't be as easy, he thought, and pulled the gun from his belt.

*

The leader raised its head, grunting once and causing the line of enormous bipeds to stop. Deep in the darkness of the mountain, the only light came from scant bioluminescent lichens, which gave everything a soft blue-green glow. Not enough for surface-dwellers to see by, but its people had adapted. The leader inhaled deeply through wide nostrils; it could smell the blood of its dead brother. Their pursuer was drawing nearer. Strangely, the darkness didn't seem to bother it; instead, it came on at a determined and steady run. A wave of rage pushed out before it, unsettling the several dozen beasts that surrounded the large pack leader.

The leader grunted, and a small band of the largest males broke from the group. The rest would seek deeper shelter, taking the body of their dead brother with them, and the females and the young.

The band of males wanted to race back to meet the coming creature. But the older beast had heard of another with this small animal's determination – the being that had driven their ancestors into the darkness. Perhaps this creature intended to do the same for the last of their great tribe. There was no hurry to find it. *It* would find them. They would wait here for it.

It was close now, and the dominant male moved to the center of the path. It drew in a deep breath, flooding its enormous lungs with the dank air of the deep cave and its own kind. Its goal was simple – to protect its species. It would not allow the small creature to get past it and reach the rest of its people.

A booming *whoop* exploded in the air around the band of males and echoed throughout the dark chamber. But it came not from the leader; instead, one of the younger males broke from the pack and sprinted to face the oncoming challenge.

The leader grunted in frustration, and held up an arm as thick as a tree trunk to halt the others, who were excited with the desire for blood and war. Unlike its younger kin, the older male sensed the need for caution. It would watch to see how the challenge was met.

*

Alex saw the creature speeding up the path towards him – a small mountain of fur and muscle. Its long yellow teeth were bared, and its huge hands knuckled the ground with such thumping force that he could feel the pounding through the soles of his boots.

Alex didn't pause, or even slow. He raised the Colt and fired two shots. The first struck the beast's shoulder; the second blew a fragment of skin and hair from its large domed skull. The creature slowed, either stunned from the shots or from the boom of the gunfire in the enclosed space.

The moment of disorientation was the small opening Alex needed. He used his momentum to ram the beast with his shoulder. Though it outweighed him by more than 1000 pounds, his speed magnified the power of his impact, causing the giant to stagger back. Alex grunted from the collision, and felt something crunch in his shoulder as he bounced off the massive torso.

The creature swung its arm and latched onto Alex's gun hand. As it took another unbalanced step back, the edge of the path crumbled beneath it. Alex braced himself, but the imbalance in weight took them both over the edge.

Alex grabbed a shelf of rock and together they hung there over the void, the monstrous beast gripping Alex's wrist with an enormous hand that could have wrapped itself around his arm three times. Alex felt his joints scream. Even though his system was flooded with adrenaline, other natural stimulants and the synthesized Arcadian treatment, his muscles weren't strong enough either to lift the creature up with him or to shake it loose.

Alex roared his frustration into the darkness as the beast threw up its other arm to latch onto Alex's bicep. It was going to use his body as a ladder. He could see its silver nocturnal eyes as it edged itself towards his upper body; they were filled with hatred and cunning. He knew that when it reached the edge of the precipice, it would bite down on his head with its cavernous jaws and crush his skull.

Alex tried again to lift himself, but it was impossible. His arm was going numb in the creature's grip. He had only one chance ...

He edged the barrel of the gun he was still holding at an angle into the beast's lower throat, and fired. The blast was deafening. The creature's eyes went wide and Alex felt its grip loosen. The large face registered something like surprise. As it slid down his arm, its hand caught the gun, stripping it from Alex's grip. He didn't know if it was deliberate or by accident, but either way he'd lost his weapon.

The massive body fell into the void. There was no sound of it striking anything on its way down into the center of the mountain. *Straight back to hell*, Alex thought.

He rolled himself back up onto the ledge, where he lay gasping for a few moments. He got slowly to his feet and rolled his shoulders. The one that had been dislocated lifted itself back into its socket, and he momentarily clenched his jaw from the pain.

He looked down the path to the band of silent, motionless creatures. They were all giants, but he easily picked out their leader, standing taller than the others. If they rushed him together, he knew he'd be dead.

Alex lifted the long blade from his belt and took a few steps towards the group, rage and battle lust making him grind his teeth. His grip on the knife handle was so tight, he felt its leather compress in his hand. He held it up in front of him.

'Come on!' he yelled at the leader.

The large creature didn't move.

'What's the matter? Prefer old women and children? Come on!'

Alex drew back his arm and threw the knife as hard as he could. The silver blade flew through the air almost faster than the eye could follow. The creature hunched but the knife buried itself into its massive shoulder. It straightened and pulled the blade free; the knife looked little more than a splinter in its large hand. It puffed out its cheeks, making a snorting sound that Alex could have sworn was derision, and dropped the blade over the edge of the precipice. It watched it fall away into the nothingness before turning back to Alex.

Alex opened his arms to show he was unarmed, and yelled his rage at the giant. But instead of charging, as he expected, it half-turned and grunted to the huddled group behind it. Begrudgingly, they backed away along the path, clearly grumbling but obeying their leader.

Alex stepped closer. 'You think I'm going to be that easy?'

The mighty beast bent to the rock wall and pulled free a block of stone the size of a small car. It strained to lift the boulder above its head, then held it there, sighting on Alex.

'Ah, shit.'

Alex doubted the creature could throw the rock far enough to hit him, but the size of the boulder and the narrowness of the path would make it a near impossible juggernaut to avoid even if it simply bounced towards him.

The creature made a whooping sound, which was picked up by the other animals now out of sight. In one swift motion, it slammed the stone onto the narrow path before it. The explosive impact brought rocks raining down from the cavern's walls, and the path itself crazed into deep cracks.

The creature pulled another stone from the wall and threw it down onto the same spot.

Alex backed up a step, suddenly realizing what the creature was doing. 'You're cutting me off? No!' He frowned and took another step back as pieces of the ledge broke off and fell away.

It fears you, said the voice in his head. *Kill it now!*

Alex tensed his muscles, filled with the sudden urge to leap at the creature. But a third rock came down on the pathway, causing a twenty-foot section to fall away into the void. The creature stood back, its chest heaving from the strain.

As it turned away, Alex, without knowing why, raised his hand, his fingers open. 'Wait.'

The large beast turned back and stared at Alex for a few seconds, then it raised its hand too, fingers open, duplicating Alex. Its eyes locked on his for a moment, then it snorted and disappeared into the darkness. Alex could hear the creatures retreating deeper and deeper into the darkness of the mountain.

It wasn't trying to kill me, he thought. *It's cutting itself and its people off from me.*

He frowned. The beast had signaled to him, had wanted to tell him something. *That there's been enough killing?*

Alex continued to stare into the darkness in the direction the giant bipeds had taken. Even if he managed to make it across the gap, what would he do when he caught up with the creatures?

FORTY-THREE

Hammerson went over to Matt and Sarah. He noticed Matt rubbing something small on his shirt, which he then held out for Sarah to see. As Hammerson got closer, he saw it was a broken canine tooth; a small yellow tusk about as long as Sarah's finger.

Matt snorted. 'Dragon's tooth – fresh. But who's gonna believe us, right?'

Sarah looked around at the human carnage. 'What are we going to say about any of it? About Bill Logan being dead – all the officers, these other soldiers? How are we going to explain why we were even up here in the first place?'

'Bear attack,' Hammerson said. 'Still get a few big ones wandering around this time of year.'

'But they were damned well shot!' Sarah said, pointing to Officer Markenson's body and the head wound that had clearly killed him.

Hammerson shrugged. 'Big rogue bear attacked in the dark ... there was a firefight. Add in some gun-happy survivalists – they all shot each other in the confusion. Believe me, it happens.' He looked at the bodies. 'Don't worry about the mess, we'll clean it up. There's a car coming for you. You've got to get to the eastern car park ... and hurry.'

He waited a few minutes to make sure they'd left, then turned to look up at the ridge. He reached into his pocket for the last foil of stimulants and ripped it open, inhaling deeply. Energy flooded his limbs, but the excruciating pain in every joint and muscle remained.

He started up the side of the ridge.

*

Alex didn't know how long he'd sat on the cold damp stone in the dark, alone with his thoughts. The only sounds were his slow breathing and the metronomic drip of mineralized water somewhere off in the distance. Not even his acute hearing could detect any sounds of the creatures anymore. They were gone, back to their nether world of darkness.

Good, he thought. They weren't suited to this modern, brutal world; it would have killed them. *He* would have killed them, *all* of them if he could. He understood why the beast had severed the link between their worlds. *Perhaps we seem even more monstrous to them than they are to us.*

They would have ended up in the hands of the scientists, and what type of life would they have known then? One of confinement and experimentation. Alex laughed out loud in the darkness. He was describing himself and his own future. Adira had told him that his own military had wanted to cut him to pieces to see how he worked. Hers wanted to do the same. He wasn't perceived as human anymore; he was some sort of extraordinary science experiment or advanced weapon.

'I should be going with you!' he shouted, and his words bounced around the cavern's walls and into the void.

Earth has enough monsters. Who had said that to him? A young woman, years ago; she had dark hair and blue eyes, but her face refused to take shape in his mind. He let the memory slide away and looked back into the dark void.

'You can't hide forever, you know,' he told the creatures. 'They'll find you somehow.'

Then he rose to his feet. 'But only if they can get to you.'

He turned and jogged back the way he'd come. Now that he wasn't focused on pursuit, he spent more time surveying his surroundings and saw that many of the alcoves he had passed without a glance on his way down were littered with debris. Not natural scree, but the rusted remains of helmets and shields and swords with jewelled handles, all now swollen with rust. There were yellowing bones everywhere too. He wondered whether these long-ago soldiers had been a last stand in the war against the giants, holding out in these tiny pockets of rock and then left behind by their generals. Such was the fate of all warriors: to be dispensable tools of war.

Alex closed his eyes as he passed the row of heads on display like trophies on a wall. Back in the main cave, he pulled from his pockets the two hand grenades he had taken from the Mossad agents' SUV after the border-crossing ambush.

Earth has enough monsters, he thought again, and popped both pins and pressed the caps down. For a second, he contemplated just opening his hands and letting the blast carry him away too.

Not yet, he told himself. *That's too easy.*

He dropped the explosives in a spot where the cave walls narrowed and the ceiling was significantly cracked from the previous earthquake. Then he sprinted to the exit and leaped out, just as a boiling orange thunderclap blew rocks out of the cave mouth like an enormous cannon.

He hit the snow-covered ground, rolled and then ran. As he'd expected, the mountain was starting to slide. In a few seconds, any evidence of the cave mouth would be gone, perhaps for another 10,000 years. The build-up of debris on the slip path below the cave caused it to loosen and fall with a thunderous rolling echo down the mountainside.

Where Alex stood there was now a sheer rock face and a drop into nothingness.

Earth has enough monsters.

He took a step closer to the edge.

*

After more than an hour of climbing, Hammerson reached the remains of the slip path. The enormous full moon had turned the peaks almost to daylight, and he immediately saw the source of the explosion and the freshly scraped mountainside. He laughed softly. *The Arcadian always does a thorough job*, he thought.

The HAWC commander examined the heavily churned pathway leading to the new drop that fell away into a mile or so of dead space. When he didn't immediately see what he was searching for, he double-blinked the lenses over his eyes to switch them to thermal vision. All around him, footprints glowed with the last vestiges of body heat. He ignored the gigantic prints of the bipeds and focused on another set – smaller and wearing a man's hiking boot. Their toe direction headed towards him, away from the precipice, but then they turned back on themselves.

Hammerson followed the prints right to the edge of the cliff. They didn't look like they'd stopped at the edge.

He changed his vision back to normal and stared up at the moon for a minute, before looking around at his surroundings. He chuckled softly.

'Not a chance, Alex. You've already been dead once.'

FORTY-FOUR

Hammerson stumbled along the snow-crusted road, limping from the wound in his leg that had burst open again. He felt like shit. His ribs and sternum were cracked, and he'd rigged a makeshift sling for his damaged arm.

He heard a powerful vehicle slowing behind him, and turned to see a big SUV with tinted windows filling the road. It went past, but pulled over just in front of him, and the front passenger door was pushed open with a boot. As he came level with the cabin, he looked in and couldn't help his mouth falling open.

He shook his head and grinned. 'You just made my fucking day.'

Casey Franks sat there covered in blood, her armor-plated suit shredded in a dozen places.

Hammerson's grin widened. 'And I thought *I* was in bad shape.'

Franks raised her eyebrows and her battered face pulled up in a lopsided smile. 'Don't ask. I'm just writing it off as another bad date night, okay?'

Beside her, the driver gave Hammerson a small salute. Seemed Sam's taxi had waited for him, after all. Hammerson burst out laughing and climbed into the cabin. He grimaced as the warmth of the interior prickled his skin and brought feeling back to the open wounds over his face and body. He turned to see Matt Kearns and Sarah Sommer in the back, looking like they were about to nod off.

The driver leaned around Franks. 'Destination, sir?'

Hammerson pointed forward. 'Into town for our passengers, I guess.' He turned in his seat. 'That okay for you two?'

Matt nodded and held up the tooth. '*Gigantopithecus schroderi* ... for Charles.'

You folks ain't gonna like the redecorating Hunter's done to that cave, Hammerson thought.

296

He sat back and spoke again to the driver. 'Take us on to Raleigh – get the medic team to meet us and we'll jump from there.'

When Matt and Sarah had climbed out, Franks moved to the back seat where she stretched out as best she could. She angled her head to look at Hammerson.

'Survivors?' she asked.

Hammerson shook his head. 'A few, besides Kearns and Sommer. Captain Senesh ... and probably Hunter, still up there somewhere.'

Franks puckered her lips in thought. 'Kearns and the Sommer woman – can we trust them? And Senesh –'

'You forget about Senesh,' Hammerson cut in, and saw Franks's eyes narrow. 'That's an order, soldier. If I know Mossad, a chopper's gonna drop outta the sky any moment to take her back to Israel.'

Franks shrugged and stared up at the roof for a second or two.

Hammerson pulled in a ragged breath. 'As for Kearns and Sarah Sommer – well, I want him brought into the fold. We can use that guy. Sommer ... not so sure. I don't know her, or how she'll hold up. We'll put her under 24/7 surveillance for the next ninety days ... just to make sure she doesn't feel the need to open up to anyone.'

Franks nodded her approval. 'So, where to now, boss? Try to pick up Hunter's trail?'

'Nope. Hunter's rebuilding his memory. I reckon he'll come back in himself eventually. We just need to make sure he doesn't detonate along the way. We'll keep our ears to the ground for anything that sounds like our man – bar fights where one guy cleans up the place, or a mugger winds up looking like he's been hit by a truck. We need to keep an eye on Connecticut too – sooner or later he might go looking for a friendly face to fill in some more blanks for him. There's a certain petrobiologist we both know who can do that.'

Franks turned and frowned. 'Great. Aimee thinks he's a corpse. When she finds out he's not ...'

Hammerson shifted in his seat. 'Yup, and that's why I think we better keep an eye out. Some people don't react too well to seeing the dead raised up.'

'Ain't that the truth.' Franks lay back.

'But right now,' Hammerson said, 'we're heading into town for a hot shower and a drink ... and to organize some cleaners for that mess up on the mountain.'

He closed his eyes, and in another few seconds was asleep.

*

Captain Robert Graham sat immobile, his steepled fingers touching his lips, as he watched the three flat lines on his monitor. Communication with his men had ceased, and his final subject's heart monitor had stopped hours ago.

He spun in his chair to face his assistant, Lieutenant Alan Marshal, and smiled grimly. 'Success.'

Marshal frowned. 'Huh? They're all dead. Either defeated by the primary Arcadian subject, or they literally burned themselves down.' He pointed at rows of figures on the screen. 'Look at their final core temperatures – 140 degrees. They must have been boiling their brains.'

Graham shook his head. 'They functioned. They carried out their orders. They just came up against a better model ... for now. As far as Wozyniak is concerned, the field test was a complete success. I'm recommending that we pursue the ARC-044 batch thread. It proves we can reproduce the basics of the design.' He shrugged. 'We just need to do some further tweaking.'

Spinning back to his screen, he looked at the flat pulse lines once more and nodded. 'A success. And now we have the original Arcadian subject wandering around in our backyard – perfect, really. Somehow that man's physiology is able to balance the enormous physical output and the psychosis and still manage the stresses to his core temperature. Now we just have to find him again.'

Marshal opened his mouth but didn't get a chance to speak.

'So, we need better base material,' Graham said, facing him again. 'And that's where you come in.'

Graham got to his feet, clasped his assistant's shoulder and steered him into the laboratory.

'Ready the next batch of ... volunteers, Lieutenant.'

AUTHOR'S NOTE

Readers often ask me about the underlying details in my novels – is the science real or fiction? Where do the situations, equipment, characters and their expertise come from; and just how much of any legend has a basis in fact? My answer is that I always build my stories around the germ of a fact or a legend – and in the case of *Black Mountain*, that something is truly enormous!

Bigfoot/Sasquatch

Stories about a giant hominid date back centuries, both in the United States and all around the world. Are the beasts a hoax? Or are there fossil remnants, as some scientists believe?

The amazing thing is that giant hominids really did exist only a few hundred thousand years ago – a mere tick of the geological clock. We know them today by a whole range of names, including the yeti, Bigfoot or Sasquatch.

The name Bigfoot is given to the legendary ape-like creature that inhabits forests, mainly in the Pacific Northwest region of North America. Most scientists discount its existence, considering it to be a combination of folklore, misidentification and hoax. Nevertheless, the legend endures, and a small minority of accredited scientists share the view that evidence collected from alleged Bigfoot encounters warrants further evaluation and testing.

Bigfoot is described by those who claim to have seen it as a large hairy ape-like creature, between 6–10 feet (2–3 meters) tall, weighing in excess of 500 pounds (230 kilograms), and covered in dark brown or dark reddish hair. It has large eyes, a pronounced brow ridge, a large low forehead, and the top of its head is rounded and has a crest similar to the sagittal crest of the male gorilla. Its enormous footprints (for which it's named) have been as large as 24 inches (60 centimeters) long and 8 inches (20 centimeters) wide. It is said to be omnivorous, mainly nocturnal, with a strong, unpleasant smell.

In 1847, artist Paul Kane reported hearing Native American stories about a race of cannibalistic wild men living on the peak of Mount St Helens, a volcano in the Pacific Northwest region, which they called skoocooms. However, they seemed to regard these beings as supernatural. In 1840, Reverend Elkanah Walker, a Protestant missionary, recorded stories of giants among the Native Americans living in Spokane, Washington, whom they claimed lived on and around the peaks of nearby mountains and stole salmon from their fishing nets.

In the 1920s, a teacher called JW Burns collected the local legends in a series of Canadian newspaper articles. Each language group had its own name for the local version of the giant hominid, but Burns coined the term Sasquatch (supposedly from the Halkomelem *sásq'ets*) to describe the creature reflected in these various stories.

Anthropologists Grover Krantz and Geoffrey Bourne put forward the theory that Bigfoot could be related to the Gigantopithecus fossils found in China. During the Pleistocene age, many animal species migrated across the Bering land bridge to North America, so it is not unreasonable to assume that Gigantopithecus might have as well.

Gigantopithecus was named by paleontologist Gustav Heinrich Ralph von Koenigswald, from the Greek *gigas* (giant) and *pithecus* (ape). In 1935, while examining pieces of fossilized bone in a Hong Kong apothecary, von Koenigswald came across something the shopkeeper called 'dragon's teeth'. Von Koenigswald thought the teeth may have come from something far more closely related to mankind, a biped that existed between one million and just over 100,000 years ago in the region that would become China, India and Vietnam. This early hominid species was said to be around 10 feet tall, 1200 pounds and extremely rare. Very few fossils of it have ever been unearthed, and those that have been found were retrieved from deep caves, leading to theories that the creature may have foraged in forested areas but lived in the shelter of a cave. The Gigantopithecus disappeared from the formal fossil record between 100,000 and 200,000 years ago, and no one really knows why. Perhaps it became more difficult for it to find food as competition became more intense; or perhaps early humans killed them off, as they did most other megafauna.

The Lazarus taxon

The current scientific wisdom is that animals, sea creatures and plants seem to have a finite evolutionary life, dying out because of climate change, a more efficient predator or competitor, or geographical separation from a mate. But Earth is a big place, and there are some areas where life forms that have disappeared from the fossil record have been found to still exist. There's even a name for it: the Lazarus taxon – from the story in the Bible where Jesus brings Lazarus back to life.

In order for any species to be considered as a Lazarus taxon, it must have vanished from the standard or agreed fossil record for a significant period of time, implying that the animal or plant has become extinct. Examples include the Laotian rock rat, which was thought to have become extinct 11 million years ago; the 90-million-year-old Australian Wollemi pine, found in a hidden gorge in the Blue Mountains area near Sydney; and the coelacanth, considered to be one of the missing links between finned fish and four-legged animals and believed extinct for over 65 million years.

The Paleo-Indians and their encounters with megafauna

The earliest humans, or Paleo-Indians, in the North Carolina area were the descendants of the first people to migrate across to and colonize North America during the Ice Age (Paleo-Indian Period: 16,500–10,000 bce). At that time, the climate and natural environments were quite different from today – temperatures were colder, making winters harsher, and hardwood tree species existed in abundance as there were more forests and fewer prairies.

This environment was home to various megafauna species – 'thunder beasts' as the Paleo-Indians called them. They included tusked mammoths and mastodons; several types of ground sloths; 2000-pound, six-foot-long glyptodon's with spiked tails and horned plating resembling nothing known today; beavers as heavy as two grown men combined; four-horned antelopes; bison-sized shrub oxen; wolves whose large heads and powerful jaws made them resemble giant hyenas; aggressive cave bears that weighed in at over 1500 pounds; and saber-toothed cats that could open their jaws to a 100-degree angle to spear their prey before tearing it apart with their enormous scythe-like canines. As the Paleo-Indians expanded their presence in the region, they relied on many of these animals for food, as well as using their bones for tools and hides for clothing.

By 8500 bce, most of the megafauna species were extinct, or found only in niche environments and soon to die out. The Ice Age was ending and the eastern ecosystem was changing. Scientists disagree about what role humans played in the extinction of these mighty animals. Climate change could have been a contributing factor, as was competition from new encroaching animal types. But humankind, the super-predator, will always be considered the main suspect.

Native American Indian legends and symbols

Lake Jocassee, tucked away in the foothills of the Blue Ridge Mountains, is one of the deepest manmade lakes in the south-east. It was formed by the damming of several large rivers – the Whitewater, Thompson, Horsepasture and Toxaway, filling a natural valley-basin – for the purpose of providing hydroelectric power for the south-east region.

Originally, the Vale of Jocassee, which now lies beneath the surface of the lake, was home to the Cherokee Indian Nation. In Cherokee, the name Jocassee means *place of the lost one*. The Oconee tribe, led by Chief Attakulla, lived on the west side of the Whitewater River; on the east side lived the Eastatoees, a rival tribe. A young Eastatoee warrior named Nagoochee was hunting in Oconee territory one day when he fell and broke his leg. He expected to die there, until he heard a young woman singing and called out to her. It was Chief Attakulla's daughter, Jocassee, and she took Nagoochee back to her father's lodge and nursed him back to health. They fell in love and Nagoochee stayed with the Oconee tribe. Later, during a battle between the Oconee and Eastatoee tribes, Jocassee's brother, Cheochee, killed Nagoochee. When Cheochee returned with Nagoochee's head on his belt, Jocassee stepped into the lake and walked across the water to meet the ghost of her lover.

*

The arrow was a sacred symbol for the Native American Indians. It was depicted in many different forms, all of which had different meanings. A broken arrow symbolised peace, for example; and crossed arrows suggested friendship.

The arrow was also used for spiritual protection. An arrow pointing to the right meant protection; an arrow pointing to the left warded off evil.

CPSIA information can be obtained
at www.ICGtesting.com
Printed in the USA
BVHW08s1938070818
523692BV00001B/24/P